"Do not be afraid to go out on the streets and into public places like the first Apostles, who preached Christ and the Good News of Salvation in the squares of cities, towns and villages. This is no time to be afraid of the Gospel (Romans 1:16). It is the time to preach it from the roof tops (Matthew 10:27). Do not be afraid to break out from comfortable and routine modes of living in order to take up the challenge of making Christ known in the modern "metropolis". The Gospel must not be kept hidden because of fear or indifference." John Paul the Great.

Sons of Thunder

SONS OF THUNDER

The Story of Joe and Paul

A Novel

Robert Epperly

iUniverse, Inc.

New York Lincoln Shanghai

Sons of Thunder
The Story of Joe and Paul

iUniverse books may be ordered through booksellers or by contacting:

iUniverse
2021 Pine Lake Road, Suite 100
Lincoln, NE 68512
www.iuniverse.com
1-800-Authors (1-800-288-4677)

Because of the dynamic nature of the Internet, any Web addresses or links contained in this book may have changed since publication and may no longer be valid.

This is a work of fiction. All of the characters, names, incidents, organizations, and dialogue in this novel are either the products of the author's imagination or are used fictitiously.

ISBN: 978-0-595-45477-8 (pbk)
ISBN: 978-0-595-89789-6 (ebk)

Printed in the United States of America

This book
is dedicated
to
John the Baptist
who shouted
from the banks of the Jordan,
"Repent!
For the Kingdom of Heaven
is at hand!"

Acknowledgements

Thank you, Holy Spirit.

Also: Manuel and Silvia Epperly, Jazmin, Johny, Chris, Matthew, Joshua, Isabel, My Guardian Angel Claude, Our Blessed Mother, St. Clare, St. Francis, St. Padre Pio, St. Anthony, the nurses at Albany Medical Center, Robert Ludlum, Patty and Silvie, Sam, Marcia and of course, my Abuela and Tia. Special thanks to Father Martin Glynn.

CHAPTER 1

▼

Joe Morrison had to pass Redemption House on his way to the Lincoln Tunnel. He had worked the day shift in the Intake and Assessment Unit before going back to his Community at 44th Street and 8th Avenue to attend Mass. He then picked up his van at the long term parking garage and was now heading down 41st Street to take the tunnel into New Jersey and his mother's house in Leonia. This was Friday and he had the weekend off.

As he glanced at the security booth in front of the Crisis Center he remembered how he had ended that particular day. He had been ready to leave on time for once when the telephone rang in his little office and the caller had asked for him.

The caller was a fifteen-year-old "runaway" that he had counseled a couple of weeks earlier. Her name was Lourdes and he had approved her release to go home after checking out her living situation. Sadly, most of the "throw-away" or "run-away" kids that came to the agency for help were safer on the streets of New York City than in their own homes. Very few went home. The lucky ones got placed in group-homes or with long term care at one of the Catholic or state facilities.

Lourdes was one of the rare ones that ended up at the agency. She was from a good Puerto Rican family in the Bronx that loved her and gave her special attention. But when her friends at school "matured" and started hanging out on the streets, her parents forbade it.

She felt like a prisoner at home and was talked into running to Redemption House by her friends. They told her that she would get her own apartment and be free to hang out. She made up a story of mistreatment at home but Joe had seen right through it after speaking to the girl's family.

Now she was on the telephone telling him that she was going to kill herself. She was crying and pleading with him to help. Lourdes' mother was on the other line and Joe was able to have a family conference on the telephone with the girl and her mother.

He had become pretty good at crisis counseling in his time with the agency. In fact, unbeknownst to him, his peers considered him an exceptional counselor, if not the best in the unit.

He got Lourdes and her mother to reach a compromise and hung up to the two of them crying together, hugging and saying I love you.

But the call had drained him and he was looking forward to getting away for a couple of days.

As he approached the entrance to the tunnel, he could see a familiar figure walking precariously along the centerline of the street and heading for the tunnel. He was clad in a monk style or Franciscan style frock and leather sandals with a thick hemp sash at the belt. The monk had shoulder length brown hair and a skimpy brown beard that looked more like a goatee than a full beard. Joe remembered the friar to be around twenty-five years old and his name was Paul.

He had first met Paul when he was bringing leftover chili, made by his Community, to the homeless on 41stStreet. They lived in large cardboard boxes in the section of 41stStreet where the Port Authority building crossed the street overhead providing shelter form the rain and snow. They also sold crack and drank cheap wine when they weren't sleeping.

He had gone half way down the block without anyone taking any chili. He was getting the impression that the homeless on forty-first didn't like beans.

In a huge cardboard box with a window cut out on the side, he looked in and saw Brother Paul. His eyes were a brilliant golden color that he had never seen before. As he approached he could see the scabbed and dirty bare feet of a homeless man lying before him on a filthy blanket.

He had never seen Paul before and was taken aback by his presence. He didn't fit in. His hair and face and frock looked clean and he had a healthy glow that you didn't see on this street.

"How about some chili?" Joe asked automatically and took a deep breath.

Immediately Paul had smiled and said, "Sure, why not!"

"It's got beans," Joe said.

"All the better," Paul said with a smile.

Joe scooped some chili onto a paper plate and handed it to Paul along with a plastic spoon.

"You're the first on the block to take some," he said. "One would figure hungry people wouldn't be picky about these things."

"Well they are and they're not that hungry. They've got soup kitchens and McDonald's dumpsters to pick from."

"Hmm, this is homemade," Paul said, as he swallowed his first spoonful.

Joe didn't say anything. He was looking at the man on the blanket. He was stunned to see a hypodermic needle in a neat little box on the floor.

Paul read his mind. "This man on the floor's name is Sayvid and he's diabetic. He's a crack head and sometimes forgets to use the needle. I just gave him a shot. He should be waking up soon.

"And no, I doubt he likes beans either," Paul said.

Joe didn't know what else to say. This magnificent looking monk, sitting on a milk crate inside a cardboard box with a homeless man at his feet, was something unreal and had left him speechless.

"My name's Paul. Thanks for the chili."

"I'm Joe. Don't mention it."

The young monk had left an impression on Joe that he couldn't describe. He had asked other community members if they had ever seen him and they had said no.

Now he was stopping his blue Chevy van and offering him a ride.

Paul didn't hesitate. He walked around the front of the van and got in on the passenger side.

They immediately entered the tunnel. About half way through came an abrupt stop. People fleeing the city for the weekend had created a traffic jam.

Joe glanced at Paul to say something but noticed his lips moving silently. Around his index finger he noticed what he knew to be a rosary ring. Paul was praying a rosary in the Lincoln Tunnel.

Twenty minutes later, and before the exhaust fumes got to them, the two men drove out of the tunnel and into the light.

Paul was the first to speak. "Where are you headed?"

"I have the weekend off and I'm heading to my mother's house for a couple of days," Joe answered.

"Where are you headed?" Joe asked.

"I don't know," Paul said, "I usually try to go where I think the Spirit is guiding me. Today it was across the Lincoln Tunnel."

"Well," Joe said, "I'm heading north on the Jersey Turnpike and getting off in Leonia, Bergen County."

"Sounds good to me," the young monk said with a smile.

They didn't speak again until they were on the Turnpike. Joe noticed Paul still fingering his pocket rosary and didn't know whether to speak or not. Paul wasn't offering any conversation. The thought occurred to Joe to tell his passenger about the "religious experience" that he'd had that morning in the chapel during the half hour meditation that the community had to do at 5:30 a.m. after Morning Prayer.

He didn't quite know what to make of it but knew that the experience had left him ebullient this morning. Maybe Paul would have some insights.

"Can I talk?" Joe asked.

"Sure, why not."

"Well, I see that you're praying the rosary and I don't want to interrupt."

"Its okay," Paul said without volunteering anything.

"Well, this morning during meditation … by the way I live in a Franciscan Community of full-time volunteers and we're required to pray three hours a day, including Mass. Well, this morning during meditation, I sort of drifted off. I was fully aware of what was happening to me and felt great. I felt very at peace. I felt myself floating upwards. Everything was like a fog at first but then the fog cleared and I found myself inside a cylindrical chamber, still floating upward. All around me were brass etchings, around 12 inches square. The etchings obviously were of someone's life, different incidences in someone's life.

"As I rose, I could gently spin and see that the etchings followed a pattern and told a story. Glancing up, I could see no end in sight.

"At first, I thought that it was the life of Christ, but then realized that it could be my life. And even though I could see the etchings, I can't recall a single specific one. Or what it said. Nevertheless, I felt ebullient when I opened my eyes."

Joe could see that Paul was listening intently.

"Well, what do you make of it?" He asked.

"I've never heard of anything like that before, but I'll look into it," Paul said.

Joe was chagrined. He expected more input from Paul.

"Well," said Joe, "The experience didn't quite end there. After opening my eyes, I felt real good and went over to a small statue of the Madonna to say a Hail Mary. I decided to light a candle and it reminded me of my grandmother. For some reason I remembered that when I was up in Albany Medical Center for ten weeks, after a motorcycle accident, my mother telling me about Abuela lighting a candle for me. The thought of my grandmother, who was not very ambulatory and had to be 80 years old at the time, going to the church and lighting a candle for me, made the tears gush out of me for at least an hour.

"I remember I had just had a 12 inch steel rod with 12 screws and a bone graph from my hip inserted in my left femur and was sitting in a wheelchair by the pay phone. I wheeled myself around the floor for an hour crying. The nurses gave me smelling salts!

"Anyway, one thought led to another and I realized that during my experience in the hospital I had made a commitment to Jesus to help others, as the nurses and volunteers had helped me. And that's how years later I ended up living in Community doing full-time service for the Lord for twelve bucks a week, a room, and three meals a day!"

Paul looked into Joe's eyes and said, "Life is a paradox. At the time you probably thought your accident was the worst thing that ever happened to you, and quite possibly, it's the best thing that's happened to you!"

"You know, you may have something there!"

Both men looked up just then as a helicopter passed overhead.

"I've had a lot of time to think about it and I do believe that I was knocked off the bike to change my life, or to save my life for that matter. I was a young man at the time and my idol was Jesse James, believe it or not. I thought Jesse was a real life American Robin Hood, a hero, I knew everything about his life.

"My favorite movie was "The Godfather" and the character of Michael Corleone. I could relate to him in a way because I was the youngest of four brothers and worked in the family business. And like Michael, I reluctantly entered the family business. We had two Ben Franklin Stores and a Plant Shop. Later on I ended up running the sales floor of the bigger Ben Franklin Store and opened the Plant Shop. We were fairly successful.

"But at the time of the accident, I hadn't gotten serious about my life yet and was planning a life of crime, selling pot to be exact. I wanted to become a big time dealer. But I guess God had other plans for me."

Paul had been listening politely. While still fingering his rosary he asked Joe how the accident had happened.

"At the end of this one summer on the Friday of Labor Day weekend, I was sitting in my attic room at my mother's house bummed out and listening to records. My friends had left earlier that day for the Catskill Mountains for the weekend and I was to follow on my Kawasaki 500 after work. The problem was the pouring rain outside.

"Well, I put on 'Born to be Wild', by Steppenwolf of course, and got psyched up to head upstate on my scooter in the pouring rain.

"And so I did. But that actually had nothing to do with the accident, although the ride on the thruway was dangerous. The wind actually pushed me to change lanes twice and I almost got sucked under a tractor-trailer. But Route 145 near Cairo was dry. The rain hadn't reached that far to the north.

"I was cruising at about 50 mph and was about five miles from my destination. I had driven over 100 miles in the pouring rain and felt good cruising on a dry country highway.

"Suddenly, just in front of me, there was a dark colored, medium sized car stopped sideways in the middle of the road. I leaned the bike to the right so hard I almost laid it down. I had made a spontaneous decision to try to go around the car. If I slammed on the brakes I had no chance. I would hit the car broadside. In that instant I actually considered doing just that and trying to jump over the car.

"But I leaned her hard right and pulled her up straight. I took a deep breath for a moment thinking that I had cleared the car. In that split second the car's headlights went on and the car jerked forward a foot. My left knee hit the right quarter panel of the car, near the headlight and the rest is history.

"I ended up in an eight foot deep drainage ditch that ran along the side of this road, with the bike a few feet behind me. I took a deep breath and felt some pain in my ribs but that's all. I was angry. I stood up to go after the culprits only to fall back down on my compound fractured left femur. Then the pain set in.

"The car that hit me actually pulled along side of me and the passenger looked down at me. Then I heard someone screaming 'Go! Go! Go!' and they actually burned a little rubber and took off.

"They left me in the bottom of the ditch, sitting on my twisted, mangled left leg. My left femur had actually come through my jeans."

Paul was now listening intently and looking at Joe as the Jersey meadowlands passed them by. The sun was now setting in the western sky.

"What happened then?" he asked.

"My injured leg blew up like a balloon and went numb. I was sitting there hoping that this was a nightmare. God wouldn't let this happen. I still had the invincibility of youth. I must wake up!

"But I didn't. The situation was real. Then looking up on the road about thirty feet in front of me was a mysterious old lady holding a leash. I couldn't see the dog.

"I yelled for her to help me, but she just stood there. Then two older men showed up and climbed down into the ditch.

"They started talking to me to try to distract me. I asked to hold one man's hand and squeezed it so hard that he screamed.

"Then an amazing thing happened. They told me who they were and where they were from. They were from Edgewater, New Jersey and I had actually gone to high school with each of their sons. I couldn't believe it.

"Finally the ambulance got there and they took me to Catskill Hospital. I had been in the ditch for over an hour.

"The two E.M.T.'s came down into the ditch with a detachable stretcher, one that they could slide under me from each side and attach. But first they had to straighten my leg. By this time, the pain had returned.

"I screamed bloody murder when one E.M.T. lifted me up from behind and the other pulled my leg forward.

"With the help of the two men, they lifted me onto a gurney and removed the stretcher. They then put me in the ambulance.

"The E.R. was dark and cold and empty. They x-rayed my leg and left me on a gurney in a freezing little room stark naked. I could see the bone sticking out of my thigh.

"I knew I was in trouble when the doctor came in with the two ambulance drivers. He showed me the x-ray. It wasn't pretty. He said that the hospital didn't have the facilities to treat me because I needed a surgeon and one wasn't available. He said the ambulance would take me to Albany Medical Center, thirty miles away, where I would have the best care.

"I remember the E.M.T. that rode in the back of the ambulance with me. He was a grown man of about 50 years old. Kind of strong and rough looking with a crew cut, like an ex-marine, but he acted quite the opposite of what he looked.

"He was soft spoken and gentle, almost shy. He tried to comfort me with chit-chat and when we talked about what had happened to me, he pulled out a picture of his motorcycle and showed it to me.

"I was aghast at first. Is this appropriate? I just crashed on one of those. I don't like those anymore.

"But out of respect, I took the photo and looked at his Harley Electra-Glide. I silently wondered why he would carry this picture around with him."

Paul was silently wondering the same thing as he looked at Joe.

"Anyway, they dropped me at Albany Medical Center where at that hour the E.R. was being run by medical students and was packed.

"For three hours they tried in vain to get me a surgeon.

"Finally they got a hold of a Dr. Quinn who told them that since the E.R. doctor at Catskill had given me a pain killer that he couldn't operate and they were to put me in traction."

"Oh boy," Paul said. And that was the closest he came to making a comment.

"They had to drill a hole through my tibia, just below my knee, with a steel pin that would extend out from both sides. This way they can attach the cable that extends up over the end of the bed on an extension pole and be connected to what turned out to be twenty-eight pounds of weight. This pulls the bottom end of my femur down to hopefully connect with the top end at the break point and give the bone a chance to heal over time.

"The intern, it turns out, didn't feel confident with the electric drill and decided to use a rotary style hand drill."

"Oh boy," Paul said again.

Joe was telling the story with intensity and in great detail and had Paul captivated.

"They gave me a shot of Demerol and while a male nurse held my leg, the intern started to manually drill a hole through my shin bone. He was obviously unsure of himself.

"Three times, maybe four times, he stopped and walked away. The last time that he walked away he returned with another intern whose opinion was to keep going. Meanwhile, I'm lying there with a steel pin sticking out of my leg.

"I actually felt no pain at the time, although besides the broken femur and the pin sticking out of my leg, my knee and ankle were both banged up and badly swollen."

"Woe," said Paul.

"So then I spent the next seven weeks in traction using a bed pan and watching TV. Every morning Dr. Quinn would come in and push down on my femur as hard a he could and make the ends meet. And everyday when I got on the bedpan I could feel the bones move apart. I had an unstable fracture because a critical piece of bone was chipped off and lodged in my thigh.

"At first the doctor would come in by himself in the morning and I would try to stop him from pushing by holding his arms. Then he started bringing two interns in to hold my arms. I was angry as hell and at God too!

"At one point, I found a little medal of the Madonna that I had taken with me to protect me on the ride and I flung it across the room.

"The janitor lady picked it up and asked if the medal was mine. I said no. Then she smiled, kissed the medal and put it in her pocket.

"The medal was beautiful! My grandmother had given it to me.

"Anyhow," Joe said, "After seven weeks of this, they did the operation. Then I spent three more weeks recovering and having some physical therapy.

"But it was the kindness and the love that I saw in the nurses that led me to make my promise to Jesus.

"There was a volunteer that I remember. A retired, kindly old gentleman named Charles Wilson. All he did was brought me the newspaper everyday. Then chat innocuously with me for five minutes, five times a week.

"He made me laugh sometimes. But to this day, I remember him and really appreciate what he did."

Paul interjected, "How long did you stay angry for?"

"For a while, I actually went back to the scene of the crime one year later, by myself, with my .22 Winchester rifle.

"I had just barely started walking. I went from a wheelchair, to crutches, to a cane and finally walking with a slight limp that I no longer have.

"I set up a pup tent on my friend's land where I slept and fried eggs in the morning.

"The first place I stopped at was a smallish Irish resort set way back from the road. The driveway leading in and out was directly in front of the spot where I was hit. This had to be where the two gentlemen that came down to the ditch were staying.

"I pulled into the parking lot in my '68 Firebird convertible. Before I was ten feet from the car, walking to the office, a kid about ten years old came running up to me.

"He said, 'I know who you are!'

"I was a little shocked but I answered, "Who?"

"He said, 'You're the guy from the motorcycle crash last year!'

"I said, 'How do you know?'

"He said, 'because I saw it. And they just left you in the hole!'

"What do you mean you saw it?

"I was astonished. He told me that his family visits there every year and that last year he saw me hit the car and disappear into the hole.

"He had walked over to the ditch with his father, who was now briskly walking towards us, and had clearly seen my face.

"I asked him if he could identify the car and he said yes, that he had seen it that day! A blue station wagon!

"He explained that a couple of guys and a girl had come in the car that very day and that "Sharon" had gotten out of the car.

"I was flabbergasted. I asked him who "Sharon" was. He explained that she was one of the babysitters that worked there at the resort. And that she worked there last year too.

"Just then the kid's father came and shook my hand like he knew me and asked how my leg was doing.

"I was stunned speechless. He told me that on the night of the accident he had heard a motorcycle coming down the road, then the crisp snapping sound of a powerful bone breaking, like a tree branch snapping, and then heard the motorcycle no more.

"He ran to his son who told him what he saw and then they went to the ditch where the two men were already helping me.

"He repeated his kid's story that the kid had seen Sharon getting out of the car.

"I asked how he could be sure. He's only a kid. But the father insisted that he believed his son and that I should too!

"We exchanged phone numbers and he assured me that he would help in any way that he could.

"I asked him where Sharon was now and they brought me around to the back of the hotel to a tiny bungalow.

"I knocked on the door. Incredibly, shockingly, I looked with disbelief as Sharon Van Dylan stood in the doorway. The look on her face told it all, the whole story. She knew!

"I was standing face to face with Sharon Van Dylan, whose brother I had considered to be a friend in high school and whom I dated on and off for at least a year. I had slept in her bed, although nothing happened.

"When I asked her what she was doing here she tried to smile and said that she worked there. She was obviously extremely nervous. There could only be one reason why. Under ordinary circumstances she would have probably screamed 'Joe Morrison!' and given me a big hug. Not this time.

"She slammed the door in my face. I asked her whom the people were that she was with in the blue car that day and she blurted, 'I don't know anything!' and slammed the door. I haven't seen or spoken to her since."

"That's incredible," Paul finally said. "Did you end up shooting anyone?"

"No," Joe said with a smile, glancing at his passenger.

They stopped at the tollbooth and Joe said, "But the story doesn't end there. There's a bit more.

"I went to see East Durham's one and only Sheriff. He happened to be out hunting in Canada someplace, but his twenties daughter was home ironing clothes and she let me in. I told her who I was and asked her if she knew anything about the accident.

"She calmly and plainly told me she did. She said she knew the car, an old blue Rambler station wagon, that everybody knew who did it, that the car belonged to two sisters that lived right on Route 145 behind a gas station, and that the sisters and their boyfriends all drove the car. She didn't know who was driving. And.... oh yeah ... Sharon knew them and partied with them.

"I said goodbye and headed straight for the gas station.

"The gas station was about five miles down on 145. I pulled in and filled it up. I then backed the Firebird up and parked it. To my right I could see the small weatherworn farmhouse with two rockers on the front porch. There were no cars in the driveway.

"No sooner did I pull out a magazine and pretend to look at it then a dark blue Rambler station wagon pulled up to the pumps.

"I immediately got out of my car and walked toward the station wagon from the back and cut over to the passenger side.

"A large, tubby, baby-faced guy stepped out the driver side and, leaving his door open, started putting five bucks worth in the tank.

"I walked around to the passenger side and stood three feet away staring at the side of the face of one of the sisters.

"Something inside me told me this was the car, this was them!

"She had long brown hair, glasses, a white tank top and cut offs. She had her legs crossed yoga style on the seat and was filing her nails. She looked at me for a fleeting moment, and then looked back down at her nails.

"I then walked over and knelt on one knee next to the right front fender where I could see the remains of a dent that had been banged out.

"Then I walked around the front of the car and stood face to face with the baby-faced country boy in his white tee shirt.

"Just as the girl made no recognizable expression of shock or recognition, he calmly looked me in the eye while leaning on his open door.

"Not a word was spoken. I couldn't be sure who actually drove that night. I could never recollect the face of the passenger that yelled go, go, go!

"He paid his five bucks, got in the car, and closed the door.

"I stood in front of the car gazing at both of them. He put it in reverse, backed up, and calmly pulled out. I wrote down his license plate number."

Joe paused pensively.

"What did you do then?" Paul asked.

"I sped to the D.M.V. in Albany. The time was 4 p.m. and the gas station guy told me they were open until five.

"I made it by five. I told the lady at the desk my story and handed her the plate number. She told me to sit and be quiet and went through the doors to the back. The time was after five now. Fifteen minutes later she returned with an envelope and passed it across the counter to me. Then I drove home.

"I got the owner's name. He was one of the guys that went out with one of the sisters. The address was in nearby Cairo, New York.

"I went to see a lawyer to see what my options were and he told me that I had three choices: hire a private investigator to get evidence, get a confession so that I could sue them, or, and he left the third choice to my imagination meaning: I know who they are and now I could go get revenge.

Joe paused for a moment, thinking.

"I let it go. I did not pursue it. But days later I heard that Sharon Van Dylan abruptly moved to Nevada where her brother was living."

"So how did you deal with the anger?" Paul asked.

"I remember exactly how, and when, I let the anger go.

"I had been misdirecting the anger. I was fighting and yelling all the time. My left leg was a half-inch shorter now and I had pain.

"I was ticked off. I blamed everybody.

"Then one day, I was reading a New Testament, Jesus' words on forgiveness.

"I had decided to give the Gospel a try to see if it worked. They say that even without faith, if you sincerely try to follow Christ's teaching, He'll infuse you with faith. I saw it happen to me.

"One day, I knelt down on the landing of my attic room, a day that I had unreasonably argued loudly with my mother. I was still living at home.

"I knelt down and forgave the guy that hit me. I sincerely forgave him.

"I immediately felt relieved. I felt a peace. I got up and went to bed.

"After that night I never felt anger toward the driver or anyone to do with the hit and run again.

"I mark this as one of my earliest religious experiences which have led to the building up of my faith."

"Excellent," said Paul.

"I believe you've responded the way our Lord wished. You've used this experience to advance on the spiritual journey.

"Why do you think that the car jerked forward?" Paul asked.

"I've considered that," Joe said. "I think the driver stalled upon pulling out of the Resort while attempting to cross the highway to the bar across the street. He or she then automatically killed the lights and tried to start it.

"As I approached, the car started up and the driver automatically turned the lights on and put the car in gear to get out of my way. Then he panicked and braked. I figure they had been drinking, holiday weekend and all.

"By the way," Joe said, "The next day was my birthday."

"Happy Birthday," Paul said and grinned at Joe.

They had turned off of the Turnpike and climbed Fort Lee Road into Leonia, the small town one mile from the George Washington Bridge where Joe had grown up, when he made a right on Oaktree Place and pulled into the driveway of an older green colonial with wood shingles.

The two men got out of the van and Joe said, "Come here. I want to show you something."

Joe's mother's house had an old-fashioned two-car garage with an open front, no doors. In the right rear corner there was an object covered in a black nylon tarp. A huge steel chain could be seen coming out from underneath the tarp and hooked to a steel eyebolt in the concrete wall.

Joe turned on the light and removed the tarp.

They stood staring at a black Harley Davidson 1200CC Super Glide.

CHAPTER 2

▼

Joe decided to take the bus back to Time Square on Sunday night. He left his van in his mother's garage. She walked him to the bus stop and wished him God-speed. She was a devout Catholic and proud of the work that he was doing. His mom then walked the two short blocks to her home.

The weekend had been relaxing and uneventful.

Friday night after "Brother Paul" had declined to come inside for dinner, Joe ate meatloaf and mashed potatoes alone with his Mom and watched the Yankee game. His mom was a big Yankee fan.

Saturday he rode his Harley out to Promised Land State Park in Pennsylvania where he ate a sandwich and took a nap on a blanket in the sun. The late August sun had felt good on his face, as did the breeze that blew in off the lake.

Saturday night he had dinner with friends, a married couple that he had known since high school. They had two young sons.

Sunday he went to Mass, had brunch with his mom, and watched another Yankee game. He also snuck in a short nap.

Now he was on the #166 bus heading back to the war zone for night prayer. That is how he looked at it. He was on the front lines of the war between good and evil.

The ruination of the children was the ruination of the future of the world. Evil was being done to these kids through abuse and neglect and he was fighting that evil with love. He believed love was the answer to all the important questions in life.

The Community that he shared with fifty-six others in Time Square was a bunker in that war zone. It was a safe haven for a group of disciples fighting that war against incredible odds.

Although he had made few friends in eight months, he enjoyed the fact that he was a member of a group fighting together for a good cause. A group committed to each other and to God. Joe believed that Christ meant for us to live in a community of agape or unconditional love and worship.

A Franciscan Priest founded Redemption House Community and members lived by the Franciscan Rule. You took vows to practice poverty, chastity, and obedience for 13 months at a celebration Mass, and you were obligated to pray for three hours a day. Most members were Catholic. Those of other faiths were welcome.

The usual day began with Morning Prayer at 5 a.m. followed by meditation. Then work as counselors either at the Crisis Center, the Mother and Child unit, or the Rights of Passage unit on 18th Street for kids in a more advanced state of recovery. Some members worked in the Community's office.

Mass was at five o'clock in the afternoon, usually celebrated by a visiting priest or the spiritual advisor, Father Anthony.

Dinner was at six. Night prayer was short and sweet at 9 p.m. Joe loved night prayer the best.

The group prayed the Divine Office, as priests and nuns are required to do, on a daily basis. Catholic Christians have done so for 2000 years. The Office consisted mostly of chanting the Psalms, which Joe loved and was good at. He had a good voice.

He also liked that Community offered a structured environment. He appreciated this and felt that structure kept him focused. There was always a schedule to keep, places to go, and things to do.

In actuality, getting into the Community was not that easy. Most applicants are rejected. The ones that are initially chosen are brought in to live in the Community for five days of discernment, and of those about half are rejected.

He thought that most people are rejected because of the reason they are trying to join a Community. If it's not to help kids while serving the Lord, then you're probably not cut out for it.

Many come to add a line to their resume. One guy admitted he wanted to go to the Alaska Community to write a book unrelated to the work.

Once you're in, you are evaluated and given a job. Joe was tough and smart and got the toughest assignment of all: the Intake and Assessment unit.

The first person the kid sees, quite often after escaping from a pimp and running from the police, was the intake counselor. He is the one who opens the door and gently nudges the kid in a direction the child never knew existed. He's the first impression, one of hope.

He saw right away that living in Community was actually "an attempt" to live as a community. There were still people there that probably joined for selfish or for the wrong reason. He didn't feel warmth and love from all corners as expected.

But they were trying and that was good.

The Priest had started Redemption House from an apartment in the West Village. He quickly moved to two buildings in Time Square that were donated.

Then they acquired the crisis center on 41st Street and Tenth Avenue and the other two units on 52ndStreet and 18thStreet.

The two donated buildings in Time Square where Community lived were on 8th Avenue and on 44thStreet. One was on 8thAvenue itself and the other just around the corner on 44thStreet, with another building dividing them on the corner. They were both five stories high and connected to each other by an outdoor fenced in walkway-bridge that hung precariously in the rear between the two buildings, high above the alley.

Their 44thStreet building was directly across from the Majestic Theatre where Phantom of the Opera was playing, one of the hottest shows on Broadway. In fact the Community lived just three blocks from the famous corner of Broadway and 42ndStreet.

From his friend Patrick's second story room one could see right into the theatre and feel like a member of the audience when they disbursed outside during a break.

Joe lived in the 8thAvenue building on the top floor, the fifth floor.

He got off the bus at Port Authority on 42ndStreet and walked briskly the two blocks to the front door. He carried a small backpack with a change of clothes and a book that he had taken to New Jersey with him.

The night was warm and humid.

As he approached his building, he noticed the two homeless men that lived on the sidewalk outside the front door of the 8thAvenue building. They were both eating spaghetti off paper plates. The Community served them dinner every night.

Joe still couldn't fathom that these two men that looked 50 years old, but were actually in their late twenties, literally lived on the sidewalk.

On cold nights, they laid an old dirty blanket on the subway grate and slept on that. The heat from below kept them warm.

He noticed that they were both shoeless. When he had left on Friday both men had on decent second hand shoes from the detox. They had on second hand clothes and had haircuts as well.

Someone had stolen their shoes while they slept! And it wasn't the first time.

Their names were Jimmy and Louis. They lived by panhandling. They lived on cheap beer and cigarettes that they bought one at a time all day long from the deli across the street. Three quarters got them a beer; one quarter got them two cigarettes.

The only time one of them would move from the blanket was to cross the street to the deli.

The younger and bigger man was Louis. He had curly, dirty brown hair, half his teeth were missing and the other half rotten. His left hand was in a permanent begging position. Elbow bent, and hand stretched out, always.

Once a week the Community let them use the shower. Made them use the shower. Who performed that corporal work of mercy Joe never did find out.

He shook hands with the men and said a prayer for them as he entered the building.

Seeing Louis' outstretched hand reminded Joe of the time he rode in the ambulance with him to St. Claire's. While they waited for a doctor to stitch up Louis' arm, he had his palm out. The waiting room was empty and only one person passed by, but Louis' hand was up in a "beggar's palm".

Louis had commented several times to Joe that he thought the waiting room was "weird". He had covered his mouth with his hand as he had whispered the word "weird" while glancing about with his eyes bugging out. He hadn't wanted the nurses to read his lips. Joe had found this to be comical.

After an hour wait, Louis had left the E.R. without being stitched up. He went to go beg at the 9th Avenue Food Festival that he had seen in progress from in front of the hospital when Joe had let him outside for a smoke.

Joe was smiling to himself as he walked up to the 2nd floor. The elevator was too slow for him. He then walked into the cafeteria.

The two young Mexican ladies were at the table by the window having cereal. They smiled and waved to him.

He washed his hands, got a bowl of cereal with milk, and sat down at their table.

Charo and Bebe were their names. Somehow, they had heard about the Community from way down in Puebla, Mexico and joined up around the same time as Joe.

Both ladies were typically in a happy mood but tonight they were quiet and somber.

"Where is everybody?" Joe asked, although he knew that a lot of the Community disappeared on weekends to visit family or whatever. Bebe and Charo's families were in Mexico.

"Everybody's away this weekend," Bebe said, "even you."

Bebe was lovely and more Castilian looking than Mexican, with long black hair and dark eyes. She had put on at least the 20 pounds that Joe had lost since joining the community.

Charo was thin and athletic looking with short black hair. She looked like she was about to cry.

"What's the matter Charo?" he asked.

She tried to force a smile and slapped his shoulder.

"Nothing," she said.

Now Bebe looked a bit alarmed. Joe sensed that she wanted to tell him something.

"What's up Bebe?" he asked.

"Don't tell me Joe that you haven't heard the latest on Father Costen?" she said, with a South of the Border accent.

"No, actually I didn't watch the news or read the paper all weekend," he said. "What's up?"

"Somebody told us that Father Costen is going to resign tomorrow," Bebe said.

Joe looked at Bebe then at Charo.

There were tears in Charo's eyes but she said nothing.

Bebe continued, "They said he thinks that all the negative publicity is killing the agency. That donations are way down and this could end up hurting the kids."

Joe should have been shaken by the news but was actually not surprised. The media was raking Father Costen, the Redemption House founder, over the coals in recent weeks.

At the beginning, he had been accused of sexual impropriety by an ex-resident, a young man in his early twenties. Then when the accusation was publicized, followed by denials from Father Costen, two more young men came forward.

There was some evidence of inappropriate behavior on the Priest's part but no proof of a sexual relationship.

The media stepped up its attack on the Priest when an investigation showed apparent improprieties by Father Costen with the agency's money. The cameras were outside the crisis center on a daily basis. They had yet to discover the Community.

Joe was praying for Father Costen.

From the evidence that he had garnered from the media and the rumors that he had heard from the secular staff at the crisis center, he sensed that Father Costen was guilty of something, of what he couldn't be sure.

When the first accusation was made one could diminish it by thinking that this was a disgruntled boy that Father Costen tried to help. That when the boy turned 21 and couldn't stay at the agency any longer, he had asked for special favors from Father Costen that weren't granted. Residents over twenty-one were referred out to adult shelters and organizations.

The only way that a resident or ex-resident can get revenge on the Priest or on any counselor for that matter was by an accusation. That's the only power an angry resident has.

Joe knew this. He also knew that it wasn't impossible for an ordained person to give in to temptation.

When one chooses to serve God and makes an outward commitment to do so, the average everyday temptation one suffers with increases in volume dramatically. The invisible enemies of goodness and love mount an army and attack.

He had never heard of spiritual warfare until his Commitment Mass. The forces of darkness don't wait. They attack immediately. The feeling was palpable that he had entered a new realm of his spiritual journey, especially in the chastity department.

He had never felt so lustful. And this attack was over a 13-month commitment. He couldn't imagine the intensity of the attack on someone called to Holy Orders. He understood why all the prayer was mandatory.

"Well, we'll see what happens," he said to the girls.

"All that we can do is pray for him. Pray for God's Will to be done. We all know the kids are what are important."

Bebe smiled at Joe. Charo was frowning. Charo still didn't comment. Joe could tell that she was sad and disappointed. He had never really had a conversation with Charo. He'd had many with Bebe, especially in the beginning.

He came to Community with the thought in the back of his mind that he would meet his one true love here. After all, the Lord had said: "seek ye first the

Kingdom of God, and all that you need you will get", or something like that. Like most Catholics, he wasn't very good at quoting scripture. He knew scripture. He knew the Gospel. But he had never spent much time memorizing chapter and verse.

He had searched all his life for a soul mate. The search had been futile. He found the girls that he went out with were confused and non-committal.

They were confused about their role in life, and non-committal to a long-term responsible relationship. He scared them off by being serious. He realized now that he didn't date but courted his women.

He also realized that women were confused by the teachings of the feminist movement that contradicted the roles that they were brought up to play. And also went against what the Bible taught.

He thought Bebe was going to be his reward for choosing to serve God full-time, a choice that he had made while praying on a mountaintop in Southwest Colorado.

He was wrong.

He tried to force it a bit in the beginning but he realized quickly that Bebe wasn't the one.

Community members were coming into the cafeteria now. Some walked across the room to the back door that opened to the suspended walk bridge and led to the 44th Street building where the chapel was. Night prayer was in fifteen minutes.

Others grabbed a banana or bowl of cereal and sat down. Some said hello and some didn't.

Joe was looking out the window on 8th Avenue. Across the street on the corner was the XXX peep show and arcade. He watched the constant flow of people going in and out. In the middle of the block he could see Club New York. Quiet, too early.

On the other corner, two hookers walked side by side in their skimpy outfits. Starting early tonight, he thought. The hotel where they took their "johns" was on that corner.

Then Patrick walked up to the table. Joe hadn't seen him come in.

"Why is everybody so melancholy tonight? Who died?"

Patrick took his backpack off and placed it on the floor.

He was a mix of Italian and Irish with an Italian last name but looked 100 percent Irish. He was the community charmer and the best looking man on campus hands down. He was clean-shaven and had short, neat, brown hair.

His humor was disarming and funny but cut to the quick.

"I guess Father Costen's fried," he said.

"Patrick, stop it," said Bebe.

Charo actually smiled.

"Well, he is, he's got to go!" Only Patrick could say this without rebuke.

"He has a bank account in his name with company funds. There's at least one million dollars in it. He's toast. Who's going to send in donations now?" he added.

Bebe looked at Pat and said, "We hear he's resigning tomorrow."

"That's not a surprise," Pat said. "I think we should get this behind us don't you?"

They all just looked at him.

"Absolute power corrupts," Pat finally said, "I feel sorry for him."

Night prayer was short and sweet. The chapel was on the first floor of the 44th Street building. There was a huge bronze mural behind the altar showing the kids and Father Costen with scenes from the gospel.

Joe found the mural gaudy. He had been strongly influenced by St. Francis of Assisi during his time in the Community. He was especially fond of the meditative book on Francis. He liked the original version that was written before the author had discovered inclusive language. All the community members, upon joining, were asked to read a book on Francis.

Francis had been simple and Joe liked simplicity. He didn't think that St Francis would appreciate the mural.

After the fifteen-minute night prayer, several Community members, including Joe, gathered near the tabernacle to pray a rosary for Father Costen.

The mood at night prayer had been deflated and this was no better. Phyllis, an older member of Community that joined at the same time as Joe, led them in the rosary.

Afterwards, they all laid down before the tabernacle in meditation. His thoughts led to Father Costen and how his resignation would impact on the agency and the community.

They all knew that Father Costen was the big reason for the success of the agency. His fundraising efforts were magnanimous. The President of the United States, stressing volunteerism during his administration, had singled out Redemption House as the number one non-profit charity in the country. He had visited Redemption House for a photo-op with Father Costen. They needed to replace him with a dynamic person that could impact fund raising in a positive manner.

What would become of Community?

He had heard that some of the secular higher-ups in the agency weren't too enthralled with Community. They could get a pretty penny for the two buildings where they lived.

He thought of the sexual accusations against Father Costen. Although he had never actually met the Priest, he had seen him on the TV news enough times, and had also seen a video of him during formation, to form an opinion of him. He felt in his heart that there was something peculiar about the man.

He thought about all the power and prestige this man had. He saw how far he had gotten away from his Franciscan vows: poverty, chastity, and obedience. He wondered how tremendous his temptation must have been.

For a moment, he remembered his temptation this past Saturday night for someone else's wife. He quickly said a Hail Mary.

And then he had been given Father Costen's cell or room in the 44th Street building. Father Costen hadn't slept there in quite some time and Community decided that they needed it. Joe would be the first person other than Father Costen to sleep in the room.

He will never forget the first time that he opened the door to the tiny cell and walked in. There on the wall for all to see hung a large crucifix of our Lord: naked!

CHAPTER 3

▼

Paul walked across the George Washington Bridge toward New York City. Leonia had been a short walk to the bridge. He could see the magnificent skyline to his right. The night was clear but humid and he could sense the energy of the city drawing him in.

Here she was: Babylon, Ancient Rome, and the center of our earthly universe. What a wonderful story she was, people from every country in the world living in peace.

Wherever she went, the rest of the world followed.

Then Paul remembered the dream. He wasn't very spiritual at the time of this dream but knew the dream meant something when he'd had it.

He was from Pittsburgh but had spent a year in New York going to school for acting. He had been badly turned off by the superficiality and promiscuity that he saw around him and had gone back home to get his degree.

In the dream, he was sitting in a red car on a bright sunny morning on the Jersey side of the Hudson River, watching the skyline.

Suddenly, the ground started to tremble beneath him, first gently and then tremendously. He could see the tall buildings start to sway and then all at once they collapsed.

The whole New York skyline leaned in his direction and fell over. The sun was behind the buildings and as they leaned across the Hudson, Paul saw the gigantic shadows of the buildings coming toward him.

He hadn't felt any fear. He had prayed about the dream. What did it mean? Was the dream prophetic? Was New York going to be destroyed by earthquake?

He had done some research and knew that there was a fault that started in upstate Blue Mountain Lake and actually came all the way down to New York City and crossed midtown. Seismologists and the media rarely if ever discussed this fault.

He felt exuberant crossing the bridge; he had fasted all day on water and felt very clear headed and energetic.

He felt confident and unafraid that he was doing the right thing with his life.

He felt Jesus at his side always.

Paul took it literally when he read in scripture that Christ said to give all your possessions to the poor and follow Him. And don't look back.

He was taking a chance on the Lord. His goal was to trust Jesus completely and walk as if the Lord walked beside him.

His journey had started with a book at a time when he was seeking truth. He had found this book on St. Francis on a park bench in Pittsburgh and only picked it up because it was starting to rain. The book was getting ruined.

He read the first chapter at a coffee shop that afternoon and was hooked. That night he read the small book all the way through.

After that, he used each short chapter at random as a meditation.

He knew that Francis, although never ordained a Priest, had by Providence inadvertently started a religious community that changed the course of history.

This Franciscan Friar had helped to renew the Church at a critical time by bringing her back to the basics: the basic teachings of Christ on unconditional love and sacrifice, a love for the poor and sick, a love of simplicity and poverty. By saving the Church Francis had helped shape Western Civilization: her art, her architecture, her music, her beliefs in human rights and equality, and her great Universities, all greatly influenced by Francis' Church.

He simply followed Christ and others followed him.

He never asked for companions. They just came.

He lived in a cave and worked with the lepers. He begged for alms and food. He fasted frequently, as the Gospel calls believers to do.

Francis believed that true freedom meant not owning anything of this world. This frees you to follow Christ, hence the vow of poverty.

Paul had privately taken the Franciscan vows while kneeling in prayer after three days of fasting on bread and water.

He smiled to himself when he thought about Francis. He had a dream to someday visit Assisi in Italy. To visit the little Friar's stomping ground.

Reading about Francis had led him to read the Gospels and then the whole New Testament several times. He would get to the Old Testament.

He'd decided to live on God's Providence and follow the Spirit wherever it led him. That's how he ended up in New York working on the streets. Good works were a form of prayer to Paul. And he had to admit he was enjoying himself. He never felt better.

He helped feed the poor by assisting at the Franciscan soup kitchen on 31st Street. And though he never begged for alms or food, God always seemed to provide.

He usually slept in the shelter with the other homeless men and sometimes took his meals with them. But he had open invitations around the city where he could eat or sleep when he wanted. These were mostly from women who had met him on the street and liked what he had to say.

He found that he never had to look far to talk to people. He could spend hours on one city block. People would stop him on the street and ask him questions. He would always pray with them.

He would simply ask people to pray. If he had prayer cards with him that day, he would give them out. He liked prayer cards the most. They were a holy reminder to pray.

That's what Paul did. He prayed with people. Right there on Broadway during rush hour, he would hold hands and pray with people. Pray for healing, pray for peace, pray for remedies to people's problems, but mostly just pray.

He loved watching the person's eyes as they looked into Jesus' eyes on the front of the holy cards and then read the beautiful Sacred Heart prayer on the back.

People would shove dollars and sometimes more into his pocket. These he always put in the poor box at church.

Prayer is what he felt called to do. As St. Paul had said: "pray always".

He always used his finger rosary to pray, although like some Saints do, he didn't count his prayers.

And although he loved the rosary and prayed it once a day in front of the Madonna, it was the Jesus prayer that he had been praying in Joe's van.

The Jesus prayer was a simple Eastern Christian prayer that went like this: Lord Jesus Christ, Son of God, have mercy on me, a sinner. Paul thought that he would teach Joe that prayer someday.

He thought about Joe and his bike accident. He knew the event to be the work of the Lord. Not to compare Joe to the great Saints, but hadn't St. Paul been knocked off of a horse and blinded too? While on his way to do wrong?

He decided that he would pray for him everyday.

He had a feeling that Joe had been chosen by God for a special purpose, maybe to serve the street kids, or maybe for something else.

Paul took a right on Broadway and headed downtown. The night was still young and he knew that he could be on 19th Street in an hour.

New York City was not as big as people thought. One could walk it clear across in a couple of hours. The city consisted of many small neighborhoods where you could see the same people all the time. Many said hello to him.

He really enjoyed this part of the city. From 145th Street north to the tip of Manhattan folks from the Dominican Republic had basically taken over. English was the second language and the aroma from marinated rotisserie chicken filled the air.

In the warm months, you could watch a vendor frying empanadas on the street, buy homemade ices and fruit shakes, and a host of other ethnic food.

There were bodegas on every corner. And Paul had been in every single one of them handing out holy cards.

When he arrived in New York, this is where he had started.

He had paid attention in high school Spanish class and could hold his own. He also had holy cards in both English and Spanish.

He loved the Dominican people. He found them to be lovely, kind, innocent, and spiritual. They would always try to give him money, even though they didn't have much. The women in their very tight pants would reach deep down into their pocket and pull a dollar bill, rolled almost to toothpick size, and offer it to him for the prayer card. He wondered sometimes if they were offering him their last emergency dollar.

They always seemed cheerful and happy.

Occasionally he ran into the "enlightened ones" that could quote the Bible and ostracized him about the "image" on the holy cards. It is true that scripture condemns the worship of images because in ancient times they actually did worship the image. Today we don't worship the image. Images help us to pray and remind us to pray to God, not to the image.

These were the Pentecostals that criticized Paul and he would take it in stride. Telling them that where there are two or more gathered in His name, He is there amongst them. He could argue with them if he wanted to, for he was a well-read and well-versed apologist, but he would choose not to.

On 165th Street, he saw a traveling sidewalk vendor that had taken the Sacred Heart card from him and put it in the plastic vendor license case that hung from his neck. He sold delicious beef, cheese, and chicken empanadas.

He smiled to himself as the short, stocky, man pushed his cart over to greet him. The man pulled the holy card out and told him in Spanish that he prays it every morning.

He then read the prayer out loud to him while holding his arm. They both smiled and Paul kept walking.

On 150th Street, he noticed the soup vendor come around the corner with a fresh cooler full of delicious fish soup. He sold pint plastic containers for $5 and sold out quick.

He saw Paul coming and stopped him. Paul couldn't remember if he had actually ever met this man or not, although he had seen him on the street ladling out his chowder.

The man twisted off the top of the cooler, which was actually meant to carry water, and scooped a deliciously aromatic hot soup into the plastic container and handed it to him with a spoon.

Paul couldn't refuse.

The chowder had fish, shrimp, and crab with a little rice and a couple pieces of carrot. He ate as he watched the man scoop ladle after ladle for people lining up for theirs. He felt good about breaking his fast with something so wholesome and delicious.

Paul briskly walked the rest of the way to 19th Street.

He passed through Washington Heights, Harlem, Columbia University, the Upper West Side, Lincoln Center, Times Square, and finally Chelsea.

He turned right on 19th Street and rang the bell that said Corcoran at a 10-story building that once housed a parking garage.

A female voice answered.

"It's Paul," he said, and was buzzed up.

CHAPTER 4

▼

Joe no longer had Father Costen's cell. In fact, he'd only had it for a couple of weeks. They had removed the crucifix after his first day in the cell when he had commented that the naked Lord made him feel uncomfortable.

He had felt a special significance about having Father Costen's old room and was disappointed when he was moved to the 8th Avenue building without explanation.

He figured it out later when the mealy mouthed guy that was given his room, a guy that worked in the community and was never hands on with the kids, was appointed the new director of the community.

After a lot of butt kissing and campaigning, Vincent LaBianco's power trip dreams were coming to fruition. Father Costen's room and old job were his.

Joe had actually gotten to know Vince pretty well and believed him to be in the community for selfish reasons.

Monday morning came quick.

He took a shower after Morning Prayer. Each residential floor of the community had a mutual bathroom with two toilets and two showers. There were men's floors and women's floors.

He felt bad about falling asleep during meditation that morning but remembered that St. Teresa the "little flower" often fell asleep during prayer. Legend has it that she prayed in her sleep.

He got dressed listening to a Billy Joel tape in his cell and went down to the cafeteria.

He had never been much of a cereal eater growing up, like most of his friends were, but had developed a fondness for fake cheerios and milk. He was still a bacon and egg man. But as necessity is the mother of invention, he developed a liking for cereal while in Community: it's all there was.

There wasn't much chatter in the lunchroom that morning. The mood was rather somber. He heard that Father Costen had announced a news conference for 3 p.m.

Joe didn't have to go in until noon that day, as he was working a mid-shift.

He walked over to 42nd Street for 9 o'clock Mass. When he got back, he went back up to his room and curled up with a novel that he had picked up.

Pillars of the Earth by Ken Follet was the book. He was enthralled with this book about Cathedral building and the villages that developed from them throughout Europe.

At 11:30 he headed out. He always took the same route. He would walk down 8th Avenue to 42nd Street (At that hour he'd be walking contrary to the masses of humanity flooding out from the Port Authority). Then he would make a right on 42nd Street past the Catholic Church where the community members often attended Holy Mass.

He always made the sign of the cross when walking in front of a place where he knew had the Blessed Sacrament, the "Real Presence."

He would then make a left on 9th Avenue and a right on 41st Street going west. There would always be a few kids from the Center hanging out on 41st Street in their new Redemption House duds.

Giving the new arrivals at the Crisis Center new clothes was one of the few fun things that were part of Joe's job.

The Center had a room upstairs loaded with brand new jeans, shirts, sneakers, blouses, skirts and shoes. All donated and all carefully inventoried. Everything was in huge piles in the tiny room and the kids could pick out two of each.

No kid turned it down.

The smaller kids sometimes had trouble finding their size and would take huge pants. This would result in the kid's pants constantly sagging down revealing their boxer shorts. Joe noticed that this was becoming a trend. The suburban boys were starting to show off their boxer drawers too.

He sensed that a lot of the new trends and a lot of the culture in America were coming from the black neighborhoods.

When he turned in at the agency at 41stStreet and 10thAvenue, he flashed his ID to the guy in the booth and started walking inside. One of the security guys stepped out of the booth and intercepted him.

He pointed to a frail, hopeless looking black kid that was standing behind the "don't cross line" holding a small duffle bag. He was wearing a wool pea coat in spite of the hot weather.

"Maybe you can help that kid, Joe," the guard said. "He's an ex-resident. He's too old now and has nowhere to go. I don't think he's feeling too good."

Joe's eyes met the young black man's eyes and he felt a deep sadness. He often felt sadness at work. But this he sensed was a little different.

He walked over to the young man.

"Hey, what's your name?" He asked.

"Huey," he said quietly. "Actually, my name is Hubert Lott."

"What's up?" he asked.

"I've been sleeping on the trains and I haven't eaten in a while."

The kid looked frail, like he hadn't eaten in a long while. He had been living on the trains. Lots of kids did that. They would hustle up a token or jump the turnstile and ride the trains from one end of New York City to the other, all night. The trains were warm and relatively safe because every train had at least one security guard.

"How old are you?" Joe asked.

"I'm 24," the young man said.

"I understand that you were once a resident here, how long ago?"

"Like everybody else, I was referred to Volunteers of America when I turned twenty-one. They helped me find a place to live and a job, but that didn't last. I've been on the street on and off ever since."

"Why'd you come back here? Why didn't you go to one of the men's shelters or to a soup kitchen? There's one right on 31st Street and Seventh Avenue."

"I don't know for sure," Huey said, "I guess I just wanted to see the place one more time. This place is special to me."

Joe sensed there was something more to this story; the young man's clothes were pretty clean and stylish.

"I have Aids," Huey blurted out.

Joe and Huey looked at each other in silence.

"Even what I do eat, I can't hold it down.

"I'm weak. I can barely walk now. I'm wearing long sleeves and pants so you can't see the cancer."

Joe knew that Aids patients died mostly from pneumonia or a cancer induced by the weakening of the immune system. The disease left terrible blotches on the skin.

He also knew that on the 4th floor there was a special unit no one talked about. He knew this unit was for the HIV positive kids. The general population at the Center didn't know this. He had heard that 30% of the residents were actually HIV positive and knew a blood test was required right after intake.

Holding the young man's arm, they walked through the building to the tiny Crisis Center cafeteria. He motioned to people in his Unit that he would be right there. He could see them through the portable Plexiglas and plastic divider walls that separated the boys from the girls in the intake unit.

Joe was a little taken aback when he saw what he would have to offer to the young man to eat. A lot of the food was donated and someone thought it a good thing to donate turkey drumsticks about once a week. The drumsticks were huge and always dried out. He thought that if there were a client uprising someday, the kids would use these as weapons.

He sat Huey down at an empty table by the entrance to the cafeteria and got him a plate. The turkey leg came with mashed potatoes, cranberry and two pieces of white bread. He asked Sean to watch the kid for him and gave him a quick heads up on the situation. Sean was a fellow Community member who was considering the priesthood. He quickly said yes.

He went back to his unit to check in and punch the clock. He was now officially five minutes late. He ran into Lorna, an experienced and highly capable counselor, who asked him to be team leader that day. He declined and told Lorna that he had to go upstairs on an errand.

She gave him a puzzled look and said, "OK". He had never declined being team leader before. This simply designated you as the person in charge that day. Any important decision had to go through you.

In reality, the person in charge was the manager, Albert Luft. He had his office upstairs and mostly did paperwork. He also sat in at the psyche meetings with the M.D. on Friday afternoons.

Joe took the elevator up to the 4th floor and walked down the hallway to the room marked 45. He was always impressed with the upstairs units. They were plush and resembled a Sheraton Hotel more than a crisis center for unwanted kids. There was a whole floor for boys, a whole floor for girls, and the special needs unit where he was now. On the top floor were the executive offices where the HR Department was and the main office. Father Costen's office was on the top floor.

Joe knocked on the boys' special needs unit door.

A counselor's voice asked, "What can I do for you?"

The door remained shut and Joe could see that he was being watched through the peephole.

He knew about the secrecy of this unit. No one really knew who resided inside. The agency was trying to protect these kids from harassment by the other kids. They wanted these kids to be treated the same as the general population.

"This is Joe Morrison from the intake unit. I have a kid downstairs that needs a bed," he said, "Just for one night, it's a special situation."

"Why's that?" the voice said.

"Cause he's over 21," Joe said.

"No can do," said the voice. "No way, you have to send him to Volunteer's on 42nd Street.

"Or call St. Agnes Hospital. They specialize in this sort of thing. They'll help him."

"Ok," Joe said, "Thanks." And he went back downstairs.

Joe's job on the unit was basically to assess the kids' needs, the client's needs. Then formulate a plan to meet those needs. And then execute the plan.

First, the immediate needs, such as medical attention. He took each client almost immediately after his intake to the nurses' office for a blood test. This would right away determine if the client needed medicine for STD's, vitamins for anemia, antibiotics for infection, or if they were HIV positive. They also determined if a female client was pregnant. He was never informed if the client had tested positive for HIV.

Usually, he could tell right away if a kid was using drugs and needed detox. But the blood test would reveal this too.

A doctor would write out any prescription necessary and Joe would pick up the meds for the client at the agency's designated pharmacy. The staff kept the meds and they made sure the kid took them.

One of the first things they did for the kid, which was very gratifying for Joe, was get the kid ID.

The same day as intake or the next day at the latest, the client was sent to get a birth certificate at the Hall of Records. Then with the birth certificate, the kid was sent to get a Social Security card and after that a state photo ID.

The kids were thrilled. Most had never had ID's before. Having a Social Security card seemed to raise the kids self esteem, giving them an identity.

This was also the first step in helping the kids 16 and up to get work. The goal of the agency was to help build the client up to the point where they could be independent, where each kid could keep a job and an apartment.

Joe unabashedly shared his faith in the Lord with the kids and would often pray with them.

He often remembered what he had read the famous psychiatrist Carl Jung had said concerning the 22,000 clients that he had worked with. The ones that were truly healed, the ones that made psychological progress and discontinued treatments, were those clients with faith, the ones that prayed.

He strongly felt that his clients had lost all faith in anything, if they ever had faith to begin with.

The tough cases and the saddest were the kids with biological psyche problems, the ones with chemical imbalances, the ones that heard voices.

Joe was actually terrified of the deep sadness that he would feel for them. What kind of future could they possibly have? And the ones that showed up at the Redemption House were always off their meds.

That was one of the standard questions that he would ask a client. Are you on any medication? Or have you recently been on medication? If so, do you have any with you or do we need to fill a prescription for you free of charge.

The answer was always no. They would rather deal with the voices in their heads than the after affects of the heavy medicine.

The medicine generally made zombies out of the kids. So they would stop taking them and start acting out, sometimes violently, and get kicked out of wherever they were.

They would end up on the street and eventually at the Redemption House.

Joe had a young lady waiting for him in his little glassed-in office on the Unit.

The Intake Unit was larger than a basketball court with a removable partition down the middle separating the boys on the left and the girls on the right. The partition's top half was Plexiglas, which was covered at night after lights out.

Each kid was assigned a foam pad and a sleeping bag and slept on the floor.

There were generally more boys than girls and the boys were easier to work with than the girls. The girls were more violent and had more fights.

It was first come first served as far as the side that the counselor got to work on. There were five counselors to a side. The first five counselors always went to the boys' side, except for Joe. It was all the same to him, so he usually worked the girls' side.

A female client that kept a shard of broken glass as a weapon had recently sliced Albert Luft on the hand and the cheek. Another time a boy held five counselors against the wall with a machete. No one was hurt.

Joe noticed that there was never any violence on days he worked. Every incident had occurred on his days off.

The young lady was husky and in an apparent jovial mood. She smiled when he walked in. She was wearing jeans and a pink windbreaker with a white tee shirt underneath. She was 20 years old.

Her name was Tanisha. She had recently lost custody of her baby girl to her boyfriend's mother. She felt fine with that because her "mother-in-law" would take good care of her.

"What's up Tanisha?" Joe asked.

"Just checking in," she said.

"I'm in a really good mood today."

"Why's that?"

"Oh, I can't tell ya," she said.

"All right then, did you go to lunch?" Joe asked.

"I'm not hungry," she said.

He eyed her suspiciously. There was something she was dying to tell him. He pulled her chart. There was a note that she hadn't come back the night before.

"Where were you last night?"

"I saw my man last night. I slept with my man," she exclaimed.

He looked her in the face. Her black eyes were bright and clear.

"What man?" he asked, "You got a new man?"

"Nope"

"You don't mean the baby's father?"

"Yup."

"Tanisha, you do remember your plan. You are supposed to stay away from him. In fact, doesn't he have an order of protection against you?"

"Yup."

"I'm going to have to document this."

"Go ahead."

"Did you stay out of trouble?"

"Almost."

"What do you mean by almost?" He asked.

"Well, I found out the hard way that he's got a new tramp, another old lady."

"How did you find that out?"

"Well, he went out for cigarettes this morning around ten o'clock. She rang the bell 15 minutes later looking for him."

"Oh gosh," he said.

"And guess who answered the door?"

"You did!"

"Yes I did."

"And then what happened?"

"I can't tell you."

"Why not?"

"Cause I'll get into trouble."

He paused, looking at Tanisha. He looked down at her hands, her sleeves, her pants, and her shoes. He saw no evidence of a fight.

"Well," he said, "If you can't tell me, then I'm disappointed. I must not be doing a good job."

"Why not?"

"Because I haven't gained your trust."

At that Tanisha got up and walked out of Joe's office and into the lounge. There was a TV playing a soap opera. Most of the kids were out of the building.

He put Tanisha's file away and locked the office. She should not have been in there without a counselor.

He walked down to the back of the Unit and went through the door to the private office where the Intake Unit secretary worked. She was an older lady, probably in her seventies. She had gray hair and always wore dark clothes as if in mourning. Her name was Jane Walsh. She was in his Community and he admired the fact that she had worked here for five years. That was unusual. Most Community members left after their 13 months. Some stayed a second year if accepted. She had found a home.

"I made fresh coffee," she said.

He grabbed a Styrofoam cup and poured a black coffee with two sugars.

"Are you going to watch the press conference?" he asked. He knew the press conference was upstairs and if they wanted to, they could probably sneak up.

"No, I don't think so," she said and smiled. Jane Walsh had a disarming smile. Some would say that she looked like an old hag and then she would smile and her inner beauty would show, catching you by surprise. Joe thought this came from love.

He didn't know that much about Jane but figured she was a widow, looking to serve Jesus and make herself useful.

The coffee was hot and bitter on his tongue. He added more sugar.

"You look refreshed Joe. Did you recharge you battery on your free weekend?"

"Some what," he said. "I took a ride up to a lake on my bike. Watched some baseball. Saw my mother. She's doing fine."

"That's good. You need to get away from here and relax sometimes. Otherwise, you can burnout pretty bad, especially you Joe. They always give you the toughest ones."

"I am feeling a bit of fatigue, but I don't mind Jane," he said as he headed out the door. "Have a great day."

He went back to his little office and sat at his desk to go through the files and to catch up on the weekend's business.

He had read his clients files first. He would then read the files on any new intakes in case they became his clients. He was checking Juanita Jefferson's file. She was a 16 year old who had two kids by her stepfather.

She couldn't take living at home with her alcoholic stepfather and her mother anymore, one big happy family.

When she came two weeks ago, they had discovered that she had gonorrhea. Joe was checking her file to make sure the staff had administered her medicine.

Then Tanisha knocked on the glass door.

He signaled her in.

"OK, I'll tell you."

He looked up at her face. She wasn't smiling anymore.

"I cut her."

"What?"

"I cut her throat."

Joe was speechless.

"You killed her?" He finally asked.

"No! No! I cut her on the side of her neck. Not in the front. If I wanted to kill her I would have cut the front of her throat, the jugular. I just wanted to scare her."

This was a first for Joe. He had never had a situation like this. He knew what he had to do. But he didn't like it. Maybe it's not true he thought.

"What happened after that? Did she fall down? How bad was she bleeding?"

"I left her in the apartment holding her neck. It wasn't bleeding that bad. It was just on the side. Like I told you, I didn't cut no artery."

"Oh boy!"

"She got to know she taking a chance dating my man."

"Tanisha this isn't funny anymore. Tell me that you didn't do this."

"I did it."

"What did you cut her with?"

"My razor."

"Your razor?"

"Yea!"

"I asked you at intake if you had a weapon, you said no. Where is the razor?"

"I have it." She said.

She could see the seriousness in Joe's face. He had never looked at her like that before. She started feeling nervous. The voices in her head started talking all at once. He was going to betray her.

"What are you gonna do?" she asked.

"I have to tell my boss. Tanisha give me the weapon."

She didn't hesitate. She reached into her windbreaker pocket and pulled out the large steel handle. The box cutter blade was slid in and not exposed. She put it on Joe's desk. Her heart was pounding.

He picked up the box cutter and slid out the blade with his thumb. There was no blood on it. He looked up at Tanisha.

"I cleaned it," she said.

He noticed Tanisha's eyes were glazing over. Not from tears but from fear. He sensed her anxiety.

"Tanisha, its policy, I have to tell my boss. I'll try to protect you as much as I can. You're sure the girls' not badly hurt?"

Tanisha had spaced out. She was looking past him. She got up and went out of the office. She grabbed a huge cushion off the couch and lay down on top of it. She then started bouncing on the cushion from the waist up, over and over. Tears were streaming down her face.

Joe watched this from his office. He stepped out and went over to his client. He stopped and remembered to say a quiet prayer: "Holy spirit help me."

Tanisha had entered another world. She was no longer where she appeared to be. He tried talking to her, but couldn't get her to respond. She started sobbing loudly, wildly.

He called his boss and then called Bellevue Emergency. They would come as soon as they could.

Redemption House never called the police on their clients. Tanisha said the girl wasn't badly hurt and he believed her.

Bellevue Psychiatric was his only choice in this situation. They would calm her down. They were used to the violent ones and knew what to do.

Sadness came over him. He really felt like he had betrayed his client's trust. But this wasn't a game. She needed help.

There had been no indication that Tanisha had a psychiatric problem. But then again she lied about that weapon too.

He knew he would never see her again. You're barred for life if caught with a weapon.

He prayed as he watched Tanisha through the glass wall of his office. She had been bouncing and crying for almost an hour now. Then the call came from the front desk. Bellevue had arrived.

The two guys in the white suits came into the Unit. One was holding a medic bag and the other was rolling a wheel chair. The wheel chair had straps for the arms and legs. They also tied the head back.

Joe came out of the office and met the men briefly. He told them to please be kind and as gentle as possible. They knew the routine.

When Tanisha saw the men she got up and walked out the door. The two men followed. Joe followed them outside. She didn't try to run. The men were talking to her. She finally spoke and said she would go peacefully if they didn't tie her down.

They all got into the ambulance. She never looked at Joe. They drove away. He never told Bellevue about the razor.

He went back to his desk. He couldn't identify the tremendous emotion that he felt. The closest he could come was sadness, maybe pity. Was it compassion? Is compassion painful?

He finished writing in Tanisha's file and closed it.

Other than Tanisha, the day had been quiet on the unit. On a beautiful sunny day, the kids usually disappeared outside in the morning, skipped lunch on the unit, and came back for supper. If they came back past 10 p.m. they weren't allowed in.

Joe walked across to the cafeteria. He didn't see Huey. He saw Sean.

"Where is he? Did they let him upstairs?"

"No." Sean said, "About an hour after you left he asked for a blanket and a puke bag. I checked his temperature, and it was almost 105. I called St Agnes. They came right away and picked him up. It seemed like they knew him."

Sean could have easily alerted Joe by calling his office. He knew the extension Thanks for nothing Joe thought to himself.

He turned and went back to his unit.

And then he realized: Huey had come home to die. This must have been his only residence where he had felt welcome, maybe even loved. A son of Redemption House had come home to die. And we sent him away.

He forgot all about the press conference. The cameras outside the agency reminded him. He ignored the reporters with their microphones.

He decided to head straight up 41stStreet to 8th Avenue then cut left to 44th Street. He had a feeling inside that this is the way he should go today.

The time was around 9 p.m. and the night was hot but not humid, a nice night. When he saw the boxes lined up under the Port Authority canopy, he realized why he came this way. He was hoping to see Paul. He had neglected to ask him where to get in touch with him and this is where he had first met him. Maybe he would be here.

CHAPTER 5

▼

Paul awoke on the floor of Gwen Corcoran's bedroom. He took the cotton blanket that she had provided him and put it inside the thin foam mat and rolled it up. He carefully slipped it under Gwen's bed and knelt to pray.

There were no windows in Gwen's bedroom but he knew that the sun was rising. His guardian angel, Claude, awoke him every morning at sunrise, as he had requested.

He said his morning prayer, thanking God for keeping him during the night and offering Him his day.

He had spent the weekend with Gwen and her sister. They lived here on the fifth floor of this renovated parking garage. Most tenants owned a whole floor and had turned it into loft space. This floor had been split almost in half with Gwen's father, a computer salesman, buying the smaller half.

They had three bedrooms, two baths, a living room and a kitchen. Gwen had the front bedroom with no windows.

Paul had met Gwen at McManus' Pub, which was right around the corner from Gwen's apartment. He had stepped in to listen to a guy playing sax that he had heard while walking by outside.

Gwen spotted him. She was a fan of Renaissance Fairs and had asked him what he was dressed up for.

Paul as usual had been wearing his cassock and sandals. He was particularly dirty and in need of a bath that night and after chatting and drinking ice water half the night, he had taken her up on her offer to wash up and sleep on the floor. She had offered the couch but he wouldn't have it.

The night was a rarity for Paul, as he hadn't talked so much in ages. They talked mostly of Francis and simplicity. Gwen had been very curious. She had become fascinated with Paul.

She had come to realize through their conversation that there was a real alternative to the only lifestyle that she knew, a lifestyle that could only be described as being materialistic and hedonistic.

She especially had loved the St. Francis prayer card that he had given her. He had given her his own personal card. The card was laminated so as to be waterproof. St. Francis was on the front with his birds and the prayer of St. Francis was on the back. The card also contained a small medal of the saint. The prayer card was a sacramental as Paul had had it blessed. The prayer attributed to Francis went like this:

> Lord, make me an instrument of Your peace.
> Where there is hatred, let me sow love,
> Where there is injury, pardon,
> Where there is doubt, faith,
> Where there is despair, hope,
> Where there is darkness, light,
> And where there is sadness, joy.
>
> O Divine Master,
> Grant that I may not so much seek
> To be consoled, as to console;
> To be understood, as to understand;
> To be loved, as to love;
> For it is in giving that we receive,
> It is in pardoning that we are pardoned,
> And it is in dying that we are born to eternal life.

Paul told Gwen that he had learned from the simple prayer not to be selfish; that when he was in a bad mood, feeling self-pity, or getting depressed about something, that the reason always was that he was thinking about himself too much, that he was being selfish, and that the cure was in giving to others, in thinking of others.

When you put others first and did something for them, you had no time for selfishness. Paul felt that many of today's modern ailments come out of selfishness, and laziness for that matter. These thoughts had rung true for Gwen.

He had talked about sacrifices. How important it was to sacrifice for others and that the word "sacrifice" meant "to make holy", and that holiness should be the goal for all people. For this is what God calls us to be.

For the first time Gwen sensed that there might be a higher meaning to life that she had never known about.

There had been a little uneasiness when he first got to Gwen's. He felt a bit uncomfortable in her father's robe while she washed his tunic. Amazingly, she had brought out a dishpan with warm soapy water and a brush and proceeded to wash his feet and give him a pedicure while he sat on the couch at 4 a.m.

Gwen had told Paul about her boyfriend and how she thought of breaking up with him. She told him that she worked for a European Bank on the east side and was considering getting her own place. She worked nights by herself and had the run of the whole office on the 54th floor.

She would pull special information from the bank records and transactions for the day and put them on hardcopy and place then on the executives' desks.

She mainly just waited hours for the information to download after setting the program and left when she was done. She started at 6 p.m. and was usually done by midnight if all went well. She always was paid for a full shift.

She told Paul to drop by some time. Gwen had given him an open invitation to crash at her place and he occasionally took her up on it. He would usually pop in when he needed to wash his tunic. She got into the habit of washing his feet. It was just something that she felt compelled to do.

Nothing romantic of any kind had transpired between them. She was fascinated by his unorthodoxy and dedication. He enjoyed her feminine energy.

The Friday night that he had rung her buzzer, he was surprised to find her crying. Gwen was usually very upbeat.

She wouldn't talk about it that night but Saturday morning she had been awake when Paul got up and she knelt and prayed with him.

She then confessed to him what her problem was. Her boyfriend Andre, whom she didn't love and wanted to break up with, had gotten her pregnant. She had two positive pregnancy tests.

She had told her sister who had commented that this was a no-brainer. Get an abortion. Four hundred dollars and problem solved.

Gwen had been raised agnostic and was not religious in any way except that she had been praying the St. Francis Prayer and had taken it to heart. Paul had told her that if she said it everyday, the prayer would change her life.

She realized now that it had.

So he had spent Saturday with Gwen, and Sunday. On Saturday they had gone to a book fair where she had bought a used copy of St. Bonaventure's story of Francis and a book on having a baby. A step-by-step guide, month by month, of what to do and what is happening inside someone who is having a baby.

This was a good sign for Paul.

On Sunday, they had gone to Mass together on 31st Street. Gwen got a kick out of seeing Padre Pio's glove on display, a great relic. Paul had told her about this mysterious miracle worker Padre Pio. He could read hearts during confession. He knew your sins before you confessed them, so you better not skip any big ones. After the Resurrection, in the upper room, Christ had given the apostles the power to forgive sins in his name. This is in John's Gospel. (John 20:23)

He had the stigmata, as Francis had, which are the five wounds of Christ. The stigmata are a sign of the great love and empathy that some Saints had for Christ's suffering Passion. He bled constantly from his hands and therefore wore gloves with gauze inside to stop the bleeding.

Padre Pio would send his guardian angel on missions of love in his place and could also bi-locate. He would visit the sick in their hospital rooms without leaving his cell. Paul had told Gwen that these were great gifts that God gave to the holiest among us as a sign of His love.

Paul had not been pushy, or overbearing or holier than thou, but he was firm in his belief that there is no such thing as a choice, that no matter what you want to call it, the fetus is human life. To abort is to destroy human life, and that's just wrong.

He told Gwen about how the abortion people had always lied about the damage abortion does to the woman, psychologically and physically. About how they used euphemisms, changing the name of something or the terminology used to describe it, in order to change its' meaning. For example, calling a baby a fetus instead of a baby makes the baby an object, not a human being. Or saying that you're "terminating a pregnancy" not destroying a child, not destroying human life, takes the sting out of it.

Paul was gentle but persuasive.

Gwen seemed happy now and leaning toward having the baby.

He finished his morning prayer and quietly walked into the living room. There was a candle burning in a jar and next to it a glass of water and half of a baguette. Gwen!

He drank the water and took the bread with him as he left the apartment.

Outside on 19thStreet the sunrise was reflected on the windows of the buildings across the street. This was a warm Monday morning in New York City, Paul thought, let's see what the Spirit has in store for me today.

He would go to the Franciscans on 31stStreet for 7 a.m. Mass. He knew he had time.

He walked up 7thAvenue eating his bread and thinking about Gwen. He hoped and prayed that she would make the right decision. A heavy set woman with dark eyes and thinning black hair came rolling out of a deli in an electric wheelchair. She stopped and looked up at Paul.

As he put his hand on her shoulder, he noticed that she had facial hair. Almost like a man.

She looked pleadingly into his eyes.

He asked her name.

"Brunilda," she whispered.

"God bless Brunilda this day with your grace and mercy. Strengthen her faith and give her an outlet for her love today so others can see her courage and good example, in Jesus name."

He smiled and walked off.

This is what Paul did. He prayed.

He reached the church of the Franciscans just before seven and went straight to the front. He genuflected solemnly and slid into the second row.

For a Monday morning, there was a nice crowd of believers on hand. About seventy-five people he figured.

The Priest said Mass reverentially and took his time. This Paul loved. When Mass ended he went back to the prayer room that held a portrait of Our Lady of Guadalupe and on his knees prayed fifteen decades of the Holy Rosary. He used his grandmother's rosary that he had gotten when she passed away. The rosary was still in the little felt pouch with the snap and the simple embroidered flowers that his grandmother had made.

Paul loved Our Lady of Guadalupe. She was the Patroness of the Americas. After her appearance to Juan Diego 500 years ago, five million human-sacrificing indigenous people had turned to Jesus.

She had left her image on Juan Diego's tilma for all of us to remember her by. He longed to visit her shrine in central Mexico.

Not many people knew that Jesus was present in the image. The four-petal flower at the beautiful lady's waist represented a woman with child. The King of Kings, the Messiah, and the Lord of History was safely in Mary's womb.

Paul thought of Mary as the Ark of the New Covenant. He thought about how the Hebrew Armies were undefeated against tremendous odds when they carried with them the Ark of the Old Covenant.

The old Ark contained the presence of God in the tablets of the Ten Commandments and the manna from heaven. The new Ark, Mary, contained God himself, the incarnation, the Savior of the World.

There was a time when Paul was reluctant to pray the rosary because he felt that he was praying to Mary and not Jesus. His spiritual director in Pittsburgh had given him a rosary and a rosary prayer book that carried a biblical quote for every two Hail Mary's.

She had told him that the rosary would bring him into a closer relationship with the Lord. She said that the rosary would increase his faith. There was no question that she was right.

The rosary is actually a meditation on the important happenings of the Gospel, saying the Hail Mary's just keeps you focused on the mysteries. And if you pray it reverentially, Paul thought, God infuses you with the purist truth of his word.

He felt that he was following Mary's advice from the wedding feast at Cana: "do as my son tells you!"

After his meditation, he headed for the soup kitchen located in the basement of the adjoining building. The Franciscans here fed thousands of people on a weekly basis. Feeding that many hungry people was a huge undertaking. He would help out in the kitchen.

He entered the large kitchen that seemed to be made of stainless steel. Everything was stainless steel: the stoves, refrigerator, prep table, and pots. He had heard that a wealthy donor had insisted on this.

He washed his hands and grabbed a potato peeler. He took a 50-pound burlap sack of potatoes and a steel garbage can and started peeling.

No one spoke to him. The Franciscan friars and brothers would let him come and help without speaking a word to him. They tolerated his presence. Some would acknowledge him with a nod or a wink. But for the most part, he was shunned.

This community didn't know what to make of him. He was a free lancer. A kook. A wannabe. Not a member of any order. He was a radical, just like Francis was!

He tolerated the friars gracefully and stayed out of their way, while peeling two hundred pounds of potatoes a day.

He wished in a way that they would ask him to serve the soup someday. The soup was wheeled out in a large stainless steel container with a ladle and 90 to 100 bowls. The hungry sat and waited to be issued their bowl of soup and two pieces of white bread. This worked better than a buffet type line, as too many people were dropping their soup to the floor on their way to the table.

But they never asked him to serve.

By 2 p.m., the friars sometimes fed upwards of five hundred people. The hungry would start lining up outside at ten o'clock and wait for the doors to open at eleven.

Afterwards, the one friar friendly with Paul, Friar Henry, would escort him to a little wooden table with a chair, in a tiny little room with a window, where the friars kept the old pots and pans and kitchen utensils.

Paul would say grace and have a bowl of soup, a piece of bread, and would indulge in a glass of ice tea. He would have wanted water as part of his daily fast but Friar Henry had insisted.

None of the other friars ever complained about Friar Henry as he was held in high regard and with great respect in the kitchen. He was the community butcher and head chef. A wide, powerfully built man with huge hands, he could carve up a side of beef as smoothly and efficiently as anyone had ever seen.

He controlled all the meat and chicken in the kitchen and knew where every piece went. When an occasional filet mignon or porterhouse found its way to his kitchen, Friar Henry would decide what hungry friar's stomach merited this treat.

Henry secretly admired Paul for his devotion and piety. Who cares what he was wearing. He was a big help in the kitchen and didn't bother anyone.

Paul finished eating and thanked God for his meal. He prayed for the Holy Spirit to guide him today as he washed his bowl and spoon.

He headed out the back way and walked up to the new bookstore the friars had set up. They once had just a couple of tables with books and holy reminders such as crosses, medals and prayer cards in another building. Now they had quite a nice little bookstore.

Little Friar Billy was there as usual, his head bent, his eyes focused on a book. The friars gave Billy this job because he so loved Lectio Divina.

Lectio Divina was a form of spiritual reading or prayer used by Monks for centuries. One could read a sentence, a paragraph or a chapter and then meditate on the message. Friar Billy had a passion for it.

Quite often they used the scriptures but were allowed to use other approved spiritual books as well, some by the Saints or of the Saints, as well as books on prayer and so forth.

Friar Billy looked up when he heard Paul coming in the door.

"Well, well, Friar Paul," as Billy called him, "Where have you been? I haven't seen you in a couple of days."

Friar Billy, Paul presumed, was the reason that the other friars were not curious to speak to him. Friar Billy was the conduit of information on him to the rest of the community. Billy was also Paul's supplier of prayer cards.

"I spent the weekend with a young lady," Paul said.

"Excuse me?" Friar Billy exclaimed, his eyes opening wider.

Friar Billy was small in stature and wore large thick glasses that made his eyes seem too big for his peanut shaped head. His hair was a thinning brown and he carried no facial hair.

His interest was piqued.

"I have a friend here in the city. She's in a bit of trouble, I suppose you can say, and needed someone to lean on and talk to. May I suggest that you pray for her tonight Friar Billy."

"William, Friar William. Call me Friar William.

"Okay."

Friar Billy waited to see if Paul would add any tidbits to his new information and sensed none were forthcoming as Paul stared at him with a grin.

"How many today?" Billy asked.

"The usual," Paul said. "Give me 20 St. Francis prayers, 20 Sacred Heart, and 20 Memorare. Oh, and one St. Francis with the medal."

Billy diligently counted out the holy cards and put them on the glass display case in front of him.

When he had them all double counted he held them in his left hand and made the sign of the cross over them while whispering a short prayer to himself, consecrating the holy cards.

He put the cards in a small clear plastic bag and handed them to Paul.

Paul reached into his one and only pocket on the front of his tunic and pulled out a scraggly ten-dollar bill that a prayer card recipient had forced him to take.

He would normally put any cash given to him on his rounds in the nearest Catholic Church's poor box at the end of each day, when he would visit the Blessed Sacrament, but towards the end of the week he would try to save a few dollars to pay for the holy cards.

Every Monday, he would try to give Billy at least $10 to cover the cost of his holy cards for that week.

Billy looked at the ten-dollar bill suspiciously, wondering if the young lady had indulged Paul.

"No Friar William, I got that from the streets."

At that, he turned and walked out the door.

Grand Central Station was only three blocks north on 7th Avenue. Paul walked up to 34th Street and stopped outside of Macy's department store.

He always found the incessant flow of people amazing. There were people of all races, colors and creeds. They were all in a hurry. No one gave him a second look.

He took out his prayer ring and put it on his right index finger. He prayed the Jesus Prayer.

Looking up at the tall buildings full of humanity, he thought of his dream. Was it an earthquake that had brought down New York? What a terrible, catastrophe that would be, a tremendous group effort would be needed to help the wounded and trapped. Surely, other nations would have to help. Maybe this would bring us all closer together.

In the crowd of people, he saw a young couple holding hands and walking slowly up 7th Avenue. The girl looked shockingly like his ex-girlfriend.

She had beautiful natural blond shoulder length hair and bright aqua green eyes, perfect features and a beautiful body.

He felt an ache in his heart.

Kathy had been his one and only. They had lived together for two years. She didn't want to get married. She and her parents had invested big dollars in her education and she felt compelled to have her career.

He had loved her with all his heart. He had been loyal and kind to her.

They had a lovely apartment, large by any standard. With an assortment of valuable antique furniture that Kathy collected on weekends. She paid top dollar for everything.

She was an accountant hoping to be a CPA someday. She wasn't making the big bucks yet but was charging up a storm as if she was.

Paul had never completed his degree in business and was managing a restaurant, a popular and successful Southern style "chic" restaurant that was frequented by what existed of the Pittsburgh "arts crowd."

He had a fondness for the humorous art on the walls of the restaurant. One in particular had a chicken rowing a boat on a beautiful day with wispy clouds on a blue sky. Upon closer observation one noticed that the clouds were actually fried eggs.

Paul by all accounts had an interesting, successful and full life. He enjoyed going antiquing with Kathy although he thought she often over paid. Kathy wasn't one to haggle when she found a piece that she liked.

He had a full size cargo van much like Joe's, so he and Kathy had no problem bringing home their treasures.

They did the usual stuff couples do. They went to the movies. They went out to dinner. They went camping. Paul thought that she really loved him. And yet, as fortunate as he knew that he was, he felt emptiness in his heart.

He sometimes found himself watching the TV preachers with the weird hair when he was alone at home. He found some of the sermons interesting.

For some reason he didn't quite understand, he found himself quickly changing the channel when he would hear Kathy coming in.

And then one day he went for a walk in the park.

Kathy was away at a business seminar when he found the book, "Francis", by Fr. Murray Bodo.

The words in the book seemed to light up the dark places in his soul. He could see more clearly into his heart. He sensed that there was a deeper meaning and purpose to life.

At first, he didn't share his feelings with Kathy. He began to seek Truth. He went to see a couple of Priests in his neighborhood but they were not very much like Francis. In fact, he felt indifference from them to his plight.

He had been raised Catholic but had drifted away. After high school he stopped attending Mass. He would still say an occasional Our Father but was otherwise too busy to pray.

The disinterested Priests did not discourage him. He knew that all of life had good and bad. He was sure that he would meet holy priests along his journey. A journey he knew had begun and almost had a power unto itself, a power all of its own. He felt drawn to Jesus and His church, to the Gospel, to the great Saints.

He found a good bookstore at a Catholic University in nearby Steubenville and began devouring books on the Church Fathers, the direct disciples of the

Apostles. He studied Church History, read about Ignatius, the Little Flower, Joan of Arc and Thomas Aquinas.

He began to understand the battle for souls that was going on in the world. How the world wanted to take God out of the culture. How the world was telling lies about Jesus' Church and deliberately trying to destroy the Church's authority.

He became convinced that he had to join the battle. He understood why he had drifted away: Sin. And the wages of sin is death, spiritual death, thus the emptiness in his heart. He had become comfortable with his sins, attached to them. He would have to give them up if he wanted to follow Jesus.

Kathy had made it easy for him. She refused to marry Paul. He had quit his job at the restaurant to work with pregnant girls at a crisis pregnancy center. He made referrals and found benefactors for pregnant teens so that they could have their babies.

He had taken a huge pay cut. He had taken a personal vow of chastity and had refused to sleep with Kathy unless they married in the Church.

She threw him out.

Around this time he had the dream, the dream of New York collapsing.

He quickly sold anything he couldn't fit into his small knapsack, said goodbye to his family, and started walking east toward New York.

The six-hour trip had taken him two days. He had accepted several rides along the way including the last one that by fate or divine providence left him off on 31st Street, in front of the Franciscans.

And who was standing outside shooting the breeze at that precise moment but Friar Henry.

At first he thought that he was seeing things. He said thanks to the driver and stepped out of the car without looking up and walked right into Friar Henry.

He was shocked to see this huge powerful-looking Friar before him, a short stout version of St. Francis, wearing the tunic and the sandals of Francis nonetheless, as well as the halo shaped haircut that the original friar wore.

Paul had simply stared into Friar Henry's large round blue eyes, eyes the color of a liquid sky. Henry didn't wear a beard and through thick lips and huge white teeth he had grinned at Paul.

"Are you the hungry one?" Henry had asked.

"What?" Was all that Paul could muster up.

"During my meditation this morning an angel told me that at 10 o'clock there would be a hungry pilgrim outside the church wearing sandals in the snow. Are you he?"

Paul looked up and for the first time realized that he was in front of a church. Then he looked down at Friar Henry's feet and noticed through his sandals that he had the thickest toes he had ever seen. They were both standing on freshly fallen snow in their sandals.

He looked up at Friar Henry and said, "I am very hungry."

That's how Paul ended up in New York City. And now he was standing at 34th Street and 7th Avenue looking at the back of the head of someone he thought he once knew.

She disappeared into the flow of the crowd.

CHAPTER 6

▼

He started north up 7th Avenue. The smell of food was powerful. The soup and bread had long since dissipated from his stomach and he was hungry.

One by one he passed the pizza, the Chinese buffets, the grilled steak, and the rotisserie chicken. The aromas were delicious. The restaurants all had opened doors or pass-through windows to attract customers who could see and smell the food.

He also knew that if he went in and loitered around a bit, most of these restaurants would offer him a plate. He found this out accidentally but had used this method a couple of times when he really needed a meal after a long fast.

Paul knew that the hunger pangs went away eventually. He also knew that fasting had made him stronger.

He had read a teaching from the Eastern Orthodox Church that said that if a person can control their appetite for food, they can better control all their desires. They can control all their appetites, especially their sinful ones.

He found this to be true for him. Amazingly, he had also found that the less he ate, the more energy he had and the clearer his thinking was.

On the corner of 40th Street, he encountered a man standing alone looking forlorn and lost. Paul approached him.

"How are you today?" he asked.

The man had a scruffy beard and dark eyes. He looked Paul in the face and then looked him up and down.

"Fine," he said and looked away.

Paul detected a Jamaican accent. He reached into his pocket as the man watched.

He took out a Sacred Heart card with a beautiful picture of our Lord on the front and held the picture up for the man to see.

The man looked at the picture and then at Paul.

There was an awkward moment and then the man reached for the holy card. He looked into Jesus' piercing beautiful eyes and then turned the card over.

His lips moved as he read the prayer.

Paul loved this part of his ministry. Something would change in the person, hopefully forever, when they read the prayer:

> O Holy Heart of Jesus,
> Fountain of every blessing.
> I adore You,
> I love You,
> And with a lively sorrow for my sins,
> I offer You this poor heart of mine.
> Make me humble, patient, and pure,
> And wholly obedient to your will.
> Grant Good Jesus, that I may live in You and for You,
> Protect me in the midst of danger,
> Comfort me in my afflictions,
> Give me health of body,
> Assistance in my temporal needs,
> Your blessing on all that I do,
> And the grace of a holy death.
> Amen.

"Can I have this?"

Paul nodded gently.

As he was walking away, he looked back to see the man carefully putting the prayer card into a wallet.

He was glad the man could read the prayer. Not everyone could. But even if they couldn't read, the powerful image of Our Lord told a story in itself. Love is what the image said, what Jesus said with his eyes. His beautiful image spoke. It would awaken or reawaken something in that person's heart that looked into His eyes.

Paul knew how powerful a holy image could be in stirring someone's heart and bringing them to the Lord. The church had always used images to teach the gospel around the world to those who couldn't read or spoke unknown or foreign languages.

Millions have been saved through holy images.

In ancient times and maybe even in some places today, he knew, people actually worshiped the image and not what the image had stood for, like the Hebrews in Moses' time and the golden calf.

Christ's Church had always seen the importance of images. In the Catacombs of Rome, where the early believers hid from their persecutors to worship and bury their dead, there were 1700-year-old images of the Madonna and Our Lord.

The earliest Christian writers had proclaimed that when the disciples got together to break bread, they hung an image of Our Lord and one of his Mother's on the wall.

Paul would have loved to be an early disciple. One of his sweetest meditations was to be walking amongst the disciples with the Lord. He could only see the back or the side of Our Lord, but the image always brought tears to his eyes. He dearly loved Jesus.

He walked across to 9th Avenue and up to 45th Street. On the corner was a fruit stand, a small shop by New York standards, but clean and with the fruit piled high.

Outside on a chair sat a boy cutting the ripened fruit into pieces to mix with other fruit to sell as fruit salad.

By the open door was Gino, the owner. His grandfather had opened the place; one of the few original fruit stands remaining in New York. Gino's was a Hell's Kitchen fixture, as this part of New York City was called.

He wore an original Brooklyn Dodgers' baseball cap over his balding pate and a large white apron with a sizable belly protruding out. He was chomping on an unlit cigar and watching his grandson cut fruit.

"Not so small Anthony", he yelled. "If you cut it too small, it squishes and they won't buy it!"

The kid didn't answer but kept cutting.

Paul could see the Italian salamis hanging in the window, and the cheeses. The smell of fresh bread and olive oil drifted out from inside.

Gino spotted him.

"Hey Paul, you got something for me?"

"I may," Paul said. "Which one do you want?"

"Whaddaya got today?"

"Who's it for today?" Paul asked.

Gino signaled Paul in and put an arm around him. He whispered to him like it was nobody's business: "She's a regular customer. She lives on 46th Street forty years now. Her husband got something in his lungs. He runs fever. She said his doctor says it's pretty serious."

Paul reached into his pocket and pulled out the plastic bag. He pulled out Mary with the Memorare prayer on the back. He gave it to Gino.

Gino pulled his reading glasses out of a case in his top pocket and slipped them on. There was tape on the nosepiece holding the lenses together.

His lips moved while he read the beautiful prayer of petition to Jesus through his Mother:

> Remember, O most gracious Virgin Mary,
>
> That never was it known that anyone who fled to thy protection,
>
> Implored thy help, or sought thy intercession, was left unaided.
>
> Inspired with this confidence, I fly to thee,
>
> O Virgin of virgins, my Mother;
>
> To thee do I come; before thee I stand, sinful and sorrowful.
>
> O Mother of the Word Incarnate, despise not my petitions,
>
> But in thy mercy hear and answer me. Amen.

Gino walked inside the store and Paul saw him put the holy card behind the counter.

Gino came back out.

"You hungry? You want a sandwich? How about salami and provolone on Italian bread, I'll put red peppers on it for you?"

Paul shook his head with a grin and looked at the child cutting fruit.

"You want a fruit salad again?"

"Eat some meat. Eat some cheese. It'll keep you strong!"

He just looked at Gino with a grin. Gino grabbed a plastic container loaded with fruit salad and gave it to him with a plastic fork and a napkin, after putting it in a plastic bag.

Paul nodded thanks. He then crossed the street and went north toward Central Park. At Columbus Circle he cut into the park to find his favorite tree.

Not far from the carousel, where he loved to watch the children ride on the colorful antique horses, he found his tree and knelt down.

He had discovered this maple tree by chance one day. Carved into the east side of the tree was a stick figure of a man with long hair and his arms open wide. On the west side of the tree was carved a six-inch by four-inch cross.

Paul knew what it meant right away. Christ was killed on a cross. The cross faced the sinking sun that brought darkness. But He rose again to give hope to all mankind, thus the stick figure on the side of the rising sun.

He knelt and said his grace before meals and then said the Universal Prayer*. The longish prayer was written by a past Pope and brought focus to him and his ministry.

He ate his delicious fruit salad which contained sliced cantaloupes, grapes, sliced melons, and a piece of pineapple, and then pulled out his Francis prayer card and prayed again. He remembered to pray for Joe, Gwen, the guy on the corner, Gino's family and Gino's customers. He asked for God's mercy on them all.

He then walked west across Central Park, past the lake where the tourists were rowing the rented boats. A lovely day was coming to a close.

In a clearing near Strawberry Fields, he saw a small group sitting on the grass while two young men in white shirts and ties stood and spoke to them. The two young men were wearing nametags. Paul instantly identified them as Mormon missionaries.

He came up close enough to hear them and sat down. They were talking about Joseph Smith and the golden plates. He listened to them speak for quite some time and then one of them turned to address him.

"And you brother, what is your name?" one asked.

"I am Paul, and I am a disciple of Jesus Christ and a member of the only Church on earth founded by Christ himself, a Church of Divine origin, the one that you call the Whore of Babylon."

He spoke these words not with disdain but with compassion, almost whispering them. He generally avoided this type of discussion, focusing instead on a simple message of prayer and agape love, but he felt the spirit move him.

"May I speak for a moment to this group?"

One of the young Mormons was going to object; the older one cut him off and said, "Feel free."

"First, I'd like to say that the Church of Jesus Christ of Latter Day Saints is not Christian. For Christians believe in the Trinity, three persons in one God, and you do not. You believe that the Father, the Son and the Holy Spirit are three separate gods.

"You also teach that the best Mormon men will someday be gods like our Father in Heaven and have their own world, their own earth. That makes your theology wholly alluring I must admit, like the snake's promise in the Garden of Eden, but this teaching is a 19th century invention of the Latter Day Saints.

"You teach that Joseph Smith will, at the last judgment, judge those souls in the western hemisphere with his twelve apostles and Jesus will do the same in the eastern hemisphere. That makes Joseph Smith equal to Our Lord and Savior. That can't be right.

"You misquote the Bible and call Christ's Church the "Whore of Babylon", this makes you anti-Christian. This is unacceptable.

"And while modern archaeology is proving the Bible true, for example they dug in the sand looking for Jericho, in the place where Scripture said it would be, and there it was. The walls were knocked down and everything.

"Meanwhile the man who ran the archaeology department at Brigham Young University for 25 years, a Mormon university, left your church because the archaeological evidence in South America disproved the book of Mormon.

"Scripture says that even if an angel were to give you a different Gospel that Gospel is from the evil one. Didn't Joseph Smith say the angel Moroni led him to the place where the "golden plates" were, the plates which led to the book of Mormon?

"I would say to you to look at the Gospel and read about the Church Fathers, those taught by the apostles themselves. Study the history of the church, but not the one written by the anti-church people. You will find the True Church there.

"One would have to believe that there has been an apostasy since the time of Christ for your church to be true. Common sense and history disprove that. You could argue that there is an apostasy today and I may agree with you. But I would argue that during the course of history, this ancient Church founded by Christ has changed the face of the earth, civilized it and made it better, much better.

"The very concept of freedom came from Jesus through the Church. The true definition of freedom that is, which is freedom to do what is right, not freedom to do whatever you want.

"Hospitals, as we know them, and universities, were all invented or improved upon by the Church.

"Help for the mentally ill was unheard of if not for some European Monks.

"I ask you to get a catechism of the Catholic Church and read it. It hums with truth. The wisdom in that book can only be from the fruits of the Holy Spirit."

Paul looked at those sitting on the grass. He nodded goodbye and walked past them. There was a lot more he knew he could have said about Mormonism but sometimes if you come on too strong or say too much, you could give a bad impression.

He admired the Mormon missionaries for their commitment and knowledge of their faith. He had spoken to them gently, sincerely and with love in his eyes. This betrayed the fire that he had in his heart to defend his church. Especially from those like the Mormons, Jehovah's Witness' and the 7th Day Adventists that called his church the Whore of Babylon. They backed this up by misquoting scripture and were able to pull unknowing believers out of Christ's church and into their cults.

He could tell you who started their "churches", when and how, what they believed and what they didn't believe. But they all had that in common. They called his church a whore.

In all the years he had been a Catholic, in C.C.D. class and in church, he had never heard a Catholic speak badly of a non-Catholic. He tried to do the same.

As he walked out of the park on 72nd Street, he passed the famous Dakota Apartments, the former home to Beatle John Lennon.

He walked south on Broadway and cut over to 8th Avenue.

He always felt a pang of guilt when he spoke to the Mormons or Jehovah's Witnesses. He didn't like getting into their history or theology but really just wanted to tell them to love Christ and the Gospel. That Jesus loved them.

This is what he decided that he would do from then on. Then he realized that he had forgotten to give them holy cards.

CHAPTER 7

Paul took a while to reach the cardboard houses on 41stStreet. He stopped and prayed and conversed with several souls as he made his way down 8thAvenue.

He ran into a young prostitute who had broken her neck and was wearing neck traction with pins screwed into her head. After speaking to her briefly, she had suddenly jumped into a car with a single older man that had honked his horn, and drove off.

Darkness had come upon the city. This night was hot and thick with the exhaust fumes of a million cars and buses. Paul felt hungry but alert.

He turned right on 41stStreet. He wanted to check on his friend in the cardboard house. From where he was, he could see Joe standing in front of the "house" looking in.

When he approached, Paul could see Sayvid sitting on the milk crate. He was all right. He looked at Joe, who wasn't.

"Hello brother," Paul said and gave Joe a hug. He put out his hand and shook Sayvids.

"Peace be with you," he said to Sayvid, who nodded, grinning. He looked high.

Paul felt instinctively that Joe had been looking for him. He looked worn out but Paul didn't mention it.

"Have you eaten?" Joe asked Paul.

"Not lately."

Joe looked at Sayvid. "Are you hungry?" Sayvid shook his head no. The homeless man looked to be around 30 years old. He was wearing fake dreadlocks that appeared quite dirty.

"Do you want a slice of pizza?" Joe asked him.

"No thanks," he said.

"Come Paul, let's go get a slice."

As they walked east on 41st Street toward 8th Avenue, Joe asked Paul what he had done after they had separated at his mother's house. Paul said that he had walked through Wood Park and then out onto the main street. Then he'd walked several blocks north and found St. John's Church where he had entered and prayed before the Blessed Sacrament for a while. After meditating on the Stations of the Cross, he'd sat underneath the huge crucifix on the north wall of the church just looking up at Our Lord.

Joe commented that St. John's was where he had spent eight years of grammar school. The crucifix had once been the main focal point of the church, situated behind the altar during the time when the Mass was in Latin and the Priest with all the worshipers faced the Blessed Sacrament.

Paul nodded and said that he had then done some spiritual reading with a book from the little bookrack in the vestibule, a book on trusting God. He'd then started walking up the hill through Fort Lee and had walked across the bridge into Manhattan.

Joe said "this way" and they both entered the Port Authority building where they had good pizza pie inside. He had a slice with pepperoni and a coke and bought Paul a plain slice. Paul drank water with his.

They didn't say much as they ate at the counter. Paul was feeling Joe out.

Then he asked, "You've got some time?"

Joe said yes, that he had worked a split and would do night prayer later.

As they walked south toward Greenwich Village, Joe told Paul about the events of the day. He told him about the Aids kid. Then he told him about Tanisha. Finally he told Paul that Father Costen had probably resigned, and why.

Paul listened attentively. He glanced at Joe and saw fatigue and sadness in his eyes. He noticed for the first time the dark circles under his eyes.

"Did you know that sadness is a serious sin?"

This caught Joe by surprise. He had never heard this said.

don't agree

"Sadness, anxiety, depression, and fear, they all come from the enemy.

"Didn't the Lord explicitly say, "Do not worry"?

"They are all emotions that come from fear, and if you trust in Jesus, you conquer fear. It's easier said than done, but pray about it and in God's time your fear lessens and your trust grows.

"I believe that this is what is meant by 'the Kingdom of Heaven is within you', trusting Jesus!" Paul said.

"They say 90% of the things that people worry about don't even come close to happening. You become conditioned to worry. This is how the opposition tries to stop you from being who God called you to be.

"Fear is what keeps you from taking that important first step that you must take to be someone special for God, that fearful first step.

"But you really have to remember to pray about it. Tell God what you want. He wants to hear it from you."

Joe thought about how sadness could come from fear. What Paul said about anxiety and depression he knew were linked to fear, but sadness? Then it hit him. He was sad because he didn't trust in God's plan for Huey and Tanisha. He felt a cold terror when he thought about their future. He would pray to trust more in God's providence.

They were quiet for some time. Joe had suddenly felt focused and more alive at hearing Paul's insight. He realized that he was being healed. That someone had just lit a light in his darkness: Paul!

"Are you afraid of the dark?" Paul suddenly asked.

Joe didn't answer.

"How about wild animals, bears, snakes and the like?"

Joe still didn't answer. Where was Paul going with this?

Paul paused, thinking.

"Well?" Joe asked. "What are you getting at?"

"Do you have any camping gear Joe?"

"Yea, I have a pup tent, a sleeping bag ..."

"Perfect.

"The first chance that you get, take your pup tent, your sleeping bag, maybe a hatchet and a book of matches and go at least three hours up a trail. Maybe up in those Catskills. Go by yourself. And spend the night."

Joe thought for a moment. "Why would I want to do that?"

Paul paused for a good minute as they walked down Greenwich Avenue toward 4th Street.

"The fear that you have Joe, the one that has got you sad and fatigued; the same fear that led you to come find me, is intangible.

"This fear is in your heart. You are in spiritual combat and haven't developed all the weapons to do battle.

"The fear that you will encounter on a mountain in the wilderness by yourself at night is tangible. If the dark bothers you, light a lamp, if it's cold, build a fire, if there are wild animals, keep your hatchet and your knife handy.

"And to sleep, repeat the Jesus Prayer. Ask the Lord for sound sleep."

"The Jesus Prayer?" Joe asked.

"Lord Jesus Christ, Son of God, have mercy on me a sinner. Breathe in slowly and deeply on the first part, exhale fully on the second. The breathing is optional.

"The Desert Fathers in the 4th century claimed this prayer contains the whole purpose of the Gospel."

Joe started saying the prayer. He messed up on the breathing but kept saying the prayer to himself.

The two men turned off of 4thStreet onto Macdougal Street. The famous Washington Square Park was on the left. They went right.

About half way down the block Paul turned and went into a small Middle Eastern Restaurant with steam tables behind glass on the right and a few tables and chairs on the left. The place was brightly lit.

Joe looked up at the sign above the door, the "Speakeasy" it said. He glanced at the food as he walked by. The smell was delicious.

A portly man in a black vest and black tie greeted Paul at the back door. He wore a white shirt and had on a white apron at the waist. His hair looked wet and parted in the middle. He wore a black handlebar mustache.

The jolly looking man shook Paul's hand with both of his and with one move slipped open the door and ushered him in. He shook Joe's hand warmly as he let him pass and closed the door behind them.

Before him Joe saw a sizable stage and about fifteen small round tables with wood chairs and dirty white tablecloths. The joint was half full.

On the stage was a man with an acoustic guitar. He looked right out of 1969 with his long hair and denim. He was singing a song called "Me and Bobby McGee".

Paul and Joe slipped across to the left behind the tables and stopped long enough to hear the end of the song. The guy wasn't too bad. They both clapped.

Then Paul led Joe into a room where the cleaning supplies were kept. Bleaches, mops, and buckets. There was a dry sink against the wall.

This room had a door in the back. Paul reached above the doorframe and pulled down a key. The key fit in the door and he opened it and they both stepped in and let the door close behind them.

They were in the dark now as Paul stepped further into the room to pull on the light switch.

When the light came on, Joe was amazed.

The room could be no larger than six feet by eight feet. There were no windows. There were narrow ledges on every wall, all about a foot apart, going to the high ceiling.

On the ledges all around were engravings hammered out of brass. They were each about ten inches square. Several of the ledges around were filled with the brass etchings. They seemed to tell a story.

In the corner of the room next to an enormous candle was a stool, a small thick wood table on which was a thin brass sheet, a ball peen hammer and a chisel.

Paul was standing facing Joe with his hands on his hips. His huge golden eyes looked exhilarated as he grinned at Joe.

"My vision," Joe blurted out.

"Exactly," Paul said.

CHAPTER 8

▼

Her sister dropped off Yasmine at the Redemption House Crisis Center. They came in a cab. She had her five-month old baby, a diaper bag, and $20.

She had come to New York six months earlier from Puerto Rico to have her baby. Her boyfriend, a drug dealer, had tried to no avail to get her to abort.

As her tummy grew larger, he had basically abandoned her in his own house. He would disappear for days at a time leaving her alone with his mother and sister. They both resented her and treated her accordingly.

She had grown up in Santo Domingo. At age twelve she moved with her mother to San Juan, Puerto Rico. At age fifteen, her mother "gave" her to the drug dealer. He was from the Dominican Republic also. They knew his family.

Yasmine, a virgin, was reluctant at first to go out with this man. She had never had a boyfriend and he was ten years her elder. Her older sister had egged her on; explaining the material benefits her relationship could have for her and her family. This man had a sizable house, two new cars, and lots of jewelry. Soon she was driving one of the cars and wearing lots of jewelry.

She never did drugs or drank liquor and felt always in her heart that something was very wrong with her situation. But what choice did she have? Her mother gave her away to this man and left her in Puerto Rico with him, returning to the Dominican Republic in pursuit of her own new man.

Within an hour of her intake she was on her way, walking up 9th Avenue with her baby and an escort to the Mother and Child Unit on 52nd Street.

Her baby was a boy that she had named Johnattan. He was a beautiful happy baby, easily entertained, with green eyes and brown hair. She was pretty and had incredible large hazel eyes. She had long black hair and a lovely olive complexion.

She was very proud of her son and his light, olive complexion, as he sat in a brand new foldout stroller provided by Redemption House.

Yasmine's bag was overloaded with baby goodies the agency had provided, including soap, skin cream, A & D ointment, a six-pack of diapers and two new onesies.

The intake person was surprised when she refused a six-pack of formula. She was breast-feeding, a rarity at the agency. Most young moms stuck to formula out of fear of ruining their breasts and losing their boyfriends.

She had told the counselor that she wouldn't give anything to her baby that she wouldn't drink herself. And besides she said, formula made babies colicky and affected the bonding between mother and child. One would never guess that someone as bright as she was had never gotten past the seventh grade, which she repeated.

She was smart. She read magazines for hours at the local drug store, especially those on babies and parenting. She had taught herself to read English. She also loved reading the mini Spanish comics that they sold on the streets. The stories were mostly about love and romance.

The fault wasn't hers that she didn't finish school. In fact, she never spent a full grade in one school. Her mother was married a dozen times by her last count and was constantly moving around. She would be left behind with a relative or friend every time her mother found a new opportunity. Often, her mother pursued work. More often she pursued men. In her own way her mother meant well and was trying to survive and help her kids. She had five children by five different men. Yasmine was the youngest and had spent the most time with her mother.

She loved her mother dearly and always missed her when apart. She missed her now. Her mother was in the Dominican Republic.

She had been staying at her grandmother's house on Dykman Street in upper Manhattan. Her grandmother loved her and adored the baby but was very strict and liked to yell.

Yasmine had tired of that quickly and wanted to move on. Her sister had heard about Redemption House on the news and suggested that she go there. They would get her into the "system" so that she would have money, and find her a place to live with her baby, probably a group home, as she was now only seventeen.

Most importantly, the news had said that Redemption House helps kids get into school. Her sister knew this is what Yasmine wanted to do.

The next day, they cabbed it down to 41stStreet and her sister gave her twenty dollars.

During the cab ride downtown, while stopped at a light, she had briefly noticed the bearded, longhaired monk standing on the corner talking to a girl with metal cables coming out of her head.

CHAPTER 9

▼

Joe had had a difficult week. The events at work had wounded his soul. He had felt better, stronger, on Tuesday and Wednesday after seeing Paul that Monday night. He said to himself many times "the Kingdom of Heaven is within you, be not afraid." But this was Friday and the sadness had returned.

He had volunteered for Morning Prayer, sensing that the community was also in a funk, and it was time to get back to basics. He had played Revel's Bolero while reading the Sermon on the Mount, starting with Matthew Chapter 5.

Bolero to Joe was like a war song, a battle march. And this sermon on the mountain was the essence of Jesus' teaching. The community had a battle ahead of it and Jesus was "the way, the truth and the life."

He had felt very self-conscious doing it. He didn't think his community got the point. A couple of people said they appreciated it. For the most part, people were down about Father Costen's resignation. The resignation implied guilt. The community had wanted the priest to fight this. In the end, the media had won. They had destroyed a good soul.

No one had seen or heard from Father since the press conference. Vincent LoBianco had called a quick meeting Tuesday night asking all to pray for Father Costen and for the community. A new boss would be announced by Friday.

The new boss was a plump little nun with a sweet round face. She'd had a lot of experience running social programs for kids and had worked with large budgets before. She visited Community for Mass and dinner and sat next to Joe during the meal.

He said nothing to the Sister during the meal. They shared a simple fare of New England Chowder and bread. The dark cloud of Father Costen seemed to permeat the air of the cafeteria, especially above their table. Conversations at other tables were nominal.

She spoke cordially about plans to bring the fundraising back to what it had been, and said that the community would remain as is for the present.

Joe sensed an inner strength and confidence inside this little nun.

After dinner, he went up to his cell to brush his teeth and read Ken Follet, but gave up after a couple of pages. He couldn't concentrate.

He wondered what Patrick was doing.

He put the book down and walked down the stairs to the cafeteria and cut across to the back door. The crew assigned to wash dishes that night could be heard in the kitchen clanging pots and pans.

He opened the door and started across the walk bridge when he was startled by a figure in a trench coat with a dirty face standing on the roof of the building just below him. He stopped and met his stare.

When he did so, the homeless man scattered back over to the open window leading to the Times Square Hotel. The Times Square Hotel was a homeless shelter where the real sorry cases took residence. These were people, men and women, who had been on the streets for years and really had no chance at rehabilitation. This was their lifestyle. The street was their home. Nothing short of a miracle would adjust any one of them back into society.

Joe entered the 44th Street building and went down to the second floor to Patrick's room. When he felt a little burnt out, Patrick was good medicine. He was full of energy, opinion and humor. He didn't take life too seriously. He was in Community discovering whether to be a priest or an artist. By the way that he was seducing the maidens in the community, Joe figured Pat would choose the latter. He hadn't been at Mass or dinner.

Pat was busy painting on a large stretched canvas. He was in his blue period and everything that he put on canvas was a shade of dark blue.

His work was icon-like in many ways but the creatures on the canvas were anything but the virgin and child. There were always fish, children, reptile people, and his mother (who he had deep seated problems with) men with helmets, and Joe noticed: each of his dozen or so works had Patrick's face in it.

Pat would sketch the painting on a piece of paper 2 ½ by 3 ½ inches and then paint it in oil on 24 x 36 canvas exactly as it was on the sketch. Joe found this amazing.

"Hello Joe-Joe", Patrick said.

Joe didn't say anything. He walked over to the window and looked out at the crowd gathering outside the Majestic Theatre. The Phantom of the Opera was knocking them dead on Broadway.

He recalled how he had borrowed a nice jacket and mingled with the crowd at intermission one very boring Saturday night, and then entered the theatre to watch the second half of the show.

He had found a great empty seat in the orchestra section about 20 rows back and had enjoyed the show for about twenty minutes, but couldn't help feeling a dozen set of eyes penetrating the back of his head.

He had thought that at any minute the owner of that seat would come back and jack him out of his chair.

So he left.

"Whaddaya think of the little nun?" Pat asked.

"How did you know she was little? You weren't even there."

"I know all Joe-Joe."

"She seems alright. I really don't know what to think."

"It's genius bringing in a nun. She brings instant credibility back to the agency. What corporation is going to say no to that sweet little face when she knocks on their door."

Pat knew that Redemption House had some huge corporate donors.

"I hope you're right," Joe answered, "I sat next to her at dinner. I got good vibes from her."

"I liked your morning prayer this morning. It was a nice touch."

"I'm glad you were paying attention. I sensed the rest of the community didn't get it."

"Don't worry about them. They're only thinking about themselves. Costen's resignation is gonna put a blemish on their resumes. They won't be so proud of their year at Redemption House any more. You done good Joe-Joe."

Pat reached down and put some charcoal blue paint on his brush. He continued to paint.

"So Joeda, do ya wanna grab the bikes tonight after night prayer and go let some steam out of your pressure cooker? You look like you can use it."

Pat was referring to the midnight bike rides he and Joe had gone on. Both nights they had found their way to the same bar in Alphabet City, where the "creatures of the night" lived and hung out. This was the piercing, tattoo, evil eye, grungy, all black leather jacketed and chains crowd that came out at mid-night and went to bed at noon.

Clean preppy looking Pat would hit on the girls and black haired bearded Joe would shoot pool. Pat didn't have much luck but was surprised at how skilled Joe was at eight ball. When they got the table they would ride it all night: free beers all night for the duo. Thanks to Joe.

Pat would shoot and miss and go chat with a "chick". Joe would wait his turn and then make half the balls. Pat would miss again and Joe would run out the table. The crowd at the bar didn't like this.

The last time they were there, it seemed like the whole packed bar watched the games. There were so many people that they were pressed up against the pool table and somehow got out of the way to let the shooter shoot.

At 4 a.m. Joe had followed the eight ball into the corner pocket and the bar went wild cheering the opposition, two young pretty ladies who happened to be quite good at pool and had played a competitive game.

Joe was sky high with excitement when they rode home that night. He was used to having lots of people watch him shoot pool and winning from the "old days" in the Jersey bars. He wouldn't tell Pat if he had missed on purpose or not on the eight ball.

"No, not tonight Patty cake. I'm going camping tomorrow and just want to hang out and rest tonight."

"I thought you had to work tomorrow," Pat said.

"Initially I was, but when I accepted a transfer to 52ndStreet they gave me off until Monday."

"52ndStreet?"

"Yea, 52nd Street."

"The Mother and Child Unit?"

"That's right."

"What the ...!"

"Lorna said that if I didn't take it, she would have me doing escorts for the rest of my life. I think she's out for my best interests. She remembers how bad my burnout was the first time."

"That's true Joeda, I remember. I thought you were going into a systems shut down. Who are you going camping with?"

"Myself."

"You're kidding me. Where are you going?"

"I'm going to pick up my tent and sleeping bag in Leonia. Then I'm going to take the thruway to Kingston and go west. There is some real wilderness up there. I remember reading that there are a couple of mountains there about 4500 feet above sea level. I'm going to go up to the top of one and spend the night."

"Have you ever done that before?"

"Nope, in Colorado I hiked and climbed a 14,000 footer with Outward Bound, Snowmass Mountain, but no, not by myself."

"Why are you doing it?"

"I think I'm doing it to learn about fear."

Patrick laughed out loud.

There was a pause in the conversation as Pat applied the twelfth coat of blue paint to what appeared to be the same spot on the canvas.

Then Pat said: "The rich man dies and approaches the gates of Heaven where he meets Peter. Peter says to him 'well, well, well, what have we here. You were a rich man and have been very blessed by the Lord with material wealth, what pray tell did you do for the least amongst you?' The rich man replied: 'Well in fifth grade they took up a collection for the poor and I put in twenty five cents.' Peter looked bemused. He said, 'I have to check with my partner on this one. Hey St. Michael, this rich guy gave twenty five cents to the poor when he was in fifth grade, what should we do with him?' St Michael replied, 'Give him his quarter back and tell him to go to Hell!'"

Joe belly-laughed as he walked out of Patrick's room.

CHAPTER 10

▼

Joe was on the New York State thruway going north by 10 a.m. He had taken the 166 Bus to Leonia and picked up the van.

The bus ride was uneventful. The day was clear and hot. He drank a black coffee and ate a croissant on the way to Jersey.

He remembered Paul as the bus entered the Lincoln Tunnel. Though he had only seen him five days ago, a lot had happened since then.

Joe had a new job and a new boss. There were two other people from the community at 52nd Street. One was Charo and the other an older man named Ken who had recently come to the community with his wife.

He barely knew Ken. He had approached him a couple of times in the community and he always seemed in a hurry to walk away. Not much of a conversationalist Joe figured.

He had been to the Mother and Child Unit a few times on escorts, but that was it. He felt ready for a new experience on Monday.

The night with Paul, Joe had to admit, was exhilarating. He didn't know what it meant that he had dreamed about these brass etchings and then met a guy who made them.

Was this a religious experience, a supernatural event? Or just coincidence! People in the community were fond of saying that there is no such thing as coincidences, that these events happened as a sign from God, a sign of His presence. These were opportunities for spiritual growth. He had had several memorable religious experiences in his life. He wanted to believe this was one of them.

Paul had simply sat down and began tapping the ball peen hammer onto the brass plate without uttering another word. Joe had glanced into his eyes a couple of times and was taken aback by his expression. Paul had been instantly transformed into an instrument of art, of expression. He became a tool for God himself to communicate with us. His golden eyes became glassy but with an inner focus. He was etching a man, a woman and a child holding hands.

Joe had thought this to be unusual. Maybe Paul had aspirations of being a family man someday.

When he got to Leonia, he grabbed his pup tent and sleeping bag, a small canvas backpack from his brother's Boy Scout days, a hatchet, and a canteen.

Mom wasn't home so he could head right out.

He went out to the garage and opened the side door of the van and put his stuff in. For a moment he looked at his Harley sitting in the corner of the garage under a canvas cover. He didn't go near it. He didn't feel "born to be wild" any more.

When he opened the driver side door he was surprised to see the little black felt rosary pouch that his late grandmother had made. His mother had given the rosary to him after his grandmother's death. The pouch had dainty little flowers made out of stitching on the flap.

He picked it up and felt for the rosary. His grandmother's rosary was inside, Joe's most valuable possession. He thought he had lost it.

He hadn't known the whereabouts of this blessed object for weeks. How did it end up here? His mother didn't know that he was going upstate. Couldn't have been her.

Then he remembered that he hadn't brought any of his prayer stuff with him and slipped the little pouch into his pocket, but not before gently kissing it.

Was this another sign from God? Was this a supernatural, religious experience? He had heard that when you're not looking for religious experiences and they occur, that they are more likely to be authentic.

The rosary made him think about his grandmother. She had died five years previous. She had passed on in her bed, peacefully. He was there.

The way he remembered her was sitting in her rocker in the upstairs bedroom of his mother's house. She would be saying the rosary.

He realized later why she never spoke when little Joey had tried to interrupt her prayer. She was on an elevated plain. She was one with the Saints in Heaven, loving God, worshipping Him. She was in the Unitive stage of the spiritual journey.

He had learned about the three stages of the spiritual journey from a book that he had read written by a monk from a monastery in Colorado.

The Purgative or purification stage is the one most of us are in, the infancy stage of your relationship with God. We wish to be cleansed of our sin, purified. We have come to know God and realize that we are sinners.

Detaching yourself from sin leads to the Illuminative stage of the journey. They describe this stage as difficult because you have entered a realm where God's light is so bright at first that it blinds you. You sense that you are still in darkness. You don't realize that you have advanced.

But in that darkness there is only God. And you learn to start trusting in God and needing God. Miracles start to happen. You begin to see God's hand directing your life. Your faith is strong. You become more forgiving, more loving. You see more the beauty in created things.

In the final or Unitive stage you become one with God. You are walking side by side with Him, hearing His voice. You are at relative peace. The things of this earth do not seem as important, eternity does. This is the purpose for our existence, to reach this level. Not many of us do.

Grandma had.

Joe had never heard his Grandmother utter a single negative or demeaning statement. She was kind, gentle, patient and generous. She was an example to him of piety. She was devout. She was holy.

His grandmother meditated on Jesus' life through the rosary for one hour every day. Then she would go downstairs to make her Cuban espresso that she would drink in demitasse cups. From 2 to 3 p.m. she would sit in her rocker looking at pictures of Grandpa, her children, and her grandchildren in frames on her little dresser. Next to those were her mini communion of saints which consisted of little tiny statues of St. Don Bosco, St. Martin De Porres, Our Lady and of course the Savior, Our Lord Jesus Christ.

She had set a personal example of holiness to Joe. She had also given him his greatest gift, his firm belief in life after death.

When he was living alone in his house in Wyckoff, New Jersey, a house that he had purchased, his grandmother, his Abuela, had paid him a visit.

Only thing was she had been dead for two years.

He came home one night after a visit with some friends. He was sober, although he drank beer occasionally in those days, sometimes too much beer.

As he entered the front door of the ranch style house, he immediately felt a presence. He felt like someone had been in his house.

He started turning on all the lights as he headed down the hallway to the master bedroom. When he opened the door and entered it was like walking into Grandma's bedroom. The scent, the feeling of unconditional love, but especially her scent, was pervasive.

He had stopped in his tracks and said, "Abuela?" And his Cuban grandmother had answered him. He heard her voice.

She said in Spanish: "Jesus allowed me to come visit you this once. To tell you that I and your Tia are fine and that you are on the right path."

That was it. He had had what he now knew to be an interior locution.

He went right to the phone and called his mother. The date was April 29 and the time was 11 p.m.

His mother hadn't blinked an eye when he told her. She was a prayerful, devout person. She said: "wasn't it nice that Jesus sent her to visit 'her favorite grandchild' on her birthday!"

He had gotten chills down his spine. April 30th was his Abuela's birthday. He had not remembered this. One hour from her birthday she had come to deliver an important message, about herself and Joe's aunt Mercedes, a wonderful schoolteacher, who also had lived with his family.

He hadn't understood the meaning of the visit until years later. One day during a meditation he had the revelation: If grandma's spirit came to visit me, he thought, there is life after death! Wow!

What a tremendous gift this was from Jesus ... and his Abbie.

Now he was cruising at 75 M.P.H. through New Paltz, New York. He watched the Shawangunk Mountains to the west pass him by. They reminded him of what he was doing, of where he was going. He felt an icy chill run down his spine. He knew this wilderness had bears, coyotes, bobcats, foxes and poisonous snakes. He knew the air would be cold up there on the top of the mountain. And that he would be alone.

He slipped a tape into the cassette player. A Capuchin Franciscan Friar was talking about the media being the enemy of the Church. Father Ben was making some interesting points. Joe had listened to the tape once before.

According to Friar Benedict, the media only publishes or broadcasts negative reports about the Church, never reporting the tremendous good that the Church does. Joe knew about this first hand from working at Redemption House. The media was all over the Church for not consenting to homosexual sex, yet never reported on the Church being practically the only health care provider assisting the gays that had come down with Aids in New York City.

This negativity intentionally tries to diminish the moral authority of Christ's Church, so that the Church eventually loses credibility and her power to be influential on issues of morality. They are trying to make the Church irrelevant. The reason being the Church's two thousand year teaching that all life is precious and that sex before marriage is wrong. Which translates to: abortion is wrong and gays should remain chaste.

He agreed with Friar Benedict's assessment. The secular media was no longer reporting objective truth but had an agenda, and this meant that the media was corrupt and dishonest!

He had met Father Benedict once when he came to the community to say Mass. When Joe had walked into the chapel there were several Priests and community members surrounding someone sitting in a chair to the side of the altar. He could clearly see a glow coming from whatever was in the chair.

As he approached, he saw a little man in a monk's tunic with a long gray pointed beard. His eyes sparkled. His demeanor spoke peace and joy. Joe was looking at Friar Benedict. He had heard that truly holy people begin to glow, that the halo in the ancient art was evidence of this.

After Mass Friar Benedict had had dinner with the community and then gave a brief talk on the importance of prayer. Prayer was the key. It opened all the important doors he said.

He had reminded the community of what his friend had once said, the little nun from Calcutta. Prayer leads to faith, faith gives you hope, faith and hope lead to charity or agape: unconditional love. Agape led to service, for one begins to love their neighbor as themselves. Service leads to peace. True inner peace. The Kingdom of Heaven.

And they all lead to the gifts of the Holy Spirit and Heaven.

Joe went west off of exit 21 onto Route 28. He stopped at the Hobo Deli and bought a large slab of Munster cheese, a lemon, and some pistachio nuts. He bought a gallon of spring water and filled his canteen.

Then he stopped at a fishing tackle store and picked up a topographical map of the area. Sitting in the van, he made his choice. Wittenberg Mountain it would be.

He drove down Route 28 for a while and then cut south down a dirt road to the base camp. The base camp paralleled a beautiful creek.

The sun was breaking through the maple trees and glistening off the rippling water. The air tasted fresh and sweet. The water looked crystal clear, cleansed and purified by the bluestone that the real Catskills were famous for.

He entered the campground. The parking area and campsites were pretty packed already and he smelled barbeque in the air.

He pulled next to the ranger station and got out. He paid his five dollars to park and told the Ranger he would be going solo up the Wittenberg for one night.

The Ranger was the outdoorsy, sinewy, lean-muscled type that one usually finds at campgrounds. He probably hiked five miles before breakfast Joe thought.

Joe had done his share of camping. He had spent ten days with a group in the mountains behind Aspen, but never alone. In fact, he had traveled by two-wheeled or four-wheeled vehicle to 46 of the contiguous United States, camping out 90% of the time. He had not been to Maine or Washington State, although he was right across the river from Washington in Portland, Oregon and was tempted to just cross the bridge and come back. But the pouring rain that day had held him back.

The Ranger was friendly enough and handed him his receipt and a simple trail map. He hung the receipt from his rear view mirror and went to find a parking spot. After putting everything in his backpack, he began walking toward the trailhead.

He was wearing jeans, a white tee shirt and lightweight-hiking boots that he had bought in Durango, Colorado the year that he had lived there. He had a red hooded sweatshirt and black windbreaker in his pack in case he got a chill.

He had spent a year in the high plains of Colorado seeking his mission in life. He had spent ten years in the family retail business and had had pretty good success by the world's standards. In fact, he was sure that he would have attained great material wealth if he had stuck to it. He was making a sizable salary with all insurances and travel expenses paid. He owned a nice home and two rental properties as well as a classic Corvette, his Harley, and his baby blue Chevy van.

He had only kept the Harley and the Van.

He had stopped going to Mass for several years and had considered himself a Bible Christian, attending different churches at different times. But he never felt quite at home. Something was missing.

He had gone to Durango to come "face to face" with God as he had put it, and he had gotten all that he could handle. About 6 months after moving to Colorado lock stock and barrel and situating himself in a single room at 7000 feet of altitude, he had begun to suffer from loneliness and then anxiety.

He realized now that he had taken two steps backward in the spiritual journey to deal with the situation. He had begun to get drunk and smoke pot again after years of abstinence. He had met a Winnebago Indian by the name of Darryl Redfeather. He thought he could help clean up Darryl's bad habits. Daryl was a twenty-six year old student at the local college.

In the end Daryl had won and Joe was doing everything but tripping.

When the anxiety hit, he visited the different Christian churches in Durango looking for help and was basically turned away.

He finally phoned St. Columba where the Priest immediately met with him, a bit reluctantly, but they got together. The Priest gave him the name of a Nun from the parish that he thought could talk to him and give him spiritual direction. He had never heard of spiritual direction, but it had sounded good.

The good sister then gave him the name of an Anglican psychologist who loved and respected the Catholic Church and gave spiritual direction, at forty dollars a pop!

He started attending Mass and went to confession. Almost reluctantly, he contacted the spiritual director.

Her name was Marcia and she changed his life forever.

Marcia was a middle aged, spunky, but devout woman whose husband was an accountant. She lived in a smallish Cape Cod style house one block up from the main street in Durango. She had a neat little office in the basement with its own entrance and a little bookstore.

Marcia introduced Joe to the rosary and gave him a scriptural rosary prayer booklet where one meditates on scripture verses pertaining to each particular mystery. When he told her that he preferred to pray to Jesus and not Mary, Marcia offered that the Hail Mary's that one recites are just a mantra to keep you focused on the great mysteries of the Gospel. That Mary and the rosary will bring you closer to Christ.

Marcia was right.

Joe credits the rosary with the tremendous growth in his faith, his knowledge of the gospel, and his close relationship with the Messiah, Our Lord Jesus Christ. Not only that, but by reciting all 15 decades before bed, he was able to sleep again. He found that, "Do what my son tells you," her words at the wedding feast when she had prompted Our Lord to begin his miraculous mission, is what Mary says in the rosary.

Marcia introduced him to the Church Fathers with books from her little bookstore. He read how these disciples of the Apostles all worshipped and taught the same way as the Twelve, with the same teachings and sacrificial worship as today, and how nothing had changed in two thousand years.

The early fathers called the Mass: the Mass. They believed the Eucharist was Christ's true body and blood. They heard confession. And they venerated Mary. They loved Mary. "All generations will call her blessed", Joe thought. As the scripture verse reads.

Marcia encouraged him to journal, which he did to this day. Not every night but frequently enough to fill several binders. And she introduced him to spiritual cassette tapes, which he learned to love and got an education from.

She was into the enneagram, which Joe had tried and didn't like. It didn't feel right. She also interpreted dreams, and quite accurately he thought, but he wasn't really into that either.

Marcia had provided Joe with the tools to help pull him out of his anxiety. He knew that Jesus had done the rest. He had prayed and fasted and meditated those last few months in Colorado for God to give him direction. What was the plan?

And that's how Joe Morrison, born of a Filipino English father and French Cuban mother, ended up on west 41st Street in Manhattan.

He had come from seven thousand feet to sea level, from the wilderness to the jungle.

Now he was beginning his ascent to the top of Wittenberg Mountain in the Catskills. A foothill by Colorado standards, but a sizable challenge nonetheless.

He paused occasionally to look around and listen. He loved listening to the soft wind bristling through the trees. Every so often, he would stop and look back abruptly, something a friend had taught him, and spot a rabbit scampering across behind him. He only passed two or three hikers on his trek.

The September day was a bit hot for that time of year and Joe had broken a sweat. He realized too late that he had drunk half the water in his large canteen.

After several hours of hiking, he came to an impasse. He was almost at the top, he knew, from looking at the map, and he felt somewhat tired. He could either boulder up the steep cliff in front of him or cut off the trail and set up his camp.

He cut off the trail to the east until he came to the edge of a cliff with about a one hundred foot drop to the forest below. He found a nice clear flat spot about 15 feet from the edge and took off his pack.

He could feel a cold chill in the air that he hadn't felt before.

He pulled out the block of Munster cheese and opened the package. He broke off a piece and put the rest in a zip lock bag. Then he took out his hatchet and looked around for some dry wood. He remembered well how to start a campfire. He could usually do it with one match.

You start with tiny little dry twigs that light up fast. Then you add bigger and bigger twigs that you've collected until you have a few little red coals going. Then you simply keep adding bigger twigs, then branches, and finally logs.

He had enjoyed doing this in the past. He remembered the amateur campers that brought lighter fluid and would douse the logs with it, only to find all the fluid used up and no campfire.

Joe hadn't planned for this. He couldn't find any wood. Not even squaw wood, which are the dry cigarette and cigar sized twigs that stick out from the lower trunk of trees. Then he realized that this area was pretty popular and had probably been picked through quite thoroughly.

He found himself hanging off the side of the big cliff holding on with one hand to a branch while hacking at some dry branches with the other. Time was passing and he had no fire. He had mistakenly picked the east side of the mountain and he was already in the shade and catching a chill.

The back of his tee shirt was drenched in cold sweat. He took it off and put on his hooded sweatshirt and windbreaker.

He felt a little panicky. He felt an icy chill. Not from cold but from fear.

The lower the sun descended on the other side of the mountain, the darker and colder it got on his side. What made things worse was that he could see Kingston in the distance in full sun with motels and hotels open. Oh boy!

He finally got enough twigs and branches together and started his fire. When he knew the fire wouldn't go out, he rushed to put up his tent. There were a lot of rocks underneath the ground and his tent stakes wouldn't go in. He had to move it.

He put the tent up close to the fire, a safe distance away, but where he could sit and feel the warmth of the fire from inside the tent. Then he realized that he had set up the tent on its' side. He tried zipping shut the entrance and it wouldn't close more than half way.

He thought about taking down the tent and setting it up again. Then he remembered how difficult it had been to dig the stakes in.

He thought about packing up and running. Could he make it back to the base camp without getting lost? In the dark? The hike had taken three and a half hours. How long would it take to run back?

Meanwhile, the wind started kicking up and howling like he had never heard it before. The howling wind seemed to circle the mountain, with the noise level getting louder and louder until it swept past his spot with a deafening roar.

He felt real fear.

The wind kept repeating this action over and over again. The cold chill of fear had entered his stomach and then crept up to his chest and throat. He didn't recall ever feeling this scared. He was alone. There was no moon. Without the fire he would be in pitch darkness.

Sitting at the edge of his tent in front of his campfire, he ate the cheese and the nuts. He hadn't brought any real food because he didn't want to have anything with him overnight that would attract bears.

Taking a pull from the canteen, he realized he was almost out of water. He put a log on the fire and crawled into his sleeping bag.

He tried closing his eyes, but all that he could think of were the open door of his tent and the possibility of a vicious wild animal entering while he slept.

He feared falling asleep. The food had settled his nerves a bit but not enough. He felt like he was outside of himself, outside of his own skin. He felt as a soul alone in this tiny space on a planet moving through the universe at 50,000 miles an hour.

His mind started to race. He asked himself why the heck he had done this.

Sticking his head out of the tent, he glanced over at the light of Kingston and thought about a queen-size bed, a remote control and hot chocolate. Not to mention a toilet.

He realized he was being tempted. His mind started racing irrationally. He thought: "why did I ever leave my job? Sell my house? Did I think I could be a saint? No way. It's too hard. Too much sacrifice and pain. I'll never be a saint. I'm an idiot!

"I should have listened to my father and taken the secure route. What the hell's the matter with me? I had it made!

"What am I doing on this freaking mountain?"

Breathing hard, Joe curled up in the fetal position. Then he felt something in his pocket. He remembered. Oh my God, he thought. Grandma, Abuela!

He gently reached into his pocket with two fingers and pulled out the little black pouch and unsnapped it, carefully pulling out the ancient tiny black rosary.

He held the beads in his left hand and the crucifix with the index finger and thumb of his right hand.

Warmth came over him, a certain certitude. He knew he wasn't alone. He smiled to himself and began to pray the joyful mysteries:

The Angel Raphael appears to Mary, a young virgin. Raphael asks her a question. She says yes, the yes that changed all of history.

God entered her womb.

He loves us. He wants to save us. He wants us to hear it straight from Him. He wants to tell us how to live holy lives.

With God in her womb, the woman fearlessly goes to help her elderly aunt, also with child.

Mary greets Elizabeth. John the Baptist jumps in the womb and receives the Holy Spirit upon encountering his Lord.

The child is born: The King of Kings, the Lord of Lords, and the promised Messiah.

Love comes alive.

Mary would have been stoned to death for becoming with child before marriage.

Joseph saves her but plans to divorce her.

God has other plans.

Angels and dreams lead Joseph, the woman, and child to Egypt.

But before that, the child is presented to God at the temple.

A wise man tells the woman that she brings the Messiah and that her heart will be pierced with a sword.

Later the boy is lost. He is found in the temple. At twelve years old he is teaching the teachers. He is going about His father's business.

These are the thoughts that passed through Joe Morrison's mind as he fell gently to sleep, the Five Joyful Mysteries of the Holy Rosary.

He arose to sunshine, warmth and calm. He packed up all his gear and hid them behind a bush. Then he scaled the rocks to the top.

The top of Wittenberg Mountain is long and narrow. The panoramic view is awesome. He hadn't expected to find so many campers at the top but there had to be twenty-five people up there, and a dozen tents.

After taking in the scenery, he scaled down the cliff and grabbed his gear. He had finished off the water and would have to make the hike down without it. Drinking from the creeks that he passed was tempting, but he remembered the stomach sickness that he had once gotten and didn't indulge.

Then he remembered the lemon, the lemon that he'd bought on impulse, not really knowing why. Sitting on a rock in the sunlight, he sliced the lemon in quarters and sucked on them. Immediately his head cleared and his thirst dissipated.

He made the trip down to his van in three hours and drank his fill of water from what was left of the gallon container that he had bought.

Then he drove down the dirt road and headed east on 28 to the thruway.

He felt different somehow. Renewed. Exhilarated. He knew that he had done something profound but didn't quite know what. Somehow, all his usual worries now seemed trivial. He had gotten a taste of something special.

In his blue Chevy cargo van, with the windows all around, driving down the New York State thruway to the most incredible city in the world, Joe Morrison asked God to take over his life, to possess his spirit. "Your will be done," he said.

Then he told God that from now on, He comes first. He will stop praying for a soul mate, a wife, and a family. And dedicate his life to service.

He would consider becoming a monk as Patrick had suggested that they both be, and lead a life of prayer and sacrifice, using his self-taught talents as an organic gardener to serve his community. He asked God to lead the way.

CHAPTER 11

▼

Paul awoke on the floor next to a thin brass plate and a ball peen hammer. He had finished the plate the night before and decided to rest a while on the storage room floor, using his arm as a pillow.

His left arm was pins and needles as he got up from the floor. He picked up the hammer and the brass sheet and set them on the table, then pausing for a moment, looked at the artwork.

He had tapped out a man, a woman, and a baby with a mountain in the background and a creek running at their feet. There was a small saltbox style house behind them with smoke coming from the chimney.

He never knew what would show up on the brass sheet when he started tapping. He let the spirit guide his hands. He was not sure what the picture meant but was quite sure that the meaning had something to do with Joe.

Paul had rested well on the floor, peacefully well. Previous nights he had been staying at the Time Square Hotel on 43rd Street.

He never slept well there. It was too noisy. There would always be sobbing, screaming, banging, fighting and occasionally a gunshot heard in the middle of the night.

He had been involved in an altercation there when he'd tried to break up a fight. One stronger man had another man down on the ground and was punching him mercilessly in the face. Paul had bear hugged the bigger man and pulled him off resulting in his being slammed against the wall so hard that the back of his head had dented the plaster.

He hadn't stayed by Gwen's in quite some time as whenever he'd pass by, her sister had said that she wasn't at home.

Stepping out of the "studio" closet, he hid the key above the door. He then passed through the janitor's closet and out into the Speakeasy lounge. The lounge was empty but the smell of smoke and perspiration was in the air.

He opened the door to the little Middle Eastern restaurant in front and found Fatima sitting at a table sipping Moroccan coffee. Her long black hair, pure black eyes and beautiful olive complexion bespoke her place of origin.

Fatima was from Iran. She had come to the U.S. when she was seven with her father, mother, and two younger siblings. They had fled the persecution of non-Muslims in Iran, walking by night out of their country and through the treacherous mountains of Afghanistan where they'd crossed into Pakistan and caught a plane to Rome and then New York. The trip had taken three months with the threat of arrest, torture, and even death always hanging over their heads.

When she was six she remembered the soldiers burning her father's face with acid, making him practically unrecognizable, and putting the whole family in prison for decrying Islam. She had clear memories of being in prison, where her parents' faith had carried them through the horror.

They were Bahai. A sect started in Iran that had broken from Islam and whose goal was world peace and tolerance of all religions. They had their own prophet who had died and his remains preserved for viewing at a special holy place. The sect was spreading throughout the U.S.

Paul respected Fatima's faith and enjoyed conversing with her. They'd met when he gave her a St. Francis prayer card one day at Washington Square Park when he had found himself standing next to her listening to two guys playing guitar on a park bench.

She read the prayer and smiled at him, giving him the once over. She then put out her hand and said: "Fatima". Paul shook her hand gently and said his name.

She asked him where he got the prayer card from and who St. Francis was.

They talked for three hours.

He gave her five more St. Francis cards for her family and her uncle and she insisted on giving him a $10 bill. He steadfastly refused the money and told her to put it in the poor box.

She then invited him to a meal at her uncle's restaurant and they've been friends ever since. Her uncle was the gentleman in the handlebar mustache.

After the meal of falafels and salad, Fatima had shown Paul the Speakeasy in the back. Speakeasy was the name of the club but it was a legitimate place. The club was a place for amateur musicians to get to play in front of an audience, mostly acoustic stuff. Her uncle inherited it when he bought the restaurant and kept it as is.

Then she brought Paul through the janitor closet to the tiny studio. Fatima's brother had decided he was going to be an artist a while back and then had given up. He had left all the materials in the room and gone off to business school. Paul tried his hand at it and liked it. Fatima gave him unfettered use of the room.

She gestured for him to sit down. He said 'good morning' and sat in the chair across from her.

"What an exquisite beauty," Paul thought as he looked across the table at her. He felt confident admiring beautiful things and beautiful people. They were works of the Greatest Master.

He saw a certain beauty in all women. He believed that he could truly admire the physical beauty of a woman without lusting for her. He also knew that external beauty was fleeting while internal beauty was eternal.

Paul looked for beauty.

He loved the beauty of the Church: her teachings, her great history, art, architecture and her beautiful people. Love made beauty he thought.

Fatima had all of it. She was gifted with a beautiful physical form and a beautiful soul. He had never seen her not joyful.

She pushed across the table a Styrofoam cup full of orange juice and a plain bagel with butter on a piece of foil.

She had bought him breakfast.

"What if I didn't come in this morning? How would you get out?" Fatima looked at Paul with pretending concern.

"I suppose I would lie down on the floor again and go back to sleep."

He then remembered that he hadn't said any morning prayers.

Fatima was always at the restaurant early, doing the ordering for the day and letting in the janitor and the kitchen prep people. She attended N.Y.U. at night. When Paul would walk in, she would always ask him the same question.

He drank half the O.J. and unwrapped his bagel. The bagel was toasted with a lot of butter. He felt guilty about all the butter but took a bite anyway. He was very hungry because he hadn't eaten since the soup kitchen the day before.

Fatima was munching a sesame bagel with cream cheese.

"Your little prayer is affecting me!" she suddenly said with a gleam in her eyes.

"How so?"

"I remember what you told me that you learned from Francis, that when you feel down, the reason is usually that you're thinking about yourself too much. And thinking of others and doing for others, snaps you out of it."

"I've never seen you down," Paul said with a mouth full of bagel.

"Oh, I get down. I used to cry every night, in private."

"Why? What do you cry about?"

"I think about the suffering and evil in the world. I especially think about the suffering in my country. My cousins never got out. My uncle has been in prison for years and my aunt can't provide. They're hurting."

Paul stopped eating and was looking at the side of Fatima's face as she spoke. For once, he saw a tinge of sadness around her eyes.

"What you told me works. My sister sees it too. We both say the prayer everyday. But there's more. I've been thinking about Mohammed, that the angel Raphael wouldn't tell Mary that Jesus was the long awaited Messiah, the Son of God, and then 500 years later tell someone else something different. That doesn't add up.

"He himself was a warrior. There's a lot of violence in Islam, and intolerance of other faiths, not to mention the lack of women's rights.

"In a sense, Moslems are like the early Hebrews were. God would tell Moses to destroy whole villages if they didn't convert, right? But then the Messiah came and changed everything, for the better. If you study history objectively and read both sides, it's obvious that Christianity had a lot to do with civilizing people, with creating a human civilization. Western civilization owes most of its greatest achievements to the Church. Not to mention the improvements in the treatment of women.

"Compare how a Middle Eastern woman is treated and how a Christian woman is treated and you can see what Christ did."

"I'm sure there's many good, loving, people in Islam", he said, "but like the Jews they've yet to accept the Messiah. Also like the Jews, their faith is exclusive; the law only applies to others of their faith.

"There is one wonderful thing that Catholics have in common with those of the Islamic faith: Mary. We both hold Mary in the highest esteem, as the scripture says about Mary: "All generations will call me blessed".

She paused, looking sideways at Paul. He was calm and gently looking into her eyes. She said, "there are two things, both faiths seem to be the enemy of the seculars."

"That is true. Islam is against abortion. And whether its admitted or not abortion is the number one issue in the world today. You are very astute to see through the revisionism of the seculars, they only fault the Church and never credit her for anything," he said.

"How do they get away with it, with changing and slanting the truth of history? The western world denies their Christian heritage, and lies about it. What's their motivation? Wasn't the search for truth the whole purpose of the University system in the first place? They've corrupted it."

"Fatima, the seculars have a false idea of the Church. Either that or they are purposely lying. And from this misinformation, other's have developed a hatred for the Church," Paul said. "They've re-written history without giving credit to the only organization on earth with divine origin, an organization whose monks spread out through western Europe teaching the peasants the best farming and building methods and educating their children in the ways of God and civilization.

"They love writing about the Crusades and how evil the Crusaders were but don't make mention that they walked thousands of miles to stop people from desecrating and destroying the Christian Holy Sites and slaughtering Christian Pilgrims.

"The fact that the crusaders got out of control was partly because they were so far away from their leadership and lost communication with them. They were jaded from warring for so long. They forgot their roots.

"They also don't mention that pagan sects in Spain, during the Inquisition, were stealing babies for sacrifice. Paganism and Satanism were epidemic, and certain sects were organizing to overthrow the Church and the government. The Spanish Church was actually very lenient with its enemies. It was really the Spanish government that became the Inquisitor.

"And lately they try to bring down a saintly Pope with fabrications and lies, a Pope who saved many more Jews than Schindler. Why, the Chief Rabbi of Rome, who Pius kept hidden in the Vatican, converted to Catholicism after witnessing the holiness and courage of this man, this holy Pope. The first Prime Minister of Israel, Golda Meir, gave him an award for being the man that most helped the Jews during the holocaust. Even Einstein thanked him on the front page of the N.Y. Times. But the big lie is still out there, fooling even the elite."

They both sipped their drinks and smiled at each other.

"You've been reading the Bible?" Paul asked.

"How could you tell?"

"Let me see, something about Moses?"

"Yes. I have to admit. I find Jesus to be the most beautiful person that ever lived. His teachings are true. I believe them.

"You told me to try living by his teachings even if I didn't believe that He's God and it works. I'm changing. I see strangers differently. I forgive easier. I feel that I'm growing in compassion for others. Love for others."

He knew this meant that she'd been praying and was growing spiritually. "What Bible are you reading?"

"The New International version, it's the only one I have access to."

"That's a beautiful translation but it's missing books. Luther took them out when he split from the Church on Halloween October 31, 1517. Do you know who Luther is?"

"Yes."

"He took out books that contradicted his views. Get a Catholic bible. The one the Apostles used."

Paul loved having these little conversations. He found that the great majority of people had no clue about the real Catholic Church, her history, her teachings and her effect on the world. And how the spirit of anti-christ was everywhere trying to discredit and destroy her. This woman had taken the time to seek.

"So anyway," Fatima exclaimed, "If Islam is not the true church then Bahai is false because the Bahia faith broke off from Islam."

Paul wasn't sure how he felt about this and kept quiet. He understood her point of view as someone who had suffered much under Islamic rule.

"This is all very joyful for me Paul but very hard too. My parents would die for their beliefs. That's the hardest thing. Going away from what you were raised with.

"Its like you're turning against your parents."

They both sipped from their drinks. He was looking straight at Fatima who was looking down at her cup. She had turned facing him as she spoke those words. Looking him in the eyes. She was thinking that if she openly turned to Christ, her family would be devastated.

"That's the hardest part of conversion, going against your ancestors. But if you truly feel God calling you, you must answer him," Paul said.

"Is that what's happening to me Paul? God is calling me to conversion?"

"Sounds like it."

They both chewed and swallowed and drank for a while.

Until Paul wiped his mouth with a napkin and asked, "Do you have access to a Catechism?"

"No, I haven't thought about that."

"The Catechism is a work of beauty and truth, truly remarkable. Take a glance at it when you get a chance."

Fatima was smiling, a beautiful radiant smile. She had perfect white teeth and full lips. "We share a secret now," she said.

"Who am I going to tell?" Paul asked.

There was a knock on the door and Fatima got up to answer it. The bread man had brought two large paper bags full of rolls. Paul watched him hand them to Fatima and walk away.

"Keep the door open," he said, "I got to go."

"Where are you going so fast?"

"I have to meet a friar at the soup kitchen. He's going to make homemade tomato sauce and I get to watch. Maybe I'll learn something."

"Oh well. I do have to get my ordering done. We're fast running out of napkins and I need to get some right away."

Paul walked out on to MacDougal Street and turned back to wave. Fatima waved back. He prayed for the Holy Spirit to show her the way. He asked that God's Will be done and made the sign of the cross.

He walked the twenty-seven blocks to 31stStreet in half an hour and entered the church, going directly for a visit with the Blessed Sacrament. Usually he didn't speak when kneeling before the Real Presence. He tried to listen. But this time he said a prayer, "I love you oh Jesus and I praise You, for by Your Holy Cross, You have redeemed the world.

"Heavenly father, I ask in Jesus name for mercy and grace for Joe, Gwen, and Fatima. I pray that the Holy Spirit fill their hearts. And as always: Thy will be done. Thank you Jesus."

He knelt for a few more moments staring at the perpetual candle in the red glass container, the candle that stood for eternal life. The light that stood for Emmanuel: God with us, The Holy Eucharist.

He got up gently off his knees and walked backwards away from the Blessed Sacrament making the sign of the cross. Then he turned and walked to the back of the church where the Virgin of Guadalupe waited, his virgin, with Jesus in her womb.

The ancients had the Ark of the Covenant and were invincible when they carried it into battle. The Ark contained the manna from heaven and the Ten Commandments. Paul believed Mary was the new Ark of the Covenant, carrying the God-man in her womb. And he carried her with him everyday in his spiritual battles.

He knelt before her and said a Hail Mary, a prayer whose words come straight from the Bible. And thanked her for talking to her Son on his behalf.

He believed that Mary had the keys to Jesus' heart. And with her prayer she could open it and graces would flow out.

He believed that in heaven, His earthly Mother had asked her divine son if she could play a bigger part in the salvation of her children on earth, because she couldn't sit still, even in Heaven, knowing of the suffering of the lost souls on earth.

He believed that Jesus had said yes, as Mary had said yes to the heavenly messenger at the Annunciation.

This was Paul's meditation time, a time when he'd pray all 15 decades of the rosary, but Friar Henry was waiting.

When he walked into the kitchen Friar Henry had six huge aluminum pots sitting on top of six gas burners on a huge stainless steel stove. On aluminum tables sat a dozen giant cans of tomato paste, cans of diced tomatoes and separate piles of chopped garlic and onions. He had just turned on all the burners full tilt and was opening a gallon container of Spanish olive oil.

"You made it brother," he said.

"I knew you would."

Paul grinned and waited for instructions.

The Friar looked healthy and rested and full of energy, as he always did. He held the gallon tin in one huge paw and began pouring some into each pot. The oil made a searing noise when it splashed in the pot.

After pouring some in each pot, he grabbed a handful of chopped onions and tossed them into the first container. Then he looked at Paul and said, "Do the same."

Paul held the large wooden cutting board, piled high with onions in one hand and grabbed handfuls with the other, tossing them into the pots one by one.

Meanwhile Friar Henry began opening the cans of tomato paste with a manual can opener.

When Paul had finished with the onions, he was instructed to do the same with the fresh crushed garlic. When he was done he figured that he'd dropped a dozen cloves in each pot.

Henry then handed him a measuring spoon and a large bag of oregano.

"Two spoonfuls in each," is all he said.

Paul followed his instruction.

The frying mixture was deliciously aromatic. When Paul smelled the oregano, he immediately felt his sinuses opening up.

When Paul was done, Henry took one large can of tomato paste and poured some in each pot.

"Keeps the onions from burning," he said.

He then handed Paul a hand held can opener as well and they both proceeded to open all the cans and pour them into the pots.

Then Henry took a large bowl of salt and with his fingers tossed salt into the sauce. Then he covered all the pots as Paul collected the cans for the garbage heap.

"We've got two hours," Henry said. "When they come to a boil, we stir 'em and lower the flame a bit. In an hour we start the spaghetti."

Paul could always tell a good cook, by the smell in the kitchen. If the kitchen had a delicious smell he knew that there was culinary magic at work.

The same held true for restaurants, especially Italian restaurants. The good ones exuded an aroma that grabbed you half way down the block. If a restaurant has a bad smell, on the other hand, don't eat there. Henry's kitchen always smelled great. And he made the best chicken soup Paul had ever had.

Henry had once made a special batch of chicken soup for some of the brothers with the flu. Paul had seen a man delivering three live chickens to him by a back door. Henry had glanced over at him and disappeared into a back room.

Moments later, he had come out of the back room with three Kosher chickens ready to cook. He had explained to Paul that these were organic chickens. They were free roaming chickens that grew up eating natural food, and because they could walk around and weren't jammed in a pen, their meat was a little tougher but had a good flavor and was better for you.

Henry had then proceeded to make a matzo ball soup so delicious that Paul had seconds for the only time ever at the soup kitchen.

Henry made the soup, he said, in honor of our older brothers in the faith, the Jews. We have something in common he had told Paul. We both love The Father.

Paul had never thought of the Jews that way. He liked it.

Now he was standing next to the wide man with the fattest toes in New York, waiting for the sauce to boil. At another stove, several other friars were preparing to cook the spaghetti. They had filled ten big pots with water and were setting them on the stove.

They had four cases of dry spaghetti open. They had opened each individual box and placed the contents into a large tin. The spaghetti was now ready to be tossed into the boiling cauldrons when the time came.

When the sauce boiled, Friar Henry lowered the flames beneath the pots and nodded to Paul to follow him. They walked outside and into another building. Up three flights of stairs and they were standing before a thick dark mahogany door with a heavy plated brass doorknob.

Henry pulled an unusual looking skeleton key from his pocket and unlocked the door. Paul followed him into the 10x10 cell. He stiffened when Henry closed and locked the great door. The room was pitched black.

With his thumbnail, the Friar flicked on a match. He then walked to the center of the room where a chandelier containing four oil lamps hung. The chandelier was from a holy place, Paul thought, as was the door.

Friar Henry lit all four lamps with the long stick match while Paul looked around.

His was a simple cell. On the wall directly in front of Paul was a fifteen-inch replica Crucifix of San Damiano, the crucifix through which Christ spoke to St. Francis when He'd asked Francis to fix His church.

St. Francis had misinterpreted the words and set about fixing an old decrepit church. This had set the story of St. Francis in motion. Jesus had actually meant it. Fix my church: Spiritually!

Below the crucifix was a small ancient-looking table made of wood and a wooden chair. To his left was Friar Henry's "bed", a simple foam cushion maybe two inches thick with a brown wool blanket thrown over it. No pillow. Paul wondered how a man of Henry's girth slept on so narrow a bed.

Against the wall to his right, he saw a square mahogany box the size of a small safe with a door that had a lock on it. On top of that was a tiny sketch of St. Francis, a tiny jar of holy oil shaped like a cross and a plastic bottle of holy water.

But it was what he saw on top of the desk in front of him that captured his attention. Leaning against the wall, resting on the table, was a painting. A lovelier painting Paul couldn't imagine he had ever seen. The woman with the child was the most beautiful woman that he had ever seen on canvas.

He walked over to it and saw that it was a work in progress, not finished. The paints and brushes were neatly stacked off to the side of the desk.

Henry spoke first.

"Do you know about Icons Paul?"

Paul thought for a moment.

"I understand that they're like a window to heaven."

"You're seeing into heaven when you look at an Icon. Jesus and Mary are in heaven. Looking at you," Henry said.

Paul was quiet. He was truly captivated by the beauty of the Madonna and Child.

"They're used for meditation," Henry added.

Then something occurred to Paul. "Wait a minute," he said. "Is this your cell? Who's painting this?"

"This is my cell of course and I'm painting that!"

Paul looked Henry up and down. He was surprised.

"What's the matter? I don't look like the artist type to you?" Henry said with a happy gleam in his eyes. But Paul sensed no pride.

Then he said, "I'd read that Icon painters from the Eastern churches fasted for days before and during their work. I pictured these haggard, limp, almost starving monks painting icons with a delirious look in their eyes."

At this, Henry laughed out loud.

"I do fast Paul," he said, "Bread and water Wednesday and Fridays for breakfast and lunch. I'm also fasting from the booze and the ladies and the TV and lots of other things. Fasting doesn't have to be just about food. I'm big because my father was big and his father before him." Henry said this with no sign of being defensive. It was just so.

"So you like it?"

"The most beautiful I've ever seen," Paul said.

"I paint about three a year and give them away. The Benedictines are onto me and want them. I gave one to my sister. She's a cloistered nun in Israel, living on a mountain. She's waiting for the second coming.

"This one's for you."

Paul was astonished. He hardly knew the portly Friar. He was humbled.

"I'm not worthy of such a thing Henry, such a thing of beauty."

"Oh but you are."

"But I own nothing. I have my tunic, my sandals, my scapular and rosary."

Henry looked Paul up and down. His brown sandals hid size 11 feet that were filthy dirty. His black tunic Henry had given him after coming across it amongst the donated clothes. He kept the tunic in his cell under orders from his guardian angel. He didn't know why until Paul had gotten out of a car one snowy day.

Paul had a small cross painted on the tunic in white paint, above his heart. And his long brown hair dropped to his shoulders. His short beard wouldn't grow but looked full enough. But it was those golden eyes that fascinated Henry.

Paul didn't know it, but Henry had had a dream that he had entered a dark cave. All he could see in the cave were a set of eyes glowing in the darkness. As he approached the eyes, he had seen their rare piercing beauty. They were a golden color. But as he got closer, he had gotten afraid. He had sensed that the eyes belonged to a wolf. He then fled the cave.

In the same dream, he was looking through a book of holy pictures. One in particular caught his interest.

The man Jesus, looking out at him with the wolf's eyes.

The next day he had intuitively had an urge to go stand outside the church at 10 a.m. Then lo and behold, Paul had exited his ride and almost gotten knocked over when he had bumped into Henry.

Then Henry saw the eyes.

"I would be most grateful if this precious work of art were to be given to me Henry. I will find a wonderful home for it where I can visit it each day."

They both stared at the beautiful Madonna. The big eyes signifying that in heaven you see much, Paul thought: the Beatific Vision, the Almighty Creator. Once you see the Beatific Vision, all you can do is stare. He couldn't imagine what that would be like.

"I work only by oil lamp or candles. In fact, I have no electricity in here at all."

And no windows Paul noticed.

"What about the door? It's the only one like it here?"

"That's a story for another day. We'd better go check the sauce."

Paul noticed for the first time that Henry spoke with a slight accent but couldn't place it.

As he turned, he looked into the eyes of the baby Jesus in the icon. They were a beautiful golden color.

CHAPTER 12

▼

"There are three kinds of people in the world," Joe was saying, "Those that make things happen, those that watch things happen, and those that ask, 'What happened?'"

"Which one are you Megan?"

This was Joe's first day at the Mother and Child Unit. He had been assigned four clients and Megan was one of them.

He was the only counselor in the office at the time and Megan was hustling him for some bottles of applesauce, which were only supposed to be doled out for the babies.

His new client was a tall fiery red head with good hygiene and meticulously clean clothes. She was five months pregnant and couldn't get along with her step-mom.

She was grinning from ear to ear. Looking down at her belly wide eyed she said, "The first one, I make things happen!" And she laughed.

"Then don't miss any more appointments young lady. Stick to your plan and you'll be alright."

Megan was the only client on the floor. Joe had missed escorting the residents to breakfast and their departures for their appointments or classes. He closed her file and opened the cabinet with the baby food handing her two jars. She said "gotcha" and laughed out loud as she exited the office.

The counselor's office was the size of a large walk-in closet and owned a large window facing 52nd Street. Across the street was St. Clare's Hospital. The building sat on the north side of the street, half way between 9th and 10th Avenue.

On the residential floors there were six bedrooms and a large storage closet full of diapers, wipes, cereal, baby food, formulas and some pharmaceuticals like A & D ointment, children's Tylenol and Neosporin. The resident's floors were the third, fourth, and fifth.

The 2nd floor was the kitchen and cafeteria.

And the 1st floor had the executive's office, her assistant's office, a bathroom, the lecture room, and the security guard's open office next to the front door.

Joe was sitting in the office on the 3rd floor. He'd had a strange feeling in his stomach since Morning Prayer, when a female community member from Germany did a strange ritualistic looking dance-prayer.

He didn't get it and thought that it was almost offensive to dance like that in church. He tried to keep an open mind though and had wondered what Patrick had thought of it. He knew that prayer didn't have to be mental or verbal and that honest work was a form of prayer, if the work glorified the Lord.

But he had never heard of dance prayer before.

Then at breakfast, the pancakes had tasted awful. He figured that the community was feeling the stresses of a new leader and the mourning of a lost one.

The dance had been bizarre. The pancakes sat like lead in his belly.

He arrived at 52ndStreet promptly at 8 a.m. and waited 15 minutes to see the unit executive. Her name was Ms. Zelda Golden and she turned out to be nice enough.

She interviewed him briefly, as her phone rang off the hook, and had him fill out some paperwork. She said that Joe had come highly regarded and was looking forward to working with him. She avoided asking him how things were in the community.

There would be staff meetings every Friday to discuss clients' progress and the plan for the following week she said.

Zelda had long straight auburn brown dyed hair that curled up at her shoulders. She wore bangs and a lot of makeup, but not enough to look gaudy, and she looked to be around 35.

She had a trim figure, wore expensive clothes and jewelry, and was six months away from her PHD, which Redemption House was paying for.

Her assistant came in with some papers and introduced herself as Gretchen O'Malley. She had a plain but attractive face and beautiful long red hair, snow-white skin, and an attractive figure. She smiled at Joe and shook his hand warmly.

He noticed that Zelda wore a wedding ring and Gretchen did not.

He then met with the head counselor. She was a handsome Jamaican woman. Her name was Beverly Sims. She had taken him on a tour of the building, including the basement laundry room. Residents were allowed to do laundry down there if accompanied by a counselor.

Beverly Sims had been very professional in her manner and gracious at the same time, making Joe feel welcome. She had sat down with him and discussed his future clients and then had given him his keys.

Joe figured out the routine right away: take care of the health of the mother and child, make sure they take their vitamins if necessary, and dole out any prescription medication. Make sure they make their appointments and hit the phone heavy to get referrals for them and find them a home in the system. 52ndStreet was a temporary stop. The plan was always to find a safe home for these girls and their children where they could hopefully grow and learn.

There was a light tapping on the open office door. Joe turned and looked into the most beautiful eyes he had ever seen. They were large and hazel with a golden glint. Her black hair was permed and hung at her shoulders. Her complexion was a lovely dark olive. She was wearing a simple black and white striped short dress with white tights underneath and around her neck hung a cotton Native American style papoose that held a very beautiful baby in front of her.

Joe felt something at once released from inside of him, something that had been squeezing his soul tight for a long time, not letting go. He didn't know what that something was, but he knew that it wasn't good.

He had experienced a similar release when he had left the mountain base camp to drive home the previous day. But that feeling had come on gradually on the drive home. That feeling he could describe as exhilaration.

This "feeling" had been spontaneous. He felt like his soul had been set free from some unknown force that had been gripping it.

His eyes were still locked on hers before he had realized that she had spoken to him. He realized that her lips had moved but that all he had heard was sound, the sound of a voice, but no words.

At once he caught himself and said, "Excuse me?"

"Are you Joe, my counselor?" She asked again, with a thick Spanish accent.

"Yes, I am," he said.

The young woman was smiling.

Through the smile, Joe saw small white perfect teeth. She glowed when she smiled.

He noticed that she had full thick lips and wore gold loop earrings. Put all together, this young woman radiated beauty, a warm dark beauty. He sensed that she had felt something too when they first locked eyes.

He glanced down at the baby and said, "You must be Johnny!"

"Johnattan," she said still smiling, "Pronounced jon-a-taan. How did you know?"

He wondered the same thing. But he had known right away.

"What can I do for you Yasmine?"

He had read her chart. He knew that she had asked for tokens to take the subway to her grandmother's. She needed to retrieve some things of Johnattan's.

"My baby's crib has been broken for three days now. He can fall out. I have him sleep with me in the bed and I get in trouble."

Joe had read that rule. Babies sleep in cribs. He didn't like the rule but understood why it existed. They wanted no accidents. The mother could roll over on the baby while sleeping or suffocate the baby accidentally with a blanket or pillow.

"Let's go have a look at this," he said.

Yasmine was in the one larger room that the floors had. This was the only room with three residents and their babies. The two front rooms that faced 52nd Street were for individuals and then there were three double rooms. This room was the last one at the end of the hall.

They walked down the hall and he unlocked the door. They both entered.

"Which one?" he asked, but then he saw that a crib had a whole side missing. They wrote her up for this he thought? They should have fixed it for her.

He lifted the side of the crib that was missing into place and had the young resident hold one side while he secured the other. Then he secured the other side.

"There you go," he said.

He was trying not to look into her eyes. He felt an inexplicable excitement inside him and he could tell now that she felt it too.

Johnattan had liquid bright green eyes and a happy smile. He was a healthy, happy baby. Joe had seen the chart. Yasmine was the only resident in the entire building that was breastfeeding. This had impressed him.

"Can I hold him?"

"Sure," she said, and removed him from the papoose.

He held the little boy for the first time. The boy felt warm and had that unmistakable clean baby scent. He then asked Yasmine if she got everything that she needed at her grandmother's.

"No. My abuela wasn't there. That's why I'm back so soon. She didn't know I was coming."

"Oh well, do you need anything for the baby like diapers or apple sauce?"

"Not right now, thank you."

He had looked back into Yasmine's face, her smile, her manner; they were ever so subtly flirtatious. He sensed that she knew that he knew.

He gave Johnattan back to her and in doing so their hands accidentally touched. The shock they both received almost made them drop the baby.

It was amazing.

Joe's right hand had inadvertently touched Yasmine's left hand and they had both received a powerful electric shock. There was no carpet anywhere on the floor. What could explain this?

Nothing was said. They just looked at each other, puzzled, both of them smiling. Then he turned and walked away.

At Mass that evening and at dinner too, he couldn't stop gushing. That's the only way to describe what he felt.

How can this be? It can't be. Love at first sight? She's seventeen years old for crying out loud. I'm her counselor. I just gave up searching for a mate. Is it a temptation? It must be, but why do I feel so good then? These thoughts raced through his head all that night, and the next day, as well as the rest of the week.

Somewhere deep down Joe knew, that something inside of him had changed forever. He knew that this wasn't a temptation. That something else was happening. He remembered reading that if God wanted something to happen; nothing could stop it from happening. Was this one of those things? But how can you tell for sure he wondered?

He had gone to work as usual and acted the best he could like nothing was happening. But something was.

On Tuesday they had touched again when he was giving her baby food and the electric shock happened again.

On Wednesday, he walked past the meeting room on the first floor where Zelda and Gretchen were giving a seminar to all the residents. He glanced in and immediately saw Yasmine. She was staring straight at him, her left breast exposed, and Johnattan suckling on it.

CHAPTER 13

▼

Joe needed to talk to somebody, somebody that he felt comfortable with. Saturday he worked until 4:30 p.m. When he got home, he went through the 44thStreet side and went directly to Patrick's room.

Patrick was painting a new canvas using all the shades of dark blue again. He had jazzy music playing loudly and had worked up quite a sweat, as none could deny, this man painted with passion.

He was in a white tee shirt and Khaki shorts with his trademark shoes: brown wing tips. Joe greeted him with a smile. Pat stopped painting and lowered the music.

"What's up Joe-Joe?"

Joe walked over to the window to watch the matinee audience breaking out.

"Not too much, you?"

"The same Joe-da, the same."

"Still in your blue period I see."

"Yes sir! Can't ya tell I'm blue Joe-Joe?"

"No, not really, you always seem the same to me: happy, sarcastic, independent."

"Sarcastic yes, but independent of what?"

"Community."

"How so Joe-da, and you'd better watch what you say 'cause I'm actually pretty sensitive."

Joe realized that the sarcastic funny side of Patrick's personality hid a much more serious side which he had witnessed. He knew that Pat had major issues with a very controlling mother who had raised two boys alone. Pat's father abandoned the family when he was four. Patrick never did see him again. That had to hurt.

His brother was two years older than him.

"Well, you're in the community, but not 100%."

"How do you mean?"

"Let's take your chastity vow for instance. Are you blatantly breaking it, and in the worst possible way?"

Patrick laughed a nervous laugh. Joe was the only person Pat knew that could speak so frankly to him and get away with it. They had a certain bond. They both liked each other in spite of their weaknesses.

"And just what do you mean by worst possible way?"

"You mean unlike the way that you broke your vows with a married woman in her own home with her husband and kids asleep?"

Pat had started to paint again furiously, with large quick strokes of dark grayish blue. A fish was materializing on the canvas along side a helmeted head of a man.

"That was an accident and you know it. That happened once. That was a night that got away. I confessed it and stopped.

"By worst possible way I mean that you are seducing brand new members of the community on the night of their initiation Mass. Or the night they take chastity vows."

"I'm a wolf Joe-Joe. They're most vulnerable in the beginning, new environment. They're not grounded yet. And the evil one multiplies his attack."

"How do you live with yourself?"

"I may have a problem. Maybe I'll even stop if you think it's so bad."

"Yes. Cut it off. Not literally. But try to stop it with Community members at least."

"I'm gonna go to confession. I'll try to stop."

Pat wasn't kidding. He was on a backward slide in that regard and knew he must stop. He was no dummy. He had a Fine Arts Degree from UCONN.

"How about Chinese after Mass?" Patrick asked.

"Sounds great to me."

Joe was unaware that his beloved Church had a serious problem in her priesthood. If Friar Costen was guilty, it was probably an aberration he thought.

He had seen and met a number of priests visiting the community that he was certain were gay. But the church didn't condemn gays. She condemned sex without marriage. She taught the virtue of chastity for 2000 years, whether you're gay or not.

But at Mass that night he had the strangest sensation when he received Holy Communion. The visiting priest was a very handsome young Italian man and had come to say the Mass with a beautiful young woman in tow. His "secretary" he was told.

She sat in the first row directly in front of the altar.

When Joe turned to return to his seat after communion, he had inadvertently looked into her eyes. She was staring at the priest's face. The look could only be described as that of someone madly in love. Could it be?

"The priest brought his girlfriend to mass," Joe said as he and Patrick took their seats at the West Side Cottage."

"How do you know? Why are you saying that?"

"I'm just going by what I saw. The way she was looking at him during Mass."

"Well, what are you going to do?" Patrick said with resignation as the two men opened their menus.

Joe had all of $12 in his pocket. This was his weekly stipend from the community for his work at Redemption House. As he eyed the menu he knew that he couldn't order everything that he wanted because he was trying harder now to live on the $12 a week. He owned a Visa card that he used to cheat with occasionally; the card had gotten him to the Catskills, but he'd chosen not to bring it tonight.

This night he was going to keep it simple and although he loved noodles in sesame sauce as an appetizer, he only ordered orange flavor chicken. This was his absolute favorite Chinese dish, with white rice and tea.

Patrick ordered chicken and broccoli with white rice and tea.

"So how's your new job going? Are you bored yet at Mother and Child?"

Patrick's job was on the boys' floor at the Crisis Center. He basically did what he had to do and went home when the whistle blew.

"No, not really, that's what I came to talk to you about."

"Oh, let's hear it. I hope it's juicy."

"It's juicy alright. You're not going to believe it."

Joe then proceeded to tell Pat everything: the feeling of love at first sight, the electric shock, the beautiful baby, the breast-feeding.

Yasmine had turned out to be an interesting person. She seemed well read for her age and knew what she wanted to do.

She wanted to go to school, she had told Joe, to be a fashion designer of infants and toddler clothes. She had heard that Redemption House helps people in her situation get into the system and into school.

Getting into the system was important. This meant getting into the welfare system, temporarily of course, to make sure the basic necessities are met: food, shelter, and clothing. And then go to school with a couple of dollars in her pocket. She wanted a part-time job too.

The last thing Joe said to Patrick as they finished their dinner was what had happened that day. Near the end of his shift, he found himself in the office alone with the mother and child when she'd come in for diapers. He had been holding Johnattan and when he gave him to Yasmine, he kissed the little boy on the fore-head. He had fallen for the baby too. Then as he had handed the baby to Yasmine, he'd had the unmistakable feeling that she had wanted to kiss him. She had even moved her face towards his.

Patrick hadn't said a word. He was very surprised and wanted to be objective and not judge. "Sounds like something supernatural to me. Does she feel the same way about you?"

"Yes. I think so."

"You're not sure?"

"I'm 99% sure."

"She's needy right now, vulnerable. You'd better let it breathe. Don't do anything foolish."

"I'll try not to."

"How old is she?"

Joe knew this was coming. He was a number of years older then her.

"Seventeen!"

"So she's legal. That's good."

"How do you know?"

"Without parental consent the legal age in New York is seventeen."

"It's eighteen in Jersey."

"It's eighteen in most states."

Joe knew what Patrick meant by this. If he and the young woman got together, he wouldn't be breaking the laws of New York State, but how about the rules of Redemption House?

Patrick read his mind.

"Don't worry about Redemption House or anything else. Deal with that when the time comes. Maybe it was meant to be. Pray about it. Meditate."

Joe's work meant a lot to him. He remembered his commitment to the Lord after the Catskill experience. "Do you think I'm being tempted, Pat, because of the commitment that I made recently?"

"Could be, or maybe the Lord was waiting for you to seek him first, as the Bible says, then all that you need in your heart will follow."

Patrick had been kind and understanding. Joe would take his advice and let it breathe. Don't break any policies. See if the relationship has life.

Joe opened his fortune cookie and read his fortune. It simply read: Go for it!

CHAPTER 14

▼

Yasmine said a prayer that night that Father God, Papa Dios, protect her and her son and that He helps them with their needs. She prayed too that her counselor finds her a place to live that is safe and where she can go to school.

A different counselor, a middle aged woman of Puerto Rican dissent named Carmen, had told Yasmine about Columbia University having a special program for kids from "the street." But first she needed her G.E.D.

She was excited about the possible opportunity. Carmen had said to wait until she gets housing before she goes for her G.E.D., this way she won't have to travel far to go to class. She can go to a local school.

Joe. Oh Joe! Her young heart wasn't sure what to make of it. She just knew that it beat twice as fast in his presence. She had never been in love and wasn't sure what was happening to her. Was it just a crush?

She had vowed to herself that she would walk the straight and narrow. Get housing, get into school, and get a job. She knew she was smart and had artistic talent. She saw what the big designers were doing with kids' clothes and knew that she could do better. There was a place for her talent somewhere.

But something painful was happening, something beyond the natural. She couldn't stop thinking about him. Even now with Johnattan rocking gently in her arms, and she singing softly to him, she still thought about him.

She put Johnattan in the crib and lied down in her bed. Her two roommates were asleep. She was making this her ritual. She wouldn't go to sleep unless they were sleeping.

She felt uncomfortable with her roommates. Right from the start they tried to intimidate her by making rules only for her. But she stood her ground and ignored them. When she got there they had taken her dresser for themselves and told her to keep her clothes in her luggage. Yasmine carefully emptied the dresser right in front of them and put her clothes in. She then handed each of them their clothes. She had claimed her piece of the territory.

She closed her eyes and thought about Joe, his jet-black hair, and his neatly trimmed beard. She noticed that he always wore a faded pair of black jeans that fit him real nice, and black shoes, never sneakers like everyone else. He liked polo shirts and had several in different colors.

She liked the way that he smiled at her, and Johnattan always lit up like a little Christmas tree when he saw Joe.

Is it possible that I'm getting my signals crossed from him? He seems to like me. I noticed that he treats me just a little more special then the other girls. Or am I imagining things?

Her last thought as she finally drifted off to sleep was of kissing Joe Morrison.

CHAPTER 15

▼

Sunday was an interesting and eventful day for Joe. After an early Mass, he took the A train uptown to 125thStreet in Harlem accompanied by Patrick and another community member, Sister Judith. They attended a barn-busting Baptist revival in a tiny storefront chapel.

The house rocked.

Joe got caught up in the dancing and singing and clapping. Patrick just clapped. The Sister seemed to enjoy herself immensely and they left feeling uplifted. They returned to Community and in the afternoon a black Baptist Minister gave a talk on racism.

Joe never truly understood what the difference between racism and prejudice was. It seemed to him that the media was using the word racist at times when the word prejudice should have been used. That racism was a stronger word with a different meaning.

He was right. The minister said that everybody is prejudiced, black folk too. But that racism is prejudice with power.

You can be prejudice and not hurt anyone. But if you're a boss and you're prejudice and you don't hire someone because of it, then you are a racist. Prejudice with power. Joe vowed to remember that.

That night he called Marcia in Durango, Colorado. Her new number had a New Mexico area code. His old spiritual director had moved.

He hadn't spoken to her since he left Colorado, but had received a beautiful Christmas card from her. The front of the card had an ancient Icon that he loved. This was the same exact Icon that he had been using at the time for meditation prayers. This was a good sign he thought; there was still a spiritual connection between them.

Before joining Community he had occasionally lit a candle and prayed before this Icon of the Madonna and Child. He felt his prayer was deeper and more powerful when he did this. A glimpse into heaven he thought. He did this when he felt confused or nervous about something and it worked. Usually he prayed the rosary. He always felt more peaceful afterward.

Marcia picked up the phone on the first ring. They were like old friends. They talked like they'd seen each other yesterday, although it had been a year.

Turns out Marcia had joined a lay ministry in Albuquerque, led by a Franciscan Priest who was rather famous for his audiotapes. Their goal was to have a contemplative community that incorporated action and contemplation.

Action and contemplation. Marcia explained that from contemplation you should find the "love action" that God wants you to put into effect. This was generally accomplished by means of serving your neighbor or the poor.

Joe thought this to be similar to what the glowing little monk had said about prayer, faith, hope, love, service, peace and heaven, in that order. Prayer leads to agape love for your neighbor, to a loving relationship with the Father, and love leads to service.

Her service was a prison ministry at the women's prison in Albuquerque. Her and Bill had just moved and hadn't started working yet.

Joe explained what was up, everything. He didn't skip a detail. He thought he was in love but questioned the timing of it. He had been praying about it and so far all was the same. No doors had been opened or shut. No message of wrong doing from above.

He knew it had only been a week since they had met, but so what? Something amazing was happening.

He asked Marcia what he should do. He was surprised by her answer.

"Don't do anything," she said.

"Let God do everything. Let the Holy Spirit do His job."

"I don't get what you mean."

"Don't do anything to pursue this girl. Just do your job. If God wants something to happen, it will."

Then she asked him if he felt like he was going to save her. Be her hero.

He said no. That he hadn't thought of it that way. That she actually had her own plan and seemed determined to go for it.

Then she explained about co-dependence and how possibly he was looking for an identity through her, as her savior. That didn't ring true to him and he left it at that.

He had finally said goodbye to Marcia and hung up the phone.

He felt confused. Something he had yet to feel about the situation.

Don't do anything?

He wasn't sure what Marcia meant.

That night he simplified his prayer. After night prayer he lay before the Tabernacle, The Blessed Sacrament, The Real Presence. He asked God simply to close the door or open the door in whatever relationship he was to have with the young woman.

He knew full well the seriousness of the situation. If a personal relationship developed between him, Yasmine, and Johny, he would have to resign his position at Mother and Child.

He felt a peace come over him as he lay there. He knew he wasn't being impetuous. He had consulted with Pat and Marcia. And he was praying about it. What else could he do? The age difference didn't matter to him. Both his father and his grandfather on his mother's side were considerably older than their spouses, and stayed married forever. Joseph was twice Mary's age.

Trust the Lord, he told himself, trust Jesus.

The last image in his mind as he fell asleep in the chapel that night was of Yasmine's face.

She was grinning and asking for a kiss.

CHAPTER 16

▼

Paul had been praying furiously all night. He had been kneeling in front of the statue of Our Lady of Guadalupe. His knees and thighs were numb. His back ached.

When he had discovered that Gwen had had an abortion he could feel the blood drain from his face. He had felt a physical pain deep in his heart. His hands had begun to tremble.

He hadn't been able to talk to Gwen for several weeks. Every time he would ring the bell either there was no answer or her sister would say she that she was out. Her sister had been very abrupt with Paul the last couple of times that he had rung the bell. When he asked where she was she had said, "none of your business," and hung up on him.

Yesterday, after finishing in the soup kitchen, he had felt an urge to go to the Speakeasy and work on a new etching. As he worked, he sensed that there was a message for him in this etching.

He then went directly to Gwen's apartment. He had no doubt that something was wrong. His heart felt heavy. He felt fear. The Holy Spirit was telling him something.

He waited outside the building. He stood across the street praying his finger rosary, reciting the Jesus prayer.

Eventually Gwen's sister pulled up in a cab and got out. She held a bag of groceries.

He came up behind her.

"Where's Gwen?"

Her sister turned and looked at him. Her face was red. Her demeanor was that of someone who had been crying. Her eyes were bloodshot and wet.

Gwen's sister was a pretty girl in her twenties with long black hair.

Her demeanor quickly turned to anger when she saw Paul.

"What the hell do you want?"

"I'd like to see Gwen."

"What the hell for?"

"Because I'm worried about her."

"What are you worried about, it's over!"

"What's over?"

Gwen's sister got in Paul's face. The anger in her face turned to rage.

"She did it okay? She got the abortion. It's her right. It's her body. And it's not against the law!

"What was she supposed to do, give up her career, to raise Andre's baby? He's a loser! She's got a great job! It's over!

"And you should go away!"

At this, she turned to open the thick glass door leading inside to the lobby.

She fumbled with her keys.

"Where is Gwen?" Paul asked gently, "Is she alright?"

Gwen's sister turned and threw the grocery bag at Paul, cans and boxes spilling everywhere.

She paused, looking up at the sky, and blurted out, "No, no, no! She's not okay. She's in the hospital!"

Then Lola did the most surprising thing. She fell into Paul's arms, sobbing, sobbing loudly for her sister and her unborn baby.

He held her gently in his arms. Autumn was in the air this late September day and the wind held a cold chill as it funneled down 19thStreet.

Lola cried and cried and cried. And finally she spoke. With her head still resting on Paul's shoulder, she confessed.

"It's my fault Paul. She was asking for you. These last few weeks she couldn't understand why you never came by. I told her that I hadn't heard from you.

"She got anxious, desperate. I kept telling her to have the abortion, talking her into it. She finally gave in and made the appointment."

At this point, Lola began sobbing again. Her tears were soaking the shoulder of Paul's tunic. Then she faced him, still in his arms.

"It was horrible. I went with her. You could hear people screaming and crying while we waited. It was chilling.

"Everything was okay for about a week. There was some bleeding and Gwen felt pain, but they said that was normal. She stayed home that week.

"And then, and then," Lola stuttered, tears streaming down her face, "And then it happened. I couldn't believe it. I saw it. That morning Gwen woke up with a fever and was having heavy discharge. We called the stupid clinic and they told us to see our doctor or go to the ER.

"And then Gwen screamed. I was in the kitchen, and when I ran in, I saw it, a little tiny foot with five toes. A perfect little foot had come out of Gwen with the discharge!"

Paul felt drained. He felt guilty. Why hadn't he waited outside for Gwen earlier? Why hadn't he visited the bank where she worked? These thoughts raced through his mind as he bent over to pick up the bag of fallen groceries.

"There's more," Lola said.

"What?" And he looked up at her.

"The doctor in the ER found that her uterus had been punctured. There's a severe septic infection. She may need a hysterectomy."

Paul tried not to convey any message with his body language that would make Lola feel even worse. He wanted to bow his head and cry but he held on. His hands trembled as he handed the bag to Lola.

He grasped Lola's arm as she turned and asked her to pray. He asked her if she believed that there was a higher power, knowing she was raised agnostic. She said that she did. Then he asked her to pray to her higher power for forgiveness. To pray that she could forgive herself, that she didn't really know what she was doing, that people were being misled, and to pray for Gwen. That God heal her.

He noticed a change in Lola's face, a relief, a healing.

Paul remembered all this as he prayed. He had to be more vigilant he thought.

He hadn't taken the time in prayer to really think of Gwen's situation. He knew that when despair set in and the woman had no positive support that this was when the wrong decisions were made.

All Gwen must have heard was "do it, do it, do it! It's your body"!

Yes, it's your body, Paul thought, but the baby's a separate body, an individual, with a soul. No one has a right to take his life. God has trusted the woman with a life.

He couldn't help but feel sad. A baby is no longer safe in his mother's womb. How can there ever be peace in the world when the innocent and most vulnerable are being destroyed!

He had tried to see Gwen, but she was in I.C.U. This was serious he thought. In the I.C.U. only immediate family is allowed in.

He was able to pass a note to her. On a piece of paper he had simply wrote: "See you when you get out. Paul." And he drew a smiley face on it.

His prayers that night led him to the depths of his soul, to thoughts that the conscious mind is too distracted to think.

He realized something very important that night. The words had come into his head as if from outside his body. As if he had heard a voice.

"The spirit of antichrist is amongst us." (1John 4:3)

"The spirit of antichrist is amongst us." (1John 2:22)

He had heard it twice, loud and clear. Then he had thought about it.

Everywhere, Christ was under attack, in the media, in the schools, within families, in the government.

The tendency was to deny the supernatural. Ridicule it. Call it superstition. Deny the existence of God, especially in the schools, in the colleges and universities.

Believers are persecuted, alienated. The peer pressure is tremendous to follow the secular humanist line.

They devalue life, teaching that abortion is a right. When no one has the right to destroy human life. They teach evolution as fact when DNA findings have shown that species once considered as evolved from one another, a succession of fossils, are actually different species. Teaching kids that we are descendants of monkeys devalues the life of human beings. We are not special in God's eyes.

Paul knew there was hope. That many scientists were facing the truth: there had to be an intelligent creator! He believed that in the future science would serve to prove the existence of God, and not the opposite.

There was hope in the student population too. New saints were on the way, young people with conviction and courage.

He knew that the Catholic College near Pittsburgh where he bought his books was sending devout souls out into the world. Souls not corrupted by the materialism and lies of the world.

The world was in darkness, he knew, people were being led by an invisible evil being whose very existence was being denied.

There must be others that sensed this underlying spirit controlling the secular forces. It cannot be identified or pointed to. But how else do you explain that when a new issue or crisis is presented, predictably these people will take the immoral and anti-church view, and make it sound like a good cause. Their favorite cause was a bastardized version of freedom. Not freedom to do what is right, which is the original definition of the word, but freedom to do whatever you want.

This evil is destroying the family, destroying the innocent, and making people depressed and miserable. Must you be enlightened to recognize this evil? Is this why so many are so easily mislead? People need to get back to serious prayer. Our Shepherd's need courage and our prayers to lead us back.

Paul remembered as a kid when a group of guys would get together in the park there was a pressure on each kid to change his personality. He found himself spitting, cursing, putting other kids down and trying to look and be "cool".

What was this "cool" that had him practicing spitting in his backyard? What spirit motivated this change in him that he would immediately forget everything that his parents had taught him as soon as he would be with a bunch of guys?

He had caught himself doing it and had tried to control it. He had stopped spitting altogether and only cursed occasionally as a kid.

But this same peer pressure is what is faced at the universities. If you don't go along with the thinking and philosophy of your professors, you can get a lower grade and not get invited to parties. You won't be popular. You won't "fit in".

You are led to believe that it is part of growing up, and that your parents thinking and the Church's teaching are antiquated. This feeds your ego; you think you're smarter than them. A part of higher education is to give up the values of your ancestors and to think of God as superstition; to believe in man, and woman, but not in God: eating from the forbidden fruit.

"Heavenly Father," Paul whispered, "make a place in heaven for the holy innocents, let them share in your eternal joy, and in Jesus name I pray for Gwen that you keep her strong. That she be healed quickly. And that she turns to you for mercy. And Lord, have mercy on Lola!"

"Amen", Paul heard, coming from behind him.

He turned and saw Friar Henry on his knees on the hard floor.

He whispered, "How long have you been there?"

"Not long," Henry said. "Come, its time to make mashed potatoes."

The two men walked quietly to the kitchen together. The other friars that worked in the kitchen were just arriving. Morning Mass had ended.

Paul and Henry each grabbed a fifty-pound bag of potatoes and sat side by side on stools. They each had a plastic garbage can with a black garbage bag liner in front of them for the skins, and large aluminum pots of water for the peeled potatoes.

Paul felt clear headed and energetic in spite of his night of praying.

Henry whistled softly as he peeled potatoes with his thick hands. Paul thought that he was pretty fast at peeling potatoes until now. Henry had him two to one.

Henry's thick hands deftly grabbed, peeled and tossed potatoes into the pots. Then he started alternating. He'd throw one into his pot and one into Paul's pot to let him catch up.

They both looked at each other and laughed.

"Have you ever heard of Athos, Paul?" Henry asked.

"I have. All I know is that it's a peninsula or an island off the coast of Greece where monks of the Eastern Rite have lived for …"

"A thousand years," Henry answered.

"What else?" Henry asked.

"I know that many popular Icons were painted there; that they are cenobic, living in groups. And that today their numbers are dwindling. That they're mostly old men."

"Oh yes," Henry said, "Old men indeed. Maybe one is the oldest."

"Athos is a peninsula and is quite a beauty. It's got the ocean and the mountains and holds some very devout holy souls," Henry said.

"What did you mean by one is the oldest?" Paul asked.

"I didn't mean anything," Henry said, grinning.

Then Henry stopped peeling, leaned toward Paul and whispered, "There's a rumor that one of the hermits there is quite old, maybe as old as the church!"

Henry was looking at Paul with an: 'I know something that you don't know' stare. Paul looked down at his potato and kept peeling. Henry did likewise.

Until Paul asked, "And how pray tell, did you, Henry, come about hearing this rumor?"

"I heard this from the Abbot at the Panteleimon Monastery on Athos."

"You've been there?"

"Yes."

There was a pause and then Henry said, "I lived there."

And anticipating Paul's next question, he said, "For seven years."

"Do you want to hear a story? We've got time. Only three hundred more pounds to peel."

"Tell me everything," Paul had simply said.

"I war born on the Emerald Isle and as a younger man I set sail on an adventure.

"I was only 17.

"My adventure took me to Portugal and Spain and Italy and eventually to Greece.

"Looking back one might call my adventure a pilgrimage of sorts but that's not what I had planned.

"I wanted to see the world.

"When in Portugal, I hooked up with some peasants that had an old pickup truck and were on pilgrimage to Fatima. I caught a ride with them, and of course, had a conversion experience at the grotto, and started praying the beads.

"I guess you'd say I was a fallen away Catholic at the time I set sail but that changed quickly.

"I went to Spain after that and ended up at the shrine of St. James Compostelo, which I found interesting, and got to chat with a lot of pious and devout souls.

"One of them told me about a Francis of Assisi and recommended that I ride with him and his wife to Italy, which was their home and home to Francis' shrine as well.

"They dropped me off in front of THE church where the crucifix spoke to Francis during his prayer.

"I loved Assisi. I stayed a month with the Franciscans, loved every minute of it.

"But then the itch to visit Michelangelo and the Pope had to be scratched and I caught a bus down to Rome. On the bus I met an old friar. He was old all right. His leathery wrinkled face and white hair made him look a hundred and ten and his tunic looked like Francis himself had worn it eight hundred years ago.

"He had been a guest in Athos, he said, of the Russian Orthodox church. They had a meeting concerning an ancient relic held by the Orthodox Church of which he refused to talk about.

"This caught my interest. I saw the sites in Rome and then thought about Athos.

"I called the Franciscans in Assisi to inquire as to this old monk and no one knew him or could recall seeing him.

"They didn't know who he was, probably a pilgrim.

"I had to stay in Rome to gather up some funds and made a small fortune when I set up a little stand and sold tiny bottles filled with olive oil to the tourists.

The little bottles held about an ounce and were in the shape of a cross. I always had them blessed.

"When I had saved enough money, I hitched a ride to the east coast of Italy and paid my way on a launch to Greece.

"I got as close to Athos as I could and then set out to find an Orthodox Church. I did and I found out that you need an invitation or a pass to go there. They don't have tourists there, only pilgrims, as the monks don't want to be disturbed.

"I told the Priest that I was seeking a profession and wished to explore the life of a monk on Athos for a week or two.

"He found me a guide, and you need a guide on Athos, and off I went. For seven years."

Henry nodded his head twice, looking at Paul and then rose from his stool to go get another fifty pound sack of potatoes.

CHAPTER 17

▼

A few weeks had passed. Joe hadn't visited Patrick's room since the night that they shared Chinese food. They had chatted several times at the cafeteria but they had kept their conversation impersonal, mostly talking about events in the community.

A lot had occurred. In that time, sixteen people had completed their thirteen-month commitment. None had apparently signed up for a second tour.

They had allowed one new person in, but she was someone that had been previously accepted into the community and had postponed her commitment due to illness.

Her name was Karen and she was from San Diego, California. She'd recently learned that she had rheumatoid arthritis and had been having tests done and getting treated before joining the New York Community.

Joe and Patrick had conversed with her on several occasions and she seemed like a genuinely kind and giving soul.

Patrick had felt that the reason that no one had signed up for a second thirteen-month stint was because Vincent LaBianco had agreed with the Redemption House Administrator to cut back on membership, part of the plan on cutting expenses.

So even if they wanted to, they couldn't come back. Each person had a private session in Vincent's tiny little office concerning this. The office used to be a closet in the cafeteria and Joe had seen a couple of community members come out of the meeting, none seemed happy.

This didn't make sense to Pat. How is it cutting expenses when you have to replace someone making $12 a week with someone making $400 a week?

He predicted the community would shrink and the two buildings would be sold for $2 million, their current value.

Joe didn't want to believe it but considered Pat's assertion as a possibility.

Of course, Pat was painting when Joe walked in. Again, Pat had missed Mass and dinner. He was wearing a white t-shirt, jeans and his customary expensive wing tip shoes.

The shoes were Patrick's trademarks. He wore them to work, to paint, or to play touch football at the community retreats.

He was the best athlete in the community hands down.

No one spoke as Joe took a seat near the window.

He could see people starting to line up outside the Majestic Theatre. This was late October. New York was having an Indian summer and people were dressed accordingly. There were short sleeves and sundresses everywhere. Why was it that I always seemed to visit with Patrick on Friday nights, he thought to himself?

"I did an escort up to Spanish Harlem today and walked over to the Cathedral of John the Divine. Have you been there?" Joe asked.

"No Jo-da, I'd like to go. That's not Catholic correct?"

"No. I'm not sure what denomination it is. But it's not Catholic. I could tell right away when I went inside. The Real Presence was missing. I actually felt a bit anxious inside too.

"The thing is I saw a real live statue maker outside, a stone carver. I'll never forget it!"

"Why, what so impressed you Jo-da?"

"This guy was intense, he was standing on a scaffold, carving away, chipping away I should say. There were three sets of four statues with all the scaffolding connected up in front of them; he could walk to any statue.

"Several forms were just the untouched cement. Others were outlined and incomplete and two seemed finished.

"He was working without a picture, from memory. The shavings fell to the floor about ten feet below. That's where I stood.

"I called up to him but he never even twitched. He was in another world."

"He was in a spiritual trance," Patrick commented, "totally focused. Amazing isn't it? What did he look like?"

"Oh my God, his hair was long and a complete dirty mess. You couldn't pass a comb through it if you tried it was so tangled.

"He was dirty and unkempt. I asked somebody about him and they told me that he was French. That there was no 'artisans of his ilk' left is what the monk said, and they were fortunate to find him in France.

"They figured he's going to be on this project for two years."

"Who was this monk?"

"Just another pilgrim like me, I ran into him around the back where this guy had smaller works. He was making corner pieces."

"So you took a little pilgrimage ay Jo-da, on Redemption House time?" Patrick was kidding.

"No. Actually, it was after four by then."

"Do you think this French artisan might have been a religious?" Patrick asked.

"No."

"What made you think the other guy was a monk?"

"Because he was wearing a habit."

"Could you tell if he was a Dominican, Franciscan, Capuchin, Benedictine or whatever? They all wear different color tunics."

"Probably Franciscan."

There was a pause in the conversation as Patrick went into the little tiny bathroom that he had and Joe looked out the window.

There was a mounted policeman in the street directly in front of the Majestic Theatre. That's funny, he thought, how few people know that Times Square had mounted policeman.

Pat came out of the bathroom smiling.

"So I guess you and I aren't gonna be monks together."

"I didn't think we ever were, really," Joe said.

"Well, think about it. It's a pretty sweet proposition."

"You don't pray any more than we do already.

"I can make wine and you can be a horticulturist, you grow the grapes. We can both be something we both love, be close to God, and pray for humanity everyday.

"There are some great monasteries in New England, very beautiful places with both woods and creeks."

"How would you keep your vow of chastity?" Joe asked respectfully, as he sensed that Patrick was being very serious for Patrick.

"I can honor my commitment if I really try, if I really want to. I'm weak right now. I'm in my blue period, as you can probably feel."

Patrick had picked up a brush and was painting vigorously on a large canvas.

"I might try some color soon. Maybe some tones of yellow or gold with the blue."

"I think my eventual ministry will be to have a family," Joe said. "I don't think I can live as a monk. I need women around."

"Speaking of women, you haven't caught me up on Yasmine. What's the news? And what did your spiritual director Marcia say?"

"My spiritual director told me not to do anything, to let God work the controls."

"Sound advice."

"So I haven't. But I'm in a dilemma right now."

"What's up?" Pat stopped painting and looked at Joe.

"A week ago I referred Yasmine and Johny to a group home in the Bronx. She's called a couple times; it sounds like it's in a dangerous area. I'm starting to regret it. She really wanted to go to the West End here in Manhattan. I probably could have got her in. But I thought it would be safer to have her in the Bronx, for selfish reasons."

Patrick knew instantly what Joe meant.

"In case you start seeing her, you don't want to be in your backyard!"

"You got it."

"I'm feeling guilty. Her roommates are a rough crowd too. Hard knocks from the street."

"What can you do about it?"

"Nothing, and apparently a real nice lady that I work with on my floor, Carmen's her name, has taken a liking to Yasmine and speaks to her on the phone when I'm not there. I think she knows the situation."

"What situation?"

"Well, at least that Yasmine has a crush on me."

"Do you know that for a fact now?"

"She tried to kiss me in the laundry room before she left."

Patrick's face actually turned red. Something Joe thought he would never see.

"Were you two alone?"

"Yes. It was a mistake. I'm supposed to take them in two's. It was sort of an emergency. Johny didn't have clean clothes. He had been sick and throwing up with the runs.

"I took them to the ER the night before. The doctors prescribed Pedialyte."

"Did he take it?"

"No."

"So how did you respond to the attempted affection?"

"I sidestepped and picked up a laundry basket. She laughed."

There was a pause in the conversation as the two men looked at each other.

Then Joe said, "It's getting complicated even though I've done nothing. I've followed instructions and just done my job.

"This lady, Carmen, passed a couple of hints that she thinks that I should keep in touch with Yasmine. She actually said that I should visit her and see how she's doing.

"And", Joe said before Patrick could comment, "there's another girl coming on to me!"

"Okay. Stop right there. Do you have feelings for two of these young ladies?"

"No. Brenda let it be known to me that she's available. And I have to admit she is sexually attractive. I'm being tempted, in my mind at least. But I'm confident that I will do nothing."

"How do you know she's coming on to you?"

"At night during room check, when we make sure everyone's accounted for and in their rooms, she has come to the door with her hair done, makeup, and wearing only a bra with tight blue jeans.

"I have not and will not enter the room. Actually, I pretend like nothing happened."

"That's good," Pat said.

"It gets worse. Somehow she found out where I live. Three times now she's been outside with her friend and two strollers, feigning coincidence."

"Oh boy, I see what you mean. It is getting complicated. What are you gonna do or not do?"

"I am never going to do anything with Brenda, but Yasmine? I'm considering visiting her and Johny. Just to make sure they're okay."

"Keep praying about it Jo-da. Does it still feel right, in here?" Pat asked, pointing to his heart.

"Without a doubt," Joe answered.

Joe looked out the window as Patrick painted. He saw a man in a tunic and thought about Paul. He hadn't seen him in weeks. He wanted to tell him about the mountain and how he had felt stronger since then. How he had had a feeling of accomplishment.

"I'll see you later Pat," he said.

"Okay. Stay out of trouble. And by the way, you mentioned that two statues were complete. Could you ID what saints they were?"

"Yes. They were St. James and St. John."

CHAPTER 18

Paul was sitting in a booth at the Speakeasy restaurant, the front part. Out the window he could see the artsy hip crowd walking past on the famous McDougal Street. A Street made famous in the 60's by the hippie crowd and folk singers. The sun had set and a blanket of darkness was enveloping the city.

Next to him was Lepido, Fatima's brother, and across the table were Fatima and her sister Sahar. They were sharing a meal of falafel, hummus, and pita bread.

Paul had only met Sahar briefly. She was as beautiful as Fatima but with brown hair. Two years younger. Lepido was home from business school. He was the youngest of the three siblings and a little hot headed.

Lepido was unaware that Sahar and Fatima were considering converting. He knew only that Paul had given them holy cards and that they were using the prayers regularly. He was addressing Paul and being critical of the Church. Paul was listening intently and politely. He was not aware if Lepido knew about Fatima's further seeking into the church.

"The Catholic Church is intolerant," Lepido was saying.

"How can there be only one way to be saved? Each culture worships differently but we all worship the same God. You mean to tell me that you believe all Buddhists and Moslems are going to hell?

"Or how about people that don't believe in organized religion but pray to God and try to live good lives. They're going to hell too?

"Jesus was special. He preaches peace and love and has had a profound effect on society and on the world as a whole, but he's not God. He was sent by God at a specific time to teach people. Just like Buddha or Mohammed. He's an avatar, a messenger.

"It's the organized church that changed his teachings and proclaimed him a part of a 'trinity'.

"And that happened hundreds of years later."

Paul had turned and looked at Lepido as he spoke. He had heard all this before and was prepared to answer him. Out of the corner of his eye, he could tell that Fatima was looking at him curiously, waiting for him to respond.

"The actual teaching of the church on salvation, Lepido, is that all holy people have a chance to go to heaven because of the incarnation of God the Father in His Son Jesus Christ."

Lepido started to interrupt but Paul gently lifted his left palm up in a peace gesture and Lepido stopped.

"It's because of Jesus and his Church that the gates of heaven reopened after God had closed them due to Adam's sin.

"We teach that it is through Jesus' incarnation, dying on the cross, and resurrection, that we are saved.

"Jesus was the final perfect sacrifice bringing on the New Covenant that Jeremiah prophesied about (Jeremiah 31:31). Did you know that after Jesus the Hebrews stopped all animal sacrifice?

"God is a merciful and loving God. And Jesus is His Divine Son. But don't forget that only Noah and his family were saved from the deluge. God destroyed the whole sinful world with the flood.

"So He is a God of mercy and love but also of justice. If you deny Him and lead sinful lives, you have to face His justice.

"Holiness is the key. That's what the Church is really here for, to provide us with the opportunity to become holy. God said: 'Be holy as I am holy'. (Leviticus 19:2)

"Christ established the sacraments through His church to bring us closer to Him and to make us holy, in preparation to spend eternity with the Holiest of Holy.

"And as an act of divine mercy, God gave us purgatory, a place of purgation, a place to purge ourselves of our sin and another chance at holiness. (Isaiah 6:1-7, Matthew 12:32).

"You see, there is only truth on the other side. All the sins that we keep hidden are out in the open. There is no more denial or deception. Your heart will only know truth and I believe that you yourself will know how you will be judged."

Lepido was sitting quietly with his arms folded over his chest and the beginning of a scowl on his face. Paul couldn't tell if he was getting through to him or not.

"So to answer your question, all holy people or those seeking holiness can be saved because of the Incarnation. So it is through Jesus and His Church that we are saved.

"And as for Our Lord being just another avatar, this cannot be. You may compare St. Francis and his influence and teaching with Mohammed and Buddha, but Jesus is either God the Son or a terrible liar.

"He says several times in scripture that He and the Father are one and that when you see Him, you see the Father.

"You see, he gave the Keys to the Kingdom to Peter. This way there would be a final authority on earth, guided by the Holy Spirit as promised, to avoid confusion and false teaching.

"I've done the research. The Catholic Church's teachings have not changed in 2000 years.

"He picked twelve Apostles to lead His church. And they in turn appointed bishops and deacons to organize Christ's church and grow it amidst tremendous persecution.

"The reason I bring all this up is because when the Catholic Church calls a Counsel to put into writing church teachings that have been handed down from the beginning, all it's doing is reinforcing a certain teaching, such as that of the Trinity.

"The church taught that Jesus was divine from the beginning, but only when challenged by heresy does it explain and document the teaching.

"Thus the ecumenical counsels such as the three at the end of the 4th century that put together the New Testament canon, are not to invent new teachings but to validate old ones already in place and handed down through the great and ancient tradition of the Church, the same tradition that brought us the New Testament.

"Lepido, Jesus is God Incarnate, the Messiah, Our Savior and Lord, the King of Kings and Lord of Lords. I believe that by love, the whole world will someday acknowledge this."

And with that, Paul grinned and almost let out a laugh. Fatima and Sahar had feint smiles on their lips and in their eyes, as Lepido had taken a large bite of falafel and couldn't speak.

Meanwhile, Joe Morrison walked up to the table.

"Peace be with you, Joe," Paul said and reached out and shook Joe's hand.

"This is Fatima, Sahar, and Lepido. This is my friend Joe."

They all acknowledged Joe. Fatima also shook his hand.

"I was hoping to find you. I haven't seen you in a while."

"Hey, I've got something that I want to show you. I hope you all can excuse us. Nice talking to you."

Paul said goodbye to Fatima, Sahar and Lepido and headed for the back room. Joe followed.

Fatima's uncle with the handlebar mustache let them both in and closed the door behind them. There were a scattered few people sitting at the tables. Some were tuning guitars, others were chatting. On the stage, a young man with a red bandana on his head was checking the microphone.

Both men slipped into the "studio" where Paul turned on the light and quickly went over to his worktable. He didn't pick up the piece that he was working on, but one that stood up and leaned against the wall.

He handed the piece to Joe.

"Does this mean anything to you?"

Joe looked at the embossing of the man, woman, and child holding hands. He remembered now seeing Paul working on it the last time he was here. A chill went up his spine and he got goose bumps on his arms.

"I think this one was meant for you. Does it mean anything to you?"

"Yes!"

"Well good. I'd like you to have it."

Joe looked at the embossing. This was unmistakable. This has to be a good sign. A good sign! He had secretly been praying for a sign from God about Yasmine and Johny. This has to be it.

The child is a little boy not a girl. The woman looks like Yasmine: full face and long curly hair. And the man wore a beard. Close cropped like his.

Joe looked up and said, "Thank you."

That was all he could say.

He looked down at the embossing that lay finished on the table. The piece showed a girl standing on a beach while in the water a small boat seemed to be taking her baby away.

"I went to the mountain."

"By yourself?"

"Yes."

"How did it go?"

"Exhilarating, I went a couple of weeks ago and I can still feel it. I feel more confident."

"Confident. Do you know what the word actually means?"

Joe didn't answer, looking at Paul.

"Con-fi means: with faith. Faith gives you confidence, courage, and conquers fear. I'll assume that you had a faith building experience up there."

"I hadn't thought about it that way. Actually, I couldn't figure out exactly why I felt more confident afterwards. But now that I think of it, I did have a religious experience. Holy cow, I'd forgotten."

"What?"

"When I picked up the van at Mom's, my Abuela's rosary was on my seat. I had no clue how it got there.

"That night on the mountain, the wind was howling, there was a cold chill in the air and I got real scared. I almost panicked. I set the pup tent up sideways!"

Paul didn't laugh when Joe said this.

"Anyway, when I started freaking out, I curled up in the fetal position in the sleeping bag and felt the rosary in the crease of my thigh.

"As soon as I realized what it was, my fear started going away.

"As I prayed the joyful mysteries I fell asleep."

"So you remembered your faith. The thought of your Abuela gave you strength and the Holy Spirit took care of the rest.

"What did you mean freak out?"

"I started all this negative thinking: regrets about the past, how I should have chosen security and material things over service. How I wasn't strong spiritually."

"Spiritual warfare."

"I guess so."

"I know so."

"Sounds like you took a few positive steps forward in your journey!"

At this point, the two men stood staring at each other. Then Paul looked down at his new embossing. He had been working on it the morning that he had rushed to Gwen's house. He had seen the message in it for him.

Joe noticed Paul's facial expression change as he looked at the piece. Then Paul made the sign of the cross and closed his eyes. He prayed for a minute with his lips moving and then opened his eyes and made the sign of the cross again.

He then looked at Joe and put his hands on his hips.

"What are we now, is this Friday night?" he asked.

"Yes," Joe answered.

"Are you working tomorrow?"

"Yes, but not until 3 p.m., I'm doing a three to eleven."

"Let's go on an adventure."

"Where to?"

"Where do you think?"

"To the mountain?"

"Sounds good."

Joe thought for a moment. He put the side of his fist to his mouth and bit on the skin of his index finger, and then he said, "Do you take subways and trains?"

"If I have to why?"

"We can take the A train up to 175th Street and then the 182 bus to Leonia. I'll pay."

"We could do that, lets start walking."

Paul shut off the light and locked the door. He noticed that Joe left his art on the table. As they went out through the restaurant, Lepido too was on his way out.

"Where are you boys going?" he asked.

"Jersey," Joe said.

"Hey, where are you going in Jersey? I'm going there too."

"Just across the George Washington Bridge, a mile from there."

"I'm going to visit friends in Teaneck. Do you know where that is?"

"Yes, of course," Joe said.

"How are you getting there?" Lepido asked.

"Subway and bus," Joe answered.

"No, you're not. I'll take you. I have my car."

Lepido's car was parked right there on McDougal, a very hard street to find a parking space. They all piled in and headed west to get on the Henry Hudson Parkway north.

The conversation was casual as they drove towards the George Washington Bridge. Lepido talked about school at first but the talk quickly switched to baseball.

Lepido was a Yankees fan and Joe was a diehard Mets fan. They both ripped each other's teams for a while and came away laughing. They both agreed that baseball was a great game.

Paul sat in the back of the old Dodge Coronet, praying his finger rosary and enjoying the ride, wondering if they play baseball in heaven.

After getting dropped off, the two men said goodbye to Lepido and wished him well. They walked up the back stairs of Joe's mother's house and could see her sitting at the kitchen table eating cottage cheese and jelly with crackers on the side.

His mom was around seventy and in good health. She wasn't startled when they knocked on the door.

She saw Joe and smiled. Opening the door, she offered him a kiss, then saw Paul behind him and said, "Come in, come in," in a thick Spanish accent. Joe's mother had lived most of her life in Cuba and spoke with an accent.

She sat back down at the table and asked him who his friend was.

"Mom, this is Paul. I know him from the city. He works with the homeless."

Joe's mother eyed Paul up and down and asked, "Are you a priest?"

"No," Paul said, "This is a bad habit that I have."

Joe's mother didn't get the joke at first but then she laughed. Joe was surprised. He had never heard Paul try to be funny.

Then Joe's mother said, "No, really, are you a monk?"

Paul shook his head no and smiled.

"Let's just say, I'm a lay Franciscan, a simple pilgrim on a journey to his heart."

"Are you boys hungry?"

"No, not really," Joe answered. "We came to pick up the tent. We're going camping for a night."

"So late? Why it's already dark out. Are you crazy Joe?"

Joe's mom had a habit of asking Joe if he was crazy. As a young man he had had a wild streak in him that his mother knew all too well.

"Where are you going?"

"To the Catskills."

"Oh boy," is all she said.

Joe started for the basement door to get the gear when Paul stopped him.

"No gear," he said.

"What?"

"No gear."

Joe looked bemused for a second and then from somewhere he heard the words: "Then we're taking the Harley."

He realized it was he who had uttered those words as he headed for the back door.

CHAPTER 19

▼

The black super-glide started right up. The noise from the straight pipes was deafening. Joe liked his bike to make noise for safety sake. If they don't see you at least they'll hear you coming was his philosophy. The bike sounded like an 18-wheeler.

He slipped his helmet on and checked the gas, full tank. He pushed up the kickstand and waited for Paul to hop on.

Paul got on rather awkwardly as a cassock is more like a dress than a pair of pants. When he divided his legs over the back seat, the bottom of the tunic came up to his knees exposing his calves and ankles.

Joe turned his head and asked, "Ready?"

He could see Paul nodding his head out of the corner of his eye.

They waved to Mom in the window and carefully navigated their way out the driveway and onto the street.

When they stopped at the corner, Joe told Paul not to lean during the turns, to stay straight up always. This gave him a more precise feel for the weight on the bike so that he could compensate for the passenger.

They took Route 4W to Route 17N through Paramus and in 45 minutes were on the New York State Thruway.

The night was perfect for a road trip. The wind felt just right against their bodies. Not too cold for a late October evening.

The men could see the full moon rising and illuminating the night sky, so bright that not a star was visible to them.

Unawares to Joe, Paul had never been on a motorcycle before. Not to mention a huge Harley screaming down the highway at 75 mph. Paul was praying Hail Mary's fast and furious and holding on real tight to Joe.

As they neared the Catskill exits, the wind started to kick up and black clouds enveloped the sky and blacked out the moon. The wind held an icy chill.

Then half way down Route 28 West there was a cloudburst, and a drenching rain began pouring down.

Joe was wearing slightly tinted sunglasses to protect his eyes from the wind, and because of the rain and the darkness, he couldn't see.

He took the next turn off, next to the giant eagle statue, and scooted down into the little village of Phoenicia. They pulled into an old gas station that now was a grocery and parked the bike under a canopy next to a wagon full of pumpkins.

They were drenched and chilled.

"Let's get a hot chocolate," Joe said.

The men walked into the tiny grocery store where they poured themselves two instant hot chocolates.

Joe paid the girl $2 and they walked back outside.

The rain hadn't let up.

"I've got a buddy only a few miles from here," Joe said.

"He's renovated an old cinder block dance hall into a home. He lives right on the river.

"He's got a two hundred year old, three story hotel on the property. It used to be a stagecoach stop. He says he's going to fix it up someday as a youth hostel to pay his bills.

"It's only him with his wife and kid.

"I've known him most of my life. He won't mind too much if we pop in."

Paul still had his helmet on and his tunic was soaked right through. All he could do was nod.

"Once upon a time, I almost bought two lots up here," Joe said, "in a one-way valley, with a creek right in front. The deal fell through when I found out I couldn't have animals on it."

The rain finally let up a bit and they headed down to George's place.

Joe thought that it must be around 10 p.m. Not too late.

They took Route 28 West to where it hooked up with Old Route 28 and skipped off onto that road for a half mile.

The light was on and George's truck was in the driveway.

George was surprised and delighted to see his old friend. He shook hands warmly when introduced to Paul and offered to put his tunic in the dryer.

When they were settled, the men sat around a pot-bellied stove in what was once the bar of the dance hall. The home was decorated around the fact that there was a bar in this room and a stage in the next room.

On the old bar George had a TV that wasn't on with books and some boxes. The old bar was just a part of the living room.

The pot bellied stove was doing the job. The two men had stopped shivering.

Paul had on George's terry bathrobe and a pair of pajama bottoms. Joe had on a pair of George's sweats with white socks.

George's wife was kind enough to put Paul's tunic in the dryer and fetched the men some clothes before she retired for the night. The boy was already asleep.

All three men held up a shot glass of peppermint schnapps and toasted the night. Paul decided that one wouldn't hurt and would warm up his insides besides. George had apparently had a few cold ones that night before their arrival. He was loose and talkative.

The men exchanged pleasantries. The mood was very relaxed. The two visitors felt welcomed.

Joe explained that he had been friends with George since 9th grade and that when most guys their age were borrowing Dad's car for a date on Saturday night, George owned a Cadillac hearse and had built a Harley chopper.

He had bought this land at the time that Joe was supposed to buy his, and then later on had moved up with his wife and kid.

They had added a new room where he wanted the two men to sleep and had put a new roof on the hotel. Tomorrow they planned to move most of their stuff into the hotel.

"So Joe," George asked, "How do you get to be a counselor without a degree?"

"Well, we're called counselors and we do counsel, but we're actually child care providers. The community believes that the Holy Spirit will provide us with the right words and actions to counsel when we need them. We also have very experienced and very educated staff members that we constantly hit up for advice and stuff. In intake we meet with a psychiatrist once a week."

"I see," George said. And Joe remembered that George liked to say, "I see" a lot.

The men talked and shared stories into the night. George telling of his vegetable garden success that he'd had. His biggest problem was keeping the varmints out of it.

He told of plans to build a garage to put his Harley's in. He had two Harleys.

George looked like a biker. Shoulder length hair and long natty beard. He had large dark eyes like a hawk. He smoked Lucky Strikes and wore heavy silver rings on every finger. For scratch he did hauling with his box van and leatherwork on the side. He was also quite a character.

He told Paul some stories about the barroom brawls that he and Joe had engaged in once upon a time, especially the one that made the front page of two newspapers because the riot squads from three police departments were called out. George declined to say that he started that fight. Luckily, neither George nor Joe had ever been arrested.

Joe had had a few sips of Schnapps and felt free to speak his mind when the conversation turned spiritual.

"George had a Jehovah's Witness lady visiting here once a week for quite a while," he said to Paul. "She fogged up his brain.

"He doesn't believe in the Mass because the word Mass isn't in the Bible. He doesn't believe that Christ was God and man. Or that Mary is the Mother of God!"

George smirked and shook his head as he took a pull on his Lucky. He never minded a little spiritual debate now and then. In fact, he enjoyed them.

"Jehovah's Witnesses," Paul began, "started in the 1800's by a Baptist Mason named Charles Russell. He never expected the church to get big. He preached that only 144,000 would be swept up and saved, but when they grew in number past that, they invented the paradise on earth thing for the rest of his followers.

"How do you tell a false prophet, George?"

George shook his head.

"Their prophecies don't come true. How do you tell a true prophet?"

George looked straight at Paul.

"Their prophecies come true. The Jehovah's Witnesses have predicted the end of the world, exact date and time, three times.

"Think about it.

"They're a false religion, separating you from Jesus, hurting you."

Paul paused for a moment looking at George. He was speaking with a firm but conciliatory tone. He continued.

"The Mass is not mentioned in the Bible but neither is 'Sola Scriptura', the belief that all revealed truth has to be in the Bible. That teaching is not Biblical.

"In fact, the church and the Mass come before the Bible. The Church started in 33 A.D. The New Testament canon was put together from Church tradition around the year 398 A.D.

"But the Mass is mentioned in the writings of the first disciples, those taught by the Apostles, in the first and second century.

"Besides, worship has always been sacrificial, since the time of Abraham. The Mass is the celebration of that final saving sacrifice: Our Lord on the cross!

"As far as Jesus being the Son of God, three persons in one God, he says many times that: 'I and the Father are one,' or 'When you see me, you see the Father'.

"Jesus as divine has been taught for 2000 years, by the church that He established and promised to remain with forever.

"If He's not God, He's a charlatan who died for nothing."

George was nodding, thinking.

"And Mary, do you call her blessed George, because in the Bible it says that all generations shall call her blessed.

"She is not literally the Mother of God, but she gave birth to a Divine Person, in a sense making her Mother of God. Is she not the Mother of the Church? Wasn't she there at the most critical moments of the Gospel? Jesus told John from the cross that she was to be his mother.

"Don't deny Mary. She's been venerated and loved from the beginning and her intercession is most powerful!"

"I see," George said, "But why would we need more intercessors if we have Jesus?" he asked.

Paul answered, "Look in Revelation. The saints in heaven take our prayers and pass them on to God, in effect, interceding. (Rev. 5:8)

"The communion of saints, we're all in this together. It's beautiful."

"I see," George said, but with a sense of urgency.

Then Joe said, "There's one thing that I want to add, the matter of authority to interpret scripture.

"My brother-in-law happens to be Jewish, not a devout Jew but Jewish nonetheless.

"I asked him why Jews doesn't give out the Torah on street corners the way Christians do. You know what he said?

"He said of course not. If you want to be a Jew, they will teach you what the Torah means. Only the Rabbis have that authority.

"The whole problem with Christianity is that we're not unified. And we're not unified because since the 16th century the false teaching that anyone can read and interpret the Bible has spread.

"So now, you have 30,000 different Christian churches all claiming to be bible based and all having different interpretations of similar verses.

"Within each Christian denomination it's pretty much up to your Pastor to be the infallible teacher of the word of God. That's confusing!

"One will be for infant baptism, one won't. One will say divorce is okay; another won't, within the same church!

"If you want to know what the Catholic Church teaches, get a catechism.

"Did you know that the readings at Mass everyday are the same in every Catholic Church in the world? We are the universal church spoken of in scripture, none other, and the only one with the authority from Jesus himself to teach the whole truth. I happen to know it's in Timothy somewhere. 'The church is the pillar and foundation of all truth'. What church? There's only one that existed at that time, the Catholic Church." (Tim.3:15)

"The key is," Paul added, "that Jesus gave the Keys to the Kingdom to Peter. 'What you bound on earth will be bound in heaven', so that there would be a final authority on church teaching, and no Vicar of Christ has ever changed a teaching from the beginning, never.

"Did you know that even up until today, every Priest, Deacon and Bishop in the Church was ordained by someone who had been ordained in a direct line of apostolic succession to Christ? Now that's authority!"

"I see," was all George could say.

"So you boys are double teaming me tonight. Ha! Ha! Maybe it was meant to pour tonight! Ha ha ha ha!"

At that point, George got up and said that he had to pee. He came back moments later with Paul's tunic and Joe's denim shirt and jeans.

"The old lady took the liberty of washing and drying your stuff. That's what took so long."

"I thought she'd gone to bed," Joe said.

Well, she went into our bedroom and read awhile until the washing machine was done. Then put the stuff in the dryer and hit the sack.

"Come on upstairs," George said, "to my new addition."

They went into the stage part of the building. The stage where bands used to perform was still visible but there were boxes stacked everywhere. This area was not being used as living space.

Upstairs, they went through a brand new door with French glass panes and into a lovely room with a new hardwood floor, wood beams and beautiful wood siding.

George took the men out the sliding French glass doors to a small deck facing the river. The rain was still coming down heavy.

"You can't see it now, but the Esopus River is right there. And boy she's running hard tonight. I hope we don't flood out."

They went back inside where the room was sparsely but neatly furnished. He had a couch and two armchairs around a glass coffee table. Against the wall was an entertainment center with a large color TV.

"The couch pulls out. There are blankets and pillows in that closet. You know where the bathroom is."

On the coffee table was a marble chess set. This surprised Joe because he never knew George to be much for brain games.

"Who's playing chess?" he asked George.

"My son, he plays my wife. He's pretty good. He beats me most times."

Paul had followed the night's conversation closely. He had paid attention. He knew that George and Joe had mutual friends going back a ways.

He had noticed that at one point, Joe's Kawasaki had come up in conversation and George had acted a bit funny.

George was heading for the door when Paul said, "Hey George, about the Kawasaki. You were friends with some of those Edgewater folks right?"

"Yea."

"Did you ever hear anything about what actually happened that night?"

"Yea sure," George said, but his blushing face betrayed him.

"I thought I told you Joe."

"Told me what?"

"I told you some news I heard about your accident right?"

"No, you didn't."

"I did a job up here for some people who were moving down to Edgewater. After the job I stopped in for a couple of beers where the Friendly Tavern used to be. You remember the Friendly right?"

"Of course."

"Well, long story short, I stayed a little too long and had a few too many when who walked in, Kevin McKee.

"He'd already had a couple beers elsewhere and was pretty loose you know."

"Get to the point," Joe said firmly.

"He told me that Karen Van Dylan was driving the car that night; that she pulled out of the driveway there, stalled out, and when she lit the car up again and put it in gear, she heard a motorcycle and stopped real quick.

"He says she and her friends were pretty wasted. She felt really bad when she found out it was you."

"Wow," was all Joe said.

"Want to know what she's up to now? She married a Mormon guy and lives in Nevada or Utah."

Joe was speechless. He turned and walked towards the sliding doors and stepped out onto the deck.

George yelled, "Well goodnight. See ya in the A.M.!" and slipped out the door.

Paul pulled out his finger rosary and sat on the armchair facing the deck. Joe came back in and slid the doors closed.

"You know something Paul? I'm not that surprised. Because I knew she was involved. But I'm amazed at the circumstances. I don't think George was even sorry to tell me.

"What made you think to ask?"

"A hunch," is all Paul said.

CHAPTER 20

▼

Breakfast was big. George ate two meals a day and ate heartily. His wife Susan had made the men pancakes with buttery scrambled eggs, bacon, sausage and a toasted baguette, which the men shared. There was real maple syrup for the pancakes.

They ate in a tiny kitchen left over from the days of the disco. Everything was antique. The stove and the sink were ancient. The walls still had the original faded yellow paint. And the floor was worn out linoleum.

But the fresh flowers on the table and the smell of home cooking made this a homey and comfortable breakfast nook.

George's son Brian had already eaten and was kicking a ball just outside the open door. A handsome boy of twelve, Joe noted he was identical to George at that same age.

The men were chowing down. Susan was pouring fresh squeezed O.J. in three cups and the coffee was percolating on the old stove when George spoke.

"How about the Apocalypse, are these the latter days or what?" He was addressing Paul.

"I do believe that these are the latter days, mostly because of the horrible genocide of abortion and things like cloning or the buying and selling of aborted baby parts as well as the terrible weapons that are being invented. God cannot tolerate these much longer. But how long are the latter days going to last? They could last 50 years, one hundred, or a thousand. One never knows.

"I think the point of revelation and the apocalypse and the whole gospel is to be ready now. Live holy lives. Your personal apocalypse, your death, could come tomorrow. The point is, are you ready?"

"I see," George said and then he wiped his overgrown mustache with a napkin.

"One can see the antichrist everywhere in this culture. Our culture. You see it in the schools, on TV, in the movies. There's a deliberate attack on Christ and Christians.

"There is a culture war going on. Our Christian culture, which created the most blessed and powerful country in the world, is in the crosshairs of the atheistic socialists.

"They've literally invaded our country, and brought lots of money with them. Money is power. They buy power through the politicians and then influence our culture through the corrupt judicial system, the media and the schools.

"Their aim is to destroy our way of life for what they perceive to be a good cause: secular humanist socialism. Or what we commonly call "liberalism". And they do have religion. Liberalism is their religion. And their beliefs are clearly against Christ."

Paul paused to take a mouthful of egg and sausage.

Joe jumped in.

"That's why the church is under tremendous attack George. The Church is the most powerful foe of these people.

"These people dream of a socialist worker utopia where most people are slaves of the state. These elitists believe that they'll be a part of the ruling class. They believe that the workers will be better off. And although the system has failed miserably throughout the world they believe that their form of government will succeed. They don't understand. When you have two workers working side by side and one works twice as hard as the other, and they both get paid the same, which one do you think will go to the other ones level?

"This is the flaw in the system. People won't be motivated to be their best. The inertia will win. All will work at the pace of the slowest. This is what's happened in Cuba.

"Cuba can trade in any country on earth except us. Why is she so poor? Those in power hoard the money and the workers get lazy.

"The Church speaks up for the most vulnerable and oppressed all around the world. The enemy considers this an attack on them. I believe that their agenda consists of controlling countries by limiting their populations through abortion and loaning them huge amounts of money and putting them in debt."

"Wow," Susan said, "You guys have said a mouthful!" And they all laughed.

When coffee was served George picked up his cup and took the men outside. As they walked towards the old hotel, Joe could see what happened.

"Oh my God," he cried.

And then Paul saw it too.

"Holy cow!"

"You mean you guys didn't hear it last night?" George said, "The sound was like a huge branch snapping, and then a bunch of branches crushing together."

George had been somewhat sullen at breakfast, and Sue very quiet for Sue. And now Joe knew why.

The hotel collapsed.

It lay all in a heap. A large chunk apparently washed away down river.

Joe could see the river was overflowing its boundaries by 40 feet.

"Oh my gosh, George. I am sorry!" Joe said.

Paul looked stunned. He wondered about the coincidence of the whole trip.

"Yea. She's gone," George said, "I heard a creaking noise at around 4 a.m. and then another. I was up taking a pee.

"I lit up a smoke and stood in the doorway. 'Cause of the full moon, I could pretty much see the silhouette of the building. I watched it go down."

George was teary eyed. He had plans for this building.

"It stopped raining around dawn. The weather channel said we got 15 inches last night. They call it the hundred-year flood.

"And look over there," George pointed to the side of the river, "The river shifted last night. It used to run over there. Now it's over here, permanently. It took at least an acre or two from me. I'm gonna have to set cement pilings up stream to divert this thing and keep it from eventually taking my home. Boy, this has to be the worst thing that's ever happened to me."

Joe and Paul were cruising east on Route 28. The Harley had started right up even though Joe had forgotten to cover it over night. The sky was clear and the air smelled fresh and moist.

He was looking for the little Catholic Church he knew was around these parts and thinking about George's plan to put all his stuff in the hotel, and maybe his family too. Joe had told George early on that the hotel was too damaged to fix up. It hadn't had a decent roof in a hundred years! He thought maybe the building's collapse was a blessing.

He turned into the little church and parked the bike. He looked at Paul.

"Give me a minute will you please?"

"Sure," Paul said.

Paul had his finger rosary going and walked over to the road to watch the cars go by and look at the Great Esopus across the street. He could see whitewater rapids from where he stood. He hoped no one had been hurt last night.

Joe walked into the church and immediately sensed something was wrong. He didn't feel the way he always did when entering church. What was missing?

And then he knew.

This wasn't a Catholic Church. There was no tabernacle. The real presence was distinctly missing. What a shame.

Then he remembered something that he had heard on one of his tapes. Protestant churches are places of fellowship. Catholic Churches are holy places of prayer. He went out and read the sign: St.Luke's church. Okay. It doesn't say Catholic. My mistake.

Paul saw the disappointment in Joe's face as they got on the bike. Neither man spoke.

As they rode east towards the thruway Paul thought that he knew why Joe had stopped to pray: to forgive Karen Von Dylan, and to pray for George, that the lost sheep come into the fold.

He prayed for Joe.

Although Route 28 ran alongside the Esopus, the highway was relatively dry. They cruised straight to the thruway, stopping once to fill the tank. Then Joe quickly got back on the road. He still had a shift to work that night.

As they cruised down the thruway, both men unknowingly were feeling the same emotion and thinking the same thoughts.

This friendship that is developing here feels good. I like this guy. I feel like somehow our destinies are intertwined.

This was meant to be.

Just then both men saw a huge arc of a rainbow. The rainbow went clear across the sky and they were moving right through the center, and straight ahead, as if being framed by this beautiful sign from God, was New York City.

After dropping off the bike the two men jumped on the 166 Bus in Leonia.

Joe didn't see his mom and figured his brother and sister had taken her out to lunch. Someone usually did on Saturdays.

Neither man spoke on the bus for thirty minutes. They both seemed to be praying or meditating. Paul spoke first as the bus turned south alongside the Hudson River, and New York City was visible on the left.

"Could you tell I've never been on a motorcycle before?"

"Actually no, I couldn't even tell you were back there. Lots of times people forget to not lean on a curve and I have to jerk the bike up a bit, you done good!"

"I don't think doing over 100 mph on the thruway was too good!" Paul said.

"I always do that at least once when I go for a scoot. It's a bad habit. But it cleans the carbon out of the system. Anyway, I went back down to 75 mph right away!"

"Not soon enough," Paul chimed in.

"Did you do your forgiveness prayer today?"

Joe looked at Paul, a bit curious.

"How'd you know?"

"Just a hunch," is all Paul said.

Moments later Paul asked, "You ever hear about Athos Joe?"

"Yes, I have. It's a peninsula off of Greece where there are a lot of Orthodox Monasteries. Monks and hermits live there. There are a lot of mountains and the ocean. It's mysterious in a way, the hermits and all.

"I heard a woman hasn't set foot there in a thousand years and that there are monasteries there that are hundreds of years old.

"Why do you ask?"

"I'd never heard of it before, until recently. A Franciscan that I know told me about it. He used to live there."

"Really."

"He was a monk there for seven years, at the Panteleimon Monastery. He started out in the kitchen and ended up painting Icons. He's good too."

The thought of Icons reminded Joe about Paul's art.

"Paul, I meant to ask you about the engravings that you do, if you don't mind. How do you do it? You just start tapping away and follow your instinct?"

Joe was curious about the etching of the man, girl and child. But wasn't ready to tell Paul why.

"Not quite, I believe instinct in my case to be The Holy Spirit. The last two in particular have meant something. I believe it's a grace, a way to identify God's will."

"I'm glad you brought that up. I need to know. How can you really tell if you're doing God's Will?"

Again Joe's question pertained to his possible relationship with Yasmine.

"Some saints say that doing God's will, will feel right. You'll feel good. No regrets, no guilt.

"I believe God is happy if you're ATTEMPTING to do His Will."

"I like that," Joe said, "I truly believe that I am."

The two men looked at each other and then looked out at the Empire Sate Building.

Paul continued.

"This monk Henry says that when he was bussing it down to Assisi from Spain, that he rode the bus with an ancient looking friar with leathery skin and long white hair.

"That he didn't realize it at first, but later thought that he had been in the presence of holiness. The old man was beautiful. He seemed to glow. He says he thought he was Franciscan because the old man wore a tunic. Except that the tunic was black.

"When he called Assisi later on to inquire about the old man they said that they had never heard of him up there. This old man told Henry about Athos and that he should go there.

"Then Henry does go there, out of curiosity, and ends up becoming a monk."

"That is quite an interesting story. Who does he think this old monk was?"

"St. John."

"What do you mean St. John?"

"I mean St John, from the gospel of St. John."

"How do you figure?"

"There are books about it saying that he never died. He was never martyred in the Bible. There have been rumors for two thousand years that he lives, waiting for the second coming of Our Lord.

"I don't know where, but somewhere in scripture Peter asks Jesus a question and he answers by pointing to John and saying something like, 'so what if he is still here upon my return,' or something like that, I have to look it up." (John 21:22)

The hair on Joe's arms and the back of his neck were standing up. He took a deep breath.

Paul added, "I first heard about it when I was investigating Mormonism. Curiously, they teach that it's true. That he walks the earth."

"And Henry saw him, you think?"

"There's more," Paul said, "In Athos, Henry noticed that every day at Mass a priest or monk walked the communion chalice up the stairs to a small private cubby that was separate from the choir, where one could see the silhouette of a man.

"He inquired as to the man's identity, and was told that he was a hermit that lived at the base of the cliff near the monastery. The cliff was at waters edge.

"He said that the only view to the hermit's cell was a three hour hike out and around the cliff almost facing it. It was incredibly hard to go straight down to his cell. You're actually rock climbing. He lived sort of on an inlet. The water was pretty rough but apparently he caught fish from there.

"So Henry takes a hike one day and after watching and waiting for a couple of hours he finally sees the old hermit. He was the spitting image of the old man on the bus. But he was too far away to tell for sure."

"Wow!" Joe said, "Amazing, I love it, the mysteries of our lovely faith."

"And there's more."

"Oh my god, I mean gosh."

"There was a rumor that this old hermit was protecting an ancient relic. Right there in his little tiny ocean front hut, possibly something extremely important and ancient."

At this point the bus had pulled up the hill into Port Authority 42ndStreet, pulled over to the curb, and stopped.

The two men disembarked quietly and walked down the stairs into the main building. They walked past the hordes of tourists from every nook and cranny in the world. They walked past the stores, the newspaper stands, even an Orthodox Priest in full black regalia and hat. They both looked at each other and laughed at the coincidence.

They pushed open the doors and exited onto 8thAvenue together where a gust of exhaust fumes slapped their faces. Paul grabbed Joe's arm sleeve.

"Henry says I should go there, but not alone, to Athos. Can you get time off?"

Joe felt the adrenaline rush through his body. He wasn't a man who blushed, but if he did, he'd be glowing red.

A hundred thoughts raced through his mind at once.

This would be an adventure, wow, and a real adventure, doing something important with this cool guy who gives his life to charity.

He looked at Paul just before muttering the words.

"Yes of course. Name the time and place, let's go."

Then he caught himself and thought about Yasmine.

Paul noticed the hesitation. But it didn't bother him. There was something special here between the two men. He knew this. He knew Joe would go.

"How much time do we need?"

"At least a week, two weeks tops."

"Where can I reach you?"

"I'll find you." At this, the two men spontaneously hugged each other and went in separate directions.

Joe headed for the community to get ready for work.
Paul headed for St Vincent's to visit Gwen.

CHAPTER 21

▼

Gwen was petite. She looked like a child under the covers when Paul walked in. Her wavy dark brown hair was cut short with bangs, easily manageable and practical, like the young career woman that she was.

She looked up from her book with round dark eyes when he approached the bed. He held a single red rose in his hand.

Gwen laid the book down on her tummy and looking at Paul, began to cry. She opened her arms wide and embraced him, holding him to her.

For a long minute they hugged each other, both of them crying. When Paul felt her releasing him, he pulled back and sat next to her on the bed.

They looked into each other's eyes silently, speaking without words. Gwen reached for Paul's hand and held it, tears still welling in her eyes.

When she went to speak, he held a finger to her lips, and as if reading her thoughts he said: "God will forgive you Gwen. He will. He does. He's all merciful."

Now Gwen really broke down and cried, agonizing tears, tears of healing.

When she could speak she said: "I've asked God constantly to forgive me. I made a terrible mistake. I wish I could have found you. I looked for you."

"I know. Lola told me."

"I just missed you when you came by the apartment. Lola thought that she was protecting me. I was home two of those times. I was in the bathroom one time and talking to my dad the other time. She never told me."

"She's very sorry that she did that. Did she tell you?"

"Yes. She told me that you have been consoling her while I was in intensive care."

She looked away when she said this. He noticed for the first time how pale she was. He caught a hint of jealousy in her eyes. Lola was younger and somewhat prettier then Gwen. Gwen probably had to play second fiddle to her in the past. He sensed this.

"Gwen I want you to know that I love you, like a sister, and would never do anything to hurt you."

Ordinarily Gwen would have taken this as an insult, but coming from Paul she understood he was different. He had different priorities and values from anyone that she had ever met. God was his most important commitment. She was starting to understand why.

"Thank you for coming Paul, is that for me?"

"Yes it is," he said, and handed Gwen the long stem rose.

She smelled it, and then began to spin it gently against her nose before pulling it away, as a single petal fell gently to her lap.

"Thank you Paul! I love you too." She said this and reached out for him with both arms again. They embraced.

"Who has been washing your tunic?" she asked as she pulled away.

"No one, it was dirtier than dirt until I got caught in the rain last night."

"Let me see your feet."

"You wouldn't want to do that. No one's been at them since I last saw you."

This brought a smile to Gwen's face. She had a toothy smile, seeing it made Paul smile.

"I suppose Lola told you about the baby's foot?"

"Yes. You don't have to talk about that Gwen."

"I know," she said, and sadness clouded her eyes.

"Lets pray," Paul said.

"Where did you get this?" He asked, as he lifted the small glow-in-the-dark cross from the nightstand.

"From Lola, who else, the future Catholic, she had it blessed and everything."

Paul held the little cross between him and Gwen.

"Lord we pray in the name of the Father and the Son and the Holy Spirit. Merciful Father, we ask for forgiveness of our sins today. By your grace, we ask for healing and peace. And mostly we ask that you help us forgive ourselves when we sin, especially because, if we weren't sinners, we would have no need for your Son.

"We pray that the Holy Spirit be our guide, our light in the darkness, now and forever.

"We pray for good health. And Lord we pray for a strong faith. We pray that we may know your Will, in Jesus name …"

Gwen interjected before he could finish.

"Thank you for Paul, Lord. Lead him where you want him to go and give him the courage to get there. Amen."

"Amen."

"I'm not ruined Paul, doctor says I can still have kids."

"That's great Gwen. Great!"

"But I think I'll try something new, an adventure."

"What's that?"

"How do you call it? Chastity?"

CHAPTER 22

▼

Joe had gotten out of work at eleven and walked straight home. From 52nd Street he cut east to Eight Avenue and then headed south toward 44th Street. The October night was cold and he wished he'd brought his jacket.

While waiting for a light to change on 50th Street, a man had come jogging up and snatched the wallet out of the front pants pocket of a short, balding man that stood in front of him. In his haste, the thief had dropped the wallet as he turned to head back in the direction that he came from. Joe couldn't help but notice that the mugger was a young black male and that he was smiling during the attempt.

The short man quickly picked up his wallet and tried to run after his assailant, only to be blocked out by a huge black man that was walking toward him.

When the short man went left, so did the blocker, when he went right, there was the big man again, in front of him.

It took a few moments but the short man realized that he'd been double teamed and turned and went on his way.

Joe watched the whole thing from the curb and then looked up into the big man's eyes and saw that he wasn't playing. His nasty stare meant business.

The smaller man must have pulled that over-stuffed wallet out in front of the wrong people, he thought, as he walked the rest of the way home.

As he approached the front door of the 8th Avenue building, he could see that Louis and Jimmy were having a party on their usual perch on the sidewalk. Joining then this night were two men and a woman that Joe had never seen before. They were obviously street people too.

They were each holding tall cans of a name brand beer that looked fresh and icy cold as they sat in a circle on a dirty old blanket. Jimmy looked drunker than usual and was laughing hysterically at something that was said while Louis chugged his beer with one hand while holding out the other in a beggar's palm.

There were several unopened beers in the middle of the circle as well as what looked like two full packs of cigarettes.

Jimmy and Louis had hit the mother lode. A passerby had probably slipped one of the boys a twenty, a rare event, and they proceeded across the street on a beer and cigarettes shopping spree. The extra beer must have attracted the crowd.

Joe said hello, but they paid no attention to him as he slipped in the door. Upstairs he found the Mexican ladies, Charo and Bebe, with another Spanish looking woman that he had never met. They were alone in the cafeteria, sitting at a table in the far corner by a window.

He noticed the stranger right away and found her plain looking but attractive. She had short black hair, dark eyes and a full but shapely figure.

"What's up Joe?" Bebe was the first to speak, and did so in her thick Mexican accent. "Come over here, I want you to meet somebody."

"Hold on, I'll be right there," he yelled, as he walked right into the kitchen to wash his hands and get a bowl of cereal.

When he came over to their table, the ladies were all quiet and staring at him. Charo and Bebe were grinning but the stranger was not.

"This is a friend of ours from Puebla. Her name is Adrianna.

"Adrianna, this is Joe."

He put his bowl of cereal down on the table with one hand while extending the other to Adrianna.

"Nice to meet you," he said, and sat down.

"So what's new Joe?" Charo chimed in. The look in her eyes told him that something had changed. She had never looked at him that way before. There was a gleam in her eyes, like she knew something that he didn't.

"Not much, what's new with you?" he said.

"Well, we have a friend in town," she continued, "only for a couple of days, and she wanted to have some fun!" Charo grinned again as she said this.

The ladies were in a good mood tonight. They were up to something.

"So what do you guys have planned?" He asked this with a mouth full of cereal. He was hungry.

"Are you working tomorrow night, Sunday night?" Bebe asked.

"No, I have an eight to four tomorrow," Joe replied.

"Well good," Bebe said. "Here's the story Joe. As you may have guessed Adrianna doesn't speak English very well. That's why she's not saying much." This time they all laughed.

"Because she usually talks a lot," Charo added, and they all laughed again.

"Anyway," Bebe said, "Adrianna was kind enough to buy three tickets to 'Les Miserables' for tomorrow night and Charo can't go. And since you do speak Spanish we thought that you may want to join us."

"Wow! 'Les Mis'? That would be great. I haven't been to a Broadway show in ages. I'd love to go!"

"Ok," Bebe said, "It starts at eight so we'll meet here in the cafeteria at seven."

"That would be fine. Thanks!"

The ladies got up to go. Bebe and Charo said goodbye, and started to walk away. Adrianna stopped next to Joe and with a big smile shook his hand and said: "See you tomorrow!"

It didn't go unnoticed that she had said this with barely an accent.

Joe finished his cereal and walked into the kitchen. He poured himself another bowl with milk and ate it standing up next to the sink.

After leaving Paul at Port Authority, he had rushed back to community to shower. He had then walked briskly to work, barely making it on time.

He'd been disappointed to find that at 52nd Street they were fed pretty much the same food as at the Crisis Center. That night it was turkey drumstick and he'd had no part of that.

When he finished quelling his appetite with cereal he rinsed off his plate and walked out the back door and across the footbridge to the 44th Street building. He went down the stairs and into the chapel.

There were no people there. He kneeled down before the Blessed Sacrament and said a quiet prayer of hello to Jesus and then sat down.

He was alone with his thoughts for the first time in a while. He wondered what the ladies were up to in the cafeteria and why they had made such a quick exit. At the same time he started looking forward to tomorrow and what he had heard was a wonderful Broadway Play.

He thought about the community. Their numbers were down to thirty-two. There were numerous empty cells in both buildings and this had had a disquieting effect. Not many were talking about it.

He'd been proud to see that the new paperback that the agency put out telling stories about the kids had an ex-client of his from intake on the cover, the latest word being that she was doing great.

He thought about a client that he had just processed for intake. Her story was that she was living in an abandoned building with her one-year old daughter.

He found this hard to believe. The client stood no more than five feet tall and couldn't weigh 90 pounds. Not the rough and tough type that can survive abandoned buildings. And her daughter was perfectly clean and healthy with no bruises and a pretty, white lacy dress. She also had a gorgeous little smile.

He surmised that she was living on the street while grandma reared her little girl and then when she needed to get off the streets she'd pick up the little girl and come to Mother and Child.

He surmised right. Upon looking up her records, he found that she'd been in Mother and Child seven times in the last six months. The last time was just before he appeared.

His thoughts then turned to his novel, the book that he was reading, "Pillars of the Earth." He thought about how the great medieval cities in Europe started with the building of a cathedral. The people that worked on the cathedral built themselves homes and needed goods. This brought the merchants and stores were built. Next thing you know you have a city. He found it interesting that all the main roads channeled outward from the church. The church was the center and heart of the city, the tallest building. Not anymore.

Then he thought about Paul. He sensed that Paul's life was an adventure, everyday something new and different. He put his life on the line for the Lord.

Some would say that Paul had walked away from the world, when in fact, he was engaging it, confronting it on its own terms, fighting indifference, alienation, and hatred with unconditional love.

He had an opportunity to be a part of this adventure and he was excited. All day he had felt it, a new enthusiasm. He felt lighter somehow. He could more easily focus his thoughts.

He remembered the rainbow on their ride home. What a wonderful grace that was, and how about the ancient man with the ancient relic? Could this be real? This thought chilled his spine. But he found it to be a good chill, not one of fear, but excitement.

This idea that he would be hopping a plane to go find one of the "Sons of Thunder" and possibly an icon of our Lord or one of the Apostles thrilled him.

But could this be? Could St. John be alive?

He contemplated this thought for a few moments. Nothing is impossible with the Lord. But I don't think this could be. We'll see.

He then realized that he hadn't thought about Yasmine since he'd hooked up with Paul on MacDougal Street. He started saying a prayer for her. He didn't think that she was truly safe where she was. The Bronx was a tough place. She was with a tough crowd.

"Lord, if it be your will, protect Yasmine and Johny. Keep them safe from all harm. Amen." Then he made the sign of the cross and said an Our Father.

He spent some more time sitting in adoration before the Blessed Sacrament, quietly, not saying or thinking anything, feeling the Peace, the peace that only Jesus brings, a peace that transcends time and space and lifts one above all the petty and into a world of beauty. In his minds eye he saw a huge castle on a mountain facing the sea. Then when he saw the great cross he realized the castle was actually a monastery. Could this be Athos that I just pictured Lord? Was it the Holy Mountain?

He then quietly rose to his feet and genuflecting, made the sign of the cross. He retreated backward as he bowed one last time and turned to leave the chapel.

Patrick was in pair of striped boxers and a white tee shirt standing before a huge canvas with a look of flushed frustration on his face. He was wearing a pair of flip-flops and had the radio blasting a raucous rock and roll song.

"Hey Joey, come in," he said, and quickly turned and lowered the music.

"What brings you to this neck of the woods?"

"What's up Pat, haven't seen you in a while."

Joe stepped into the room and turned to look at the canvas. He saw multiple layers of different tones of dark blue, nothing else.

"What are you up to Pat? This is quite a good sized canvas!"

"I sold a painting."

"Did you really?"

"Yessie Joseph, I sold one to a collector from here, from Manhattan. I just have to paint it and deliver it."

"How did you sell a painting that's not painted yet?"

"He commissioned it. I've been coating this for three hours now. Is there such a thing as painter's block? I showed the guy my mini sketch that I always make before I start and he commissioned me to do it."

Patrick reached over and handed Joe the small 2 ½ by 4-inch sketch. Joe was always fascinated at how Pat could sketch something so tiny and then put it to canvas exactly as it was on the tiny sketch. He never seemed to have a problem doing that.

"Maybe I know what the matter is," Joe said.

"What's that?"

"Have you ever sold a painting before?"

"No."

"Well, looking at this sketch tells me that this is very personal. This is your heart and guts, your pain, warts and all. And you're about to sell it to a stranger. Maybe never to be seen by you again."

"You might have something there, Joey!"

"I see you, your mother, your brother. I can only guess who the wretched figure heading out the door is."

"I'm starting to see what you mean."

"How much did you sell it for?"

"Eight thousand."

"Say what?"

"Eight thousand American," Pat said laughing.

"Holy smokes."

"I went to see a swanky art show on the Upper East Side and was approached by an older gent who asked me what I felt about some piece of crap painting that I was standing in front of. The painting was awful but he seemed to like it so I filled his ears with a load of B.S.

"We started to chat and I told him that I painted. I ended up bringing him here to my "studio" to show him some stuff and he saw the sketch. He said he wanted it huge for a gothic room that he has in his million-dollar apartment on 5th Avenue in the Village.

"After careful consideration and remembering that the crap at the art show was priced at $35,000 and up, I quoted him ten grand. He offered eight and we had a deal."

"Wow. That's unbelievable. God bless you."

"I'm pretty sure he's gay. And he invited me to a dinner party at his house next week."

"Pat, Pat, Pat. Be careful. Are you going?"

"Of course! Hey, this fella believes in me. He says the blue period stuff of great artists becomes very valuable."

"You knew that."

"Yes, but I liked being qualified as a great artist. And he's a collector with friends that are collectors."

"I see," Joe said. He thought about George for a split second.

"Well Pat, ask the Lord to help you paint. Go down to the Blessed Sacrament."

"I think I will."

Joe took a seat by the window and looked out at the Broadway show crowd. He was stunned by what Pat had just told him. One minute Pat wanted to be a monk and the next he's going to dinner parties with the rich.

"I'm going to see 'Les Mis' tomorrow night."

"With who, Bebe, Charo, and their guest?"

"Yes, how did you know, all except Charo."

"I went to the cafeteria and made a coffee and chatted with them for a while. They seemed excited about something. They asked me where you were."

"Oh."

"Hey Josie, are you going to try to re-enlist or what? I've decided that I'm not but I worked it out that I can stay on as paid staff at $12 an hour."

"You've been busy Pat. What else have I missed?"

"I'm looking for an apartment right here in Hell's Kitchen. I saw one for $750 on 47th between 9th and 10th Avenue. It's tiny, smaller than this room."

"I'm speechless. I am unprepared to comment on any conversation that occurred in the last few moments. But I can say I've been leaning toward re-enlisting but I don't think anyone has been allowed to. It hadn't occurred to me to go paid-staff."

"Think about it Josie. I may need a roommate."

It was Joe who stopped by the tabernacle on his way back to his room. He knelt in prayer and asked God to protect Patrick from the world, from temptation.

As he was leaving the chapel he could hear plain as day the word "Athos" being whispered three times. Or was it his imagination.

CHAPTER 23

▼

Yasmine was sitting on her bed talking quietly with Charo who was standing by the crib watching Johny sleep.

Unbeknownst to Joe, Charo had secretly developed a mentor/student relationship with the young lady and Yasmine had confided in her about her feelings for Joe.

At first Charo had thought it humorous that Yasmine liked Joe, he being quite a bit older than her and a member of a Franciscan Community at that. But she had started taking it seriously when she learned that Joe was calling Yasmine daily and planning to visit her and Johny.

"I tried to kiss him two times," Yasmine was saying with a sweet Spanish accent, "But he turned away."

"I know that he cares about me. He treated me special at Redemption House. Other girls were jealous."

"He's a good man," Charo said, and added, "He's honest and devoted to his work. In fact he doesn't know it but there's a big fuss happening on the second floor ever since he covered it the other day."

Yasmine looked at Charo, "Why? What happened?"

"He went through all the charts and found problems. The counselors weren't following up. They were slacking in their work and he corrected it."

"How?"

"Well, for example, the five year old child of a client needed glasses before starting school otherwise he wouldn't see the blackboard. The appointment was made but the prescription for the eyeglasses wasn't filled. It was in the folder for two months. That's just one of many examples that I heard about."

"How did you hear this?"

"I walked into the office on the 2nd floor the next day during a shift change. Joe's notes were rolled up in a ball on the floor. The supervisor works that floor with her friend and was embarrassed. I think she wants revenge. He better watch it. They might go after him."

Yasmine sat digesting what she'd just heard. Johny had stirred and Charo had picked him up and was humming to him.

"When do you start G.E.D classes?" Charo asked.

"I have to bring the papers Monday. I'm taking an English course too."

"Good, very good."

"Hey Charo, Lourdes on 52nd Street mentioned that Columbia University was offering classes to people in my situation after I get my G.E.D. Can you get the information for me?"

"Sure, I will."

Johny was awake now and smiling as always. He was crawling on the bed.

"Yasmine, were you baptized? Are you Catholic?"

"I was baptized in my older sister's church. She was a very strict Christian, sometimes. My mother says that I was baptized in the Catholic Church in D.R."

"Your sister was a strict Christian, sometimes? How is that?"

"When I was twelve my brother who was fourteen and I were sent to New York to live with her. I spent two years with her in the Bronx. She was very cruel to us. She left us for days at a time without food while she went with men. She would bring these terrible men home that were using drugs and make us call them daddy. We would be locked out for hours at a time in the freezing cold while she was inside with them. She preached one thing and did another. Her actions made me hate the Christian church for a while.

"She would tell my brother and me how evil we were and that the devil had us under his spell while doing all kinds of evil herself. I hated it."

Charo saw tears in Yasmine's eyes and quickly changed the subject.

"So how do you like it here so far? How are your roommates?"

The tears flowed even harder.

"They're terrible. They don't know how to take care of their babies and don't seem to care.

"They're very mean to me. The two of them gang up on me and threaten me. The overnight lady always takes their side. But I do have a friend. Miss Stella is showing me books from the library. She wants me to go to her home for a weekend where she lives with her mother. She's very nice. She works days."

Charo felt bad for Yasmine. She remembered her upbringing in a loving, stable family in Puebla, Mexico and felt bad for her and the way she was raised.

Little Johny crawled up to mommy and tugged at her sweater. Yasmine instinctively pulled up her sweater to feed him. For some minutes the room was quiet as Charo looked out the window and Johny nursed.

"Don't feel sorry for me Charo," Yasmine said.

"I have a plan. I want to raise my son and go to school. I have talent. I know that I do."

"What is your talent? What is it that you want to do?"

"I want to design children's clothes, infants and toddlers."

"What do you know about that?"

"I've seen all the magazines and visited all the good stores. I see what they're doing. They're all copying each other, some better than others. I am original. I can do better than them."

Charo looked carefully at Yasmine, wondering if she really had it in her.

"Have you done anything towards that end?"

"I have. Look in the top drawer there, the blue jean overalls."

Charo opened the drawer and pulled out the tiny denim overalls.

"Oh my God," Charo said, "These are beautiful! How did you do this?"

Charo was holding a pair of denim toddler's overalls that were embellished with a large sunflower across the front made from beautiful quilted fabric. The stem from the flower reached around to the back of the outfit where a cute gingham watering can was shown watering the flower with sequins of water.

"I've never seen anything like this before. This is wonderful."

"I know," Yasmine said. "I know."

Yasmine and Charo spoke for a while about some other ideas that the young lady had for a whole line of kid's clothes. Strictly from size six months to size five.

Charo was very impressed.

"This is what I've been doing in all my spare time," Yasmine said.

"This is great, just great. But I have to ask you, where does Joe Morrison fit in to this equation?"

"Charo, I don't really know, but I believe in God and God seems to have sent me Joe. I believe that God did. And so far I believe in Joe. I believe that I love Joe and I hope he loves Johny and me."

"That's nice," Charo said, "really nice."

CHAPTER 24

▼

Joe had a lot to think about. He was on his way to take his first major step with Yasmine. Weeks had become months and he still felt the longing in his heart. Sometimes he trembled at the thought of her.

Their many phone conversations had led to this moment. He felt anxious. He couldn't wait any longer.

He looked out the window of the subway train that had just crossed into the Bronx from Manhattan. For a moment his thoughts went to Adrianna, the Broadway Play, coffee and pie afterwards, and a few moments alone in her room at Community.

The play had been wonderful. The best he'd seen. The company was smart and funny. Adrianna was educated and had a good job and her own condo in Puebla.

Upon arrival back at Community, Bebe had quickly excused herself and retired to her room, leaving Joe alone with Adrianna.

Thoughts of Yasmine had faded away that night. He felt that somehow this had been set up, especially when Adrianna invited him to walk her to her room, and then asked him to come in to see a "book" that Joe had shown interest in earlier.

He felt regret as he looked out at the mass of brick buildings from his bench seat on the train. They had kissed. He had felt welcome and took advantage of the hospitality offered. They lay on the bed and kissed, but that's all. He had made a move to take it further but she had resisted. He felt guilt. He felt human.

He told himself that he hadn't made any commitments to Yasmine and felt better. Then he realized he had almost broken his pledge of chastity to the Community.

They had planned to meet at a park by the subway stop. This was not too close to the residence where he might be noticed.

The train was slowing now; he could see her pushing Johny in a stroller not far away. She looked radiant, even from a distance.

He walked down the long, steep subway steps to the street as she was pulling up with her son.

They smiled at each other.

He patted Johny on the head and took her hand. They walked into the park together, Yasmine pushing Johny with one hand, and found a bench.

The afternoon sun did not melt the coolness in the air on this November afternoon as the couple sat together silently on the bench. Not a word had been spoken.

Joe took the stroller and faced Johny in the opposite direction and applied the breaks. Then he looked at his love, and seeing his future children in her bright hazel eyes, reached over, with one hand gently cupping her face, and kissed her.

They kissed for a long time. And then kissed some more.

During these moments he felt like he was floating in the air, like he was lighter than air. He felt good and sensed from looking at her eyes, that she felt it too.

Unbelievably, after a very long while, the first words were Joe's, "I got to go."

The sun was setting and he wanted her inside where she was safe. After all, this was the Bronx at a time when the thugs ruled the streets.

He walked her part way and they parted. He kissed them both goodbye and headed home.

CHAPTER 25

▼

Paul and Henry were sitting on crates in the stainless steel kitchen peeling what was left of six huge bags of potatoes.

Paul was intent on what he was doing, shaving the potatoes with slow deliberate strokes, careful not to shave the skin off his hand.

Henry on the other hand looked like he was having fun, like this was child's play, as he deftly peeled potato after potato, in rapid succession.

Paul was waiting for the right moment to tell Henry about his planned trip.

This large monk, who always seemed joyful, fascinated him. He sensed today that Henry wasn't quite his happy self.

"You seem a little down today friend. What can a fella do to cheer you up?"

They had previously been discussing the desert. Henry said the desert was a great place to find the Father. There are few distractions.

He had talked about the beginning of monasticism in the fourth century. He explained how the great hermit monk St. Anthony had taken to the desert after Christianity had been legalized by Rome and the Great Persecutions had ended.

He hadn't liked what he saw. Anthony felt that Christians were losing their fervor and turning more to worldly things, so he took to the desert in protest, living in a cave in the desert of Egypt, fasting and praying, and was blessed with the gifts of healing and prophecy.

Soon Pilgrims came to him for healing and a large following developed. Many joined him in the desert and had to be organized and given a rule to live by. He was credited with many miracles as well as creating the first monastic rule, Henry had said.

The later Franciscans had reversed the isolation and contemplative manner of early monastics and had gone out into the world to live out the gospel by helping the least amongst us, while returning to the monastery when work was completed to live and pray.

Paul was taken by what Henry had said concerning his vocation:

"You came to a desert called New York City to exemplify holiness at this critical time when materialism is dominating the culture. To you this is a desert, a wasteland really, and you're alone with the Father. You're serving Him from your heart and trusting Him. You have supernatural courage," Henry had said, and almost made Paul blush.

Paul never thought about things that way. He found that since he had committed himself to relying on providence that he rarely thought about himself. He lived in the present and his life felt like a miracle.

"So I look a bit down to you do I? Maybe I don't feel like my usual self.

"I got a message about my sister yesterday. She's a nun of the Carmelite order and lives on Mt. Carmel at the ancient monastery. I got word that she's not well."

"I'm sorry to hear that Henry. Is she sick?"

"I suppose that you can say that, but she's not physically sick. I guess that you can say that she's having a spiritual sickness."

"How's that Henry?"

"Well, she's very troubled by the spiritual darkness enveloping the world, in that part of the world in particular, and she went on a long fast, taking just water and the Eucharist. The note said that she's on her ninth day."

"But she's okay right? Others have fasted similarly and been alright," Paul said.

"Yes, this is true. Actually, there's a woman saint whose name escapes me, that lived solely on the Eucharist for years, and gained weight.

"The fast is not the problem. It's what is happening to her that could be problematic."

"And what's that?"

"She's uttering some kind of prophecy of some sort; the note didn't go into detail."

"Is this why your thoughts are on the desert today?"

"Yes of course," Henry said.

Paul took the burlap sacks and rolled them up and took them outside to the kitchen dumpster. Then he came back in and swept the floor in the area where the men had been working.

Henry meanwhile was dropping the taters in the large boiling cauldrons with the help of two other monks.

Paul walked over to Henry while he was adjusting the flames on the stove and simply said: "I'm going on a journey!"

"Oh really," Henry said, turning to Paul, "and would that journey be taking you anywhere near a magnificent tongue of land that projects out into the Aegean sea?"

"That would be correct."

"When do you plan on leaving?"

"Soon."

Paul bent over to help one of the monks lift one of the heavy pots that held the potatoes. When he attempted to lift, the monk stopped, and looking him in the eye, shook his head. Paul got up and stood away as the other monk came to help.

Henry got busy in the process of making mashed potatoes so Paul took a stroll outside to 31st street.

The day was clear and bright and cold. He could see his breath as he stepped out the front door of the church. So far his wool tunic and the long johns that Gwen had given him were working against the cold. He felt like he was cheating St. Francis by wearing the long underwear and wool socks with his sandals, but forty degrees in windy New York City could feel like the Artic.

As he looked down the steps of the church he saw a curious man staring up at him. His was a strange appearance of sorts as his bushy curly hair sat wildly on his head and his beard was a mess of hair going in all directions.

His eyes were bulging and he didn't blink as he followed Paul, walking across the front steps of the church.

Paul sensed the man behind him and turned to him.

"Hello, what can I do for you?"

The man smiled with grisly yellow/brown teeth that were rotting from his mouth. His stench was that of a wild animal. He gazed into Paul's eyes without speaking and then bowed his head gently and looking up at Paul he asked, "Are you a priest?"

"No I am not," Paul said.

"Then are you a monk?"

"No," Paul said and felt some apprehension at the site of this creature. He noticed that the man had little black crosses tattooed on the tops of his fingers just below the knuckles.

"Then why are you dressed the way you are, are you an impersonator, an imposter?"

Paul trembled as those words were uttered, not for the words, but from the gaze in the bulging black eyes, pure evil, he thought.

"Are you an actor, playing make believe like all those Hollywood idiots who think they're so bright playing make believe and repeating someone else's words?"

This struck a chord with Paul, the wrong chord. For a moment he began to doubt his mission, who he was, but only for a moment.

He swiftly pulled out his rosary, his blessed rosary, and a sacramental. The enemy hates sacramentals. Paul only wished that he carried a bottle of holy water with him.

The creature seeing the rosary spit at Paul, missing him, but in turning to flee he tripped on the bottom step and fell to the ground hitting his head on the cement. A wound opened on the man's forehead and started to bleed.

Paul hesitated as the man jumped to his feet cursing him. The blood dripping down from his forehead onto his face made him look grotesque.

"You will pay imposter, you will pay," the man screamed, as he ambled down the Street.

Paul turned to go back up the stairs and into the church. As he opened the entrance door he looked to his left and saw the monk from the kitchen standing there, a sinister look on his face.

He entered the church and went straight to see his mother Mary. There were several people in the small room praying, all the kneelers were in use. He felt crowded. He had sensed evil before, when he was working the crisis pregnancy center, he'd seen it in the eyes of some of the "boyfriends" that wanted the girls to get abortions, one in particular he never forgot.

When he began helping the young lady her young man looked amiable and kind. Later his persona took a turn and he was unmistakably changed. He simply looked evil. Turns out he had shot and killed someone outside a bar and was later caught and arrested for this crime. The change in his looks and demeanor after the murder were as different as night and day.

He saw the same look in this creature's eyes.

Paul felt distant and anxious. He knew the feeling. He had unwittingly entered a Wicca store looking for candles and had exited feeling the same way as he felt now. Is this what they call "discernment" he thought? Is the Holy Sprit warning him by this "feeling" to defend him against an evil attack?

He turned quickly away from the Madonna and bumped into a smaller man wearing a cassock. Looking down at the bangs of hair and thick glasses he recognized Friar Billy.

"Excuse me Billy!"

"It's William," Billy said, as he straightened his glasses.

Billy looked into Paul's eyes and saw something he didn't like. "What's the matter Friar Paul, you look like you've seen a ghost?"

"I'll be O.K.," he said, but realized he was clutching Billy's crossed arm.

"You'd better come with me," Billy said.

Billy didn't ask what happened. He led Paul to the far end of the church where there were no pilgrims.

Paul realized that he was still clutching Billy's arm. He slowly took a deep breath and tried to focus. Then he realized that since the incident outside that he had been repeating to himself the words: "the lord Jesus Christ is my savior, the lord Jesus Christ is my savior!"

When they arrived at the far wall the friar turned to Paul and simply said, "Kneel."

Paul knelt down before Billy. Billy looked pious and devout. He looked strong to Paul; with his eyes closed he was moving his lips in prayer while holding his left hand on Paul's head and making the sign of the cross with his right.

Paul could hear the whispered words of the prayer of St. Michael on the breath of the friar. Then Billy reached into his tunic and pulled out a tiny plastic bottle of holy water. He put some on his fingers and blessed Paul, making the sign of the cross on his forehead, uttering words that Paul couldn't make out. Paul remembered now that Billy was a Priest, not just a monk.

He felt peaceful and at ease sitting in the last pew of the church. As soon as Billy had touched his head, he had felt warmth emanating down through his body and the anxiety quickly disappearing.

He knew that anxiety was the grave enemy of faith. Anxiety was fear and fear came from the evil one. Jesus taught, "Be not afraid". At every mass a prayer was said against anxiety. Fear was the enemy against having the courage to do God's Will. To seek His will, to take that first big step towards eternal life.

At that moment, the bells rang and the Priest came from the sacristy with his altar server to begin the late afternoon Mass.

Paul was thankful for the blessed timing. He needed the Eucharist right now. He had never felt doubt about his mission before.

CHAPTER 26

▼

The two men took a train to the airport and walked together up the long ramp that led inside to the international flights.

Paul was wearing his usual black tunic with the small white cross painted over the heart, with his long johns, wool socks, and sandals.

Joe was wearing black jeans, black leather shoes, and a black leather jacket with a black hooded sweatshirt. He was clutching a small carry-on leather bag.

They walked silently in thought about what they were leaving behind and the adventure they were about to embark on.

Joe was thinking about Yasmine. She'd cried on Thanksgiving when he told her that he would be gone a week. They were sitting at the table in her grandmother's Section 8 apartment on Dykman Street when he mentioned it, and although it was still a week away, she'd become emotional.

Their relationship had grown in these past weeks. He visited her and Johny whenever he could. They would sit outside her building on a bench in a small park that had a beautiful waterfall. The Bronx was quite a place at one time. Even now the Italian neighborhood nearby was a neat clean enclave of immigrants from another era where one could safely walk the streets eating a spumoni after a delicious meal of linguini with clam sauce.

They still kissed, but not in the park. He would walk her to her door inside the ramshackle building where she stayed and they would kiss and hug for what seemed like eternity until the "mother" of the house, usually the mean one, would come out for Yasmine. He was feeling at peace with his decision to take this relationship to the next level.

He had said goodbye to Patrick who had collected his $8,000 at one of the many "cocktail parties" in the West Village that often was a party of two.

He had questioned Pat about this and hadn't felt like he'd gotten a straight answer. What was going on here? The man was obviously gay. Was Pat "playing" him to get his foot into the proverbial door of the "art world"?

Pat swore that the man never made a pass. Joe thought that hard to believe.

Pat gave him $100 to bring him a tunic from the gift shop in Karyes. He'd read on the Internet that they had one in the small village where one shows their papers. The tunics were black.

Paul was holding the passport that Fatima had bought him and saying a prayer of thanks for that and for Gino from the fruit stand who was gracious enough to have paid for the flight.

He hadn't asked either person for help. Providence had opened conversations with the two that led to their offers.

Gino had won a Pick 4 for $1500 and wanted to give the money to Paul for his mission. They worked out a deal where Gino made the reservation on his credit card and gave Paul some cash for the trip. Paul had refused the cash, but when the grocer insisted, had held on to it and slipped it to Joe on the train to the airport.

Fatima had laughed out loud at the Speakeasy one morning, after one of the many nights that Paul had slept there recently, when she realized that he didn't have a passport. She took him by the hand one day and got it for him after sending for his birth certificate.

He was thankful that Gwen had returned to excellent health and was attending daily Mass, accompanied by Lola. Paul promised to attend with the sisters and inconspicuously explain to them what actually was taking place. They knew that they were taking part in something sacred, especially because they had a reverent Priest, and the human heart craves the sacred. But they were hungry for the details.

Gwen had given the baby boy a name and prayed to the Father for forgiveness. She kept the glow-in-the-dark cross and the dried out rose on her dresser as a reminder of him. Sometimes she suffered terrible pangs of guilt when she would think about what he would have looked like, how big he would be, and what color his eyes were.

Then she would utter the prayer Paul had taught her: "Lord Jesus, Son of God, have mercy on me a sinner", and know that through His mercy, God loved her and forgave her. This, she had found, helped her cope.

The doctor had given her a clean bill of health and both her and her sister were being chaste. She'd found that the most important thing to do in seeking chastity was to control your thoughts. So at every temptation the girls would say the Jesus Prayer and try not to put themselves in a tempting situation: "avoiding the occasion of sin", Paul had told them.

The men had had their passports stamped and had entered the Greek airliner. The airplane would take them to a city near the Aegean Sea.

From Thessalonica they would bus it to the coast where they would catch a launch to the port of Daphne, on the southern coast of Athos. From there a bus would take them to Karyes, where they needed to procure the permits necessary for their visit.

The men would then bus it back to Daphne where they would take another launch to their destination, the Russian Orthodox monastery named Ponteleimon.

The jet was a Lockheed L1011 and Paul had the window seat. The chairs were comfortable.

Paul took out his finger rosary and gave Joe a long look. Joe looked at Paul and at the same moment both men realized, "Holy cow, I'm going to be with this guy for a week!" And they both laughed a gushing, relieved laugh.

Then the men were quiet, locked in thought, until the plane had taken off and the "fasten seat belt" sign was turned off.

Joe was the first to speak, "I'm Joe Morrison from Leonia, New Jersey," he said, and put out his hand.

Paul shook it and said, "Paul Johnston, Pittsburgh, PA, actually McKeesport if you want to get technical."

"Johnston, is that English?"

"So it is."

"My father's father was English," Joe said, "his mother was Filipino, while my mother's Cuban with French ancestry."

"Very interesting," Paul said, "How'd that come about?"

"My dad's father was in the Spanish-American war in the Philippines. He loved it there and after the war he stayed. That's where he met grandma. They were both schoolteachers.

"He got sick in his lungs and boated it to the U.S.A. via San Francisco and eventually to the American desert of New Mexico. He took my Dad with him.

"After a couple of years his lungs cleared up and then after spending some time in Oklahoma they ended up in Minnesota.

"Yes, Minnesota."

Joe had read Paul's mind and answered his question before he asked it. "Then they sent for his mother and brothers and sisters. Four years later.

"My dad got a job with an American company and transferred to Cuba because he could speak Spanish.

"My mom actually has French Cajun ancestry from France, her people fled the persecution of the French Revolution via Louisiana, where they stayed for about a hundred years, and then landed in Cuba, the so-called 'honeymoon capital of the world' when my dad was there."

"It's amazing how many people don't know about the murdering and pillaging that went on against the Church during the French Revolution, how nuns and priests were slaughtered by the so-called 'enlightened,'" Paul added.

"Ditto!"

"Well, my story's not as interesting so I'll just tell you that my family at one time worked for the steel industry, but in the accounting department. Pencil pushers.

"My ancestry came from England about mid-1800."

At that moment the pilot came on the intercom and asked that seatbelts be put back on. The flight attendants continued dispensing Uzo and a small Greek salad with feta cheese and black olives to the patrons.

Joe had his salad with a coke and Paul drank a bottle of water.

Both men became quiet during and after the meal. They both ignored the movie playing. Paul kept fingering his rosary with his eyes closed. Joe pulled out a plastic rosary that his mother had made and put in his pocket after their good-byes. He had slept at home at the insistence of mom and had had a home cooked meal of keilbasa with sauerkraut, cooked apple slices and boiled potatoes. The meal was a favorite of his from the days his mom was learning gourmet cooking from distant lands.

They topped it off with apple cobbler and whipped cream.

The timing for his trip was perfect as he was due for a week's vacation before Christmas. There had been no problem arranging it with the Agency and Community.

Joe said the prescribed five decades for the day and when he saw Paul still fingering his rosary, he just kept going.

Fifteen decades of rosary later, he opened his eyes and turned to see Paul happily staring at him from six inches away with a huge grin on his face.

"Hey what's up?" Joe screeched, backing his face away, "What's so funny?"

"Nothing, I'm feeling joyous. I was watching your eyes move under your lids. What were you looking at?"

"You really want to know? I was looking for the lost twelve-year-old Lord. The last …"

"I know my friend, the last meditation in the Joyful Mysteries."

"That's right."

"Did you find him?" Paul asked, and both men laughed.

Joe had never seen Paul so giddy. He truly seemed like a different person.

"I feel great Joe. There's an incredible battle going on right now, one like never in history, and we're in the fray. We are warriors, warriors in the spiritual combat.

"I read once that if there's something wrong in society or in the world, something bad or evil, those with the ability to take action have the responsibility to take action. I believe that."

Paul's energy was contagious. In his heart Joe knew exactly what he meant, but Paul took it to another level.

"In about 20 hours we are going to be on a launch into a great mystery. We are going into an ancient land of holy monks where there are great secrets to be discovered and great mysteries to be unveiled.

"I've been led to believe by a righteous man that there's an ancient person on the peninsula with a great story, perhaps the greatest story of them all. And that he may hold an ancient relic of our Lord's, a relic that may have incredible powers, and consequences, for believers and non-believers.

"I know I've let my imagination run loose Joe, but imagine if it's His sandals or His cloak; or something from the Passion like the Crown of Thorns or a nail from the cross. If this man is St. John there's no telling what we're going to find!"

"If we find him," Joe said.

"Oh, we'll find him."

Both men sat staring straight ahead. Paul had a smirk on his face and felt ecstatic. Joe felt exhilaration mixed with doubt.

"You don't really think there's a 1900 year old man fishing the Aegean Sea from a hut at the foot of Athos hiding a powerful ancient relic, do you?"

"Don't you?" Paul said, and closed his eyes to nap with a smile on his face.

CHAPTER 27

▼

Some time later, the flight attendant inadvertently woke the men while chatting with an elderly gent in the next row who needed a pillow. Neither man knew what time it was as neither wore a watch. They both knew it was late into the night.

Joe spoke first: "You mentioned earlier the great battle that's going on; you mean the battle for souls right? The battle for righteousness?"

"Yes. One soul is worth more than the entire universe."

"That reminds me," Joe said, "a number of years ago a Cardinal form Poland made a speech in St. Louis about the final battle beginning between Christ's Church and the anti-church, ultimately the final battle of good versus evil, a battle that can only be won by love, by living holy lives, and of course that man is now our Pope, our Poppa, our Spiritual Father.

"What bothers me the most is the attack on youth. Kids are inundated with sex and violence from all sides. They're not being mentored on this and taught that our culture is sinking and becoming a culture of filth, and that they don't have to be a part of it. They can change it. They're dummying down the schools and secularizing them. Did you know that the downward slide in young people's test scores began in the 60's the year after they stopped school prayer? It's not a coincidence; they're taking away the motivation to learn. Kids are graduating high school that can't write a paragraph!

"Then they glorify the wrong things in the movies, like prostitution. I know first hand how sad that really is. One hundred percent of the prostitutes that I have counseled were sexually abused as children. Many of them are drug addicts. And these 'porn stars' are no more than prostitutes."

"They're teaching kids foundational lies, Joe, in school. They teach evolution not as the unfounded theory that it is but as a fact. That devalues human life. People start acting like monkeys if you know what I mean. They teach over-population as universal and blame over-population for starving children, when it's greed and politics and possibly racism behind this."

"I understand that you can give every person in the U.S.A. a twelve hundred square foot house and fit them all into Texas," Joe added.

The flight attendant, a plump Greek woman with jet-black hair, offering them drinks, interrupted their thoughts.

"I'd like a coke," Joe said.

"I'm good, thank you," said Paul.

Joe went on talking about the cultural corruption of youth and Paul went on listening. What Joe was saying was true, was it deliberate? Were forces corrupting and alienating our youth purposely, knowing the destruction of our society would eventually ensue. To be replaced by what? A secular, pill popping, materialistic, pornographic, socialism where anything goes? After a while, the attendant came back and took Joe's empty can for the trash.

"It starts with the individual," Paul began, "if people change, if they repent, meaning return to God for meaning and guidance, then others change. You truly can't change others, they have to change themselves, with God's help, but by you changing your attitude to one of love for instance, others react to that. Do you understand what I mean Joe?"

"Yes, I do."

"That's what our Holy Mother Church needs, individuals to outwardly attempt to live holy lives, and to speak up for truth and injustices in a loving manner."

"The church would change," Joe added.

"The world would change," Paul exclaimed.

Both men sensed after a quiet moment that the other wanted silence for a while. Paul's thoughts kept coming back to the ancient disciple and the relic. Joe was daydreaming about Yasmine and wondering if he should mention her to Paul.

After a while Paul said: "What do you know about relics Joe?"

"Not that much really, just that it's a piece of clothing or something belonging to a great saint."

"Since Old Testament times," Paul said, "the relics of holy people have been venerated. Relics actually come from a word that means remains. First class relics for example, are taken from the remains of the person, usually pieces of bone.

"Second class relics are something the Saint actually wore or used when alive, and third class relics are usually a piece of cloth that has touched a first class relic.

"People are fascinated by relics and lots of miracles have occurred from relics. I happen to recall that there's something in 2 Kings, I believe chapter 13 about this.

"And in Acts 19," Paul said, "I was reading where cloths touched to the skin of St. Paul when applied to the sick cured diseases and drove out demons."

"The Church has some great relics in their possession, right Paul? I heard we even have the swaddling cloth of the baby Jesus!"

"That's true, we also have relics from the Passion like the Holy Shroud of course, which false science has tried to defame."

"How so?"

"The secular, corrupt media is passing disinformation on the shroud that a carbon dating test put it at seven hundred years old."

"I heard that too."

"Number one, they did a carbon dating test on an Egyptian mummy that we know is at least 3000 years old and it came back at 1000 years old. In fact did you know that the man who invented carbon dating, a Catholic, said from the start that the readings could be horribly inaccurate?

"Number two, high heat effects carbon dating and we all know that the shroud was in a fire and was singed by the flames. Heat affects the carbon count in the cloth, resulting in an inaccurate reading."

"Wow," is all Joe said.

"We have the Holy Stairs. Those are the twenty-eight marble steps from Pilate's palace that our Lord had to climb on his way to be scourged on the night of His Passion. We have the scourging post, pieces of the holy cross, and the holy nails.

"Think of it Joe, it is in the Bible that relics have a supernatural power. Why doesn't the Church use a holy relic to perform miracles and convert people, especially at this critical time in history? I bet non-believers would come and miracles would happen. We need miracles today more than ever before."

"I'll say," Joe said, nodding his head.

This put Joe to thinking about what else Paul knew about the old man and the relic. Was he planning to have the relic and return it to New York City?

"What's going to happen if we do find a holy relic?"

"I don't know. I really don't know where this is leading us. Only that Henry insisted that I'm the one chosen to do this. I believe that the way we met and other "coincidences" are signs, and I feel in my soul that we're doing the right thing."

Joe put out his right hand with a smile; Paul shook it firmly and warmly.

"Christ is risen," Joe said.

"Truly risen indeed," added Paul.

This they both knew was the standard greeting in Athos.

"So," Paul said, "what did you find out about the Holy Mountain?"

Joe had mentioned that he had found a book in community on Athos and that he had spoken to Patrick about information that Pat had found on the net.

"The Holy Mountain is consecrated to Our Lady, she is the protector. There's lots and lots of beautiful churches, each one with their own group of monks, each one self-sufficient. And off the churches are "sketes" which are small groups of monks that live outside the walls of the monasteries. They too have an abbot for life. Then there are individual hermits that live in isolation, some of them in silence, who are subject to the abbot, and pitch in with work for the monastery like growing potatoes or shepherding goats.

"For quiet a few years there were dwindling numbers amongst the monks but there's been a recent surge. There is quite an interest today in monasticism from what I read.

"And let's see, they don't eat meat."

"Really?"

"Yup. They eat beans, veggies, olives, fruits and bread. Fish on feast days."

"Then what are the goats for?"

"Good question. I would guess for milk and cheese. And they drink wine. A fine quality homemade wine from what I understand.

"Athos is part of an archipelago, thirty-five miles long; with three branches in northeast Greece, one of them being Athos. There are twenty monasteries; seventeen are Greek Orthodox, and the oldest one was built in the tenth century. Their chapels are quite ornate. The Orthodox chapels are quite lovely with lots of beautiful Icons, chandeliers, and lots of brass and gold from the pictures that I saw. They're into Icons as opposed to statuary. There are few if any statues in the chapels."

"Tell me what you found out about Orthodoxy?" Paul asked.

"Not that much really. The Church spilt in two around 1054. Ostensibly because of disagreement over a passage in the Nicene Creed, but it's believed to be more a matter of geography and lack of communication.

"The Orthodox were separated from Rome by seas and mountains and communication was difficult. East and West split apart and the East made Constantinople their headquarters and the "Patriarch" of Constantinople became their leader."

"What was the issue with the creed?"

"That the Holy Spirit descended from the Father and the Son, which is what we believe. While they argued that the Holy Spirit came from the Father. There were other issues too. They also questioned the authority of Peter and his successors."

"Are they considered apostolic, direct disciples of the apostles, as we are?"

"Yes. And of course they have the true Eucharist, the body and blood of Christ, the holy sacrifice.

"I found it interesting that in order to shepherd a flock, to be a Pastor, one must be married. Their priests are allowed to marry while their monks are not."

"Interesting. So we share all the great saints until the eleventh century or thereabouts."

"Yes, that's true, I hadn't thought of that," Joe answered.

"My friend Henry had his conversion at Fatima in Portugal, but later while visiting Athos actually became an Orthodox Monk."

"How did he end up a Catholic Priest?"

"Francis. He never forgot Francis. Something occurred in Athos that he never told me about. He felt drawn to New York City and Francis.

"His sister's on Mt. Carmel you know, she's a Carmelite, a contemplative."

"Wow, that's cool."

"She lives in an ancient monastery right on the side of the great mountain."

"Wow, the splendor, the greatness, the history, the miracle that is our church, all so interesting," Joe exclaimed!

"We haven't even discussed the great influence of the Church in art, architecture, science, music, medicine, and the universities," Paul added.

"I've heard it said that the body of western civilization breathes with Catholic lungs. That is if you can cut through the prejudice, propaganda, and lies."

"Did you know Joe, that the first geologist was a monk: Albert the Great! The first chemist was Roger Bacon: a monk. Gregor Mendel, a monk, invented genetics, even the "Big Bang" theory!"

"A monk!"

"No a priest: George Lemaitre."

"If only the world knew the truth."

"We'd all be Catholic."

"Have to be" Joe said and both men laughed heartily.

After a few moments Paul said: "The road is narrow and few there are who find it."

"That's sad."

"Strikingly."

"I guess in a way, that's why we're both sitting here 30,000 feet over the Atlantic Ocean."

"We want to widen the road."

"Or squeeze more souls through it."

The launch that got the men to Daphne had a motor on it. The boat the men rode to Athos had a cowled monk with two oars.

They greeted the monastic in the traditional way, "Christ is risen," Paul had said. "Risen indeed," had replied the monk.

Joe, usually talkative, was speechless and in awe upon their arrival on the craggy shores of Athos. Paul on the other hand was self-assured, seeming to glow. His golden eyes were piercing. The monks whose paths they crossed all had stared into his eyes.

The men had had no trouble acquiring their permits in the monastic city of Karyes. The small city of narrow winding roads with projecting balconies overhead was the administrative center of Athos.

They'd returned to Daphne where they shared a meal of rice soup, bakkal fish, with beans and homemade red wine. Both men enjoyed the meal enormously, which was served to them at a tiny Inn where they'd spent the night.

The next day at noon they met up with the cowled monk on the rowboat. The only other discourse they'd had with the monk was when the monk asked them what they were seeking. Then he had answered for them: "Most seek eternity. Prayer has led them to glimpse it." And that was all he said.

The men had remained silent the rest of the way as the foamy, jarring, sea seemed like it was going to flip them over and devour them at any moment.

The monk, who of course spoke English, had silently led them up the rocky paths in a fine drizzle, with the wind hissing and whistling; passing caverns and crags and dark cedars that led them deeper into the mountain.

The twin limestone peaks of Athos, cold and wet under a cloudy sky, finally became visible in the distance.

There was a mist all around them as they approached the massive wooden doors; doors that were reinforced with huge iron rods on the inside and big metallic plates on the outside. These were the outer doors. They were open.

The gatekeeper met them, a monk with a peasant face and jovial eyes, whose job it was to open the doors at sunrise and close them after sundown. The doors were the only way in or out of Panteleimon, the largest monastery on Athos. He also checked permits.

There were two sets of doors or gates. The monk led the men through the cell that separated the two gates and through the second set of massive doors. Then he took them to the main hall.

There a monk who was the chief host of the monastery met them. He offered them water, coffee, or tsipouri, a Greek drink made from pressed grape.

They signed the visitor book and were escorted to their room to rest. Their host, a monk by the name of Constantine, had instructed the men to meet in the main courtyard at 16:30, or 4:30 pm.

The room was small and quaint. There was a Byzantine crucifix on the wall over a small wood table that held a ceramic bowl and a pitcher with water.

Against each wall was a straw mattress on the tile floor. Next to each bed were a huge pillar candle and some stick matches. Each mattress had a rough looking wool blanket over a cotton sheet.

Paul went to the window and looked out, taking in the authentic beauty all around him, the spires, cupolas, and crosses that were Ponteleimon. Joe lit his candle and took a seat on the bed.

"Did you notice the silence? Silence on the boat, up the trail, at the gates, and inside the gates as well."

"I did," Joe said.

Paul looked out at the swaddling clouds passing overhead. Then he looked down below and saw two cowled monks walking silently, each carrying a woven basket filled with grapes.

"Wasn't the vineyard beautiful, and the olive grove? I love the thought that these holy men are totally self sufficient, living off the land." Both men talked just above a whisper.

Just then a huge black bird, the size of a full-grown bald eagle landed on the open window ledge where Paul stood. Frightened, he stepped back. Joe looked at it too. The bird was enormous. No such species existed. It stood looking at Paul, then at Joe, with eyes like a burning fire. And at once it turned and flew off.

Going to the window both men looked out but the huge winged creature had disappeared.

Later as planned, the two men met Constantine in the main courtyard. He took them on a quick tour of the grounds ending up at the spring water building, which is next to the church. This is an important building, housing the monasteries holy water and the place where it is blessed.

After vespers, where some of the monks had gathered in the incredibly ornate church for the chanting of the liturgy of the hours, the men gathered at trapeza for the meal. The meal was just as Joe had said: beans, veggies, olives, fruit, and bread, served sparingly and washed down with delicious fruity homemade wine.

A reader read from a pulpit as is the custom during meals. They usually read from a great old sermon or from the Gospel. Today was an exception. They read from the Old Testament.

When the reader got to Joel 2:28, the two men looked at each other, a knowing look. Paul's held an air of confidence; Joe's look had a bewildered certainty:

"And afterward I will pour out my spirit on all people. Your sons and daughters will prophecy, your old men will dream dreams, and your young men will see visions …"

CHAPTER 28

▼

After dinner the two men were led, along with several other Pilgrims, to the main church, where Constantine welcomed them. The Holy Remains of the great saints of the monastery had been removed from the monastery safe and put in the sanctuary for the guests to pay their respects. One in particular got the attention of Joe. The 500-year-old skull was honey brown and had a pleasant scent.

They were also allowed to admire the great and holy Icons that hung in the sanctuary. Some were said to be miraculous, especially those of the Virgin Mary.

Later in the courtyard, Constantine spoke to the men. Athos as it turned out was called "The Garden of the Virgin Mary". The men were both stunned to hear the monk say that according to legend, the Blessed Virgin Mary and St. John the Evangelist, on their way from Joppa to Cypress where they were to visit Lazarus, encountered a stormy sea that forced them to take refuge on Athos. The Virgin so admired the wild beauty of the place that she asked God to give her the Mountain as a present.

At the time the voice of God was heard to say, "Let this place be your lot, your garden, and your paradise, as well as a salvation, a haven for those who seek salvation." Since then Athos has been considered "The Garden of the Virgin Mary".

Words cannot describe how the two men felt the moment they learned that St. John had not only been linked to Mt. Athos, but had actually been here in the past, this according to an ancient tradition. The men were astonished.

At the time of Mary and John's visit Mt. Athos was pagan, and at once converted to Christianity.

The monk went on to say that in the Fifth Century the first monks came to Athos in the form of hermits who had been bored and disappointed with communal life elsewhere and thought Athos the ideal place to worship.

Russian monks had founded the monastery of St. Panteleimon itself in the Eleventh Century. The richness and great wealth of the monastery had been bestowed on the monks by past Russians Czars who gave their blessing to the monks.

St. Panteleimon was a greatly revered young saint of the early Russian church. As a boy, he was blessed with the gift of miracles: healing the sick, raising the dead, and curing the blind. And still as a boy he was inhumanely martyred: after being tortured, he was beheaded. This boy saint, who gave healing and comfort to his countrymen, is still highly honored in the Eastern Church.

Constantine went on to say that many great relics were being kept on the Holy Mountain including the largest piece of the true cross. The wealth of books and holy Icons on the Holy Mountain were second to none, he said, although the great libraries aren't used much because their way of life is dominated by prayer and work. Lectio Divina or holy reading is not a part of their lifestyle.

The monk reminded the men that their visitor permits were good for four days and if they wished they could stay outside the walls of the monastery in one of the small huts or kalyves, where groups of hermits lived, but to give the hesychasteris their privacy. The hesychasteris were the most austere hermits who lived in caves on the cliff face or in lonely huts deep in the woods. The two men gave each other a look at the mention of this. For to visit such as these is why they came.

The thought of staying in a Kalyve, consisting of several hermits living together, excited the men. They were both extremely curious to visit with and actually talk to a hermit. Hermits were a fascinating lot, and there were different types of them. They ranged from vagrants to ascetics and lived like the earliest hermits, the ancient anchorites of the desert, giving glory to God, mostly in silence.

The excitement of the possibilities for the next day stayed with the men as they found their way to their room. Constantine had departed to go pray the "secret rule", which is solitary prayer that the monks say in their rooms before retiring.

Once in their cell, the two men lit their candles. They had no idea what the real time was as the monastery ran on the clock of the ancient East and was about five or six hours ahead. The monks also ran on the Julian calendar and were fourteen days behind the rest of the world.

The two men sat on their beds looking at one another. Joe could see jubilation in Paul's eyes. Paul saw worry in Joe's.

"Relax Joe; everything's going to be all right. If our hermit doesn't want to speak to us, when we find him that is, we will respect that."

"But you heard what Constantine said, not to bother them."

"It won't be a bother. I assure you!" Paul said confidently.

The men had many things to ponder. The Sacred Remains had been eerie. They had been told that after a monk is buried, his remains are dug up three years later. If all they find is bone, the monk had led a holy life. If anything is left on the body, the monk was not quite so holy. The bones of the holy monk were removed from the earth, labeled, and stored away. The other was reburied. This fascination with relics was new to the two men. Not much thought and attention is paid to these types of artifacts in the Western Church.

Both men had decided after the long trip that rest was essential and they wouldn't attend matins at 1 a.m., but would attend the Orthodox liturgy at 6 a.m. Constantine had arranged for a monk to come get them at the appropriate time.

After an hour or so of prayer, the two men blew out their candles and fell fast asleep, with both of them thinking of an ancient apostle.

Six o'clock in the morning was really one o'clock in the morning to Joe and Paul, but when the bearded little monk with the braided pigtails entered the room, both men awoke.

The little monk identified himself as Simon and led the men silently down to the main church.

The main church was truly an awesome site with tremendous crystal and gold chandeliers and Icons of incomparable beauty. The men quietly knelt in a pew in the front row on the left and simply admired their surroundings. They had been in the church before but hadn't taken the time to really look around.

Then the abbot came in leading the monks in procession, and they all quietly took their seats. There had to be several hundred of them. Joe noticed Paul looking back straight to the far corner of the church where a great pillar stood. Barely visible from behind the pillar was a solitary monk. He was sitting apart from the others. His face couldn't be seen and instead of the black tunic of the monastery, he wore a very faded, bleached white tunic with what appeared to be a brown wool wrap around his shoulders.

The Mass was fascinating, primitive and ancient. Was this what the original worship was like? According to the Orthodox, it was. Constant chanting of prayers, profuse incense burning, bowing, and the sign of the cross repeatedly made. Nobody was sitting.

The Eucharist, consisting of unleavened bread cut into pieces, was kept in the sanctuary, the Holy of Holies, where only priests could enter. The priests and monks repeatedly went in and out of the sanctuary behind the altar.

The reverence for the Holy Communion was spectacular. A monk saying prayers and in an apparent ecstatic trance doled out the Body of Christ, immersed in his blood, the wine, with a long spoon, while two others held a white cloth under the chalice and under the chin of the receiving monk. The two men did not receive.

The celebration was impressive, the chant mesmerizing, a glimpse of heavenly worship on earth, as described in Isaiah. (Isaiah 6:1-4)

The homily was on passionlessness, a favorite teaching on Athos. Passionlessness is freedom from anger, hatred, bitterness and all other negative emotions. A major goal of all the monks on Mt. Athos: passionlessness.

Paul had the urge to again look back for the ancient man and resisted. But as soon as the Mass was over he was out of his seat, with Joe in pursuit, heading for the rear of the church.

Once outside in the daylight, the two men went out of the gates of this Byzantine Castle, known as a monastery, and caught a glimpse of the brown wrapped man turning the corner toward the entrance to the olive grove.

They both jogged past the olive trees and turned just in time to see the lonely figure of a man entering the dark cedar forest at the periphery of the monastery grounds.

From this distance the man's long white hair seemed ethereal.

He seemed to almost turn to look back upon reaching the forest but hesitated and continued on. The two men reached the cedars quickly and could now make out the footprints of the man in the cold, damp, earth. They couldn't see him ahead so they followed the footprints as fast as they could.

After some minutes, they reached a thicket of bushes and flowering yellow gorse where an opening in the thicket had just moved. They raced to the opening and into the thicket following the narrow trail through the scrub for what seemed like too long a time, until they came upon a large rock and the stony crags that signaled the top of the ocean cliff.

But wait! They heard a sound like an echo of a rock hurdling into a hollow cave. They followed the sound and sure enough, at the base of the huge rock, was an opening. You had to get on hands and knees, but there it was, with fresh prints where a man had knelt and entered.

Paul knelt first and peeked under the rock. He could see what appeared to be a tunnel possibly lit by flickering candle light. Paul stood facing Joe and looked into his eyes. Both men instinctively reached out and held hands. Paul whispered, "Father, guide us, protect us, teach us. May it be your will that we are following. Amen." They made the sign of the cross and knelt to enter the cave.

Paul crawled in first. He pulled himself up by a ledge and stood. The tunnel was wide enough for two people to walk side-by-side and tall as the average man. About twenty feet away he could see a flickering light coming from around a corner.

Just then, Joe entered and stood. His eyes were open wide. He stared down the dark chamber toward the light. The salty smell of the sea permeated the cave.

Paul whispered, "Let's go!" And the men walked carefully toward the light. The tunnel was all stone of course, possibly a limestone, and the walls were cool to the touch.

They reached the turn where the candles flickered and stood looking at a ledge in the rock where many a candle had burned. The small mountain of wax was melted and spread around. There were all different colors. The monk must leave these candles on until they burn out.

From this spot they could see down an incline that turned dark for a stretch and then lit up again one hundred feet away, where another candle was flickering.

The men looked at each other knowingly and headed down the dark tunnel toward the light.

When they reached the second candle ledge, they looked to the left where the shaft jutted sharply downward at a much steeper incline. The salt air was much stronger here and the walls and floor of the cave were beginning to feel damp. At the bottom of what seemed like a hundred foot incline was another candle. This one seemed to be encased in glass.

The men carefully worked their way down toward the light. Their minds were blank save for the great anticipation that they felt in their hearts. In a moment, they were at the bottom.

Looking to the right, the men expected to find the path continuing but only faced a dark wall of rock five feet away. Glancing around it seemed they'd reached a dead end. The walls looked solid all around. But on second look, the wall before them was not solid but actually a pile of rubble, seemingly where the tunnel had caved in.

The two were puzzled. They had followed the tunnel to its end. Guided, seemingly, by candlelight and had reached a dead end.

Then suddenly the last five feet of tunnel that jutted to the right lit up and an ancient cowled face with powerful, deep, penetrating eyes looked upon them. The men were speechless; their hearts were doing drum rolls. "Come," was all the man had said.

As they stepped down the last few feet of tunnel, they realized that the dark wall on the right was actually a door. A thick wood frame had been constructed and a simple chestnut door put in place.

The men had to stoop to enter the monk's cave. The floor was stone but was covered by a heavily faded grass mat. In the back corner was a simple pile of pressed down dried straw where the monk probably laid his brown shawl and slept. His pillow was a flat stone. A large pillar candle sat on a square shaped rock next to the "bed".

In the other corner was a natural stone table abutting the wall that held a wooden bowl filled with small red potatoes. Next to that was a small burlap sack that lay open and had figs coming out the top. Near the front of the cave, which was really a crevice with a plank roof overhead, was a weathered wooden plate that held a small fish that was apparently sun-dried, as there was no other form of cooking visible in the ten by ten space.

Looking out the opening of the cell, the great ocean was visible, the Aegean Sea, a transparent emerald green. But obviously missing was the front door.

The monk had stepped aside to allow the men in and Paul had walked directly to the missing door. Looking down from the opening, he could see the ocean crashing upon the rocks sixty feet below. The rock that the plank roof sat upon extended out from both sides beyond the roof, protecting the cell from the wind. He could see the path that the ancient monk must take to go below and catch his meals.

Paul turned and looked at the man. Joe had stepped halfway into the cave and had turned and just stared. The monk had pulled down his hood.

His hair was shoulder length and silver. His eyes were bright and penetrating, the color of the sea. His beard was braided and came to his waist. His hands were strong, his fingers long. He held the countenance of a much younger man.

Then the man with skin like a tanned hide spoke in the soothing voice of wisdom.

"Walking with the Savior was pure joy, miracle after miracle. He was love incarnate. He spoke the wisdom of eternity. Whenever we needed something, it would appear. He healed thousands. Always spoke of the love of the Father. Everyday He needed to be alone with the Father for a time of prayer.

"He was a plain looking man, tall for the time, wore His hair and beard long as most men did. His voice was warm and yet captivating.

"His eyes were distinct. His look could melt gold, and this was the color of His eyes, a liquid gold, the same as Mary's. He looked quite like Mary.

"You would describe His hands as strong, yet supple, tender. One could sense that He felt the pain of those that suffered.

"He walked on water, the blind could see, cripples walked. The dead awakened.

"He is God's Messiah, the Son who died for our sins.

"He is the Way, the Truth, and the Light. Through Him you must pass to reach the Father."

As the man had said these words, he had looked from Paul to Joe and back. Now his gaze was at the distant sea.

A moment passed and then Joe blurted out, "Are you saying that you are the elder, St. John, who wrote the Apocalypse?"

"Does it matter? Everyday is someone's apocalypse. Are they ready? The Lord's message is, 'be ready'. When you cross to the other side, be ready, He's waiting for you."

With reverence and looking into the man's eyes, Paul asked, "How about antichrist?"

Without hesitation, the man answered, "Antichrist has been on Earth since the First Century, he's a false spirit contrived by the demons to corrupt humanity. The evil one knew he had to spread his lies alongside Christianity or be crushed by Truth. He knows he's been defeated by the resurrection, but wants to destroy as much as possible.

"The spirit of antichrist is everywhere. His goal is simple, take away people's belief in the supernatural, and they lose faith. One must battle him from within with your heart. Fast, pray and lead holy lives of love. Avoid the things and thoughts that cause you to sin. But above all, ACT! Feed the poor, help the sick, and never forget he came to heal us.

"He is the Healer. We are healed by His love; His ministry was one of healing. And because of that, we must live joyfully. If you love Him, know that all things that happen to you are good. Trust Him for He is merciful"

The man walked by Joe and Paul to the opening that faced the sea.

Joe piped up, "Do you see Him? Does He visit you?"

The man turned and with the sea and sky at his back, looked like a god himself.

"Yes, He does often. Now you must go. I have spoken much for one who is silent."

Just then both men realized they were hearing him in their own language, much like Pentecost.

"But you, whose eyes I recognize, this is for you."

From inside his sleeve, the man produced a key; handing it to Paul he said, "You'll know what to do. Do not worry! Now go!"

As he said this, he made the sign of the cross, much as a priest at the end of Mass, blessing the two men.

The men walked up the tunnel and out of the cave. Paul led the way. Once outside, Joe followed Paul up the path through the thickets and the dark forest until they reached the olive groves.

The great bells from the monastery were ringing signaling the end of the morning labor and calling all to the 1 p.m. light meal. This couldn't be, Mass had ended at 7 a.m. Six hours had passed. What happened to the time? Both men were stunned as they marched up to the refectory for tea and a piece of bread.

After tea, where the reader had read from the Gospel of St. John, the men silently separated. Joe went to their cell and Paul went to one of the small chapels to pray before the Blessed Sacrament.

Joe looked out the window where the huge black bird had landed and recalled reading something in mythology, or was it Christian myth, that these appearances by large black birds signaled an important time in ones spiritual journey, maybe even a miraculous time.

As he looked out at the enormous monastery he realized that on the walk back from the sea, neither man had spoken.

He thought about the old monk and wondered if he'd dreamt everything. And what happened to the time?

Paul had different thoughts. He thought about Henry. The mystery of Henry had broadened. He thought about the missing door to the cave, was this the door that Henry had in his cell at the Franciscans? And what was this antique looking key for? Why would I need a key and what has this key to do with Henry?

With that last thought, Paul let his mind relax as he knelt and bowed before Jesus.

CHAPTER 29

▼

"Christ is risen," Paul had said.

"He is risen indeed," said the red bearded, red-maned monk chosen to row them back to Daphna.

The two men had spent the rest of the afternoon and evening of the third day working and praying with the monastery monks. They harvested olives in the grove, watched, as some were virgin pressed for fine quality oil, and got to go to the wine cellar with one of the cooks to have an early sampling of the dinner wine. The wine was a robust red fruity wine that was delicious.

Joe and Paul were doubly impressed by the reverent manner in which the monks acted and their happy countenance despite their grueling schedule. The young monks recently joining the monastery had been a refreshing change to the overall mood and had taken quite a bit of the workload from the older monastics.

After Mass on the fourth day, they had ventured outside the walls and had encountered a threesome of ascetic hermits that lived together in a small hut near the vineyard. They were a fascinating crew and welcomed the men into their tiny home and shared their meager space and food with them.

There was no conversation as the three hermits were silent, but regardless, did not speak English. Joe and Paul worked with them cultivating in the vineyard and prayed with them each time the bells rang. One hermit with a beard so long he had it wrapped around under his arm and tied to his long salt and pepper hair in the back, worked with one hand and with his other hand fingered his prayer rope and repeated the Jesus prayer, praying constantly as St. Paul inspires us to do.

They ate grapes and figs and a tiny piece of bread, a meal that the three hermits had eaten with reverence after solemnly blessing the food.

The two men had then reentered the walls at sunset and retired to their room to rest for the long trip the next day.

The emerald sea had been choppy, but the red-haired monk was a powerful rower and soon they embarked on the dock at Daphna, where the silent monk had left them with some curious words, "The hermit that lives on the cliff by the ocean, he's a strange one, thinks he's one of the Holy Apostles!" With those words he had winked at the two men and rowed away.

The launch back to the mainland and the drive to the airport had been uneventful. Joe had bought Patrick the tunic he had asked for as well as a prayer rope and a tiny icon of the Madonna. The driver of the car only spoke Greek and didn't engage the men. The plane was the same wide-bodied L1011, but this time their seats were in the center row.

The conversation to this point had been topical. Both men had commented on the passing countryside and the beauty of Greece during the drive. The weather had been pleasant to that point. They'd stopped at a restaurant for a classic Greek meal that even Paul partook of as both men felt as if they had fasted for four days.

Now they were at the airport. Once they'd been seated and were up in the air, Joe spoke first. "Wow that was an amazing experience. I will be digesting this for days and weeks to come."

"It was. It really was," said Paul. Joe noticed he was fingering his prayer ring.

Then Paul said, "What do you figure about the red bearded rower?"

"I don't know. I'm fascinated thinking about it. If he had made the statement without winking, did you catch the wink?"

"Yes, I did," Paul said.

"If he had just made the statement, you would have to consider the truth of it, that maybe the hermit John is deranged, but the wink left it open. It could be true!"

"That's how I see it Joe. But why did he make the comment? We never spoke to anyone about our visit with the lone hermit, and we all looked up at his cell as we passed it, including the rower, but the hermit wasn't there and no one said anything. So it wasn't like we tipped him off or anything."

"No definitely not."

"His words were simple and direct. Just as one would think that the words of an Apostle would be. His statement on the supernatural gets right to the point, to the bottom line. Eliminate belief in the supernatural and you eliminate God."

"True. I've never looked at it that way."

"Neither have I."

After a moment, Joe said, "And that ties in with what you spoke about before. The Church has these wonderful miraculous relics. If people became aware of them and the Church in some way used them to show the miraculous, these religious experiences would enhance the faith of the people."

"That is what I believe," Paul said. "We need miracles today. We need signs. Signs are supernatural, as are miracles of course. They point to God our Father. That He's watching. That He cares. That He wants us to do better. But we must not forget that trying to live holy lives is a sign too, a sign that there's an alternative to a life of sin, an alternative to materialism."

"An alternative to the other 'isms' too," Joe added, "Relativism, secularism...."

"We need men and women warriors," Paul interrupted, "prayer warriors. We need our parishes to be real, living communities of brothers and sisters that love each other and are unafraid to fight the godlessness at any cost, whether by engaging it or by a living example. We also need strong shepherds. And I believe God will send them."

Then they were quiet.

Both men slept. They slept right through the meal. Hours later, they both awoke to the pretty, young Greek flight attendant offering then drinks. Joe asked for coffee and a coke. Paul got an orange juice and a club soda.

Joe had been dreaming about work and Yasmine. He felt some apprehension now for the first time as he thought about her. Was his relationship with her unethical if God was calling for it? He thought not. She was of age and not his client anymore. He also kept thinking about "the kids".

Then he remembered what one of the visiting priests at Mass in community had said. He had been paying close attention because this young priest had been radical. He had long black hair and a black beard and was saying the Mass with great reverence and deliberation. But what had caught his eye was that the Priest was barefoot. He hadn't seen a Priest say Mass barefoot before or after that day.

During the homily, he had talked about "the kids", as many visiting priests did. What he had said was that God was calling these kids but that they didn't know where to look for him. And because they didn't find him, they turned to drugs and alcohol to take up the emptiness. He said that the depression that most of these kids suffered from was a sign that they couldn't find God.

Joe shared these thoughts with Paul. Then Paul said, "At some point in everyone's life they need something, something to help us cope, and something to deal with fear. If you turn to God, he gives you strength, he gives you faith and hope, but others choose to escape the issues through drugs, alcohol, or even music, television, sports, and video games.

"The main issue of course is our purpose in life, why are we here? Where are we going? What are we to do? In other words, one either turns to God or something else."

At that precise moment the plane hit an air pocket. There was no warning. The fasten seatbelt sign was off. People that were unbuckled flew up and smashed into the high ceiling, including all the flight attendants, who were working the aisles. For a moment some were lengthwise against the ceiling, only to come crashing down horizontally onto their seats or other people. A baby had actually bounced off the ceiling and onto a man's lap.

Joe and Paul were strapped in.

The plane had dropped thousands of feet in just seconds, before the pilot got control. Then another air pocket hit, but not as strong. This one lasted but a few moments and no one flew out of his or her seats.

A female flight attendant strapped herself into her seat on the wall facing the passengers and announced in two languages, with her voice breaking up and her eyes filled with tears, for all to fasten seat belts. She was clutching her side, in obvious pain.

Joe had the aisle seat. He had been an E.M.T. for three years as a volunteer ambulance technician and wanted to help the older woman in the seat ahead of him. She was moaning loudly and hanging over the side of her chair.

But he knew he'd better wait. If he unbuckled and was sent flying, he couldn't help anyone and matters would be worse. He was always trained that an accident could become a catastrophe if helpers entered an unsafe scene and were themselves hurt.

Moments later the pilot announced that it was safe to help the injured. Fortunately, only a few passengers had been unbuckled, but all the flight attendants had kissed the ceiling. Joe turned to the lady in the front. He got her situated and strapped in. Her breathing and pulse were just a touch fast and she said her ribs hurt but that she would be all right. Paul held her hand and prayed for her.

It turned out that no one was seriously injured and the pilot asked for everyone to put on his or her seat belts again. The plane then turned southwest to avoid another dark cloud.

The terrible turbulence had occurred when the pilot had flown directly into a black cloud. When the plane hit the air pocket, it was like a roller coaster plunging down the steepest incline, where one's stomach is pushed up into his chest. That feeling lasted about nine long seconds and made it feel like the plane was nose down going to crash. People had screamed hysterically and others had obviously screamed prayers in Greek.

After the first air pocket, Joe had realized, he and Paul had held hands.

When the plane arrived in New York, paramedics came aboard and took out the injured. The two men finally got off the plane an hour later and went through customs.

On the noisy subway back to Time Square, they sat across from each other, occasionally looking up and smiling at one another, a happy, serene look on their faces.

Something supernatural was occurring. Something who's meaning God would reveal in due time, in due time.

CHAPTER 30

▼

Joe was drinking a flat cold beer out of a dirty mug while Patrick chugged on a Bud longneck. The boys were sitting in a tiny, skuzzy bar on a side street not far from the Port Authority building on 42nd Street.

Pat had been surprised after dinner in Community when Joe had agreed to go out for a cold one. A long time had passed since the two went out together.

Joe was bummed. Moments after he'd arrived at Mother and Child on his first day back, he was called into the executive director's office where he was then summarily suspended for alleged improper conduct with a client. He was given a date a few days hence to come back for a "hearing" and then told that they would see him then.

He sensed the whole community knew about it except for Patrick. He'd caught people giving him "looks" in community and others approaching him for idle chatter that had never done so before. Of course, Vin LaBianco had been informed and from there word must have leaked out.

So when Pat suggested a beer, Joe's guard was down and he agreed. But why Patrick had chosen this place he'd never know. He said this was the closest bar to Community that he knew had a pool table.

Both men had put two quarters on the table and their names on a chalkboard and were waiting their turn.

Joe watched the two men shooting eight ball and sensed something was up. The smaller man with rat's eyes and a cigarette in his mouth seemed to miss on purpose while the larger man, with an unintelligent expression on his face, obviously couldn't sink a ball if he tried.

There were two black hookers standing at the bar with fabulous long blond wigs and see-through chain link miniskirts that clearly revealed naked backsides.

Pat was making sarcastic small talk, something about going on a date, when Joe blurted, "Don't you know I'm suspended?" This caught Patrick by surprise and all he could say was "whoa".

"I've been accused of improper behavior with a client."

"Yes, I do know. But I've been waiting for you to open up about it." Pat was holding a cue stick as he talked.

"That's why I asked you to come out. Everybody knows."

"And how does everybody know?"

"Well, for one, you haven't gone to work all week. You're walking around Community in old sweats and socks, no shoes, and when you come out for meals you look depressed or guilty."

"Oh boy, everyone thinks I'm guilty?"

"I didn't say that. You are being quiet. Not talking. I guess they think if you were innocent that you'd be angry."

"I am angry, somewhat angry."

"Do you think it's about Yasmine?"

"Yes."

"How do you know?"

"I didn't think that this could be about anyone else."

"How about that girl that you said was hot for you, the one with the bra?"

"No, nothing has come close to happening there!"

"I know Joda, but didn't you say that you rocked the boat when you covered that other floor? Remember, kindness or truth isn't always appreciated. Someone might have been embarrassed and wanted revenge against you. That's how the world works. And put somebody up to accusing you."

"That sucks," was all Joe could muster.

Rat's-eyes had just made the eight ball on a cross table bank shot and now it was Patrick's turn.

"Hey bud, want to play for a couple of bucks?" The man with the eyes of a rat said.

"Naw, I stink. I'm just here to entertain my friend."

"Come on pal, let's make this fun, a buck a ball. How about it?"

Joe noticed the conversation had caught the attention of the two hookers. The hustler was probably a regular and they had seen his work before.

"No thanks. But maybe my friend will play you. He's pretty good."

Patrick obviously had no clue what was going on. Joe did.

"No thanks. I never play for money. I play for a beer sometimes. But that's it."
Then Patrick pulled out a twenty-dollar bill.

"C'mon Joda. You know you're good. Take him."

"Patrick, stop it."

"Okay, we got a game here. Twenty bucks it is. I rack, you break," Rat's-eyes had come alive.

Joe looked out over the table where Rat's-eyes went to get a sip of what looked like club soda. No alcohol for this hustler. He noticed the rat had two body-guards, Big Boy, who couldn't shoot, and another mean looking young guy dressed all in black with a toothpick in his mouth. He was drinking shots.

"Come on Joda. Let's have some fun," Patrick said, still holding his cue stick. He offered it at once to Joe who declined and went to get a stick that wasn't obviously warped.

Rat's-eyes made a tight rack of the balls and walked over to his table where Big Boy handed him a slim leather case that held his personal cue. He unzipped the case and made a show of screwing the two pieces of his stick together.

"One game," Joe said, "That's all I'll play."

Joe broke them. A loud, solid crackle could be heard. He'd hit it good. The balls went flying all across the table with two going in, both solids. He then picked off two more before barely missing a bank shot to the side pocket.

The hustler put in five in a row at a blistering pace. He hardly took time to look at his shots. Then he made the mistake that most guys do that causes them to lose the game. He had an easy shot and a more difficult shot. Take the easy shot next to the pocket and set up your next shot. This was how Joe played. But macho pride got the hustler.

He didn't take the "easy way" and missed the cross table shot.

Now it was Joe's turn. He needed to make three balls and the eight ball. Rat's-eyes didn't get another chance. He tried to distract him when he banked the eight into the side pocket, but Joe was focused.

The bar maid, a huge woman with a bigger hairdo and heavy on the eye makeup, came over to Joe with a smile and handed him the forty dollars she was holding, Patrick's and the Rat's.

"Come on man, double or nothing. Let me a chance to win back my money."

"No sir. I said one game." Joe said this respectfully.

"Listen man, you've got to give me a chance to win back my money."

"No, I said one game."

Joe turned and walked back to his table. His mug was empty. He walked up to the bar for a refill.

The hustler put his cue away and pulled out something else, a switchblade knife. The knife slid open when the jukebox was in between songs, making an unmistakable sound, swoosh!

Joe heard it and turned. Bad boy was coming his way waving the weapon like a maestro waves his wand. The look on his face had turned unmistakably evil, a darkness created a dull glow from his eyes. He was casually approaching his adversary. Joe turned facing the man, with the empty mug in his hand. When the bad guy was five feet from him, with his two buddies trailing him, Patrick came up from the side with a cue stick in his hand.

"Put it away Buddy. We don't want any trouble," and without hesitation, Patrick slammed the thick end of the cue stick into the man's hand knocking the knife out where it went sliding across the room.

From behind the punk came the big dumb guy lunging at Patrick. Pat grabbed him by the shirt and swung him sideways, sending him crashing to the floor. Then the mean little guy with the toothpick jumped on him from behind. All this while the Rat watched, not making a move.

Joe thought the better of it and put down the mug. The bigger guy had come back at Pat from the front while the little guy held him from the back. He went for the big guy. He bear hugged him from the back and spun, throwing him to the ground. The little guy still had Pat from behind but was now in front of Joe.

Joe grabbed him off of Patrick and wrestled him down to the floor pinning him down on his belly while holding his arms outspread and separating his legs apart with his own legs.

He looked up to see his friend struggling with two of them again. The hustler had decided to join in and was piggybacking Patrick and trying to choke him. The big guy was trying to hit him but couldn't, as Pat kept ducking and moving, trying to shake off the rat.

Then the hookers joined in. One came up behind the bigger guy and put him in a headlock. The other one grabbed the hustler and pulled him off of Patrick, getting him in a bear hug from behind.

It was over.

The barmaid came out from behind the bar with a mini baseball bat, one that she could whip around and do a lot of damage with.

"You boys are banned for life. Get them the hell out of here!"

Joe let the toothpick guy up. The three men headed for the door trying to save face, threatening, cursing, but five against three didn't work for them. They left.

The barmaid looked at Joe and Pat and said, "The next one's on me," as she walked back around the bar. The two hookers went back to their thick mint drinks, laughing and giggling, and Joe looked at Patrick and said, "Was it worth the twenty bucks?"

"Hey you won. That was a great game, under pressure."

"You didn't know they were trying to hustle us?"

"Of course I did. That's why I let you play him."

"Oh boy!"

The men drank the free beer, tipped the barmaid, and headed out. Walking home Patrick wondered if the two hookers were really girls. One couldn't help but notice the arm strength they used in subduing the two thugs.

By the looks of the two of them, the fact that they'd been in a fight was obvious. The big guy hadn't missed every shot after all. Pat had a nice black and blue on his left cheek. Not to mention his ripped tee shirt and the red claw marks across his chest from the Rat. Joe looked unscathed.

As they walked in their door past the two barefoot men sleeping on the sidewalk, Joe couldn't help but wonder what was happening to his life.

CHAPTER 31

▼

New York City is an amazing place, full of energy and excitement. There's always something to do and interesting people to meet, a cultural center for all people. And in spite of the millions of people and cars and noise, there are still nights that are quiet, nights where the streets seem to be in slow motion.

This was one of those nights. The howling, freezing, December wind had died down and warmer air had descended on the people. Some didn't trust that the warm air would last the evening and were overdressed with thick coats and scarves, with hats and gloves, especially the elderly. Others always hopeful of summer were underdressed with only tee shirts and open denim jackets, especially the young, and they felt the cold.

Paul was in a chess shop off of Washington Square in Greenwich Village. He had always been fascinated by this store when walking past, but had never entered. He wasn't feeling himself today and was looking for a distraction.

This was a unique store. The left side of the small shop had old glass cases full of gorgeous chess sets of all types and sizes. Behind a short wooden counter sat the proprietor with his cash register.

The right and larger side of the quaint, earthy store held small tables of all shapes and colors, each with two unmatched chairs, where men of all stripes were playing some serious chess.

Across from a potbellied, garrulous man who resembled Santa Claus with his long white hair and beard, sat a beady-eyed mouse of a man with thick glasses and a wool hat. Playing against the guy in the suit was a hippy looking guy in black sweats. Sitting across from the only woman in the place, and an exotic beauty at that, was a young man in a monk's habit with a faded white cross painted on the chest.

"Boanerges," Fatima was saying, "That's the word that he used. The word means 'Sons of Thunder' he said."

Paul made a move and said, "check". He was intent and focused on playing his best game as Fatima was nonchalantly crushing him. She was telling him about the homily that she had heard earlier that day.

"He said that James the Great and St. John were Galileans and that Galileans were the strongest defenders of the Jewish Nation. Galileans had what he called 'energy of temper and vehemence of character', they were no-nonsense, in your face, hearty, brave and industrious."

Fatima moved her king out of harms way. The pieces of the chess set that she'd rented were made of granite and the board was glass.

"Checkmate," Paul said, moving his knight to take Fatima's queen.

"No way," she said smiling, looking at the board, but she wasn't happy.

Paul had made an unlikely comeback. The chips were down and he came through with only two knights and a bishop left from Fatima's assault, as well as a few pawns and his king.

"Wow, you got me," she said.

Paul looked at Fatima and smiled, "Boanerges you say?"

"Sons of Thunder."

He started gathering the pieces together to return to the manager. There were others waiting to play.

"He went on to talk about 1John 4:3 and how the spirit of the antichrist was already in the world then," Fatima exclaimed.

They both stood, Paul holding the chess set, and walked over to the counter. He said thanks and they walked out onto 6th Street towards the park.

"What do you think about that Paul, about the antichrist?"

"Funny you should ask. I've been thinking about that a lot. I'm not really sure what the official church teaching is, as I haven't looked it up in the Catechism yet, but I know there are books out there saying that he is a person, and that he will rule the world for some time. Before our Lord Jesus comes again and dethrones him.

"My personal belief is that it's a spirit. A pervasive evil spirit that spreads disbelief in our Messiah through subtle and sometimes obvious means, and that that evil spirit is all pervasive in our society today and in others.

"Does it ultimately take human form or possess a person and give him power? Maybe. But you know what I think Fatima?"

"What?"

"I think believers are going to win. There's too many of us and more are coming. There are young people today of strong faith, 'Sons of Thunder'."

"And daughters," Fatima interrupted, "And daughters of thunder that are going to come out and give their lives to Christ to save humanity. I believe we will win as well, I believe you," she said, and held onto his arm with both of hers.

As they traversed Washington Square Park, Paul reached into his only pocket and pulled out the key, the key from that far away place.

He thought about how, after his return from the Holy Mountain, he went to see Henry. Only Henry wasn't in the kitchen. But the evil looking monk was. The one he remembered seeing when he'd had the incident on the church steps.

The mean monk had given Paul a dirty look and removed his apron, throwing it on a table as he abruptly walked away.

On his way to Henry's room, Billy had intercepted him.

Turns out that Henry had left to see his sister, the nun on Mt. Carmel in Israel. This is what Billy meant to tell him when Paul had encountered the evil man outside. The thought of that man chilled Paul's spine and gave him a sick feeling inside of things to come, almost haunting him.

Billy had bad news too. The Provincial wanted to see Paul. The boss, the chief, had some questions for Paul. And the Bishop may be involved.

Paul took in these words silently. Henry's gone and they're calling him on the carpet. Are they going to bar him from making soup? He'd have to see. A date and time had been left available for him for the meeting. He had agreed to it.

He clutched the key, knowing Henry was connected in some way.

A black man with long dark braided hair who simply said, "Ganja", interrupted his thoughts, Fatima quickly responded, "No thanks."

"Pot," she whispered, "they sell little bags of marijuana here. They have for years. I hear they mix it with oregano."

"I believe it rots your brain, gives you a false sense of reality, and smothers a person's motivation," Paul said.

"That's why they call it dope," Fatima answered.

They entered the Speakeasy together. A young couple sat at a table eating garlic hummus with pita. They stepped through the open rear door to the club and sat at a table together in the back. A lone woman in cowboy boots, hat, and pigtails strummed a guitar and whispered a song of loneliness from the stage.

"I want to join the Church Paul. I want to convert. All I find is beauty and truth, and the person of Jesus Christ, when I do my research."

As she said the words "Jesus Christ", tears welled up in her beautiful eyes.

"He's already changed my life. I changed my major at school. I want to do counseling. I want to help. I don't seek financial security, Jesus is my security."

Paul was looking into those gorgeous dark eyes. He felt a warmth in knowing that he had a part in her conversion. But that's all, a warmth. He wouldn't allow himself pride. He knew that the Holy Spirit was at work in her soul.

"Those are lovely words Fatima."

"I'm volunteering at a rehab, a nasty one. They detoxify street people. It's ugly. At first I wanted to puke because of the smell, the open sores, the horrible missing and broken teeth, but I sense something inside of all of them, something that wants to be loved, and something that seeks kindness and mercy too."

"There isn't enough kindness in the world. It takes guts to be kind and merciful," he said.

"My family is suspicious, but hey, Bahai claims all religions are leading us to the same place, so what's wrong with picking one of my own?"

"Nothing, nothing at all."

He reached out with both hands and held Fatima's hands. They were warm and soft. Then he let go and they both stood and hugged as the singer sang about the emptiness of her life.

They both went inside Paul's little studio, and when he turned on the light she saw that he was embossing a pair of sandals. She recognized them as being of a style from the Middle East.

"I like the sandals," she said.

"Thanks."

Paul put the finishing touches on his art while Fatima sat leafing through a book she found on his table called "The Philokalia". The books' theme was spiritual warfare, how to defend yourself against attacks from the evil one. She noted that it referred to people from the Eastern Church and wondered how and where Paul had gotten this book.

There wasn't much conversation left in Paul that night and she knew that once he began embossing, he became almost trancelike, so she sat paging through the book.

She found "The Philokalia" intriguing and stayed late into the night. There was spiritual wisdom in those pages. Then at once she placed the book down and left with a smile.

Paul had finished the "sandals" by then and had started another embossing. This one was starting to look like a chapel on a mountain.

He stopped and took a break for a moment, looking around at the different embossings on the walls. He loved his little studio. He knew the room really wasn't his but was happy to have a little place like this where he could come and create. He felt peace here. And because he had the buffer of the mop and bucket room, he had relative quiet.

Just then he heard the outer door close and then came a soft knock on his door. When he opened it, a beautiful young woman was standing there.

CHAPTER 32

▼

The letter from Adrianna was well written, Joe could tell, although he didn't read Spanish very well. She was catching him up and inviting him to come for a visit to her condo in Puebla, Mexico.

He'd had a great time with her he had to admit. What was not to like? She was smart, attractive, had a good job, a real good job by Mexican standards, and her own condo and car. She liked him and he knew it. He liked her too.

Under normal circumstances he would jump at the chance. After all, after the United States, Mexico was his favorite country. He'd snorkeled and bodysurfed the Pacific side many times and had acquired a few friends in the small village of Zihuatanejo. He'd driven far into Mexico in his van when he lived in Colorado. In his travels in Mexico, he'd enjoyed the happy people, the slow pace, the cobblestone streets and the culture. There were always festivities, generally celebrating something to do with their Catholic faith.

But he was smitten and he knew it. Yasmine was going to be his girl, his woman, and Johny his boy. He'd had a lot of time to think, not working and all, and realized that this was meant to be. And besides, the Lord hadn't closed any doors yet.

He tried not to talk on the phone with Yasmine too much during his time off, so he kept it to twice a day, occasionally three times a day. They talked about silly things, what's the best diaper for Johny, why didn't Joe like malta, a Latin malt drink, and how many hours since they'd been together.

Joe was still worried for her safety in the place where he had put her and he still felt some guilt for what he had done.

Yasmine was keeping busy. She got a part-time job at a donut shop on her corner. The two owners had loose hands and were being fresh with her and this bothered Joe immensely. He planned to go have a chat with the boys.

She was going for her G.E.D. but felt at a disadvantage because the classes were in English. The Spanish ones were filled.

He thought about a character in his book, "Pillars of the Earth," which he had finally finished reading. There was a wild woman living in the woods outside the town that eventually comes into town and becomes a successful textile merchant.

He thought that Yasmine could be a success too.

Joe had butterflies in his stomach today, as this was the day of his hearing. He stopped by the cafeteria where Luis sat alone drinking an orange juice. He was a community member contemplating joining a new order, founded by the little monk who glowed, called the Franciscan Friars of the Renewal. He had just returned from interviews with some of the Friars.

Joe spilled the beans about Yasmine. Luis was not a priest yet but heard his first confession that day. He especially liked the part about the electric shock when they touched, also the love at first sight, and the fortune cookie telling Joe to go for it.

He respected Joe for praying about it and seeking guidance. He advised him to go for it. He said, "If God wants something to happen, nothing will stop it." Joe had heard these words before.

His heart was rushing as he entered the building on 52nd Street. They buzzed him in and he walked straight back to the executive director's office. She wasn't there but her assistant was.

There was an accusation he was told; a counselor had asserted that Joe was carrying on a relationship with a client, that she had visited him at his home, and that he had an unprofessional relationship with her on the premises. The client's name was Brenda.

They wouldn't tell him who the counselor was, but he had a pretty good idea. And he thought that the next time he covers their floor their charts better be up to date or he would fix them again.

He categorically denied everything. Brenda, to her credit, had not corroborated the fallacious story. But other clients claimed that they saw her and Joe together, talking, away from the premises, probably when he encountered her outside his home.

Another had stated that Brenda opens the door of her room to him half dressed and he doesn't reprimand her. Joe told a white lie and denied this. This was Patrick's advice. Resign or deny everything.

He was flabbergasted. He had innocently updated charts and pointed out errors in the follow up, all in the best interest of the clients. Because of this, things got personal, and hateful. He would later learn, to his great disappointment, that this is the way of the world. One could predict a person's response to a situation by guessing which of the cardinal sins would be acted out. The evil one still ruled the roost.

He felt alleviated as he walked home. The charges had been uncorroborated and dismissed. His denial was the icing on the cake. He was reinstated.

CHAPTER 33

▼

Sahar looked upset, Paul thought, as he closed the door gently behind her. He gestured for her to sit and took the stool across from her.

Turns out that she had been out on a date with her young American boyfriend and he had tried going too far. When she turned him down, he had gotten angry and told her to get out of his car, which was parked on a dark street outside N.Y.U., not too far from the Speakeasy.

She had complied and walked over to the restaurant hoping to find Fatima. When she didn't, she knocked on Paul's door.

"You did the right thing Sahar. One must practice self-control at all times, especially in such a serious situation. Sex is very serious and can have grave repercussions."

"He was trying to feel me up."

"Of course, that's the first step. And if you advance, then he will expect step two, three and four, without commitment or responsibility of course. It's best to keep it chaste."

"I'm not going to see him anymore. What he did was very selfish and rude. He shouldn't treat me that way."

"No, he shouldn't."

There was a moment of pause as the beautiful Sahar looked about the room. She had never entered this space before.

"What do you call these again?" She said this motioning to the artwork on the walls; she remembered that Lepido had planned to do this type of thing.

"I've recently learned that they call it embossing."

"You're pretty good. How do pick your subject? What do you use as a guide?"

"The Holy Spirit. I always pray before I work and ask the Spirit to guide me."

"What are those, sandals?"

"Yes."

"Why did you do sandals?"

"I don't know. I don't know yet I should say."

"Who are the man, the girl, and the baby? Anyone you know?"

"Actually, yes. I gave this to my partner Joe. I believe it has something to do with his future but he hasn't told me if it does. I gave it to him a while back but he forgot it."

Sahar looked into Paul's brilliant golden eyes. She felt a penetrating love, a deep love. She knew that he cared for her and a lot of other people too. But his was a chaste love, a holy love, and an unselfish love, which comes only of the Holy Spirit that he's always talking about. In her heart she too wanted this Holy Spirit that gave Paul so much strength. She kissed his cheek.

"The time is late. I will walk you to a cab."

"Thank you."

The days flew by and it was time to go speak to the Prior. As he walked up Seventh Avenue, he saw a very distraught middle-aged woman walking towards him. She had a black veil over her head and was carrying a single withered rose. She looked up at Paul and almost smiled what would have been a sad smile.

He stopped before her and reached out his hands, palms up. She looked down at his hands, and took one in hers while the other still held the rose.

"Why are you sad?"

She looked into his eyes and hesitated. Then she looked at the rose and then at Paul's hand that was holding hers.

"I lost my son, my only son, to drugs."

"I am so sorry."

"I wasn't watchful. At a young age I let him have bad friends. I knew they were bad but I let him and hoped. But they won. They say that once you are an addict, you are always an addict.

"Heroin! From Afghanistan! Heroin from Afghanistan! Heroin from Afghanistan!" She was whimpering loudly as she said these words.

Paul didn't comment but just looked into her eyes.

"It's a terrible thing, a terrible tragedy."

"Now I have no one. His father was my second husband and he left years ago. I have no other children."

"But you have friends don't you? And relatives?"

"I have a few friends," she said. Paul noticed that her lips were extremely chapped, and what hair he could see was unkempt.

"I am not alone. But I should have more children. I should have had them when I could. But I didn't."

Then her look became severe, "I aborted three children. I killed my family. All to have a better life," she said, "better life my eye!"

She glanced away at the traffic when a car horn blared. Her eyes were now glazed over.

"You need support. There is support. What is your name?"

She looked at him, "Hilda" was all she said.

"Right here around the corner is a church. They are open now. Tell them that you need help. Tell them what you told me. They can help. They will help you Hilda."

Hilda's eyes teared up. Then she closed them when he said, "Let's pray".

"Almighty God, Friend and Father of all those in need, lead Hilda to the help that she needs to get strong. The help that she needs to relieve the guilt that she feels. Let her know that to the sincere heart, there is always forgiveness. That we are still and always will be your children. Give her courage, Lord. We ask all this in Jesus' name. Amen."

Was it his imagination or had Hilda's cold hand suddenly felt warm after the prayer? She opened her eyes and looked at him. Her lips moved without sound as she said thank you.

She walked away in the direction of the church.

He continued up Seventh Avenue.

The Prior's office was on the top floor of the building east of the chapel, a building Paul had never entered.

A smiling Franciscan led him up the stairs. He wore a crew cut and was eating an apple. The Franciscan knocked gently on a large ornate wooden door and then opened it saying, "Go ahead in, they're expecting you."

Paul walked into the room. The Prior sat at the large mahogany desk with a priest standing at either side. Behind the men was an image of the Crucifix of San Damiano and to the left on the wall was the traditional rendering of St. Francis with the bowl hair cut and the animals at his side, an image Paul considered almost whimsical.

"Good afternoon, Paul is it?"

"Good afternoon. Yes, I am Paul."

"Have a seat if you like, Paul."

Paul was nervous and said that he would rather stand.

"Do you know why you were called here Paul?" The Prior was speaking in a very neutral tone, passionless, but yet authoritative.

"No sir, I do not."

"There has been a serious charge against you. One where there are two witnesses, one being one of our own monks and the other a layperson. The incident took place in front of our church."

"Go on." Paul had an image in his mind of what this was about but couldn't put his finger on it.

"You have been accused of representing the Church and particularly this Parish without the proper credentials."

Paul was stunned. This never happened.

"Specifically, that you claimed to be one of our monks and told a man that he had demons and needed an exorcism. This event took place on our front steps and was witnessed by one our own. As you might know, you wouldn't be standing here if but one person had accused you, but two makes it an issue."

"What you are saying sir, with all due respect, never happened, none of it." Paul said this with a serenity that he didn't know he had.

"Do you know, Paul, that there are steps one must take within the Church and under the authority of Church leadership in order to represent the Roman Catholic Church, in order to preach accurately the teachings of our great Church?"

"Yes, I do."

"Have you considered it?"

These words came as a shock to him. On the one hand he was being falsely accused of something and on the other hand this Prior seemed to be sending an olive branch. At these last few words, Paul couldn't help but notice the monk to the left flinching.

He spoke tentatively, "I haven't sir, but it is possible that maybe I should."

"That would be fine. Come see me when you've thought it over. But in the meantime, I am going to ask you not to come to our kitchen, although we do appreciate your assistance, and no proselytizing in or around our grounds.

"Of course you may attend our Worship and Adoration as well as pray before our lovely Virgin."

"I understand that you give out prayer cards?"

"Yes, I do."

"You are of course welcome in our bookstore always. How is your prayer card ministry working out?"

"Fine sir," was all that he could muster.

"Well, I believe that we see eye to eye on this, and I wish you godspeed."

"Thank you," Paul said, and left.

As much as he felt the urge to enter the chapel, he couldn't. For at the moment he felt as an outcast. He didn't know whether to laugh or cry. On the one hand, he was falsely accused, and maybe the Prior knew it, and on the other hand, he was given a vote of confidence, almost an invitation, to join the Franciscans.

All he knew was that he must pray about this.

As he walked across on the sidewalk in front of the church, he saw a familiar face waiting for him, Friar Billy.

"Friar William, what are you doing out here? It's rather cold out."

"Waiting for you. How did it go?"

"Well, let's just say that I won't be peeling potatoes for a while. But I will be in for Holy Cards."

"Alright, but tell me, will you still worship here?"

"Just like always."

"I meant to tell you why Henry left. His sister is having visions of annihilation, of great destruction, suffering and death. It's driving her mad. She's bedridden. She'll eat only Eucharist and cries a lot. This is what Henry said.

"Where can I reach you if I hear from Henry?"

"I'll always be around, God willing, Friar William."

With that, Friar Billy looked down with his peanut shaped head and reached into his tunic. He pulled a small stack of Holy Cards out and handed them to Paul.

"These are on me. I blessed them."

"Thank you Friar Billy, err … William."

"You're welcome."

As Billy walked away, Paul looked down at a Holy Card. He didn't recognize the picture. This was one he hadn't used. They were all the same, all ten. All ten Holy Cards were of St. John the Baptizer.

Paul read the words on the back to himself as he walked:

John the Baptist lived as a hermit in the desert of Judea until about A.D. 27. When he was thirty, he began to preach on the banks of the Jordan against the evil of the times and called men to the penance and baptism "for the kingdom of heaven is close at hand". He attracted large crowds and when Christ came to him, John recognized him as the Messiah and baptized Him saying, "It is I who need baptism from you."

When Christ left to preach in Galilee, John continued preaching in the Jordan Valley. Fearful of his great power with the people, Herod Antipas, Tetrarch of Perea and Galilee, had him arrested and imprisoned at Machaerus on the Dead Sea.

John was beheaded at the request of Salome, daughter of Herodias, who asked for his head at the instigation if her mother. John inspired many of his followers to follow Christ. He is presented in the New Testament as the last of the Old Testament prophets and the precursor of the Messiah. His feast day is June 24th.

How is it that a prophet such as John seems to be all but forgotten in our times, Paul thought? He'd never realized that John was a hermit, living like a wild man on the banks of the Jordan, and that's when he realized, as was the case with Francis, that those who radically live the Gospel of Jesus Christ, who aspire to new heights in the Spiritual Journey, that live solely on Providence, stand out, they attract a following, they're leaders. They change the world.

We need leaders, he thought, and turned south on Seventh Avenue.

CHAPTER 34

▼

"You are only fifteen years old. You are just now becoming responsible for your actions and the things that you've experienced, the bad things especially, were not your fault. Do you understand?"

Joe's words brought tears to the young pregnant girl's eyes. She had always believed that the terrible abuse that she had suffered since a very young age was all her own doing, her own fault. That's what the "adults" had told her.

"The things that you're ashamed of, these horrible experiences with your stepfather and your uncle, were not your fault. You were a child and they took advantage of you."

Now the tears were running down Shameeka's cheeks, tears of healing. She tried to speak but couldn't. She choked up.

"But you must not be ashamed. They should be ashamed. They should be in prison."

Joe was careful not to point the finger at the young girl's mom. She would figure out for herself her mom's culpability in the crimes committed against her. But he must not alienate her now. Now was a time for healing. He knew that no matter what happened that she would defend her Mom.

"These deep, deep hurts, the ones you keep secret, painfully secret, you have to bring them up out of the darkness of your soul, into the light, the light of love, God's love."

With this he gestured with both hands outwardly from his heart.

"If you keep them hidden they fester, and continue hurting you. You must bring it all out, all the hurt, all the anger, all the tears, and let God heal you.

"You have to forgive yourself especially. Forgive those things the you blame yourself for, and then begin the long process of forgiving those who hurt you."

The young girl reached for the box of tissues that Joe kept on his desk. Her cheeks were wet with tears.

"Are you a priest?" she asked him.

"No. But I am a member of the Christian Community that founded Redemption House and so I can use the Lord in my counseling.

"Do you understand what I mean? Don't be afraid to talk to me about what hurts inside. None of it was your fault. You were a child. You're still a child."

He wished he could hug the girl and hold her hand. She seemed so vulnerable, so alone. Shameeka was five months pregnant and had no clue who the father was. She had a regular boyfriend but had been very promiscuous, including still having an occasional fling with her uncle.

There is a misconception about child abuse, that the abuser waits until the child is of a certain age before beginning the abuse. This is not so. These kids are abused as babies.

"Your life can start right now if you want it to. This could be the first real day of your life. The past is past. You can start building a future for you and your baby."

"What should I do? How do I start?"

"Well, why don't we make your goal to be independent, to be able to take care of yourself, without relying on boys?"

The look on her face told him that she hadn't thought of this before.

"Let's make a plan to get you the schooling or training that you need so that, let's say, in three years you can have a good job that pays a lot more than minimum wage, that is of course, after we get you a safe place to live and the right people to help you."

"That sounds good!" she whispered thoughtfully.

As he wrote in Shameeka's chart afterward, Joe prayed. He hoped that the young girl followed her plan and succeeded, but he felt pain in his heart as he wrote. He knew this pain well. He felt it when he wrote in the charts and realized the difficulty that his clients faced in sticking to their plan. How would they react to the setbacks, to the peer pressure, the pressure to go back to the streets and the futureless life of despair that the streets offered?

But somewhere in that pain he always had a spark of hope, that if they fell, they could pick themselves up and try again. He had to have this hope.

Walking back to Community his thoughts drifted to his future. Christmas was around the corner. In March his thirteen months were up. Patrick had talked to him about staying on at the agency as paid staff and getting an apartment together in the neighborhood. He hadn't responded but had noted that a frequent visitor to community, a wormy little guy that rubbed him the wrong way, was pushing Patrick to get a room with him. Joe thought that the guy had a crush on Patrick. Could that be?

Community was down to an unbelievable twenty-two people. There were around fifty when Joe came around. No one was re-upping. The two young Mexican ladies were arguing over what to do. They had hoped to go another year but were informed that it wouldn't happen. They couldn't decide whether to return to Mexico or extend their visas and get a job in New York. Joe still had no clue that Charo knew all that was going on with Yasmine. Her and Yasmine spoke almost daily.

He would later realize that this was a good thing. Charo, as it turned out, was on his side, in spite of the fact that he had kindly rejected her friend Adrianna.

Since returning from Greece and being accused of impropriety, he had let his relationship with Yasmine cool a bit. They talked on the phone daily but he had only visited her a handful of times.

Tomorrow was Saturday and he planned to go to Jersey early for his van and then pick up Yasmine and Johny and spend the afternoon at Bronx Beach. He had never heard of this little beach before. A community member had talked about it at dinner a while back and he had remembered. He looked it up in his Road Atlas before pulling out of his Mom's driveway that morning.

The time was 11 a.m. as the blue van ventured across the huge bridge. Down below he could see several tug boats pulling barges and freighters on the Hudson River. This was a clean and beautiful December day, the temperature just above freezing, and a perfect day for the beach. They would have it all to themselves.

He picked up Yasmine and Johny and in minutes was parked yards from the beach in the parking lot of a fish and chips restaurant.

He still couldn't believe that he lived just on the other side of the George Washington Bridge all of his life and had never heard of this place, Bronx Beach, a small town with a beach and fresh seafood twenty minutes from Leonia.

After crossing the bridge onto the tiny island, they passed seafood restaurant after seafood restaurant on the main drag, then some homes that reminded Joe of the beach houses near the Jersey shore. At the end of Main Street was the ocean.

They placed Johny in the stroller and wrapped a soft wool blanket around him. He smiled when Joe pinched his cheek.

Joe loved this little guy. He was an amazing looking child with sparkling gray-blue eyes and always a happy disposition. Sometimes he wasn't sure who he loved more, the little boy or his mother.

The three stepped out onto the boardwalk and smiled a knowing smile at a couple passing by. They all knew this was good. An off season visit to the beach always meant peace and quiet, and time to look into each others eyes and express the thoughts that only come when one knows that you're alone, together.

They passed by the viewing machines that serve as binoculars and put some quarters in. The sea was calm yet robust. The salt air filled their lungs with freshness and a happy feeling as they gazed out at the Connecticut Sound and watched the fishing vessels troll the depths, probably fishing for shad.

The two lovers hadn't said much on the way. They both had looked at each other and smiled when they noticed little Johny was lip-synching the words to an Ednita Nazario song that they both liked. The song was in Spanish.

They both knew something had to happen soon in their relationship. She was in a dangerous situation with her roommates and her neighborhood. She had quit her job at the donut shop. He had come to see her and had walked in, taking her by the hand, and told the two owners that she wouldn't be needing the job anymore. He came short of telling them off, but they got the message.

On his end he really wanted to be with them all the time. He wanted to take care of them. He was at a point in his life when he needed to be needed. Joe was a very giving guy and wanted to give of himself on a more intimate level, like a man and wife maybe?

She knew he'd be leaving Community soon and had hinted at living together. He flatly told her that he didn't believe in that. Not without a serious commitment. He knew that when couples live together before marriage their chances of divorce increase.

As he stepped away from the telescope, holding Yasmine's hand with his left and pushing Johny with his right, he noticed a figure to his right. There on the black steel fence sat a huge black bird, for a brief second looking directly at him, before flying away with its great wingspan. He looked at Yasmine, but she was looking out to sea and hadn't even noticed. When he turned again the giant bird was nowhere to be seen.

A sign! Another sign! A spooky one at that, but it had to be a sign. He had to try to remember to look up what kind of bird this was. He seemed akin to the one he and Paul had a visit from on the Holy Mountain.

They sat on a bench facing the sea and wrapped themselves in the blanket they carried. They kissed frozen kisses to keep warm and held hands underneath the blanket.

Yasmine felt the warmth of Joe's hands keeping her skinny fingers warm. Then she felt something like a small box with a bow around it slip into her hand. She giggled excitedly and pulled out her hand holding the box. She was grinning from ear to ear. She loved surprises, especially when they included a small gift or two.

"Can I open it?" she asked, with an accent less thick than usual.

"Of course."

She held the box with both hands. Her fingers sticking out from the fingerless winter gloves that she wore, and carefully opened it.

She gasped when she saw the beautiful silver heart and chain necklace. The charm was truly lovely. Joe was not partial to gold and had discovered this piece in the window of a small boutique on Eleventh Avenue, a bohemian place.

"Does this mean?"

"What?"

"That we're going out. Like boyfriend and girlfriend?"

"Yes. And I think it also means Merry Christmas."

Yasmine's eyes glazed over as she reached and kissed Joe. He gently pushed her back and took the necklace, slipping it around her neck. It draped out over her turtleneck sweater beautifully.

After getting a chill on the bench, the couple with the small boy stopped in the restaurant to warm up with hot cocoa and fish and chips, before heading back to make the young lady's curfew.

Joe walked the two to their door where Yasmine gave him a huge kiss with a look in her eye like the cat that ate the canary, or was it something else?

He drove back to Jersey feeling strong and confident and praying for God's will to be done in his life, and that he was doing the right thing.

CHAPTER 35

▼

Paul missed Friar Henry and the kitchen at the Franciscans. He realized now that his work in the kitchen was a form of security for him. He would see a familiar and interesting face in Henry and was guaranteed a meal.

At first his meals were rather sparing but once he realized that this might be his only meal of the day, as it often was, he began to eat larger portions. He rarely had seconds, but just larger portions.

Since he had stopped working in the kitchen he found that there were days when he wouldn't eat solid foods. He had discovered where there were several water fountains around the city where he would take a drink when very thirsty, Macy's was one.

This area around 34th Street had now become his favorite part of the city in which to hand out holy cards and pray with people. There was an excitement there that he felt, especially now with all the Christmas shoppers.

Macy's had gone full blown this year in their decorating and their display windows reflected this. Santa and the elves were everywhere with their moving parts, assembling toys, while robotic figures of Christmas carolers sang "Joy to the World".

Paul was stepping through the crowds and out to the street when he saw her. He remembered a long time ago thinking that he saw her pass by this very spot, but this time it was she, none other. He knew this because she was stopped ten feet in front of him and looking directly at him.

He kept walking toward her and she stepped toward him. She was alone and holding two large bags with gift-wrapped packages inside.

"Kathy?"

"Paul? I can't believe it. Is it really you?"

Kathy had never seen Paul with a beard and long hair, not to mention wearing a monk's tunic. They didn't speak for moments that felt a lot longer.

"I'm in New York shopping."

"I see that," he said looking at the bags.

She hadn't changed much he thought, the same beautiful green eyes and long natural blond hair. There was a sweetness to her face that he had misread. He thought it meant a wife, a mother, a soul mate. But it meant a fancy car, expensive clothes and jewelry to match. But he still loved her. He had butterflies in his stomach.

"Can we go somewhere and talk?" she asked.

"What's wrong with here, are you alone?"

"Right now I am. My Mom and Dad are at the hotel. I never heard from you again. I called a few times. Your mother said you were in New York experimenting on what it would be like to really follow Jesus, the Gospel, and that she only heard from you about every couple of weeks. She said that you sounded fine."

"I suppose that's how she understood my explanation for what I'm doing."

"She thinks that you'll return home after you get your fill."

"God bless her. I think she'll understand my mission someday."

As soon as he said it he wanted to take it back. My mission? But he was a little nervous; there was a lot of history here standing in front of him.

She couldn't let his words slide by.

"Your mission? So you're on a mission?"

"Of sorts, I'm simply trying to follow the Lord. I believe the world needs disciples to contrast the materialism, the secular, and to show that there are still those who believe in the transcendent, so much so, that they give their lives."

"Give their lives for what?"

"Not for what, but for whom, for Jesus the Christ, the Messiah of God, Our Savior."

"Uh-huh. I started going to church, you know, we found a cute little bible church not too far …"

"We?"

"Myself and my fiancée."

In spite of everything he believed, everything that he lived for and loved, she could still put a lump in his throat and butterflies in his stomach. Fiancée?

"Do I know the man?"

"No."

Then Kathy looked away and Paul did too. He noticed dusk was approaching and the air was chilling. He felt his chest tightening too.

Then she looked at him.

"He's going to be an investment banker, or he is an investment banker."

Paul nodded his head and looked right in her eyes. She knew what he was wondering. Does she love him or love his career, and the riches their future would hold. She glanced down.

"I wish you well Kathy."

She gave him a quick unexpected kiss on the cheek and darted off north on Fashion Ave.

He headed south, wondering what would have happened if he'd gotten the messages and called her back.

He walked slowly south towards19th Street. The excitement that he felt earlier replaced by emptiness, emptiness that he couldn't remember feeling in a long time.

What was this he was feeling? Then he realized the line had been cut. Kathy was no more. There was no going back to her. She was in the past.

Amazing how the Lord had set this up. In a city of 12 million people, two people that knew each other from 500 miles away meet for a moment in time in a ten-foot square area of a very crowded street.

He knew now that he was totally the Lord's. Not that he'd really thought about Kathy that much, but she was his first true love and still held a place in his heart, and maybe, somewhere deep, deep down in his soul, he had harbored the thought that eventually she would be his again, some time in the distant future, and under different circumstances. He now knew that this was not to be.

These were Paul's thoughts as he rang Gwen's bell.

CHAPTER 36

▼

Yasmine was a good girl. In her heart of hearts she knew this. She was different from her sisters. Her sisters saw men as sources of money to be hustled. After all, how many Dominican men stay faithful and loyal? Her lifelong experience told her not many. So if their intention is to use you, what's wrong with using then in return? This was their logic. Love never entered the picture.

She was in love, with Joe. She felt incredibly fortunate to have met this man. He was a good man. He would be true to her.

At times she wondered if he had money. She figured his family did from the description of his mother's house and the family retail business, but how much of this was his? To her it didn't matter.

And especially she loved him because of how he treated Johny. She could easily see that he loved the little boy. He was not bashful about holding and kissing the little boy and always brought him a small gift.

He had handed her a gift-wrapped box when he dropped her off after the beach. Johny's Christmas present. She didn't wait, she couldn't. Inside of the box was a New York Mets baseball uniform, complete with a hat and jacket. She put it on him right away. He looked so cute.

Her sister who was closest to her, the one that dropped her at Redemption House, was pushing her to hustle Joe. To find a means to have sex with him and get pregnant so that he's obligated to take care of her. But she couldn't do it.

Yasmine's roommates were very jealous of her, as was to be expected. Their "men" did not treat them with the respect that Joe had for Yasmine, and they noticed the little gifts that Johny was bringing home. The Mets uniform was the crusher.

On an afternoon a few days after her rendezvous with Joe at the beach, she was making some pasta for her and Johny when Sonya stepped into the kitchen. She had come home past curfew and missed her turn at the stove. Each girl had a scheduled half hour in the evening for cooking. Sonya missed her turn and now was supposed to wait until the others went.

She was in a particularly nasty mood as her "man" had stood her up, and in searching all afternoon for him, discovered that he was with another girl getting high. She couldn't catch him and now was looking for someone else to take it out on.

Yasmine's roommates, due to her kind and gentle demeanor, had mistaken this for weakness. Sonya thought she could push her around. Sonya was wrong.

Yasmine was facing the stove when Sonya walked in.

"Hey bitch. What's cooking?"

Yasmine looked at her, and then back at the boiling pasta.

"I'm making bow ties."

"Hey, did ya make enough for me?"

"No I'm afraid I didn't, the box was not full."

Sonya stood next to Yasmine looking at the pasta. Yasmine stood around 5'5" tall and Sonya was at least an inch shorter but probably thirty pounds heavier. She was an enigma. She had the facial characteristics and hair of an African-American and spoke distinctly ghetto, but her skin was white as powder. She had deep blue eyes that had a mean look to them and a mouth that was always in a snarl. She came from a broken home and foster care and had been in many a scrape.

"How about you let me have this pasta and you make something else, being as it's my turn?"

"You lost your turn Sonya; you can have the stove as soon as I'm done."

"No, I'll have it now."

With those words she pushed Yasmine hard to the side and took her place in front of the boiling water.

"Sonya, please move. My son is hungry and he needs to eat."

Johny sat in a high chair waiting, by the far wall of the kitchen.

"Give me the spoon; I need to stir my dinner." Sonya said this and reached across for the spoon. Yasmine pulled back her hand with the spoon and at the same time reflexively slapped the pushy girl in the face with her other hand, a loud slap that could be heard in the next room where Miss Stewart, the meaner of the two childcare workers, was sitting.

Sonya attacked. She lunged toward Yasmine grabbing at the front of her blouse. Yasmine fell back and smacked the girl in the head with the thick wooden spoon.

Yasmine then turned to the side and pushed Sonya down to the floor. She turned and picked up a saucepan and as Sonya stood she bounced the aluminum saucepan off the top of her head, denting the pan.

This only made her angry. She bull rushed Yasmine and reached up and grabbed her long black hair and yanked down with both hands. This was a favorite fighting move of Sonya's, and it worked.

She was holding Yasmine, bent over, by her hair, when Miss Stewart walked in and screamed, "Let her go, now!"

"She hit me first!"

"Now!"

Miss Stewart grabbed Sonya by the back of her neck as she released her hold on Yasmine. She led the girl out of the kitchen and up to her room.

"No dinner for you tonight! And maybe no breakfast neither!"

Yasmine felt relieved. Somehow she wasn't really afraid of these girls from the streets. She had fought before in her youth and had a pretty good idea what to do. Her sister was a wild woman when she fought, including using a weapon if necessary, and always protected her. She knew that she had Joe in her corner too. So these girls didn't scare her, as rough as they were. This was the first time one of them had "tried" her.

She didn't know why she had a delayed reaction to the fight, but after she and Johnny ate and she went to her room, she closed the door and started to cry. She waited until Johny was asleep to call her "man".

CHAPTER 37

▼

Paul and Gwen had arranged a signal. On the corner of 19th and Seventh was a subway entrance with an old stairwell. Next to the wrought iron fence that protected people from falling into the stairwell was an old streetlamp that was quite possibly used with gas at one time. If Gwen wanted Paul to come by she would reach up as far as she could and wrap a piece of duct tape around the lamp. He was happy when he saw the signal. He didn't want to spend Christmas Eve alone.

When he walked into Gwen's apartment he got warm greetings from everyone but one person. The woman that he'd never met looked him up and down with disdain.

Lola had answered the door looking ravishing and gave him a hug and a peck on the cheek. Then she introduced him to her friend Louis, who for some odd reason had the nickname "Big Dog".

He shook Gwen's father's hand warmly as he turned to introduce Paul to his new girlfriend, the owner of her own computer networking company.

"Nice to meet ya," she said, in a thick Brooklyn, New York accent.

"What are you, a priest?"

"Not quite."

"He's a sidewalk preacher," Gwen's father interjected, "and quite an interesting chap."

The woman, Jody was her name, gave Paul a limp handshake while continuing to eyeball him. She was the owner of a fancy hairdo and expensive but tasteless clothes. The gaudy rings on her fingers spoke volumes. Paul tried not to pay attention. He was still feeling the lump in his throat from seeing Kathy.

Then Gwen came out of the bathroom, which was off of the kitchen, in a white terry bathrobe and white towel wrapped around her head. As usual she was the last one to get ready and as usual she was upbeat and smiling.

"Hello Friar, you got my signal?"

"Yes I did."

"Excellent. Give me seven minutes and we can eat."

Gwen had actually done all the cooking, a first, and a sign of the change in her.

The table was already set. A large ham sat in the center surrounded by a dish of sliced pineapple, a large white porcelain bowl of mashed potatoes, a small bowl of gravy with a ladle, and a plastic platter of what looked like a large store-bought salad, sumptuous yet simple.

Jody caught Paul eyeing the table setting. She held a glass of white wine that was obviously not her first glass of the early evening.

"I made string beans with crispy onion rings. Where are my string beans? Did I leave them in the car?" There was panic in her voice.

"No," Lola said, "they're in the oven heating up. I'll get them."

Louis took a seat next to the head of the table. He was a round-faced man with a crew cut and long sideburns. He was wearing a New Jersey Devils jersey. He put his can of Bud on the table and looked up at Paul and smiled. Paul saw a bit of defiance in the smile. What did it mean?

"Well," Paul said with resolve, "Merry Christmas. I hope everyone's enjoying themselves. This is a happy time of the year."

Gwen's dad motioned for Paul to take the chair across from Big Dog. Lola came in holding the beans with two oven mitts and placed them on the table.

"Watch out, hot," she said.

Looking past Lola, Paul could see a beautifully decorated artificial Christmas tree. It had what looked like handmade ornaments hanging from it as well as beautiful gold garland and silver tinsel. On top was an angel with a sword.

"Lovely tree," he said.

"We just finished decorating it," Lola answered. "Your timing for dinner couldn't have been more perfect. We're going to Midnight Mass; do you want to join us? Just me and Gwen."

"Sounds good, I was planning to go."

"We've been going to a church not too far from here. You're welcome."

"Thanks."

Gwen's father was a balding man who wore rimless glasses and carried a mustache. He was looking across the table where Jody had sat, staring at Paul, after refilling her wine glass.

"So, why are you dressed like that?"

Paul's eyes had been following Lola across the room when Jody addressed him. He took a deep breath and looked her way. For once in a very long time he wasn't in the mood to get drilled. He just wanted to enjoy the gathering and forget the feeling of gloom that he had in his heart.

"This is a gift from a friend, a priest, a monk, his name's Henry."

"But don't you have to join a group or something, be a member, to dress like that?"

"Last I remember, this is still a free country," Gwen's dad piped in.

"I feel it's appropriate for what I do," Paul answered.

"What do you do?"

"I pray with people."

"I pray with people too. I don't need to dress like a nun to pray with people. You don't have a job?"

"Technically not."

"So how do you pay the bills, how do you eat?"

"I don't have bills as I don't live anyplace and I rely on God's providence and the mercy of others for food."

"Have you ever had a job?" She asked this after giving him the once over again.

"Yes."

"What did you do?"

"I managed a restaurant."

"Where?"

"That's enough Jody, don't get too personal. Paul's one in a million. He's given his life to Jesus and he's on the street everyday helping people. And he doesn't look like he's in the mood for your grilling."

Paul didn't think anyone could tell. He was wrong. His somber disposition was obvious.

"I'm just curious. So you're Catholic? That faith's going down the tubes, too judgmental. How can there be only one way to be saved, with all the different cultures in the world?"

With that Lola came to Paul's defense. She'd been studying.

"Jesus' sacrificial death, for all our sins, opened up the gates of heaven for all. He was the atoning sacrifice. He was God's son."

Jody looked at Lola and then at Paul. "What is this? This guy's converting people or what?" She asked this and looked at Gwen's dad.

Apparently Jody was new to the family and didn't have much background on the girls. Lola piped in. "What if he is? It's an improvement for me and Gwen, believe me!"

"Gwen too?"

This was her cue. Gwen came out looking dashing and yet conservative in a blue gingham blouse and blue khaki's, neatly pressed. She had a gardenia in her soft brown hair.

"Jody giving Paul the third degree? Don't worry Lola; he's a big boy. He can take care of himself." She looked at Paul and winked. Paul smiled.

"Come on," Gwen said. "Let's eat."

The conversation turned to talk about the food. It smelled delicious and tasted just as well. They talked about how Gwen had cooked the pineapple and made homemade mashed potatoes for the first time ever. Lola helped her peel the potatoes.

When all were served Gwen surprised everyone and said a blessing.

"Bless this food, Oh Lord," she began, as they all held hands around the table. Even Jodie closed her eyes and bowed her head.

"And bless those at this table."

Paul could see a smirk on Big Dog's face. He was enjoying all this. Paul wondered how many beers he'd had.

"We hope for peace. We pray for peace. We thank you Jesus for all you've done. Amen."

"Wait, wait, wait," Lola added, "I want to say thank you Lord for our friend Paul. Who helped bring peace to our home. Amen."

Dinner was delicious. One could tell that Gwen put a lot of effort into it, and Paul had to admit that the old stand-by green bean dish made by Jody was good too.

The conversation centered on Gwen's plan to volunteer one evening a week to visit those unfortunate at St. Vincent's hospital that had no one to visit them. Lola was considering the same.

Gwen's father was quiet while Jody discussed how she was going to grow her business and eventually take it public and make millions.

Big Dog drank two more beers over dinner, and then excused himself to step outside "to burn one." He had hardly spoken a word but had kept looking at Paul with the same smirk.

"Well Paul," Jody said, "you barely spoke a word at dinner. What's the matter, cat got your tongue?" With these words, Jody burst out in a mocking, cackling laugh. Paul simply looked at her peacefully and didn't reply. He'd had a serving of everything on the table and was enjoying the after effects of a good meal, one he hadn't had for quite some time.

"So Paul, what's so wrong with our society that you decided to drop out?"

Lola was first to answer. "He didn't drop out, he dropped in. He's facing up to the problems in society and helping people cope with them. He's teaching people the truth that you'll never see on T.V. or read about in the paper."

"He teaches people that there's another way to look at things," Gwen added, "a spiritual way, one with real meaning. There's an alternative to materialism."

Paul was embarrassed. He didn't realize that this is what he might be doing. He hadn't had to explain what he was doing on the street and he preferred not to. Keep it simple. Follow your heart. Trust Jesus.

"I believe Jody that people are not adjusting well to modern technology. Even and especially things that we take for granted like the T.V.

"Because now we can be constantly distracted by T.V. and radio and other inventions we cut back on the need for other people in our lives. We can live precariously through the T.V. and forget about others until we go to sleep and wake up to go to work or school. On our way to work we're distracted by the radio. Then we're occupied with work. We put on music on the way home and then the T.V. again.

"People don't generally go out anymore, only to shop. We don't want to know who our neighbors are. We have no sense of community, and most important we don't take time to pray."

"So that's why you chose a prayer ministry, right?" Gwen asked.

"Probably. The T.V. culture, what they preach on T.V. is a culture of pleasure, physical pleasure as well as the pleasure that comes with owning a new car or an expensive home. It's a selfish, narcissistic lifestyle that leads to people becoming alienated, especially people that can't afford a new car or a trip to Aruba.

"We have to set limits. Pick what T.V. shows we're going to watch and then turn off the T.V. Read a book. Do research. Keep learning. But also knock on your neighbors' door. See how they're doing."

"So modern technology is causing the alienation of our society?"

"Yes. And with alienation is a lack of giving and receiving love. And I believe that at the root of many of society's problems is a lack of love. People need to love and be loved. But it's a lot easier to sit on the couch with a remote control."

"That sounds more like selfishness and laziness to me," added Lola.

"In a nutshell," Paul said.

"So what's that thing you're spinning around on your finger?"

"A finger rosary."

"Oh really. Why do Catholics pray the rosary?" Jody asked.

"The saints call praying the rosary a sign of predestination to heaven. I believe it."

"Are you going to heaven Paul?" Jody asked.

"I hope so."

Jody got up and walked over to the kitchen counter to get yet another glass of wine. Paul felt relieved.

Gwen's father leaned across the table at him and whispered that Jody had been seeing a psychiatrist for a lot of years and told him not to let her bother him.

"I heard that," she said with a laugh. "And what's wrong with seeing a shrink? Everybody I know sees a shrink. And what's wrong with that?" she asked, looking first at Gwen's father, then at Paul.

Paul didn't want to answer.

"Well? Is something wrong with that?"

"Not necessarily," Paul relented, as the eyes of Gwen and Lola were upon him. They wanted to hear his opinion too.

"Shrinks don't acknowledge sin. So you go to them to confess your sins and they try to make you feel good about your sinful life. So you don't stop the sin and you don't get better. You end up going to them forever. And of course they don't tell you to pray.

"Did you know that Dr. Carl Yung himself admitted that in the 20,000 plus cases that he studied in his career, those that were consistently healed and didn't have to continue therapy were people of faith? I believe only God can heal you Jody and he wants you to ask for healing. He wants to hear from you. In prayer."

"Hogwash," she said. And as she said this white wine shot out through her teeth onto the table. Lola chuckled, and then the whole table burst out in laughter, even Big Dog, who after coming back from his cigarette break, had yet to utter a word all night.

Gwen signaled for Paul to follow her as she rose from the table. He followed her into her room, which was just off of the dining room.

"I want you to see this," she said as she closed the door behind her.

There, next to her bed, Gwen had set up a little altar. She had a white table-cloth over the little table. On it sat three glass votive candleholders with three lit candles. "Representing the trinity," she said. She had a beautiful card size icon of the Madonna, a small plastic bottle of holy water, and of course her glow in the dark crucifix. Above it on the wall was a St. Benedict crucifix and on her bed he could see a prayer book.

Paul knelt. She knelt beside him. They prayed quietly together.

Gwen got up first and sat on the bed. Paul stood and sat next to her.

"I didn't want to say it in front of Jody, but I'm also volunteering as an advocate for pregnant teens," she whispered.

"You're not going to believe it, but because of my experience, the girls listen to me. I already talked one girl out of an abortion."

"Wow Gwen, you saved a person's life!"

"I never knew these places existed where they'll pay for all the doctor's fees and help you put your child up for adoption." Tears welled in her eyes as she said this.

Paul reached for her hands. "All things work out for the best for those who love God."

They were quiet for a few moments. He holding her hand and looking into her eyes. She whispered, "Thank you", with cheeks now wet from tears.

The three knocks on the door were loud. It was Lola.

"Hot apple pie and ice cream, come and get it!"

After Midnight Mass Paul walked Lola and Gwen back to their place, gave them both a hug and wished them a Merry Christmas. As they slipped away each lady put a tiny gift-wrapped box into his pocket.

He actually blushed as he looked at them both backing into their building smiling together. They knew he was a Franciscan who owned nothing, at least in his heart he was, and wanted only that.

CHAPTER 38

▼

The time was after 2 a.m. as he walked to the corner of Nineteenth and Seventh. This was the corner where he met Gwen; and there stood the pub where they'd met.

The sound of laughter and a guitar echoed from the bar. There was a happy, festive Christmas crowd inside. The sign on the door said, "Merry Xmas-open mike".

Paul was curious and stepped through the doors. He recognized the old Irishman who owned the place standing on the small platform that held the mike stand.

"Who's next?" He spoke into the mike.

"C'mon, who's next, who will be the next brave soul?"

Paul found himself standing in front of the puffy, balding Irishman. "How about you preacher?"

He stared into the eyes of Mr. McManus and had a thought. He'd sing a song for Jesus on his birthday.

As he had told Joe to take to a mountaintop for inspiration at a trying time, this could be a little mountain for Paul at his trying time.

He stepped up and took the mike. He started the song without music but quickly a young longhair that knew the chords grabbed a guitar and started softly strumming.

The crowd quickly grew quiet. And out of those listening, one at a time they chimed in, softly singing, until it sounded like the whole pub had joined in to "Here I am Lord."

Paul opened his eyes at the close of the song and looked around him. There was hearty applause and happy laughter. Some whistled. He felt a natural high.

"Happy birthday, Jesus," is all he said, and stepped through the crowd and out the front door."

He didn't go to the bowery that night to sleep at the shelter where he'd been the last few nights. As much as he loved Jesus and the poor, the shelters were still a big challenge for him.

For one, he never slept well for fear of being attacked. Things could get violent inside. And he found himself more often than not awakened by the cries of a desperate man, wailing and crying to himself.

The attendants would go to the aid of the person and then call Paul over for prayer. He never failed to respond. But it didn't make for much sleep. And sometimes he needed to recharge his spiritual battery.

The shelter smelled of industrial cleaning fluids and urine, not an attractive smell, but one he would put up with.

Often times, the attendants were indifferent to the homeless men. In his heart, Paul forgave them for this. It probably comes with the territory he thought, tough job.

This night he felt inspired. The stars were shining bright and there was something in the air. He went south on Seventh Avenue where his little studio awaited him. He knew the Speakeasy was open late tonight. He needed it to be because he didn't have a key to the front door.

His thoughts switched to the great dinner at Gwen's and how Jody had suddenly become very quiet during dessert and thereafter. Paul had seen it happen when a person drinks too much, they suddenly and inexplicably go quiet.

Big Dog on the other hand got loud with inane chatter. He tried to talk about the hockey team, some cool bars he'd discovered where one could get drunk on the cheap, and the "fast as hell" motorcycle he planned to buy, but no one would engage him, not even Lola. Turns out he was an acquaintance of hers that had nowhere to go on Christmas.

When the threesome had left for Mass, ole Big Dog had slipped into McManus'. Little did Paul know that Louis had been way in the back of the pub, out of view, sitting at a table with three girls: the life of the party. He'd had no clue who it was that sang the "Happy Birthday" song.

Now his thoughts were on Fatima. Wow, do things happen fast. Feels like yesterday that he had met her at the park. Now she was half way through the New Testament for a second time and reading Psalms. She was working, going to N.Y.U., and volunteering at a detox three nights a week.

A detox. Wow. She didn't fool around. That's a tough place. Not a place for the rich, but for the destitute, the street people.

He had wondered how and why God would put Fatima to service in a detox. A few days earlier he had found out why.

It had to be him. He hadn't seen him in his cardboard box on 41st Street in a while, and who else had a name like Sayvid?

Fatima was telling him about a diabetic black man with long Rasta braids who claimed to be "touched by the Lord". Upon discussing how his conversion had taken place all Sayvid could say was, "The monk with the golden eyes, he saved me, the monk with the white cross on this chest. He carried me here, on his back."

Fatima was stunned. This could only be Paul. Who else? Was there anyone else in a city of twelve million like him?

Paul was just as stunned. He thought Sayvid was one of the hopeless cases, a body to someday be scraped up from the street and put in a nameless grave at Potters Field. Amazing. A miracle. And according to Fatima, he was determined to make it through. His reward? He wanted to see Paul on a regular basis when he got out. He wanted to be on the streets with him.

God bless him and keep him, he thought.

He was thinking about the little gifts in his pocket. What could they be? He became curious. He stepped into the entrance of a little café that was closed but had a bright light by the door.

He opened Lola's first. Oh my, how lovely. In the tiny box was a carving of Our Lady with Child, The Christ Child, our future Lord. Intricately carved. Beautiful. He carefully closed the box and put it in his pocket. Then he opened Gwen's.

The simple brass lapel pin was of John the Baptist, the hermit of the desert, who declared for all to repent. He put the empty box in his only pocket and attached the pin above his left breast, John the Baptist. As he pulled his hand from his pocket he felt something familiar rub against his fingers.

He kept walking down Seventh Avenue. Then his legs started feeling heavy and he felt like he was walking against a strong wind, though there was no wind to speak of. He felt like a swimmer trying to swim upstream, like he was going the wrong way. And then he abruptly stopped. He was suddenly staggered by a thought, the thought of a beautiful Icon; the one Henry had painted for him.

Was it still in Henry's room? I need to see it again, he thought. I don't know why, but I need to see it right now!

He turned north on Seventh as a light snow began to fall.

CHAPTER 39

▼

"I'm thinking of taking you up on sharing a place around here after our thirteen month commitment is up."

"Are you Joda? That's good news. Only my new little friend is way ahead of you. He's already started looking."

"But we have three months to go yet!"

"He would move in now, he's currently living with his parents, and I'd join him later."

Joe felt a touch of jealousy. He couldn't help it. But he fought it off.

"Well, whatever happens happens."

They were sitting in the cafeteria at a table by the window. Both men dressed in their Sunday best. This was Christmas Eve and Community was going all out. All the big benefactors were invited, including the generous lead rock star from a local New Jersey band and his family, to a fabulous Midnight Mass.

Joe was wearing his favorite sweater with black slacks and Patrick wore a preppy button down light blue shirt with pleated khakis and of course his trademark shoes.

Joe was expecting his married friends from Jersey, who were bringing his mother. Thus he felt a bit nervous. He was one who never liked all the attention on him. They were coming into the city at that late hour just for him and this made him feel uncomfortable.

"I got a job commitment from the agency Joda. I am going to be the new Ombudsman while still in community. Then I'll go paid staff at a measly $25,000 a year." Ombudsman was an important position. He'd have the final say in any disputes on the status of any resident, including whether to expel them or not. Joe was surprised they had offered this to Pat, although he knew that Pat was very popular at the agency.

"Hey, that's not bad for a single guy."

"It's more than you're going to make if you go paid staff at Mother and Child. I hear they'd offer ten dollars an hour. What's that $20,000 a year?"

That was less than half of what Joe was making when he left his work to head for the Rockies and then Manhattan.

"You can take the 20 grand and then Redemption House will pay for your finishing your degree. They're big on that. You can get your degree in social work right here at Hunter College. The agency has a lot of students there. Then eventually you can do private counseling to support your future or should I say, 'current' family, in a finer fashion."

Patrick laughed after he said this, but the laugh of a true friend.

Joe looked out onto Eight Avenue and the masses of people, most of them holding bags full of freshly purchased goodies. A fine sight, a happy sight, he thought, but are they remembering what we're celebrating? Many of them are, he hoped.

"Merry Christmas," Sister said. "Merry Christmas," Patrick answered and Joe looked over.

Sister Jude sat down with the two men. She was wearing her habit tonight although she usually dressed civilian.

"This is the last time I'm probably going to wear this."

The men were silent.

"I'm taking a leave from my order. I've done my discernment. I'm getting a small apartment and have a job lined up at a hospital. I'm going to look for a new order, one that's more relaxed, and if not, I'm going civilian."

Joe knew that Sister loved the Church, the Mass, and Community, although she didn't see eye to eye with Vinnie LaBianco. So this came as a surprise.

"You've got to go where the Spirit takes you," Patrick said.

"That's right," she said, looking at both men's faces for a reaction.

Joe tried to keep a poker face. In many ways, with as much life experience as he had, he was still a trusting soul, naïve and inexperienced in the ways of the world, partially due to being in a family business his whole life.

But Patrick, who was more in tune and realistic about the world, had opened his eyes to some things, especially in the Church, that Joe was ignoring.

Joe still couldn't believe that a well-known visiting Priest had left a note on Pat's pillow inviting him to visit his upstate New York parish as his guest. And when Patrick did, the Priest had tried to seduce him in the Rectory. This was ugly to Joe and turned his stomach, literally.

Patrick implied that the Priesthood was loaded with non-celibate homosexuals and someday this would have to surface and cause the Church a lot of harm.

Joe refused to believe this and felt Pat's was an isolated incident. But he had to admit to himself that a good percentage of the visiting priests that came to Community to say Mass appeared to be gay.

Then again, the older lady in Community, the one that he prayed with a lot before the Blessed Sacrament, had implied on several occasions that she believed the third secret of Fatima had to do with a renewal of the Catholic Priesthood. Why did it need renewal?

He pondered this oblivious to the short conversation that Pat had with Sister Jude. She got up, said Merry Christmas again with a forced smile and walked away.

"Another one bites the dust." Pat exclaimed. Joe looked at Pat knowingly. "Another confused religious leaving the religious life."

"Father's next," Patrick said.

"What?"

"Our singing Priest."

"He of the outrageous liturgy, the sung Mass, the most beautiful I've attended?"

"Correct."

"What makes you say that?"

"I'm assuming."

"Why," Joe asked incredulously.

"He's got the hots for his cello player and she for him. You can't tell by him, but do you see how she looks at him?"

"I do actually."

"Well?"

"Stop assuming Patrick."

"We're in a stage, and not for the first time, when we need renewal in the Church."

"And God always sends holy people, right? At the right time holy people rise up to save the Church."

"Also correct, but it may take a while."

"No doubt," Patrick answered, and the two men rose and headed out to cross the walk bridge and walk down to the chapel.

Joe's friends and mother arrived at the Forty-fourth Street doors just in time for greetings and to be escorted to the balcony. His Mom brought him a gift, obviously a gift-wrapped book that turned out to be "The Imitation of Christ" by Kempis. She was excited and obviously very proud of her son.

The Mass was spectacular. Every word sung beautifully, accompanied by a beautiful cello. There was a flutist and pianist as well. The conversation before Mass only put a slight damper on the evening for Joe.

The chapel was packed and the incense still burning when he stepped to the podium and read the first reading, Isaiah's prediction of the coming future King.

When the Gospel was read, his thoughts turned to Johny, who he was determined to raise into a fine lad. I'll make sure he learns a trade Joe thought, just like Joseph did for Jesus. As he thought of Johny and Yasmine, he had a warm, special feeling in his heart. This must be right. God must want this.

Then he realized something. He should resign his position.

Or should he? He remembered meeting one of the psychiatrists contracted by the agency to work with kids a few hours a week and his wife of 10 years, an ex-resident. She's African-American while he's white and possibly Jewish and quite a number of years older than her. They have no children but seem happily married nonetheless. Was there something wrong with that?

Okay, stop thinking so much, he thought, and focus on this beautiful celebration.

After Mass there was cake and coffee in the cafeteria. His mother couldn't stop raving about the Mass. He loved to see her so happy.

They said their goodnights and he retired to his cell. He lied on his back on the bed, thinking. He thought about Paul and wished him a Happy Christmas.

The year was soon coming to an end. Some major events were churning in his life and about to unfold.

When he couldn't sleep, he put on shorts and a tee and went down to the chapel. He lied down before the Blessed Sacrament and quickly fell asleep.

CHAPTER 40

▼

Days later, Paul was coming out of Gino's fruit stand on Ninth Avenue with a beautiful Italian prayer card in his hand, quite a beautiful prayer card of Our Lady of the Rosary. The tables had turned. Now Paul had a partner and benefactor in his prayer ministry: Gino.

Gino, being the businessman that he was, had discovered a wholesaler to buy prayer cards on the cheap. He had a small turntable rack that held about 40 different cards on his checkout counter and sold them for a dollar or gave them away for free when necessary. The dollars he gave to Paul to put in the poor box. He also had an unlimited supply free for him.

As he stepped out to the street a familiar face was passing by at that exact moment, Joe Morrison.

The two men hugged and patted each other on the back like the good friends they'd become. They didn't know what to say to each other. They gave each other smiles and started walking south on Ninth Avenue together.

"It's been a while," Joe said.

"Yes, it has."

"A lot has happened."

"Same here."

"You have time, Paul? Let's catch up!"

"I've nothing but time!"

"Join me, I was escaping Community for lunch at one of these neat little international restaurants that this street is famous for."

"Alright."

"There's a little Filipino place that I've been meaning to try. They have a small steam table with just a few homemade dishes to pick from and about six or eight tables, its family run."

"Let's do it."

Both men crossed the street and went down the other side. This was a crisp, cold, New York January day. The sun was shining bright.

A string of jingle bells hanging from the door announced their entrance into the small ethnic restaurant, now empty in the mid-afternoon. A diminutive, aging Filipino man with jet-black hair and a white apron came out of the kitchen with a grin.

"Hello," he exclaimed happily.

"Hello," the two men answered in unison.

Joe eyed the food while Paul eyed the proprietor, both of them grinning.

The Asian man grabbed a large porcelain plate and announced the contents of the food on the steam table. Joe chose the rice noodles with chicken and mushrooms and ordered two.

The men sat at the small table that was covered with a soiled linen tablecloth, soiled but not too dirty to eat from. Joe was served a can of coke and Paul an ice water.

The food came immediately and after blessing it the men chowed down.

"You left your embossing in my little studio, 'The Man, the Woman and the Child'. You need to come get it."

"I will."

"What does it mean to you?"

"Dead-on the biggest event in my life to date is all. I met someone. She's an ex-resident. She has a baby boy. And I fell in love with her. I believe they are my future."

Joe said this with a mouth full of food and Paul couldn't help but notice. "You said a mouthful."

"Yes," Joe answered knowingly, "I believe I'm being called to a family ministry. I mean that I'm being called to have a family as my ministry."

"I knew what you meant," Paul said, stabbing a piece of chicken with his fork and placing it in his mouth. The thought of Kathy crossed his mind for just an instant.

"I've prayed about it. I've sought counsel, discussed it with a close friend and a future priest. Its all systems go.

"I even had a fortune cookie tell me to go for it."

"Sounds great."

"But things haven't been so smooth since our trip, our incredible trip! I got suspended from my job for four days. A counselor accused me of improper behavior with a client. The charge was dismissed. And to top it off, I was in a barroom brawl."

The last statement made Paul stop his fork, which was almost to his mouth with another piece of chicken.

"And how did the brawl come about?"

"Ah, it was over in a minute. It was over a pool game. The guy tried to hustle me. I beat him and he got a little angry."

There was a break in the conversation as both men drank from their cups and digested what Joe had just said.

Paul was happy for Joe, of course, especially since he knew the embossing must mean something current, but on the other hand, he had fleetingly entertained the thought of Joe joining him on the street.

"Where do you stand in your relationship right now?"

"She was just recently in a fight with a co-habitant at her group home."

Paul almost coughed up his water. This didn't go unnoticed by Joe.

"Yes, she's young, but her heart is in the right place. She's smart and responsible."

"God works in mysterious ways," Paul said, adding a light touch.

"Yes He does. I want to be with them all the time. But at the same time, a friend from Community wants me to get a place with him and keep working at the agency when my commitment is up."

"So you have some decisions to make."

"Yes."

"Fast and pray and the answer will come. And by the way, you're not the only one who needs to fast and pray."

"Why, what's up my friend?"

"I came home from our trip and was kindly asked to stop making soup and ministering near the Franciscans on Thirty-First."

"No."

"Falsely accused like you. But there was a catch. The head priest, I guess it's the Abbot, practically invited me to join them, legally you know, through the right channels."

"Say what?"

"For me to preach legitimately I need to be a member of a fraternity and be examined and approved by the Minister General. Then I would receive the order of Preacher."

"Do you need degrees in theology and so forth?"

"I'm not sure about that."

They both paused and ate and drank, both thinking.

"Holy cow, are you considering Holy Orders?"

"I have."

"Wow!"

"And no, I like what I'm doing. Right now, I definitely do not feel worthy of Holy Orders. I love the Mass, but don't feel ready to say the Mass."

"You could be a deacon right?"

"Yes, but then I'd be tied to a parish and I couldn't work the street. I love the street. I love what I'm doing."

Joe couldn't help but think of his own job at the agency. Did he love his job? Not really, but he liked it a lot. His problem was that he had difficulty not taking his work home with him and this would tire him and burn him out.

He truly enjoyed counseling and helping the kids. He loved praying with them and helping them to forgive, but he couldn't say that he "loved" his job.

On the other hand he knew he couldn't live on the street like Paul. He was convinced that he personally needed structure and routine to keep his life straight. In Colorado he didn't have this and ended up with anxiety.

Joe dropped his napkin to the floor inadvertently and when picking it up noticed the unique and ancient looking sandals on Paul's feet. The leather was almost white, possibly bleached by the sun, and they were obviously hand made.

"Wow, where on earth did you get those?"

Paul looked Joe straight in the eye while he finished chewing and then took a gulp of water.

"I have to tell you what happened. I haven't told anyone yet."

This got Joe's attention.

"What's up? What happened?"

"Everyday I feel the Lord's presence by my side. He's in my heart. And everyday I experience the wonderful and the mundane with an exquisite joy. I've put my trust in Jesus and I've never been happier.

"And everyday I experience minor miracles and have mystical experiences, such as today meeting you at that precise moment on the street. Whenever I really need something I pray for it and just wait, and God gives it to me, from the words to say when praying out loud with someone to finding a drink when I'm thirsty.

"But nothing major had happened since I'd been on the street, until now."
Joe got goose pimples as Paul paused to take another drink.

"Christmas Eve I went to Midnight Mass with Gwen and Lola. The service was lovely. Their church has a huge organ that kind of dominated everything but the Mass was very spirit-filled and the homily was excellent.

"I walked the girls home and then planned on going down to the studio to sleep a while, when I passed by that bar on the corner of 19th. They had open mike and the place was jamming when the guy on the mike seemed to call out to me to sing a song. Something came over me and I stepped up to the mike and sang Jesus a song for his birthday."

"What song?"

"Here I am Lord."

"Good choice."

"As I sang a guy pulled up with a guitar and half the bar joined in."

"That is a nice experience. You must of slept good that night!"

"No, I never made it to the studio. As I headed down seventh, I reached into my pocket and discovered the key."

"Oh wow, the key that St. John gave you!"

"Yes."

"What did you do then?"

"I got an irresistible urge to go to Henry's room at the Franciscans to retrieve the Icon that he'd given to me as a gift, an incredible rendition of the Madonna with Child. I sensed that this was meant to be my Christmas present from him."

"And then?"

"I turned and went straight to 31st Street. About three blocks from there I got a bad feeling in my gut about three young guys that appeared drunk and were walking straight at me. Sure enough, they deliberately didn't move out of my way. One of them, the biggest one, pretended to pass me then grabbed me from behind and threw me to the ground. One of the other guys then put his foot on my chest and said something crazy like 'beware, you are headed for trouble,' or something like that. Meanwhile, the third guy took a liking to my dirty old sandals and ripped them off my feet."

"Holy cow!"

"Yea, they left me barefoot. Then the big guy spit at me but missed."

"You were alright?"

"Yea, but that didn't stop me. I continued on. By now it had to be three in the morning. I went to the side entrance to Henry's building and found the door open."

"Unlocked you mean?"

"No, open, with a light on."

"Like an invitation for you. Like someone knew you were coming."

"Exactly how I felt. I walked up the stairs to his room with the massive old door and found it too to be open."

"And no one was around?"

"Not a soul."

"So you went in?"

"I did."

"And what happened?"

"Well, let me tell you, I never felt as alive as at that moment. I felt vibrant. Excited wouldn't be the right word, more than excited."

"So what did you do?"

"I stepped in and closed the door behind me. The room felt warm. I felt the Holy Spirit. I faintly smelled incense. There was a lit pillar candle, new and hardly melted, on his table. Next to it was a package wrapped in paper with a note and string around it."

"What did the note say?"

"Simply, 'for a dear friend, keep seeking his will'."

"It was the Icon?"

"Yes it was."

"Then what?"

"Man, I felt as if I was on auto pilot. I never felt like this before, like I was in the presence of pure holiness. I felt totally at peace and knew there was more for me to do.

"I turned to an ancient box that sat to the right of me on the floor. I knelt before it and removed the key from my pocket. I inserted the key that somehow I knew would open the box. The tumbler turned and the lid snapped open a bit.

"I put both hands on the box and closed my eyes. Words of prayer never came, just a warm feeling, and I felt light headed but in a good way, elevated.

"I opened the box slowly and peeked in, and there these were," Paul said, glancing under the table at his sandals and gesturing for Joe to do the same.

"My good friend, I'm telling you the truth, when I reached inside and held the sandals, I heard a voice, loud and clear. The voice said,

"The wind is what they see in your eyes,
    The free wind, the wild wind. (John 3:8)
Preach to them repentance,
    That they return to Me.
What's in your heart can change
    The world.
Preach to them repentance,
    For the Kingdom of
    Heaven is near."

"Holy smokes!"

"Yea, then I sat on the floor and put them on. They fit exactly perfect. Funny thing is my feet were clean, when moments before they were quite dirty. Then I got up to close the box and peeked inside."

"Oh no!"

"Yea, there was a small Icon inside. I recognized it as John the Baptist. So I closed the ancient box and set the Icon on the top of it and knelt to pray.

"I prayed for Henry and his sister. I got the strangest feeling that I would be seeing them both soon."

"On Mt. Carmel?"

"Yes. Then in the reflection of the glass over the Icon, I caught a glimpse of a pair of radiant, stunning golden eyes. At first I didn't realize they were my own. They made me remember the dream that Henry had about seeing these eyes in a cave, thinking they were a wolf's, and then realizing that they were Jesus'. And I remembered what St. John said about seeing my eyes before. What could he have meant?

"Then my thoughts turned to the Apocalypse, and what he said about it being personal to each of us, that we're all called to be ready for our apocalypse at all times, to be holy.

"And I thought about how terrible these times are. Spiritually blind people, all the sin, the denial of sin, and then I realized...."

There was a pause. Both men sat staring into each other's eyes, Joe's dark brown eyes looking into the brilliant liquid golden eyes of Paul. Their food was now cold. The Filipino cook was standing behind Joe, listening.

"Yea, you realized?"

Paul glanced down at the table, then at the cook, then to his friend.

"That the priesthood is not my calling, the street is. I'm to announce the coming of the Kingdom, as John did. Here in this desert of loneliness they call New York."

Paul paused looking up at the ceiling. Joe glared at him with a feeling in the pit of his stomach that this wasn't really what Paul had been about to say.

"I must be free and unencumbered to do this, to live the pure gospel with God's help, to the best of my humble ability."

"Holy cow," was all the Filipino cook could muster as he walked back behind the counter.

"That's amazing, what happened next?"

"I put the little Icon back and closed the box, leaving the key inside. As I walked out the Great Door the candle inexplicably went out. I turned to look back and could see only the darkness, though I thought I saw a shape in the darkness, like an angel, but I couldn't be sure. I spent the rest of the night walking the streets, praying, it was hours before I felt my adrenaline come back to normal."

After a long pause where the two men ate, the conversation turned lighthearted as the cook shared some faith stories with the men. He turned out to be a good and devout Catholic who owned a fish farm back in the Philippines and whose sister was a nun there, working with a small leper colony.

The men finished their meals. Joe paid and they walked out on 9th Avenue heading south. Joe spoke first.

"Tell me your thoughts; about Henry, the ancient box, the key, Athos. Put it together for me."

"I think Henry got the box from St. John. Under what circumstances, I don't know. I have a feeling that he took it and ran. I'm not sure why, but I believe that St. John somehow knew that Henry had something to do with our visit and gave us the key.

"Somehow it's all tied in together because remember, the whole reason Henry went to the Holy Mountain was because he met an ancient monk on a bus, sort of the way Henry and I met."

"How so?"

"He had a dream about the wolf and Jesus and the golden eyes. Then he claims an angel told him to go out to 31st Street at a certain time just as I stepped out of a car. That's how we met."

"This all sounds like a conspiracy to me. The Lord puts St. John and Henry together, then you and Henry, then you and St. John, and finally you and what could be the sandals of St. John the Baptist."

"That's about right."

"Sounds like He has a plan for you, Mr. Johnston."

"Sounds like it."

"St. John said Jesus comes to speak with him. Do you think Our Lord told him you were coming?"

Paul looked up to the now cloudy sky and fingered his prayer ring. He never did answer the question.

Walking along beside Paul, Joe remembered the first time he set eyes on him. He was in the cardboard box, under the shelter of the Port Authority, helping a helpless man, and wondered what his own place might be in the Master's plan.

He said a short prayer, asking for God's Will in his life and especially Paul's, a prayer that ended with, "Jesus, I trust in you!"

CHAPTER 41

▼

There's an atmosphere of good cheer in New York in early spring. The anticipation of the good weather, the greening of the parks and the early street festivals may be why, or it could be that all are tired of the bitter cold winter with its blustering, bone chilling wind.

People pull the old dead plants from the pots on their balconies and fire escapes and replace them with fresh pansies and ornamental cabbage that they hope will survive what is left of the killer frosts.

On those special days in March where the thermostat hits the 60 mark, one can see the hopeful congregating in Central Park to be seen and to catch some rays.

On upper Broadway the Dominican population can be seen setting up their card tables in the center median, while wearing their colorful bulky sweaters, eager to begin the round robin domino contests.

The homeless might appreciate the warmth most of all as the fear of freezing to death is replaced by a calm hopefulness, a hope that the coming days may get better, and a cause for celebration.

On such a day, Lola and Gwen walked together to church with great anticipation. On this day they would meet for the first time Paul's "other" friends.

They both wore matching denim jackets and jeans with brand new white sneakers, and while Gwen wore a white turtleneck sweater underneath, Lola wore a black cable knit sweater.

They felt joyful as they walked. First Gwen and then Lola had joined the R.C.I.A. program at their local parish. This is the Church's program for people interested in joining the Roman Catholic Church. They were being fast tracked and making up for their missed classes by studying hard together, as they had joined after the program had started. They were both now looking forward to an Easter Baptism and Confirmation in the faith.

Gwen was still saving lives at the pregnancy center while Lola had taken Gwen's spot at St. Vincent's visiting the unwanted sick.

The opportunity to love! They had both put themselves in situations through their service where they could love and serve their neighbors, and never felt happier!

In an unbelievable turn of events Lola had continued seeing Big Dog and had persuaded him to enter into a 12-step program for alcoholics. He was accompanying Lola once a week on her rounds at the hospital.

They both continued living at home and were praying for their father's conversion. Jody had since taken a powder and their Dad had taken up going to bars to deal with his loneliness. They were hoping this wouldn't become a habit.

They walked together down 7th Ave. with happy anticipation.

Fatima and Sahar, when happy, walked with a bounce in their step. Men seeing these two beautiful women walking down the street may mistake this for arrogance and conceit.

But it was joy that drove them this day. They couldn't wait to see Paul's "other" friends too. It was Fatima who had suggested that they all meet and Paul who had suggested a Mass together. The girls had brought Lepido along as he was becoming more and more interested in the change that he'd seen take place in his sisters' lives.

They both were changing their majors and doing volunteer work. Fatima was making plans to go for her Master's in Social Work, with an emphasis on addiction. She planned on getting her certification as an Addiction Counselor at the same time. She was still volunteering at the detox where she was having some success getting through to the so-called "lost causes" that she was assigned to.

There was one client that she was happiest about. She couldn't believe the hand of God could be so obvious. The diabetic street urchin named Jayvid, whose resolve to stay off the stuff and off the street had so impressed her, turned out to be the same Sayvid that Paul had mentioned to her in passing to pray for, only Paul had mispronounced his name. Jayvid was not only off the stuff but back on the street already, praying and giving out prayer cards with Paul.

Though not ready to join any "organized" religion, he felt the powerful call of the Holy Spirit to serve others, and who better to serve than the street people that he had known and lived with for the past five years. He spoke their language. He cut through their denial and their lies in a patient, loving way that Paul had been profoundly affected by, impressed by, for Jayvid was truly a walking miracle. His were eyes that once looked empty and now had life in them once again.

But Jayvid wasn't the only person to join Paul on the street. Every Saturday a passive little monk with a peanut shaped head walked the streets with Paul and Jayvid, serving those in need. Friar Billy hit the streets with permission from his superiors; he had asked for Saturdays free and informed them that he was going to serve with Paul.

The Provincial, with the wink of any eye, had granted his request.

"Only go beyond 31st street," he had said.

Sahar was changing her major to pre-med and had declared a moratorium on boys. Both girls had discovered that by switching off the TV and carefully choosing the movies that they went to, they were able to wash away the sex-saturated mind control of the secular media and better control their thoughts and their habits. (Matthew 5:28)

Sahar was taking a wait-and-see approach about joining the Church, as in "wait and see what happens with Fatima", although she knelt in prayer every day, prayers that included the prayer of St. Francis, and attended weekly Mass with her sister.

Both parents had become concerned about the girls changing their majors. They had both anticipated their girls to be up and coming business majors and were being challenged to understand the change that the Savior had brought about in their hearts.

This is what made Lepido curious. His big sisters were less cranky and didn't pick on him as much. They seemed surer of themselves and down to earth, especially Fatima. He respected the fact that Fatima was putting some newfound belief into practice and not just talking about it. He admired that in her. This is how he wanted to be.

By Divine Providence they all arrived at the corner church at precisely the same time and from three different directions, Paul and Jayvid arriving together. Paul was surprised to see Lepido and was overwhelmed by the awesome power of the Holy Spirit to bring this group together.

Lola and Gwen and Fatima and Sahar exchanged hugs and tearful smiles upon their introductions. One could sense a feeling of euphoria as the group stood in a circle looking one another over with gleeful smiles. There was a feeling in the air that something special was happening here, that this was the beginning of something.

The look of contentment on Paul's face said it all as he looked at once to the miracle that was Jayvid and then to Fatima. She was the only one to give Jay a warm welcome as he approached the group, for in spite of his turnaround, he still hadn't developed the habits of good grooming and cleanliness. He still looked and smelled like a homeless person. His clothes were dirty and had holes in them. His missing teeth added to this persona.

The group stood looking at each other inquisitively, as Paul, who wasn't one to talk much about people, had not given anyone any details on each other's lives. Just that they were all seekers and lovers of Truth.

Then the church bells rang and Paul said, "Let's go in," then he paused a moment and said, "One thing, no talking in church, even if everybody else is, we must remember our Lord is present in the Tabernacle."

The group entered the beautiful gothic style church and promptly took their seats in the front row. They all knelt in prayer. Some in prayers of thanksgiving, others remembered to pray for loved ones, Paul was asking forgiveness and mercy for his sins and of those of his crew. Then the explosive roar of a V-Twin Harley engine could be heard coming from outside the church.

"God, he made it," Paul thought. The girls looked around wondering what the racket was. Jayvid was motionless and in deep prayer with his hands clasped before him and his head bowed down. His thick, long, reddish brown dreadlocks, reflected in the bit of light coming from the stained glass high above them, seemed like the royal headgear of an ancient warrior.

Joe had been seeing Yasmine regularly now. After the fight, for her safety, she was transferred to West End, the Group Home on the Upper West Side that she had always hoped to go to.

Right in the middle of a beautiful neighborhood stood the brick five-story building called West End, looking like any other apartments on the Upper West Side, except for the fact that young girls, some with babies and others pregnant, were the only tenants seen going in and out. And the doorman didn't just open the door, but he checked ID"s and made sure the girls signed in and out.

Yasmine was as happy as can be. She was getting her GED and planning to attend the special classes for youth at Columbia University, which incidentally was a short ride north of her new abode.

She had put the plans to be a designer on the back burner for now although in that regard she was taking sewing lessons. She had decided to study photography instead. This was not a very practical decision as Joe had pointed out, but as she had pointed out to him, she had a passion for it, and he himself had told her he believed the secret to happiness was finding your passion and pursuing it full tilt. If your work was your passion, it wouldn't be work, but love, you're doing what you love, he had said.

Johny was doing great and was officially a toddler now as he had taken his first steps. Yasmine's grandmother was happily watching him today and making sure that he ate his share of chicken, rice and beans.

Joe had picked her up on Dykman Street right in front of Grandma's tenth floor apartment. They could see Johny and Reina, as she was called, waving from the window as they thundered off. He had made a left on Broadway and cruised straight down to Greenwich Village where the church was.

He wore his typical black jeans with a black hooded sweatshirt underneath his black leather motorcycle jacket. Yasmine was dressed to ride too with thick black leather boots and matching jacket that Joe had gotten for her. He was very safety conscious since that long ago accident.

They both wore full helmets and leather gloves and Yasmine had taped a mini flag of the Dominican Republic on the sissy bar that drew some whistles and applause when passing through Washington Heights.

Joe was feeling happy. He had his girl on the back, heading to a beautiful church to meet some good people, and feeling good about what he had decided to do. April 1st he'd be moving into a luxury high-rise apartment on 48th Street near Broadway with his buddy Patrick. They landed a spacious one bedroom with a balcony for the total amount they each would have paid for tiny studios of their own. They flipped a coin and Joe had gotten the bedroom. Pat would have the living room for his space.

As Pat had projected, Joe was offered a fulltime position at mother/child for $400 a week plus benefits. He took it.

March 31st was their official last day in Community. This was a sad time for Community. The building on 44th with the chapel had already been sold for over 1 million sorely needed dollars. Community had use of it until May.

They were down to a dozen or so members. Word was Community would survive but in much smaller numbers, and new quarters would be found for the crew.

The Mexican girls had both decided to return to Puebla and were leaving any day now. Charo still spoke to Yasmine regularly in secret and supported her growing relationship with Joe. She told Yasmine that she saw Joe as an honorable and loyal person and wished her well.

This day was special to Joe for another reason. He'd always dreamed about what it would be like to ride his hog down Broadway, New York City, with a gorgeous girl on the back. This was the perfect day for it, as the happy smile on his face would attest.

As the Harley crossed 14th Street he saw a lady at the curb that reminded him of Carmen, his fellow counselor at 52nd Street. His heart filled with joy and thanksgiving knowing now that it was Carmen that had arranged Yasmine and Johny's transfer to West End.

They parked the scooter by the side entrance and he locked the front end and then chained the bike's frame to a utility pole.

They went in through the side door and blessed themselves with Holy Water. Joe immediately spotted his friend in the front row and pointed him out. They both genuflected to the Tabernacle and entered the second row just behind their friends.

Just then the bells rang and Mass began.

In the earliest part of the second century St. Justin Martyr describes the Mass in a letter that he wrote to his persecutors just before they put him to death. He wrote of the Holy Sacrifice of the Mass, the celebration of the Lord's Supper, the Breaking of the Bread. "Do this in memory of me," the Savior had said. "Unless you eat my flesh and drink my blood you have no life in you." These were words that had caused many of His followers to depart from Him. (John 6:53)

After professing their faith in the Holy Trinity, asking forgiveness for their sins, and praying for the Church and the world, the congregation hears the Liturgy of the Word. The Liturgy of the Word is the inspired word of God as written in the Holy Bible.

The first reading is from the Old Testament, often a prophetic reading from Isaiah predicting the coming of Jesus hundreds of years before his Incarnation. Then it's the Psalmist's turn. The third reading is generally from a letter of Paul. These readings from Holy Scripture generally connect with the proclamation of the Holy Gospel, sending a concise message. These same readings are read at every Mass celebrated this day throughout the Universe.

After all stand for the proclamation of the Gospel by the Priest, the words of Jesus Himself, there's a teaching, a homily, usually a short message connecting all the readings, a message that one should remember long after the end of the celebration. This day the message was about stewardship, loving thy neighbor.

Then comes the Liturgy of the Eucharist, the Real Presence, considered to be the Body, Blood, Soul, and Divinity of our Lord since the beginning. The disciples of our Holy Apostles spoke and wrote of this. Truly.

During the most important part of the Mass, the highlight, God is called by the Celebrant to send the Holy Spirit to change simple bread and wine into the Body and Blood of the Christ, to create the Banquet of the Lord, spiritual nourishment for His children. This is the most important event in the world every day. Anyone who truly thinks about what happens here must go to his or her knees in awe.

Those receiving Jesus in the Blessed Sacrament must be baptized Catholic, must confess to a Priest with true contrition, and be forgiven for any serious or mortal sin. One must also fast for at least one hour before the start of Holy Mass.

After the Consecration the worshipers hold hands together and recite the prayer that Jesus taught us. Paul and Joe and their friends all held hands. Fatima reached back to join hands with Yasmine to fully connect the group. They said:

> Our Father,
> Who art in heaven,
> Hallowed be thy name,
> Thy kingdom come,
> Thy will be done,
> On earth as it is in heaven.
> Give us this day our daily bread,
> And forgive us our trespasses.
> As we forgive those who trespass against us,
> And lead us not into temptation,
> But deliver us from evil.
> Amen.

After the Our Father, as is the custom, the group exchanged smiles, kisses on the cheek, and handshakes. Yasmine felt shy and a little out of place, but again Fatima stepped out and gave her and Joe a hug.

Paul was quiet and deliberate shaking everyone's hand and saying "the peace of Christ be with you". He felt an indescribable exhilaration in him, an outpouring of joy at the friends that God had blessed him with.

When he came to the city he was but one, now there were nine, ten if you count Gino. Not all had joined him on the street but were serving in different ways. His thoughts turned to forming a prayer group and a discussion group with all his friends, to encourage each other, to share, to love.

Only Joe and Paul received Holy Communion, as both men had been to Confession. Paul knelt in reverence afterwards, eyes closed, and prayed from his heart for God's mercy and grace for all, especially for his friends.

As was his custom, Joe sat when he returned to his seat and glanced around joyfully at all those who took the time on this Saturday afternoon to come to the Banquet of the Lord. He loved watching the Communicants coming up to receive.

There was happiness in the group. There was a beautiful energy that they all felt. Life had a purpose. We are real. We are alive. We are fulfilling our purpose.

They all stood and bowed their heads for the blessing. Just then the sun turned a corner and broke through a huge window on the southwest corner of the church, high up, and bright sunlight shone down like a spotlight on the group. It was surreal. At the same remarkable moment three beautiful white doves came gracefully flying down the center aisle, as one front door had been left open, and circled about the altar, as if deciding where to land.

"May the Lord bless you in the name of the Father," at that moment a dove landed on the shoulder of the priest, "the Son," a second dove alighted upon the shoulder of a surprised Paul as he made the sign of the cross, "and the Holy Spirit". The third dove, to all their amazement, had flown toward the back of the church where it stood upon the peanut shaped head of an agitated little Monk wearing glasses.

"The Mass is ended go in peace to love and serve the Lord."

"Thanks be to God."

All of them knew that something extraordinary had just occurred, something supernatural, something good. The girls were smiling brightly as they genuflected and walked for the door.

They all looked at each other as they walked and could see the radiant joy on each other's faces. Only Yasmine looked a bit apprehensive.

Paul had a knowing look of confidence as he watched his friends exit, but also was concerned as to the presence of the tenth member of the group. He had stayed on his knees in the church, praying, as they filed by.

Outside they all quickly agreed, at the urging of Fatima, that they would meet at the Speakeasy for some food and beverages. The place would be empty at this time.

Jayvid walked ahead with the group. Joe left his bike chained up and did the same. Paul waited outside the church.

Finally the little Monk came out. He had a look of consternation on his face as he held the banister and walked briskly down the steps to Paul.

Paul stood with his hands clasped together in front of him. Billy grabbed Paul's hands and looked into his eyes, the golden eyes.

The look on Billy's face sent a chill down his spine.

"What is it?"

"I got word from Henry, his sister's in a trance, she won't eat or drink, except for the Eucharist, she may die!"

"Yes, and?"

"He wants you to go. He wants you to meet him there at the Monastery."

"Why, what could I possibly do?"

"She's prophesying Paul. Henry thinks you're in great danger. She mentioned you even though he never told her about you."

"What?"

"And there's more!"

"What else?"

"She knows who the antichrist is!"

Paul gasped! He fell to one knee with his eyes closed and grabbed the banister, bowing his head. He felt faint. He could hear Billy mouthing words of prayer above him. He whispered to himself, "Lord Jesus, Son of God, have mercy on me, a sinner."

Then he stood and looked Friar William in the eye, "Then I must go." Without blinking Billy replied, "And I must go with you."

The End. (For Now)

The Universal Prayer

Lord, I believe in you: increase my faith.

I trust in you: strengthen my trust.

I love you: let me love you more and more.

I am sorry for my sins: deepen my sorrow.

I worship you as my first beginning, I long for you as my last end,

I praise you as my constant helper, and call on you as my loving protector.

Guide me by your wisdom, correct me with your justice, comfort me with your mercy, protect me with your power.

I offer you, Lord, my thoughts: to be fixed on you; my words: to have you for their theme; my actions: to reflect my love for you; my sufferings: to be endured for your greater glory.

I want to do what you ask of me, in the way you ask, for as long as you ask, because you ask it.

Lord, enlighten my understanding, strengthen my will, purify my heart, and make me holy.

Help me to repent of my past sins and to resist temptation in the future.

Help me to rise above my human weaknesses and to grow stronger as a Christian.

Let me love you, my Lord and my God, and see myself as I really am: a pilgrim in this world, a Christian called to respect and love all whose lives I touch, those in authority over me or those under my authority, my friends and my enemies.

Help me to conquer anger with gentleness, greed by generosity, apathy by fervor.

Help me to forget myself and reach out toward others.

Make me prudent in planning, courageous in taking risks.

Make me patient in suffering, unassuming in prosperity.

Keep me, Lord, attentive at prayer, temperate in food and drink, diligent in my work, firm in my good intentions.

Let my conscience be clear, my conduct without fault, my speech blameless, my life well ordered.

Put me on guard against my human weaknesses.

Let me cherish your love for me, keep your law, and come at last to your
salvation.
Teach me to realize that this world is passing, that my true future is the happiness
of heaven, that life on earth is short, and the life to come eternal.
Help me to prepare for death with a proper fear of judgment, but a greater trust
in your goodness.
Lead me safely through death to the endless joy of heaven.
Grant this through Christ our Lord. Amen.

—Pope Clement XI

The Hail Mary

Hail Mary, full of grace, the Lord is with thee.
Blessed art thou amongst women, and blessed is the Fruit of thy womb Jesus.
Holy Mary, Mother of God, pray for us sinners, now and at the hour of our
death. Amen.

About the Author

Robert Epperly left a successful career with all the trimmings for a mountain in Colorado where he rediscovered his Catholic faith and grew in love for Jesus Christ. After a year on the High Plains Desert, his calling was to the streets of New York City and its homeless young people, the street kids.

After serving in New York as a missionary for two years and several bouts with severe burnout, this dedicated champion of youth met his one and only and traded in his Harley for a mini-van and eventually a pile of kids.

A man of prayer, Robert, has been blessed with the grace of witnessing first hand many events that can only be described as "supernatural." At the precise moment when he informed his son Johny of his intention to write this book for the Lord, the power went out in his neighborhood and a huge rainbow burst across the sky above them.

Every diabolical obstacle to this work followed in an attempt to halt the completion of this book, including Robert being a passenger in a car wreck that should have ended his life, instead emerging almost unscathed after being extricated with the "jaws of life." By God's mercy the author never quit and the result is a page-turning story of mystery and romance that witnesses and teaches the love of God and His concern for His creatures at this critical time in history.

Mostly based on real events, including his horrendous motorcycle crash, and originally penned in long hand, the work was intended for young adults and the unlearned in the faith, but is written in such a style as to be of interest to all.

The author, a Catechist for three years, has been asked in recent years to consider the Deaconate but has had to decline in order to focus on his ministry as a father of five children.

He now writes from Western North Carolina. You can contact him at epperlyrobert@yahoo.com.

978-0-595-45477-8

0-595-45477-1

Printed in the United States
104915LV00003B/106/A